*To Da...*

*Enjoy The Yarn!*

# SECRETS,

# LIES AND

# DREAMS

## Karl Manke

author of *UNINTENDED CONSEQUENCES*
*& THE PRODIGAL FATHER*

**Alexander Books**

Alexander, N.C.

Publisher: Ralph Roberts
Cover Design: Ralph Roberts
Interior Design and Electronic Page Assembly: WorldComm®

Editor: Ralph Roberts

ISBN 978-1-57090-275-8

**Alexander Books**—an imprint of *Creativity, Inc.*—is a full-service publisher located at 65 Macedonia Road, Alexander, NC 28701. Phone 1-828-252-9515, Fax 1-828-255-8719. For orders only: 1-800-472-0438. Visa and MasterCard accepted.

This book is also available on the Internet at **Amazon.com**

# Contents

*To my beautiful wife Carolyn
for her immitigable patience*

# 1 — A MYSTERY BEGINS

*Drip, Drip, Splat, Drip, Splat.* The sound and the delicate sensation of feel are fusing themselves into an incessant, unmelodious happening. The dripping water is hitting the forehead of a semiconscious man, cascading down the creases of his tanned face to a spot on the back of his head.

Cold, wet clothing and a strong need to urinate further force his struggle against unconsciousness. His eyes are open but see nothing. It's totally dark. His body battles any movement against the pain it produces. Forcing his way to a sitting position, strictly guided by a man's primordial need to stand to relieve himself, he powers himself to his feet.

With this task finished, it's quickly replaced by the awareness of an overwhelming headache and lower back pain. "What's happening? Where am I?"

His bewilderment intensifies. Questions speed through his mind aimlessly as if caught in some web of unexplained confusion. Stumbling around his surroundings, his brain further focuses on yet another unexplained need—to do something to move himself out this horrific environment.

The smell is the unmistakable odor of damp earth. Frantically his eyes search around and around for something to focus on.

With no apparent foe to fight, the dominant mind set is to flee. "How do I get out of here?" Finally a light from above catches his eye. It's reflecting off the side of what is apparently the side of a hole. A closer inspection indicates that this shaft is not straight down, but rather on a slight incline.

Even through the unrelenting physical pain, his body is following the impulse to begin to climb. Clambering up the incline proves to be a much more arduous task than he is presently capable of performing. After about twenty feet of climbing the shaft takes a sharp upward turn. To add to an already near impossible task, the material beneath his feet has changed. Instead of stone and gravel, it's turned to a mixture of loose dirt and gravel allowing only precarious footing.

What's giving him hope is that the further he climbs the wider the light. At the same time it's becoming evident that the light is still another twenty feet up with no good footing to reach it.

Somewhere in the recesses of his mind is an awareness that this is a perilous situation, but with no context as to how dangerous — that is until his footing slips out from under him pulling him back to the bottom.

Nauseousness over takes him. His head is still fiercely pounding along with sharp pains shooting down his legs. Retching violently, and with no other choice, his body shuts itself down throwing him back into coma.

It's a fitful slumber. In this nightmare-like trance, he hears a voice. It's calling a name that's unfamiliar. "Joey, Joey, can you hear me?"

It awakens him only long enough to be conscious of it happening, but not enough to process its meaning. He does not answer.

Not knowing how long he has been in this predicament, he awakens to an incandescence above him. It's a noon sun penetrating its way through the gloomy darkness. He lies there. Everything still hurts. What is becoming certain is that his mind as it is, is unaware of anything other than this present reality. He has no recollection of a past beyond this hole.

He also notices something else he had missed earlier. In the shadows appears to be rope. It's dangling, but from where can't be determined. Cautiously pulling on it, not knowing what to expect, it doesn't give. Adding more of his weight, it still doesn't give way. Determining that it must be fastened to something out of sight, but secure enough, he wraps his hands tightly around its circumference and begins to lift himself.

It's only fifty feet, but when the body is exhausted with pain shooting from nearly every extremity, it may as well be fifty miles. The only thing that drives him on is a tenacious desire to survive. After several attempts, he finds the precise footholds that give him victory.

Emerging from his would be tomb, he is awestruck by the sudden change in his environment. The cold dampness has yielded to a sun-warmed breeze heavy with pine scent.

But the victory elation from emerging safely from his certain tomb is yielding to the haunting question of "Who am I?" Nonetheless, the one-time danger of the mine shaft has morphed into this new and just as perplexing situation. Looking around nothing is familiar. It's as though he's emerged from a birth canal with no recollection of any former life.

Checking his pockets reveals nothing. There is nothing at all to give him a hint as to who he is, how he came into this dilemma, or for that matter, where he is. Reaching around to the back of his head brings a gasp as his hand retrieves a handful of dried blood. Anxiety has taken over where certainty has left a void.

Gathering what wits are left him, he's mindful of the rope that miraculously appeared and saved him. It does have a beginning and it's mindfully attached to a small tree outside the entrance to the shaft. In addition is the conspicuous presence of a backpack and a sleeping bag attached.

He stares at it in silence. First at the rope then at the backpack. Shaking his head from side to side in an attempt to clear his thoughts. "What the heck is wrong with me? I can't remember any of this."

Littering the contents of the backpack across the ground in front of him, he takes a quick inventory. Two liters of bottled water, a half dozen bags of dried fruit, three bags of salted peanuts, a buck knife, and a butane lighter.

Seizing a bottle of water, he cracks the twist top, emptying half its contents in a few large gulps. Tearing open a bag of fruit, he crams his mouth full. Temporarily satisfying his hunger and thirst, his mind turns back once again to what devilment brought him to this dark and threatening predicament.

Straining to remember anything, he habitually looks to his wrist for a watch, but it's gone. His brain still contains its cognitive skills, but no past memories come to mind.

"Have I lost my mind?" he asks himself nearly screaming. The overpowering feeling of being lost has him in a firm grip. The thought that something out of his control has taken him over is more than terrifying.

"Something is very, very wrong here!" His panic is not diminishing. Frantically searching his thoughts for anything from the past, they land on a vague recollection of the faint sound of a voice floating over him calling, "Joey, Joey are you down there?" A mystery can be an enjoyable exercise until it threatens sanity, and now not able to discern this as a reality or a dream, he retreats into a paranoia.

His gaze wanders. First slowly then frantically as he searches for anything that looks familiar. It's bad enough to awaken in a strange place, but then discovering that he has no recollection to an identity trumps everything else.

His attention turns from his surroundings to an examination of himself. The dried blood matting his hair is puzzling enough and now he's looking his at clothing. He's never seen them before. A pair of filthy jeans, a hooded sweatshirt, and a pair of work boots. Wetness still clings to all of it.

What has caught his eye is a trail some fifty feet directly below the cavern. What happens next is another new experience. He hears voices. It's the voices of several men coming up the trail. Excitement over takes him. "Maybe they are looking for me," he thinks out loud. A second thought shoots through his mind obliterating any previous thoughts. "What if I'm some kind of fugitive!" he declares to himself. "Maybe I'm running from the law." In a heartbeat excitement changes to apprehension. A wave of fear rolls over him causing a momentary paralysis.

Terrified to show himself, he throws himself to the ground behind some scrub brush and rocks. Remaining completely hidden, he's able to peek through enough to still see and hear them coming. They are too far away for him to understand their conversation, but what he sees adds yet another layer of insecurity. One of the men is carrying a torn college varsity jacket. Adding even more to the mystery is that it looks as though it's covered in blood. It's clear to him that their attention is directed around the jacket, but one of the men seems to be purposely lagging behind the others. His look is woeful. His thoughts don't seem to be with the group as he stops for a moment looking intently at the cave. He soon drops his head and continues slowly down the trail.

# 2 — A BRIEF HISTORY

The year was 1857 when a disillusioned Missouri sod buster left to join a caravan of Joseph Smith's followers westward. His name is Hiram Mueller. He was born in Pittsburgh, Pennsylvania in the year 1827. In 1847, like many other young men of his era, he grew restless. Choosing to leave the safety of the East and along with young wife, they headed West with the hopes of a new and prosperous life. The promise is a plot of land he can call his own and nothing more.

After ten years of hard toil he has lost a son and a daughter to a flash flood and more recently his wife to pneumonia. Being left alone and no family to work for, he abandons the homestead and heads West with a group of Mormons in the hopes of a new start. Not being a particularly religious man, he is more taken by their kindness. At this time in his life a little kindness goes a long ways.

With everyone of the same mind set, he finds it easy to join their movement. After all it has some fascinating aspects. Each member seems obsessed with doing what they believe to be God's will. Good works are held in high regard. In particular no one ever grows tired of expounding on what the Prophet Joseph Smith has proclaimed

"When the Prophet speaks, I feel a burning in my heart," says Millie Winston as she shares her feelings about this new American religious phenomenon.

All Protestant and Catholic faiths agree that this group is too innovative to be called Christian and find justification in persecuting them.

"The Mormons" or rather "Latter-day Saints" as they insist on being referred to, are as yet a small sectarian assemblage. The prophetic encyclicals of Joseph Smith included polygamous marriages insuring that within one generations their numbers would be sufficient enough to ward off any continuing persecutions.

By the time the caravan reaches the Great Salt Lake, Hiram is betrothed to Millie. July 5, 1857 they produce a son whom they named Abraham.

Abraham in turn produces a son named Levy who by September 23, 1942 with one of his wives produces twin boys who they named Ezard and Jacob.

Having broken away from the Church of The Latter-day Saints over continuing the practice of polygamy, Levy's family has settled in Alaska, joining a little known fundamental Mormon sect referred to as "The Pathway Of Christ"

In 1963, Jacob Mueller marries his first wife Lena Stroub, whose family also claim to be fundamental Mormons. She gives him four sons. By the time Lena is in her fifties, she has gone through menopause and hasn't had a child in ten years.

In 1983, he takes a second wife. Rena Stroub is a younger sister to Lena. At the time she is barely sixteen years old. In spite of the vast age difference between them, Jacob hopes to find a soul mate with this younger wife. Lena has always hoped Jacob would not take another wife much less have it be her younger sister. Finding it impossible to hide this fact, Lena holds a resentment against her sister that festers over the years. Since polygamy is the central tenet holding this sect together, she could glean very little sympathy from other members of her community. This is her cross to bear alone.

Lena's boys are a robust lot. They all carry the stocky, sturdy build from their mother. They are also verbose and quick to anger, often among themselves.

On the other hand, Rena's children are smaller, more delicate in their features and of course much younger than their half brothers. They, by comparison, are also more pensive in disposition than the other family.

The Muellers have proceeded from farming to the black smith trade and now in recent years, Jacob has morphed the business into a precious metal smelting operation. Mueller and Son's Smelters is set in a valley around the region of Whitehorse, Alaska along the Tintina belt. This area is rich in natural resources with gold, silver, and platinum all leading the way.

As a good Mormon father, Jacob has attempted in various ways to bring his sons into the family business. The division of labor is generally based on aptitude and maturity. Rupert is the eldest son of Jacob and Lena, he also of late has become general manager of Mueller and Sons Smelters. He's forty-three years old and still single. "I prefer it this way," he's been heard to say.

Sam is Lena's second oldest son. He tends toward trying to control all the siblings from both families. It would hardly be a stretch to refer to him as the family bully. He spends much of his time in the field buying precious metals from independent miners.

Justin and Levi, full-blood brothers to Rupert and Sam are in charge of operations in the plant as well as maintenance.

Joseph "Joey" and his younger brother Benjamin "Benji" are the sons of Jacob and Rena. Joey, in spite of his young age of only twenty-five, has a gift with numbers. He is the plant comptroller managing all monies coming in and going out. His natural self assurance under propped by being Jacob's favorite son is unbearable to his half brothers. It is one thing for a parent to have a favorite child, but yet another thing to minimize it's effects on the rest of his siblings. There is also an underlying arrogance on Joey's part in how he comes across as a know-it all.

Benji, at seventeen, runs a fork truck and is also materials handler. He also shows promise of a greater potential, but for the time being, he is content.

Jacob has been diagnosed with macular degeneration. At this juncture, he can no longer see to read, but still is able to see at distances. Even with this discouragement and discovering more and more limitations everyday he still finds ways to thank God for his many blessings. As the days go by now, he becomes more determined to give more and more business responsibilities to his sons.

Each of these men are capable in their own way. It's the hope of this father that they will grow the business and some day include their own sons and daughters.

Looking back across the years, remembering what it took to build a business to support a family of this size, he can't help but wonder if his offspring will maintain such a haven of financial support for their families.

His success has been the quiet envy of many of those within and without his circle of believers. Even though his religious community piously supports a life of doing good works, they along with every other human being, possess the fallen flesh that envies. For fear of recrimination from their church leaders, this is the kind of sin that is best kept to oneself.

# 3 — THE FAMILY

So as to not draw an overt amount of attention to their unique family arrangements, Jacob has built two houses. One for himself and Lena, the other for himself and Rena. He likes this arrangement because it allows him special time with each family. This is Jacob's week to be with Rena.

He usually slips out of bed earlier than the rest of the family for a quiet devotional period before breakfast and work. Heaving himself off his bed, he heads for the bathroom to relieve himself, then splashing a hand full of cold water in his face, he enters the kitchen, grabs a mug and heads for a cup of Mormon coffee, Postum.

Unseen for the moment is his son Joey. He's sitting at the kitchen table warming his hands around a hot cup of herbal tea.

"You're up early, son," exclaims a surprised Jacob sitting himself across the table. His smile makes it obvious that he is pleased to see him.

"Ah, I am," says an affable Joey, "I wanted to be sure and see you before you leave for work. I just want to thank you for the great varsity jacket."

Looking very pleased in turn, Jacob says, "Well, it's not every day I have a son graduate a certified public accountant with top grades from a major university. It's not much but I thought you'd appreciate it."

Continuing to smile at this prodigy, Jacob recalls the special talents this young man has always possessed. Even as a toddler he demonstrated a special intelligence by learning the entire alphabet before he was two years old. He was promoted from seventh grade into high school, skipping eighth grade altogether. Now after working full time at the plant and taking an online-master's program, he has graduated summa cum laude at the top of his class.

Both comfortable in each other's company despite their age difference, they continue to sit in a harmonious silence more as brothers than father and son.

Jacob is the first to break the silence, looking Joey straight in the eye. "I'd like you to take a greater responsibility in the company," he says.

An invigorating shot of energy shoots through Joey like electricity. He's very competitive in every aspect of his life and this is the kind of stuff he thrives on.

A boyish grin begins to spread across his face as he considers this new twist. Looking his father back eye to eye, he exclaims "Sure Dad you know I'm always up for a challenge." Setting his cup down, giving himself a moment to digest this sudden new change in events, he wipes his fingers across his lips as though it were a slate that needed cleaning before moving on. Giving his father his complete attention, he leans forward waiting for the assignment.

Jacob paces for a few moments. He's struggling for words. "Joey I don't know quite how to put this." Pausing even longer now. Finally, he clasps his hands together on the table as he surrenders to the words he's hesitant to put together. "We have a 50% increase in new miners over the past few years, but only showing a little under 20% gain in profit. Somewhere between the miners and the plant some product is vanishing into thin air."

His voice as well as his face reflect a deeper concern than Joey has remembered coming from his father. There is an accusing tone in the voice, but his face almost looks sad.

"What are you trying to say Dad?" says Joey shifting himself around in his chair as if a new angle will help get a better perspective on his father's words.

With a pervasive look Joey has yet to see in his father, Jacob begins. "This has to stay between you and me Joey is that understood?"

"Agreed," says Joey assuring himself that he is able to handle anything his father has to throw at him.

"I want you to keep an eye on what may be going on in the business that can explain this variance. It may mean you'll have to go out in the field with Sam." It pains Jacob to have to say these words. The unspoken message is all over his down cast demeanor. He looks like he would like to explain further but can't bring himself to say the words.

Contemplating what his father is saying and still staring at his father, he continues to listen. He's picking up on what is not being directly said. Sam has never been Joey's favorite brother. He recalls the disparaging words Sam uses when he talks to either himself or Benji and now their father is indicating as well, that this brother may not be trustworthy.

Joey has no exact plan on how he proposes to manage his father's appeal, but he knows that he will some way. He has always taken it for granted that he is up for any challenge life throws at him and certainly much smarter than his brothers.

"Does this mean leave no stoned unturned?" asks Joey looking to his father for confirmation.

Far from comfortable, Jacob frowns for a moment giving his decision a final consideration, then nods, "Yes, I want you to be through, but please try and remain friends with your brother." With a reluctance, he pauses for moment, "I'd take care of this myself, but my eye sight..."

Jacob's world is black and white. This new development with his eyes, and having to depend on others to do what he would normally do for himself, is unsettling.

Seeing his father struggle, Joey assures him, "Don't worry about it Dad, I'll take care of it." Wearing his new jacket he heads toward the door.

He quickly calculates several scenarios in this, seeming delicate assignment. To his thinking, achieving success at these kinds of tasks will eventually assure him the senior position in the family business.

Employing the following thoughts, he adds, "Without pointing fingers at this time, I'm confident we can solve this dilemma."

No more words are needed. Jacob nods, which is the most assurance this son needs.

A few years ago when Joey began to show up around the plant no one paid much attention. It was dismissed as a father attempting to show his son the business. He was usually given some menial office job that no one cared to do.

That's quickly changed since he graduated from college. Recently it's becoming more and more apparent that he's being given a more authoritative voice.

Sam in particular has taken notice. His aggressive personality is clashing more often with his much younger brother's slower, but much more calculating persona.

The second oldest brother is a short stout man with short stumpy legs. At first glance he could be easily mistaken for a laborer. There is nothing about him that can be described as handsome.

His hair is ill-kempt, stuffed under a hat, wildly flying from its brim as though its design is meant to keep him from tipping one way or the other. He's a straightforward man, accustomed to intimidating those whose agenda may threaten his own.

His voice is rude and arrogant. He's as menacing as any common street thug. He likes to give the impression that he's a tough negotiator. In spite of his short legs, his gait is quick and determined. He's all the time barking orders at anyone unfortunate enough to be in his path.

Sam takes to leading much quicker than he does to following. He's a quick thinker and able to perform arduous task under pressure. He's dexterous enough to get more work done in one day than two other men. He's capable of either doing a great good or a great evil.

Jacob sees this son acting as though the world is his stage in which he is the director. Not only is he in charge of the actors, but also the lights, the curtain, the parking lot, and everything in between. If only the actors would remember their lines, it would be a great show.

His father has always hoped he would outgrow his mean streak. Instead, in these later years his contempt has evolved into mindless insolence. Some have even gone so far as to suspect he may have traded his soul off to some unseen demon.

Sam's frustration usually comes to a head when his agenda crashes head long into opposition. Nonetheless, his father is well aware of his strengths and weaknesses and hopes he can be rehabilitated.

In stark contrast, Rup's life revolves around good intentions. He aspires to high moral values, but rarely ever meets them. He considers his penchant to compromise for the sake of peace a superior trait. This allows him to regard solving problems much like one who kicks an old empty can down the road.

Parents are usually the better umpires when it comes to determining the integrity of their children. In spite of Rup's high regard for his "ability to compromise" his father compares this son's character to water. "That boy is like water—he always shapes himself to whatever container he finds himself in." The uncertainty of this trait has made him hard to trust.

Since the old gold rush days when the Yukon demanded a blacksmith's repair skills, they have given way at Mueller and Sons to a state-of-the-art smelting operation and purifying metals according to federal standards. The Muellers have established themselves as premier precious metals extractors and Jacob wants to keep it that way.

Doubting the integrity of Sam when he was young was to be expected but now that he is an adult, he had hoped for more. From time to time he has had words with Sam—usually for minor problems, but this is the first time he is questioning his honesty.

# 4 — DREAMS FATALE

The Mueller smelting company structure is not the more recent pole-barn design. Rather this one dates back to an era of brick and mortar when the permanence of a building of this kind was the premier symbol of success. The original blacksmith shop had been built of local field stone and is to this day buried in the structure as part of the office complex.

Entering Rup's office unannounced Sam goes into a tirade. "Rup when you gonna get off your dead ass and do somthin' about these guys standin' around the plant doin' nothin'. They act like they own the place."

Rup looks up from a grungy desk piled with assay samples. He knows his next younger brother all to well. Once he gets rolling on this kind of rampage, it goes to some sort of unpleasant conclusion. The knot forming in his stomach tells him that this confrontation is not going to end well.

"So what do you expect me to do about it?"

"You tell me. You're the one in charge of the plant when Dad's not here." Not waiting for an answer, something catches his eye. Maintaining the same generalship, he peers out a dirty office window. "Well here comes Daddy's little Wonder Boy!"

Rup slowly places his pen and glasses on his cluttered desk. He runs a hand through his straggly hair. This is all very painful to him. The last thing he wants is for Sam to start something with Joey, especially at the plant in front of the employees and certainly not behind the closed doors of his office.

"Okay, okay Sam don't get all riled up, that won't change anything."

"I can't believe your taking his side," says Sam.

Rup can hear the contempt. "It's incredible how you can manage to turn this shop upside down every time you come through the door. Why don't you just go back to the field and leave the plant to the rest of us. We can manage quite well."

Just as suddenly as he appeared, Sam turns on his heel not bothering
to close the door and he heads down the corridor to his own office. Before
he can sequester himself behind its walls, Joey is at his entrance. Resting
one hand on the door frame, he confronts him. "Ah Sam you're just the
guy I want to see," announces Joey. He's wearing that "churlish grin" that
Sam finds boorish and irritating.

Trying his best to ignore him, Sam enters his office shuffling papers
around as though he's on a mission that can't be interrupted. "Get with
me later, I'm busy right now," he says in best big brother voice.

Since Joey has become an adult, he no longer allows Sam to bully him
like he did a few years ago.

"This won't take more than a minute Sam," says Joey wearing the
same grin.

Sam's attempt to conceal his feelings is falling apart. His look says
that he probably is not going to like what he's about to hear.

"Dad wants me to learn more of what goes on in the field. His suggestion is that I ride with you until I catch on," says Joey in a very matter
of fact tone.

For the moment Sam stops his busy work trying his best to digest
this twist. Not convinced he can't outmaneuver Joey, his mind races for
a way out.

This process stops as quickly as it starts. What he hasn't noticed is
that his father is suddenly standing unannounced in the door behind Joey.
For all of his bluster, the barefaced appearance of his father neutralizes all
attempts to manipulate his younger half brother. His Mormon upbringing has taught him to regard the commandment to "Honor your Father"
seriously. It's Jacob's tradition, to embrace his family members with a hug
after a separation. Sam relishes any attention his father consigns to him.
For the moment his meanness is quieted.

Jacob has always been able to anchor any tacking that Sam may attempt. But this does not mean Sam won't venture a random shot now and then.

Always wanting to appear fully capable of any task his father assigns, Sam acquiesces. In spite of this second son's deference, there is something in his eyes that disturbs Jacob.

"Fine," says Sam, "when do you want to get started?" His look is saying something other than his words.

"Let's start today," says his father. He knows this son well enough. Realizing this is not sitting real well with Sam, he leaves as quickly as he appeared, leaving Sam alone to deal with the dark shadows looming over his thoughts.

With a bland, blank look and a blunt tone, more of an imperative than a request Sam says, "Be ready to go at 7 a.m. tomorrow." His thick hand closes his office door leaving Joey standing outside alone.

"Damn, damn, damn," says Sam pounding his littered desk top, simultaneously attempting to avoid its contents bouncing to the floor. Releasing this kind of pressure is what keeps his head from exploding. His life has been one of continuous hitting, banging, kicking, twisting, and bellowing at everything and anybody that stands in his way.

Joey is fifteen years younger than Sam and for this reason Sam has mostly dismissed this younger brother. He's always felt that his father has favored Rena's children more than him and his brothers, which has further legitimized his loathing. And if this weren't enough, Joey's gentle nature rebuts his own brashness causing even more disdain. Nonetheless, Sam can not hide from the fact that he also fears his younger brother's sharp intellect.

Within minutes of Joey's departure, Sam bursts back into Rup's office.

"Sam, can you please stop barging in here. I've too much work to do," says a startled Rup.

Paying little attention to his brother's request, Sam continues his bombastic ranting, only this time he targets his father.

"Do you know what the 'Old Man' wants me to do?" Not waiting for an answer, he persists, "He wants me to take his prima donna out in the field with me. I think he does this just to piss me off."

"Good grief. Sam calm down. You're gonna blow a gasket!" Rup is well aware of his brother's dislike for Rena's children. At times he's shared some of the same feelings, but Sam always takes it to a level Rup finds uncomfortable.

Still not ready to lighten up, Sam continues his diatribe, "You don't get it do you Rup? The 'Old Man' wants me to train this school boy to take my job—I know what he's up to."

Fear feeding a paranoia always results in an unreasonable form of insanity. Sam is plunging head long into its grip.

"Come on Sam get a hold of yourself." The concern in Rup's voice is unmistakable. "You don't know any more than I do Dad's motives."

Sam does not intend to allow Rup to dissuade his thinking any time soon, so he switches tactics.

"Rup, you're a naive wimp! If you don't see what's plain as day how can I depend on you to watch my back?"

Sam reverts to what he knows Rup will respond to—guilt.

This statement causes Rup to sit with his mouth slightly agape and to blink rapidly. Sam doesn't have to wait too long for the expected response. "You know I love you Sam. You're my brother."

By this time Sam knows he's gained the upper hand, he can already hear the doubt in his brother's voice.

"If that's true Rup you wouldn't leave me swinging in the wind with this pissant half brother." Again not waiting for an answer and starring straight and hard at his older brother, he delivers the knock out blow. "Rup I'm asking you to take my back—can I depend on you?"

Defeat is written all over Rup's face. It's carried forward in his voice. With ever recurring confusion and convoluted allegiances, Rup caves in. "Yes, Sam – you know I'll do all I can."

In an unprecedented move, Sam embraces his brother, "I knew I could depend on you." It's not a hug of affection for his brother rather one of triumph for himself.

Satisfied yet once again that he is capable of bullying his older brother, he returns home. There is much more that must be thought through.

At present, Sam has only one wife. Her name is Mattie. He had another named Rebecca. She had decided she was more willing to risk the fires of hell than to stay with a tyrant one more day. On a cold winter night several years ago she was able, along with their two daughters, to make their escape. So as not to involve government social workers, he was advised by their religious leadership not to pursue them.

More out of fear than love, Mattie stays with Sam. They have a son, Jonathan, and a daughter, Sarah. She is much younger than her "sister wife" had been and for the time being is willing to remain compliant to the demands of a much older husband.

Joey on the other hand is not sure at this time whether a polygamous or monogamous relationship is in store for him, he remains open. Having recently graduated from the University of Alaska, he's more interested in the business than having a women in his life. Living at home with his family is also a preference. It provides a defense against the outside world.

Joey has arrived home from the plant and is confiding in his mother. "Ma, I'm going out with Sam tomorrow. Dad wants me to keep an eye on Sam's dealings with the miners." Joey isn't merely announcing this fact for the sake of sharing information, he's also hoping for a reaction.

There has been tension between Lena and Rena for years over Sam's bullying. Ever since they were small boys, Sam has taken great delight in sending her boys into risky situations, if for no other reason than to amuse himself.

Sam is no stranger to Rena's fury. There are many awful memories of Sam's meanness toward her sons. She is only a couple of years older than he is. Many times she has thrust herself as one would a lion tamer's chair between him and her boys. This has caused undue wear on the sisters' relationship.

Lena has always been a rather plain woman, lacking in both looks and personality. After raising four sons, she's even worse for wear. At the time she and Jacob married, she proved to be a fit match. She appealed to his need for a strong, healthy mate.

Later, Jacob's eye turned toward the prettier sister. She was not what any would describe as a stylish woman, but much more of a slender build and prettier facial features than her older sister.

To Jacob, both choices fit a need, but his special smile and joyous reaction is reserved for Rena and their sons. Of course this display of affection hardly goes unnoticed.

"Don't worry about it Joey, you'll do just fine." Rena's voice is slightly hushed in a reassuring motherly tone as she lightly pats his hand.

Both father and son are up at their usual 5 am. "Good morning, Joey," says Jacob on his way to the tea kettle.

Joey sits quietly staring at his hands wrapped around his cup of hot chocolate. His cup seems to interest him more than his father's greeting.

Not waiting any longer for a response, Jacob asks, "You all right ,son?"

Joey has a very puzzled look about him as though he has something to say, but not sure how to start. He finally speaks. "Dad, I don't know how to explain what happened to me last night." He's still sitting with his head hanging staring at the table.

Jacob can tell there is something pressing on Joey and is willing to give him the patience he needs to bring it into words. He sits across the table content to drink his Postum and wait.

"I really don't know how to start. Last night I had the most intense and vividly clear dreams I have ever experienced in my life," says Joey still struggling for words. "It was more like a vision than a dream. It was so real that somehow I actually lived this dream."

He pauses, continuing to stare. The silence continues as Joey tries to resolve the meaning of this mysterious vision.

Jacob's waiting has come to an end, and now his curiosity has come to a head. "Well, let's hear what message this dream is trying to tell you." Jacob leans forward resting both folded forearms on the table giving Joey his undivided attention.

Joey raises his head, looking directly at his father and begins. "I am in a huge office building much like a big city skyscraper. My office is on the top floor, I'm in charge of many things it seems. Suddenly you and all my brothers are sitting in chairs around my desk awaiting my orders."

Both continue to sit and stare at one another. Jacob is stunned. He can hardly believe the implications this dream will lead to if his other sons get drift of it. Favoritism in families is unavoidable, but its effects are unquestionably divisive. Jacob has unwittingly shown favoritism to Joey over the years, something he imagines is under his control. Now this dream is giving him serious second thoughts.

It has been brought to his awareness by Lena as best she can that her sons also need an equal portion of their father's attention, but now this has gone to another level. Jacob realizes that this son has also subjugated him. "What have I created," becomes his thought. His next thought is even more glaring. "If the other boys hear of this dream, it could be a game changer." It will certainty aggravate already strained relations.

"I think it will do well to leave this dream between the two of us for now," says Jacob.

Joey, looking hurt and puzzled at his father's abrupt reaction speaks up, "Dad it's not like I forced this dream on myself—I can't control everything."

"For now let it rest. We'll talk about it again later," adds his father trying to be as diplomatic as possible.

What isn't apparent is that Benji has overheard the whole conversation. Not aware of all the family dynamics at his age, it's not going to be like him to keep a secret too long, and in this case it proves to be a correct assessment.

By the time this sixteen year old enters the plant this spring morning, he is chomping at the bit to tell Justin and Levi their brother's stupid dream. Rup and Sam overhear the laughter, soon making their way over to this part of the plant.

"What the heck is so funny?" challenges Rup.

Benji is astonished and pleased at the attention his older brothers are paying him. More than ready to relate the story yet once again, he describes in great detail all he overheard.

Sam is the first to comment. "Does this peckerwood actually believe we are all going to be sitting at his feet blinking our eyes at his every word!?" As usual Sam's assessment is swift. The rest of the brothers smirk a bit as a first reaction.

Rup is the first to respond. "I know our brother has always had a high-minded opinion of himself through the day but now he even dreams about it through the night."

"Do you really think he believes all this?," ponders Levi.

"Knowing him, he probably does," responds Justin.

Not being in competition with his older brothers, as Joey is, Benji's left somewhat surprised that they aren't as amused as he is at their brother's folly.

"You guys are really taking this stupid dream too serious. I told it to you because I thought we'd all get a good laugh and then forget about it," says Benji.

He'd thought the reason they always dismiss him is because he's just a kid. Now he's beginning to see there may be another dimension to their condescension.

# 5 — A CONCOCTED STORY

The calendar may indicate that spring has arrived, but in Alaska that only means that temperatures during the day are high enough to thaw the nightly freeze into slimy mud. Shaded from the sun, snow remains on the north side of everything as the wooded areas slowly give up their white covering for the dead brown from last fall's die off.

The focus this morning is for Sam and Joey to team up and get out into the mine fields. Sam particularly feels the tension. He didn't sleep well. Stressing over Joey doing a ride along kept him awake most of the night. If that weren't enough, having Benji reveal Joey's dream further entrenched his resentments. After all having to work with his much younger brother in an area that has been his for most of this kid's life is enough to put him in a terrible pout.

On the other hand, Joey is anxious to get out into the field for a "hands on" opportunity. Not able to explain it, he has never doubted his abilities. It's as though he possesses a kind of self assurance that never doubts itself. He's never been able to shake the strange and very alluring feeling that he's being led by some unseen force.

The ride out to the mine field remains silent. It's not the kind of silence that occurs when no one speaks, but rather the silence that's not being spoken.

Sam has his own way of dealing with these placer miners. "The last damn thing I need is for this still-wet behind-the-ears young punk interfering with my business," is the thought that keeps bouncing off the walls of his mind.

The Mueller business paradigm worked out over the years is to offer presmelting wholesale prices. The idea is to offer cash on site, expecting the margins to be great enough to make a profit. This in turn gives Sam a lot of flexibility with a lot of discretionary cash to make the deals.

What is giving their father all the concern is that there has been a greater percentage of cash going out for the amount coming back in spite of the increase in the number of new clients.

Sam has the maps for all the claims in the region. There are at least 1,700 to date with more being added every time the price of gold spikes. Their first stop is in an area that can best be described as uninhabited. It's muddy, uneven terrain, steep hills, and a hard packed gravel stream meandering through a spot on earth that offers a brand new challenge every few yards.

Joey possesses an athletic ability that Sam hasn't been blessed with. He deftly follows Sam's more trudging gait as Sam plows his way through this unfriendly territory. It's not soon enough before they come upon the best that civilization has to offer.

It's a group of crude structures. It's obvious they're not meant to be permanent. Some are old vintage army tents, probably from WW2, others are a mixture of wood and blue plastic tarps formed into lean-to type structures, along with what can best described as sheds. As a center piece is a large propane tank fueling the generator that's used to power a portable pump that operates an ingenious looking sluice box.

The three men that greet them, in spite of their age difference, all have similar characteristics. They all have straggly hair and beards. They all are wearing clothing that more than likely at one point in time was of differing colors but now have been neutralized by the common earth tones of the region. In other words they're filthy.

Sam introduces Joey and himself as gold buyers to this grandfather, son, and grandson team. Soon they are negotiating on a price. Sam has run out of the chemicals he needs to run some tests. Turning to Joey, he barks an imperative, "I'm running out of acid, run to the truck and grab some for me."

Quickly returning to the truck, Joey not sure where Sam keeps these supplies tries to be as efficient as he can. Sam's truck bed is covered with a customized shell that can be locked. Hastily unlocking the secured door with the key Sam had given him, he begins by carefully sorting through things. This rapidly turns to inefficiency as his sorting is turning into a clumsy pawing. Now thoroughly frustrated, he begins to open every bag and box. The sulfuric acid shows up, but not before he comes across a locked container that Sam is sure he would not find.

"What the heck is this?" Joey mutters to himself. It's way too heavy for it's size to have only a few tools or assaying equipment. After carefully tucking it back in its hiding spot and remembering the concern his father expressed to him earlier about a gold shortage, he ponders the possibilities of this discovery. His mind is traveling a mile a minute on his way back to the claim site.

Sam completes his transaction. He's bought the gold, weighed and tested on site. He then marks the information in a log book. Joey's not certain of everything Sam is doing, but suspects something could be amiss.

"Sam you sure know your business," says Joey trying his best not to sound condescending or patronizing. "I know I can learn a lot from you. Let's see how much I remember. You first test the ore for purity, then begin your negotiations to buy. After you make the deal, you enter it all in this log book."

Catching Sam off guard, Joey reaches across and snatches the log book from Sam's side of the dashboard. Not expecting this maneuver, and not wanting to appear anxious, Sam checks his reaction from initially intending to break Joey's arm to just a nervous chuckle.

Sam's attempting to keep his mind on his driving all the while Joey, exhuding innocence attempts to tie his suspicions as to how Sam makes his entries.

Sam's eyes are moving nervously from the road to Joey freely thumbing through his log book. It's apparent he does not want Joey snooping. The anxiousness soon surfaces. Holding the steering wheel with one hand, and with one quick snatch, he manages to grab the ledger away from his brother. Clutching it to his breast as one would something held dear, he shouts, "Don't screw around with this. I don't want you messin' it up."

Up until now, Sam has forced himself to be civil, but now the gates are open for him to return to his normal impatient demeanor.

Realizing how upset Sam was getting, Joey more or less surrendered the book to Sam, but not before, he was able to notice some discrepancies. Sam had shorted the weights of a few transactions that morning, registering them fractionally lower than Joey remembered them.

Not wanting to appear suspicious, but definitely on alert, Joey pays close attention to Sam's agitation, especially his nervous body language. Meanwhile he's content to keep the talk low key.

In the early evening, after work, they go their separate ways. Sam's natural paranoia kicks in as his fear of Joey knowing too much feeds on itself. Not sure what his brother may have seen, he opts to check his special box hidden away in the bed of his truck.

The first thing he notices is that the box has been disturbed. An unsolicited panic wave is inundating his thoughts. He had it safely tucked away under assorted toolboxes, now to find it disturbed leaves him shaking.

"If the family ever figures out what I'm doing, they'll run me out on a rail," he confesses to himself. Not wanting the risk, he removes his hoard from his truck to a locked shed behind his house.

The next morning Joey arrives for work. Realizing he'll be working with Sam again, he tries to be nonchalant, not wanting to raise any unnecessary suspicions. He knows how out of control Sam's paranoia can rapidly get. What he doesn't realize is that suspicion has already come to fruition.

Sam, on the other hand, hardly able to disguise his temperament, is unusually short with Joey this morning.

"Take your time office boy. We've got a lot of work to do today and you're acting like this is a pleasure trip," snarls Sam.

Since Joey has become an adult, Sam's bluster has become non-intimidating resulting in a boldness Sam finds disconcerting.

"Slow down Sam, you're gonna' blow a gasket," chortles Joey.

It's also become apparent to Sam of late that Joey is intimidating him more than he's capable of returning. This frustration is further feeding his insecurities.

Joey manages to stay out of Sam's way for the most part, but is not remiss to notice Sam trying to remain unnoticed as he continues to shave fractional amounts of gold weights in his log book.

Another day together is winding to an end as they make their way back home. Joey surreptitiously, while trying to remain naive, begins to question his half brother about some discrepancies he observed.

"I know it's probably just an over sight, but I think you recorded the weights wrong on some of the gold you bought today."

These words sting Sam. Joey is too close for comfort. Slamming his brakes, Sam brings the truck to a halt. The sudden jolt nearly sends Joey through the windshield.

"Just what the hell are you inferring?" demands Sam in a tone Joey has yet to hear. The very thing men like Sam are guilty of creates the illusion of innocence in their own mind. Not waiting for an answer he grabs Joey by the shirt collar, "Your ass is mine little brother. I'm tired of your shit. You and I are going to have it out here and now."

Without a pause, Sam is out of the truck and around to the passenger's door, throwing it open, and with one monumental thrust has Joey on the ground bashing his head with a nearby rock shouting, "Die you bastard, die!!!"

All the pent up resentments, anger over Joey finding him stealing, and his own guilt causes this already unstable man to continue to punch the limp, defenseless, seemingly lifeless body of this hated half brother. His thoughts come pouring through, taking a life of their own as he continues his diabolic rant. All the special attentions and favors that he feels should have been his are doing this helpless body no good at all. "You got what you deserve. Joey the big shot hah!" As his brother is laying crumpled on a dirt back road in Alaska's wilderness

The picture that comes flying into his consciousness is a dead Joey and now everything will be wonderful. Not only is he sick in his mind, he's sick in his heart.

These are always the perverse thoughts of the self-centered. They rest comfortably in the thought of how necessary their misdeeds become.

Since Sam has justified his actions, all that needs to be done now is to rid himself of the body. His mind is working at warp speed. Scanning the terrain his eyes focus on a spot just above him. It appears to be the opening shaft to a long abandoned mine. It's late in the day with dusk promising to conceal those deeds done in secret.

With the strength that only the possessed are able to muster, he tosses the limp body over his shoulder and climbs the short distance to the cave's gaping mouth. Once there, he unceremoniously dumps his brother down its steep throat, hearing only the angry sound of disturbed rock and gravel as it marks the body's downward tumble.

Ever mindful of the lies he's going to have to concoct, he picks up Joey's varsity jacket from where it had dropped in the struggle carrying him up the hill. It's covered in blood. Abruptly an idea spawns. Within minutes he has made his way down a trail winding its way through a wooded ravine. His eyes rapidly survey the location. Picking a medium-size tree, he ties the two arms around its lowest branch. Satisfied he hastily backtracks to his truck and makes his way home.

# 6 — LIAR, LIAR, PANTS ON FIRE!

The mining season in Alaska is short at best. In some areas the permafrost allows only a short, muddy window of opportunity. Many more fortunes have been spent looking for the elusive, yellow ore than have been made finding it. Nonetheless, the fortune hunters continue to pour into the region year after year. Some confess they originally came for the adventure, but ultimately find they too are bitten by the "gold bug." Only those with exceptional survival skills succeed. It's a rough country. The terminating fate of many is that they live and die here broke.

The days are getting longer again as the promise of warmer and mud free days lie around the corner. This night though is unusually dark when Rup arrives back at the plant. With each moment of lost illumination, darkness becomes the ruler as muted shadows slowly twist themselves into unpredictable shapes.

Rup, Justin, and Levi are working overtime when Sam arrives. Rup is the first to notice his next younger brother's strange demeanor.

"What the heck is the matter with you Sam? You look like you been rode hard and put up wet," says Rup. Still chuckling he asks, "What did you do with our little brother Joey, make him walk?" Rup knows all too well Sam's dislike for their younger half sibling.

"He ain't coming back," says Sam in a flat, matter of fact tone.

"Wadda' ya mean he 'ain't commin back'?" asks a puzzled Rup.

"Just like I said, he ain't comin back."

Rup's expression is one of apprehension. It's occurring to him there's going to be more to this than he's wanting to deal with.

"Why is he not commin back?" It's the only question that makes sense at this juncture.

"Cause he's dead," answers Sam with a just as dead tone.

By now Justin and Levi have joined Rup's inquisition. They are all aware of Sam's temper. The three of them stand dumbfounded, staring at Sam. Each has the same question, "How did Joey die?"

When one is fully aware of this family's dysfunction the potential for violence lies very close to the surface. One can only hope for the best, but expect the worst.

"I killed him. It was an accident," says Sam in the same flat tone.

It's becoming clear to each of the brothers that if they're going to bring this fiasco to a head they are going to have to keep asking the questions. In unison the next logical is, "How?"

Sam's delusional mind begins to 'spin' an explanation.

"He started that crap about his stupid dream. He said God wanted him to take over the business. I told him the rest of wouldn't put up with his 'bullshit' dream. He said that Dad was behind him and if the rest of us didn't like it that was too bad, and that we could leave. That's when I lost it and hit him. When he went down, he hit his head on a rock."

Rup, Levi, and Justin are left speechless. They stand apart in this little group, alone from the rest of the world. Confusion and frustration are the only emotions they all share at the moment.

"Where is he now?" is the next question.

"I dumped his body down an abandoned mine shaft." Sam's answers are beginning to sound a bit more desperate as the questions sound more hostile.

"YOU DID WHAT? WHY?!!"

Pausing long enough to measure his words hoping to gain as much understanding as possible.

"Because I know Dad would blame me." Sam's eyes shift from brother to brother, carefully watching their reactions. Not satisfied, he drops one more falsification hoping this one will prevent any deeper interrogation.

"Not only all this but it could bring the law in and you know how Dad feels about that!"

Rup's mind is speeding full throttle trying his best to process all this. "How do you know he's dead? Did you check his pulse or his breathing?" are Rup's next questions.

This question catches Sam off guard. Not wanting to elaborate on how badly he had beaten Joey and how if he wasn't dead from all that, he would certainly be dead from the fall, Sam concocts yet another lie.

"Yes I did. I even did CPR for at least an hour. I'm sure he's dead."

From the look on his brother's faces, Sam feels he is accomplishing what he has hoped for all along—their trust and cooperation.

Levi asks the next pertinent question, "How do you ever imagine we can keep this from Dad and Rena?"

Sam's confidence is building by the minute. "What I'm going to tell Dad is that Joey went off by himself and didn't return. Tomorrow we are going to organize a search party. We will then return to where the accident took place, sending Dad and Benji down the road a ways. The four of us are going to find his blood-soaked jacket. We'll then inform Dad that he has been mauled and carried off by a Grizzly." Sam states this with the full confidence that he has spun his brothers into his web of deceit.

In spite of Sam's siblings believing that he is capable of murder, they also possess a sense of brotherly fraternity.

The tensions between the two sister's children has finally run its course. All these years of unresolved resentments have led to this moment where hurts have turned to an anger that has produced a rage that proceeded enough to committed a murder.

Acting in fraternity, the four of them agree to stick to Sam's description. The next step is to inform Jacob. It's not unusual for the four boys to show up when it's his week at their mother's house.

"Good to see you boys. This is a treat to see you all together. Your mother will be happy to see you," says their father greeting them at the door.

Rup being the oldest, and out of tradition, assumes the role of spokesman when they have family business.

"Unfortunately we aren't here on a social call," says Rup as he nervously clears his throat.

Jacob is developing a weak smirk that appears when a smile is beginning to wane. It's the face every parent wrestles with when their mind is being smothered with a wave of fear.

Still trying to maintain a calm persona, Jacob asks the question he fears. "What's happened?"

"Joey's missing."

"What do you mean, 'Joey's missing'?" Jacob's face tells that fear is having its way.

Rup looks at Sam with that look that says, "You take it from here."

Sam begins his story, sticking to his basic script.

By time he finishes, Jacob is putting a plan together. He's facing his worst fears with action. He starts by gathering his family around him, invoking God's protection for his missing son. At the end of the prayer they all shamelessly add their "amen" along with their father.

Agreeing to meet the next morning at the plant no later than 6 am, Jacob and Lena leave to break this distressing news to Rena and Benji.

When all that is known is divulged, predictably Rena is heartsick. Jacob holds his younger wife trying as best he can to console her. She reaches for a dish towel hanging from a magnetized hook on her refrigerator, wiping her eyes, she whisper to her husband, "I have a very bad feeling about this Jacob."

She is mindful of bad blood between her son and Sam. The circumstances surrounding this rift has been festering for years. Jacob has always hoped that having a strong Mormon home would insulate them from the problems of the outside world. Unfortunately, this thought remains a myth.

Nonetheless his faith remains unwavering. At times like this, both wives are very grateful for their husband's spiritual leadership. Holding both Rena and Lena, he reassures them, "We can't prevent these bad things from happening, but our response can be different. Our God will not abandon us."

Benji, meantime, has retreated to the living room. Jacob finds him sitting alone on the couch. He has a reflective look about him, determined not to be dismissed.

Alarmed and half crying he blurts out, "Dad, I told my brothers about Joey's dream. Sam was really mad."

Puzzled as to how in the world Benji knew about Joey's dream, he sets this thought aside for the moment. It's obvious this youngest son is distraught.

"What are you trying to say, Benji?" questions his father.

Benji is old enough to be aware of Sam's dysfunctional nature.

"I mean I don't trust him." He says this with a perception that can't easily be dismissed. After all, he's experienced Sam's mean streak first hand as a young boy growing up.

It's Jacob's nature to try and dismiss the things he seems powerless over. The tension that has grown between the two sets of children is one of these things. The best he is able to conclude is that it's normal sibling rivalry.

Still hoping to console his youngest son, he puts a positive face on the status quo, "Don't worry Benji, your brother is an Alaskan man, he knows how to take care of himself." Jacob finds these positive statements console him as much as they do Benji. He prays he's right.

The next morning arrives on schedule. It's been a fitful night for most of them. Unrelenting human emotions have won the battle against sleep. The only one who has slept soundly, it seems, is Sam.

# 7 — THE PLOT THICKENS

Sam may be an oaf of a man blundering his way through life, but when it comes to deception, he's on top of his game. He's been heard to say, "Even a dumb fox can steal a chicken once in a while."

Sam is leading his father and brothers to a remote region where he claims he and Joey stopped for a break. The only ones not aware of this deception are Benji and their father.

"I stopped right here, Dad. Joey said he wanted to survey the valley beyond that next ridge. I said I'd wait here and finish some paper work.

"This was about 2 pm in the afternoon. I began to get a little worried when he didn't show up by 4 pm so I tried yelling for about an hour. By this time it's beginning to get dark so I figured I better head home and get some help."

Jacob is listening earnestly along with Benji. The other brothers are also listening as intensely; they are amazed at how smooth their brother can lie.

It's an astounding weakness in the human condition that consents to stand behind a lie when it's such a fugacious refuge. These brothers are no exceptions.

Jacob and Benji agree to search in a designated region while Levi and Justin, along with Rup and Sam search an adjacent territory.

As soon as their father and younger brother are out of sight, Sam leads the others to the old abandoned mine. He parks in the same spot where the day before he committed his unspeakable crime. The bloody rock is still lying where he recklessly tossed it. Lost in their own thoughts, each of them are dealing with the deception they have unwittingly agreed to.

Rup, unnoticed by the others, has retrieved a bunch of gear from his truck. It's a basic survival pack Alaskans carry in the event they become stranded in the wilderness. It's a strange toiling to be watching. It prompts a response from Sam.

"What the hell are you doing Rup?" It's clear Sam's aggravated over his oldest brother's behavior.

From the slamming Rup is initiating, it's apparent he's not in the mood to be answering questions. He's exasperated. Finding himself pulled into Sam's fraudulence is most uncomfortable.

"I'm not convinced from your account that you could be sure Joey was dead and I'm not willing to take that chance. He could still be alive."

Even more aggravated Sam bellows at Rup, "Do what you want, I'm tellin' you: he's DEAD! The Old Man and Benji are not going to be gone forever and I've got other things that need to be done."

In spite of Sam's timetable, Rup cannot be dissuaded. He makes his way to the mine shaft to begin his vigil.

"Joey, Joey, Joey can you hear me?"

Rup continues with his purported task, dropping the survival pack at the entrance as well as securing a line to a small tree and sending the other end uncoiling down the shaft.

"For Pete's sake Rup, quit that damn hollerin'—he's DEAD I TELL YOU!!! Now come with me, we've one more task to finish," says a contentious Sam starting out on his own. Like the lemmings they've become, his brothers fall in line behind him, following him down into a nearby ravine.

Holding his hand in the 'halt' position, Sam takes on a slight smirk—the kind taken on after a job well done. Pointing to a tree where a tattered, bloodstained yellow and blue University of Alaska varsity jacket hangs, he boasts, "I hung it just high enough for some critters to tear at it. It looks like they found it okay."

Rup, Justin, and Levi, remain dumbfounded at their brother's crass reaction to his part in Joey's demise.

"We are going to take this back to the Old Man and tell him it appears Joey has been attacked by a Grizzly and dragged off somewhere."

The three weak-minded brothers each feel they have reached the point of no return. Sam has successfully pulled them into his deceptive quagmire.

As they make their way back up the trail, Rup lags behind. He doesn't have the stomach for this stuff. With a woeful gaze, he turns his doleful eyes up the hill in the direction of the mine shaft as he thinks to himself, "What am I hoping to see? At this time I don't even know." Startled for a second when he believes he's seen movement. Finally settling on it being only his imagination playing tricks, he catches the rest of his brothers. Besides Sam is on full-court press to get this bloody jacket in front of his Dad and get this episode down the road.

It's early afternoon when they finally meet up with their father and Benji. Without a word exchanged, all eyes are focusing on the blood-stained remnant.

"I'm afraid we've bad news Dad," says Sam thrusting Joey's jacket out.

Jacob's eyes as bad as they are immediately recognize it as the one he has recently given him. Hoping against all odds that if he looks away, it will also make the jacket go away, that this whole incident will prove to be only an illusion. It, of course, is not to be.

"Oh dear God what has happened to him?" His voice quivers. It's nearly hushed. He is struggling hard for control. Turning his grief inward, he fights back the tears, continually clearing his throat.

"You tell him, Rup," says Sam feigning overwhelming grief.

This request startles Rup. Sam is proving very successful in aligning his brothers as far into this ploy as he wishes.

"It looks like either a Grizz got him or a big cat. There were both tracks. We couldn't find his body. We think he was probably dragged off," stammers a visibly shaken Rup. Not shaken with grief, but not nearly as good at lying as his brother, he's shaking with the fear his deceit may be detected.

Justin and Levi stand quietly praying that Sam doesn't suck them any deeper than they already are. This is not to be.

Jacob's heaviness of heart prevents him from stopping—his disconsolation demands feeding. He turns to these two sons with a look that begs for an opposite witness.

Both look at the other, hoping to be spared. Stammering over the top of each other, they validate Sam and Rup's account.

Jacob finds himself at a point in life no aging parent should have to find themselves, mourning the loss of a child.

The skies have darkened, shutting the sun out for the moment.

# 8 — THE ARTFUL LIAR

It's a late spring afternoon now. Our newborn from the cave is endeavoring to understand his new life. For him the past is as recent as this morning.

He's paid a high price for his youthful arrogance. His dream had a certain impact on his father and brothers. Certainly not angry enough for all to murder, but angry enough for his some of his brothers to be conplicit in Sam's deed.

Doctors would diagnose his condition as "Declarative Memory loss" caused by a severe head trauma. It means he has completely forgotten his personal identity, but retains learned skills. It shifts from a neurological condition to a psychological state of mind or in simple layman's—Amnesia.

This hapless vagabond is as fearful as any lost person. Not only is he lost to himself, but also lost in a strange wilderness. For him this means there is no contextual beginning. In other words to look forward is to take the next step.

He's struggling to allow his instinctive senses to take command. In this new unfolding reality, he senses that he would prefer being the 'discoverer' rather than the 'discovered'. He's already had one encounter with some strange men earlier in the day, but remained hidden.

As any newborn, survival becomes the meaning of life. It's crucial that he pay attention to useful things. For the moment that means determining what he is going to do and how he is going to use those things he's discovered at the mouth of the mine shaft.

The immediate attention to his hunger and thirst have been met. Now the incessant question returns to plague him "WHO AM I? Am I insane? Have I lost my mind? Have I committed some kind of crime and am now a fugitive?" More unanswered questions relentlessly bombard him.

At least for the moment, he opts to retreat back into the entrance of the mine shaft. Remaining huddled there for no other reason than it's his only connection to something familiar and predictable.

The next morning he awakens to the sound of trucks coming down the road. It's the same trucks carrying the same people he avoided the day before.

His instincts kick into full force telling him to get moving. Engaging these strangers is out of the question. Gathering all his equipment, he opts to follow a trail deeper into the wilderness and away from the road.

The trucks are parking along the road in the same spot they had yesterday. As the men exit the sound of slamming truck doors echoes through cool dawn. Gathering together, Jacob's voice can be heard. His face is drawn and pale. He's a visibly shattered father.

"As best you can, take me back to the spot where you found Joey's jacket. I just want to bring him home. He doesn't need to be laying out here alone away from the rest of us."

Sam makes a quick knowing glance at his three coconspirators and begins the trek. He's leading them past the scene of the crime for the second time in two days. The details remain his and his alone.

Rup takes advantage of this time to break off from the rest for the time being and check the supplies he had left the day before. THEY'RE GONE! He's standing in the same spot loaded with provisions only twenty-four hours ago, now it's becoming more and more apparent from all the disturbed stone and dirt, along with boot prints that someone crawled up out of this shaft. Even the rope is missing.

"My God he's alive!!" His first reaction is to alert the rest of his family. Then his second thought comes screaming at him, "He may already be on his way home." Realizing how deep he's buried himself into Sam's lie, his thoughts begin to sicken him as the just effect for one whose deception is beginning to unravel.

His mind harks back to how content he had been only a day or two ago. Now he's grieving the day he was born. In his mind, he has no other choice than to live with his horrific guilt, hoping somehow to redeem himself sometime, someway.

Catching up with his father and brothers, his demeanor has changed to match that of his father's and Benji's, but for totally differing reasons. Theirs' is to mourn the loss of a son and brother, his is to mourn his possible resurrection.

Sam is heartlessly running his father and youngest brother around all day. His pretense is blatantly guiltless as he artfully dupes them into searching one location after another, all the while keeping their hopes high that it will be possible to locate his remains.

After a day of Sam's nonsense, they all agree to go home. Rup has been spending most of his time trying to get Sam aside to inform him of his discovery. With the rest of the family absent, he seizes the moment.

"What did you say?" says a startled Sam.

"I said Joey is alive."

"What makes you so sure."

"All that stuff I left there is gone, including the rope. It's real obvious someone crawled out of that hole."

"I've got to see this for myself," says a disbelieving Sam. Both return to the mine entrance. Sam is clearly shook looking at the battle Joey put up clawing his way out of what was thought to be his tomb.

This is the closest to sheer panic Rup has ever seen Sam.

"Where in the hell do you think he went?"asks Sam. The tone of his voice accompanied with a dumbfounded stare reflects how truly unnerved this turn of events is making him.

Rup has the potential to be a thinker, but unfortunately for him worry always trumps his thinking. This secret Sam has forced on him is bringing him close to a complete breakdown.

"What if he has made his way home and we have to face him," laments poor, distraught Rup. He's beginning to take on the pitiful character of some poor thwarted misunderstood child who just doesn't know better.

"I'll kill him, I'll kill him again!!" blurts Sam.

Rup stands staring at Sam, trying to make sense of this impromptu confession. Not only stunned, but also confused at this new revelation prompts the question, "What do you mean Sam 'you'll kill him again'?"

Sam can't believe his failure to protect his crime, but under strain even the best liars fall apart. Like all equivocations, sooner or later they begin to disconnect.

Quickly trying to reconstruct this damning admission he says, "I mean, 'I feel' like I murdered him, I don't mean that I actually did."

In practice, Rup doesn't have enough character to lose his character. Rather than have anymore disconcerting confrontations, he's willing to let it all slide.

The ride home is silent. Not sure how they are going to react if their presumed dead brother reappears. Neither sleep well that night.

# 9 — NEW LIFE BEGINS

Crashing through the woods, tripping over fallen logs, plowing through tangled brush—fear and panic are having their way with this newborn.

Forcing himself to stop, he realizes his mind is going in a crazy direction. "Think, Think, Think," he finds himself shouting. He's developed enough history in the past twenty-four hours to grasp the need for a plan. The only thing that is presently facing him is survival.

The sun is much closer to the horizon. He's not dressed for the cool nights, but then it occurs to him, "I know how to build a fire."

Capable of cognitive thought, he's also cognizant of predators in the wild. Using his buck-knife to cut a six-foot sapling, he slices enough of his rope to lash the knife to the pole making himself a make shift spear. Not the best weapon in the world, but hopefully adequate enough to thwart off a more than curious predator.

Building his fire in front of a large fire tree allows him to not have to worry about covering his back as he wraps himself in his sleeping bag, leaning back against its sturdy trunk. He soon falls asleep.

He awakens the next morning to the rustling sound of an uninvited guest. It's a black squirrel trying its best to steal a package of peanuts. With the reflexes of a cat, he swats his spear at the little invader. With the reflexes quicker than any cat, the would be thief darts off.

With his adrenalin already spring-loaded, he's up tending to his fire. Knowing that birch bark has enough creosote to burn even when wet, he gets his fire hot quick enough to take the morning chill off.

The mystery surrounding his past is hastily replaced by coming up with the skills he needs to survive. His primordial instincts are sharpening. At this point, he feels very vulnerable to everything. Everything needs studying. "Stay focused, stay focused!" has become his unceasing mantra.

Staying alive is all consuming. Food, water, and shelter are first and foremost. These are taking more and more of his days. He's even managed to use his shoelaces to make snares, allowing him a rabbit from time to time.

A week has past and so far he hasn't moved around much. He's gained a sense of security in his present surroundings. Not certain of his standing in a civilized community, he opts to continue his wilderness makeshift.

When things aren't too pressing, his mind travels back to a lone male voice calling down the mine shaft. He distinctly remembers a name this person was calling over and over. "Joey, Joey."

"Is that who I am? Is that my name?" Pondering this thought has no significance other than to lead to some other unanswered questions.

With no one else to talk with, he's taken to talking to himself. "I know I gotta get out of here, but where?" A natural curiosity is pushing him forward.

One morning when filling an empty water bottle, he takes notice of how the stream is flowing in a direction. A plan begins to develop. "I'll follow this sucker and see where it takes me." It's a joyful epiphany. The first he's experienced in his short memory. The thought of it causes him to break out in a staccato laugh, "ha, ha, ha, ha." As if this isn't ridiculous enough, he begins to twirl around in a purely instinctual, impromptu dance. He has the appearance of a primal man who has lost his mind—but after all isn't this the case?

His elation soon turns to hard work. Trying to maneuver a meandering, brush-lined stream is an arduous task. Two full days of trudging and he's traveled at best ten miles—half that distance as the crow flies.

A lack of the proper foods for this kind of undertaking along with the natural obstacles of rock, fallen trees, and steep inclines is taking its toll on this already battered and compromised body. Not to mention a mind partially destroyed by a beating he can't recall.

The day wears on. The sun once again promises to surrender to the dark of night. At about this time its become second nature for Joey to prepare for this inevitable event.

Beginning a scouting expedition for a suitable camp site always requires a keen eye for dry firewood, safety from predators, and suitable drinking water. Suddenly, after breaking out into a clearing, he is taken back by a chill raising the hair on the back of his neck. It's a lone cabin stuck out here in the wilderness. Instinctively, he takes a step back into the tangled brush. Peering out like frightened animal, he's cautious and defensive—careful not expose any part of himself that can't be defended. His eyes dart from one point to another, surveying every aspect of this small compound.

The structure is both very inviting and at the same time prohibitory. There remains a strong conflicting voice in his head that is attempting to restrict him, "This is not yours—Thou Shalt Not Steal." Without connecting these words to any past experiences and after a careful vigilance, he makes the decision to move in for a closer inspection.

The grass-less packed earth surrounding the cabin have no human tracks, but on the other hand it has every other kind of critter tracks one can imagine. Carefully making his way ever closer, he cautiously peers through a curtain-less window. There is no sign of life, human or other. There appears to be a small table and chair, a wood burning stove, a couple of bunk beds along the wall, a wash basin and most inviting of all is a door-less cupboard exposing cans of baked beans.

Making his way to the cabin's only door, he finds it stacked with dry wood on both its sides covered by a small tar papered roof, supported by a couple of poles and a floor from rough cut cedar. After pulling the wooden peg fixed in the latch, he swings the door open. The smell is a musty odor that tightly-constructed cabins take on from the lack of circulating air.

The can opener he discovers on a counter below the open cupboard is quickly becoming a high-priority item. In less than a minute, Joey has spun the can opener around a can of pork and beans. Not bothering to search for a spoon, he tips his head back, pouring its contents down a welcoming throat followed by an enormous sigh of contentment. Having this strong prohibition against stealing buried deep in his psyche, he's hoping his needs will be small enough to be overlooked.

Catching a glimpse of himself in a small wall mirror brings a startling response, "Good grief!" It's the first time he has seen himself. Running his hands across his unshaven face, it's difficult to distinguish the tan, beard, and dirt. Not sure how old he is, he imagines compared to the men on the trail the previous week that he is probably younger.

It takes only a few seconds of study to discover a crude hand built rocking chair. Rediscovering the seeming lost simple creature comfort of rocking has overtaken him.

Before long it's dark. Opting not to build a fire, content with stretching out on a bunk and feeling only the warmth of his sleeping bag along with the safety of the cabin soon has him in the soundest sleep he could hope for.

Morning arrives. The nearby "caw" of nesting crows awaken him. The moment his eyes open, he bolts out of this bunk terrified its owner will try and reclaim it with him still in it. Panic stricken guilt drives him to the window searching the landscape for the cabin's possible possessor.

What catches his attention is a small out building. Knowing (but not remembering) what this building's use is, he quickly makes his way to its small door. Poised before it as a Spartan warrior with lance in hand, he thrusts the door open ready to do battle with any resident varmints. Satisfied it's empty, he accepts its gracious invitation to be seated.

It is the quintessential "one holer." The outer sanctuary. The annex to all libraries. It's well stacked with old newspapers and magazines. *Dawson City Gazette* catches his attention. It's the inscribed name across the top of every newspaper. With the intended use of this building behind him, he carries a stack of these newspapers back to the cabin. Rocking with nervous energy, he scans each of them for any clues to his identity. So far all he's been able to conclude is that he's in Alaska somewhere near Dawson City. As to his personal identity, it remains a complete disconnect.

Instead of this communique' satisfying his curiosity, it only serves to intensify his frustration. Finally slamming the papers on the floor and with this continual festering enigma surrounding his identity, he succumbs to it all with a shout, "Why don't I know who I am!!?"

Left over thoughts continue to bubble through from some unknown source, again leaving him with more questions, "How do I know these other things, but don't know me?" Deciding there is nothing he can do to change things, the moment passes and his thoughts hastily turn back to some immediate needs.

Looking amongst the jumble of tools in a chest, he picks out a hammer and nails. Doing a once over around the outside of this old cabin, he centers his attention on any loose board he can find. He is so intent on what he's accomplishing that he fails to notice he's being watched. Being remiss in this environment where eyes and ears are the most important tools for survival could prove to be fatal.

Sensing something, he swings around and comes eye to eye with what appears to be either a wolf or a wolf-dog mix. It's just sitting at the edge of the clearing watching him. His first thought comes with no effort, "WHERE'D I LEAVE MY SPEAR!" His second thought comes with the realization that this critter is not aggressive—it's merely sitting. Fear soon turns to curiosity.

There is forlornness about this mangy creature. The more he allows himself to scrutinize the situation the less fearful he remains. "Hey Buddy, how ya' doin'." It's all he can think of to say.

A primitive caution soon returns to both as Joey retrieves his spear from its resting spot, the critter turns on its heels and disappears into the brush.

# 10 — AN UNLIKELY NEIGHBOR

Taking advantage of the obliging benevolence of this roadside inn is indeed tempting. It, for certain, provides most of the amenities he needs to survive. Compared to modern conveniences this refuge falls short, but when compared to the open wilderness, it provides all the advantages of strong hold. The decision to stay one more night is made. Besides, he's growing accustomed to trespassing.

Overall, he's been very pleased with his day. It's furnished him with a kind of rest that is impossible in the wild. It's a pleasant retreat.

In the area designated as the kitchen, he has discovered the ingredients for hot chocolate. Lowering himself down into the rocking chair, he's content to sip and rock, staring out the curtain-less window and watch the night fold in around him.

Imagination can do wonderful things or terrible things. Joey is finding the secret to being alone without becoming lonely. Content and grateful for this unlikely reprieve and crawling into his sleeping bag one more time, welcoming it's security, he drifts into a somniferous doze.

The break of dawn brings to mind the need to organize a farewell to this roadstead. Restlessness is once again overtaking him. In the short time he's been here taking notice of a few useful items that is hard to pass up.

Catching his attention is a nail with a worn pair of Carhartt coveralls along with an equally worn coat hanging from it. Slipping them on, he continues his search for other useful objects. Under a bunk is a pair of hunting boots. They prove to be a size too big, but by stuffing some newspapers into the toes, they're at least wearable.

Joey is far from comfortable with this form of thievery. There seems to be some vague moral vestigial that continues to haunt him. Not completely overtaken by this conviction, he continues to search for usable items. Happy to find a small hatchet, he places it in his backpack along with a few cans of beans and fruit. Making his way to the door, he secures it back the way he found it and heads down the slight incline to the creek.

It's a cool morning. Feeling the of the warmth of his newly-plundered clothing against the chill is a welcomed luxury. The sky seems to be struggling with either forming clouds or ridding itself of them.

While bending down to fill his water bottle, he catches a glimpse of movement in the brush on the opposite side of the creek. Instinctively grasping his spear, he watches intensely for a recurrence. Nothing happens. Satisfied that whatever it may have been has moved on, he continues his routine. It's as though he's being driven by some unconscious system that knows if it's done right it will end right.

After only this one-day sabbatical, he feels a renewed sense of strength and vigor, ready to move ahead. To what though, he's not sure. Nonetheless he's looking forward to the rest of the day with a tremendous excitement.

Talking to himself as though he's speaking to an entire committee, he comes to an agreement. "I think I'm going to stick to my original plan follow this stream." Searching around for the least impeded path he soon discovers a game trail that parallels the stream. For most of the morning it's been a good choice. By noon the terrain has changed from a fairly flat trek to a sudden rocky out cropping. Leaving the stream a 100 feet below, it continues it's tendency to meander, bearing its course to that of a least resistance.

By late afternoon after scaling several of these grenadiers his clothing is soaked with perspiration. Not having taken a bath in his memorable history he's becoming well aware of that certainty by the aroma emanating from under his coat. Slipping it off he feels the cooler air against his skin. It's a simple pleasure. Tossing it over his shoulder, he makes his way down the stony precipice to the stream's edge. It's formed a natural dam at this point creating a small lagoon. He has the resolve at this time to take a bath and wash his clothing.

Common sense directs him to build a good hot roaring fire before he leads himself into these chilly mountain waters. Stripping himself naked, he slowly lowers himself into the icy waters. Every organ in his body is individually protesting. "Whoa! This crap is cold!" With this awareness he grabs a handful of his stinky clothing, ceasing to dip them around only after he can't stand the cold another second.

Satisfied that this mission is complete and after hanging his wardrobe on a make-shift clothesline, he plunks himself still naked on a log near the fire.

Something catches his attention. Looking in its direction he's pleasantly surprised. There sits the half-breed dog not fifty feet from him. Neither do anything. They sit across from each other and stare. Holding his hand out as a friendly gesture Joey forms the only words that come to mind, "Come here doggy."

The dog thrusts its twitching nose in the air as though it expected to smell food. Concluding nothing is being offered, it once again turns back into the woods.

Disappointed at this turn of events, Joey finds himself yearning for companionship even if it's only shared with a feral dog. The lightheartedness he had earlier in the day is giving way to a somberness.

Not wanting to dwell on this disappointment any longer, he quickly busies himself drying the rest of his ragged wardrobe.

While retrieving a rogue sock that managed to stay behind near the stream, Joey takes notice of a strange churning behind the dam that created his swimming hole. The water is crystal clear, perfect for observing the cause of all this commotion. "My gosh those are salmon!" He can't hold back the emotion. Within seconds he's grabbed his spear and is back on the banks. "Gotcha!" shouts a delighted Joey as his spear sinks through the spine of a ten pounder.

Taking great satisfaction in this conquest, he handily prepares this river denizen on a stick over his fire. In spite of once more having a full stomach the concern for inadvertently inviting a bear in with the pungent smell of roasting fish is a very real trade off. Rather than risk one of these late night camp burglars the decision is made to take the leftovers to the water and let them wash downstream.

Before this plan can be set into action it takes another turn. This fish fry has caught the attention of another neighbor. Joey is once again sitting face to face with his canine friend. Getting a much better look now, this creature is far from being a thoroughbred, smaller than a wolf but bigger than a German Shepherd. It's fur is made up of some gray, a little brown and a black like mask around it's face.

Not to let this new acquaintance slip away again, he tosses the fish head to this seeming dinner guest. Sticking its nose in the air, this four-legged cur cautiously, with a down turned head and neck hair standing straight up, approaches the handout, snatches it and immediately makes a retreat.

Within minutes this shy dinner guest is back for seconds. This time Joey pitches a piece of the fish at half the distance of the first. Wasting very little time the mangy daredevil approaches the piece of meat, sniffs it and gingerly carries it back to some predesignated dining area.

Though not returning for thirds this simple amusement satisfies Joey's craving for fraternity—at least for the time being. One thing he is learning is that nature has its own agenda. Either one learns how to adapt or it will reject a person without a trial.

With his camp cleaned of leftover fish, the emphasis changes to gathering fire wood. Little by little the cumulative effort is met. Carrying the last armful back to camp, he is stopped dead in his tracks. In his brief absence a large brown bear has taken charge of his bivouac. Separated from his spear, and without a lot of thought, he does what he believes to be the next best defense. Waving a stick and hollering, he charges the bear. Brown bears, as many wild animals do when confronted by humans, either run or attack.

The beast has already made its decision. Baring its teeth as it twists its head from side to side, and with a loud growl it begins a rush in Joey's direction. Its bone-hard clear that the bear stands between him and his spear. He unconsciously begins a backward retreat with no plan at all, when suddenly as from nowhere comes the charging mangy half-breed cur. With hair on end and teeth bared, this new ally begins an attack on the hind legs of this 300-pound behemoth.

As if on cue the bear's attention is immediately off Joey and directed at this more apparent adversary. Joey's wits have prodigiously returned as he makes a mad dash for his weapon. The smaller half-breed wolf-dog is out maneuvering this much larger foe as it manages to bite its nose.

Successful in retrieving his weapon, Joey is positioned close enough now with enough adrenalin surging through his muscles to sink his spearhead deep behind the bears left front leg and piercing its heart, but not before a front paw caught the cur sailing it through the air. The large brute and the mongrel slump to the ground simultaneously. One dead, the other out cold from a blow to the head.

Joey's eyes dart from one creature to the other. At this point not knowing what to expect from either and with his adrenalin still in the attack mode, he gingerly pokes the bear with the end of his six-foot spear. Satisfied this one's dead, his attention swings back to this new-found hero. With an overwhelming obligation to help this poor fallen creature, Joey drops his spear and rushes to its aid.

The poor critter is struggling to get to its feet. Staggering for a few steps, it stumbles back to the ground. Grabbing its rough course fur with one hand, he steadies the creature giving it time to regulate its unstable gait.

"There, there big fella calm down now," says Joey in his most comforting tone as he attempts to cradle the still struggling ally.

Giving in to the moment, the fallen hero seems to sense the caring hands firmly encircling it. Unconsciously yawning several times before making a successful attempt at standing, the poor thing wriggles loose, shakes a few times, spots the downed bear, and resumes a growling posture. Joey makes no attempt to dissuade this four-legged warrior from having the satisfaction that it killed this interloper. Sensing its yet weakened condition, the canine remains satisfied to perform this ritual at a distance.

Why this unlikely ally suddenly came to Joey's aid can only be hypothesized—it will remain a mystery. But what is apparent is this animal is deciding to stand by as Joey cuts out the heart from the beast and feeds it to this waiting guest. With a mug saturated with blood and still licking its chops the much-welcomed patron stretches and lays down in the middle of camp.

Satisfied with this curious new friend, Joey feels much safer going to sleep with this sentinel on duty.

Morning arrives. His guardian has disappeared. Joey's attention turns to salvaging the backstraps from the stiffening carcass. The night had been cold enough to cool the meat sufficiently to cut and pack it into a gallon-sized plastic milk jug he had found. Cutting it in such a way that it retained a hinge and closing cover assured its security.

Joey is beginning to take confidence in his survival abilities. He has been thrown headlong into a stone-aged existence. Like the men and women preceding him that were forced to make the incertitude of survival their primary concern, creativity had become their passion. This strengthening confidence gives him a sense of oneness with his universe. This is a man who finds his being in control as a gift from some power other than himself. He can't shake the notion that his life is not his own, but rather being directed from some outside force.

This sense of being led that had begun at some unremembered point in his life continues to be an inexplicable mystery. It continues to haunt him. At this juncture, and not sure why or where from, he takes great pleasure in its undeniable calming presence. It's something that goes way beyond a feeling — it's more as if it is an awareness of the presence of God. It continues to puzzle him, but in a comfortable way.

He is brisk and very business like in breaking camp, double checking for later needed overlooked items. Taking a last bite of bear meat and coaxing the last pieces of green beans stuck to the bottom of an other wise empty can into his mouth are the last acts he will ever perform in this camp.

The address he's headed for is yet unknown. Just putting one foot in front of the other is good enough for now.

# 11 — A TORNADO OF INDISCRETION

Nearly two weeks have passed since Joey's disappearance. Jacob is standing staring out a kitchen window. Even though his view is that of beautiful, rugged, snow-capped mountains, his look is vacant. Reviewing his own life, he has tortured himself with remembered unrepentant indiscretions of his own.

"My son is missing." Unable to pronounce him dead, Jacob refuses any consolation that carries that kind of finality.

"Now I'm being punished," he continues to hopelessly cry out.

"God will punish those who don't obey. Now I'm suffering the consequences for my sins." This is the mantra that will not leave his head, and also the sum of his religious upbringing. He had been warned of these punishments by his religious leaders and has dutifully passed these verdicts on to his own sons. These are the thoughts that keep him in the basement of life.

"God why have you taken my son? I'm the one who needs punishing. Punish me, take my life, end this slow death."

His memory harks back to how he deceived his twin brother to gain the family business and has never done anything to correct this with his survivors. The impending justice of God is expected. Now he feels alone and not deserving of love. "My sins have come home to roost," he tells Rena.

As long as Rena has known her husband, he has been a man of integrity. She understands none of this.

"Please Jacob hold me. Tell me Joey is all right. Tell me he'll come home," sobs Rena. Along with her husband, she can not bring herself to believe that her eldest son will never return. Despair looms all around them. Even the heartfelt consolation each try to give the other cannot replace the hole in their hearts.

Rup, Sam, Levi , and Justin are all back to work. Each in their own way are living with concealed lies and deceit.

Rup, at best, can be described as the brother in charge of the office. In spite of the distraction of the past few weeks, he is trying to keep the appearance of business as usual. It continues to be a challenge.

He went along with Sam's stupid plan believing he could return to rescue him. Now his heart stands still, buried under layers of lies. There is no one more aware of his weakness of character than himself. He is disappointed that he cannot hold to his public convictions in his private life.

Now he's purposely avoiding his father. It's a wearisome time and his father is deeply hurt that these sons are not being more supportive. These sons have been raised with the purposeful obligation to honor their father. On this occasion they are noticeably remiss.

This morning Levi and Justin have found their way to Rup's office. Being alone with their guilt is resulting in uninvited tensions to surface. Mormons lie like every non-Mormon, but are very sensitive to the results of this sin.

"I know we should be paying more attention to Dad and Rena," says an anxious Levi, "I found Benji crying the other day. I couldn't even bring myself to console him. I feel like such a phony."

Rup sits quietly listening. Aware of his role as oldest brother, his tradition dictates he should be playing a more active role in the lives of his younger siblings, but for various reasons due to his weaknesses of character, he can't.

"Levi, I've got to get this report done, it's over due. Get back with me later." Despite this younger brother's desperation, he feigns a business deadline to cover his incompetence as a consoler.

Levi's disappointment can be read in his stooped shoulders as he is dismissed by this inept brother.

Trying to put himself back into a normal routine, Rup takes a sip of bottled water. A sickening feeling is coming over him like a wave. Leaning back in his chair, he folds his hands and tries to pray, but his thoughts are to muddled. He yearns to be a man of strong character, unfortunately he can't pull it off.

Guilt can be a great motivator. It's bugged Rup all afternoon that he's been so calloused that he hasn't spent any time with his father and Rena. Up until today, he has consciously opted not to do that. Not visiting them is a conspicuous indication that there is a questionable reason, so slipping out of work, he makes his way to Rena's where he expects his father to be for the week.

"Anybody home?" he calls out as he enters the house. Looking around he sees no one. Unannounced, a head suddenly appears from over the couch. It's Rena.

Rubbing her eyes and wiping the wet from the corners of her mouth, she replies in a rather sleepy voice, "Yeah, I'm here."

Rup stops dead in his tracks. "Oh gosh, I didn't mean to wake you." His voice is full of apology as he takes a step ready to leave.

"Oh no—don't worry about it. I haven't been sleeping too well lately. Your Dad's off somewhere and Benji's at work, so I laid down for a minute and fell asleep," says Rena bounding off the couch and fussing with her hair. It's a desperate endeavor to keep him from leaving.

The sadness in her eyes is shocking. She and Rup grew up together, not being far apart in age. They had a crush on one another as adolescence, but as is the custom in these polygamous communities the young women, and especially the attractive ones, are kept away from the young men and held in reserve for the older men. She eventually was promised to Rup's father, Jacob.

Rup's feelings never changed. She was a pretty girl when they were young and he still finds her equally attractive as a grown women. She in turn, although always trying to be a faithful wife to Jacob, still finds herself having feelings for Rup. Her being his aunt, the younger sister to his mother is not troublesome enough to avoid a physical attraction. In some of these closed communities, incest is viewed differently.

"How're you doing through all this?" he asks. Rup doesn't have to fake this part. With more than a mere inclination to display sympathy, he opens his arms and lets her lean in as close as she is willing.

It's a moment that could support a legitimate purpose as she responds to his question. "Not very good Rup. I just keep hoping and praying that I'll look up and see Joey walk through that door with a big smile." Pausing for a moment her eyes wander toward the empty door. "I sure do miss that smile."

This brings a flood of tears. Rup knows exactly what he's doing. Holding her as she uncontrollably sobs into his chest is the same feeling a predator has when it has a grip on a vulnerable prey.

The feeling is mutual. She has fostered a secret attraction for Rup and has often found herself daydreaming about a liaison and what it would be like.

Still sobbing she pushes her body tighter to his. "I've always known I could talk to you Rup. I've always appreciated how you listen."

He can feel his breathing becoming labored as the sweat begins to trickle down his sides. This phenomena is ignored at the overwhelming urge to take this occasion to another level.

Not having to wait long, he feels Rena's body beginning to tremble slightly. Looking up at him she responds with the most wanton and needy expression they have ever experienced together. Without a cue their lips meet. It's the kind of kiss that quickly turns to their lips pawing at each other's mouth. They break long enough to exhale and then begin again.

If blood is required for clear thinking, their blood has left their brains and settled in a lower extremities. Rena has always been strong enough to set aside her attraction to Rup and hold to a higher moral obligation toward her husband. But as the days are beginning to stretch into weeks with no sign of her eldest son, she is along with these empty days becoming weak and vulnerable.

Her imagination is painting Rup as a much stronger man than he really is. The truth in this instance has become nothing. What she perceives truth to be, becomes everything. To her he has become a man of strong character, who understands her need.

Desire is controlling Rup's hands as they deftly move across her hips. With rough force, he pulls Rena's dress up around her waist. In an unhesitating synchronized move, she has kicked her panties aside. Both are still struggling to keep their lips locked as if not noticing what they are doing makes it not happening.

Rup's hands next go to his own pants. He has them down around his ankles and with one sudden burst of strength, he is lifting Rena's whole body as she in turn wraps her legs around his waist allowing herself to be penetrated.

It's soon over. Still panting for air, they stand speechless in front of each other not knowing what to say or do. This account has been settled and neither feel the better for it. No man or women can steal the character of another, it can only be thrown aside by its owner.

The luxury of working out the ramification of this liaison between the two of them suddenly comes to a halt as they hear the familiar sound of Jacob's pickup truck pull into the yard.

Neither has any regard for the other at this particular moment. Rup can't get his pants up fast enough. The sweat is pouring out of him, his hair is soaked, his face is flushed red, his lips are swollen and sanguine. He has the look of a man whose guilt is so great that it becomes impossible to disguise it. Both are a mess in so many differing ways, but also in similar ways.

Rena has run from the room, stripped herself down and is showering as though a thorough full-body baptism will rid her of her sin. At best it's giving her time before she comes face to face with her husband.

Jacob enters the house. Rup tries his best to adjust to the situation and appear nonchalant. Standing up from the couch, that minutes before was the back drop to his indiscretion, shaking, he greets his father. "Hi Dad, glad I caught you home. I just stopped by to see how you and Rena are doing."

"About as good as can be expected," says Jacob all the while looking long and hard at his eldest son.

"What's the matter with you Rup, you look like you've wrestled with a Grizzly bear," adds his father not taking his eyes off his son.

"I haven't been feeling good lately. I've been running a fever off and on. I think it just broke on the way over here," says Rup hardly able to meet his father's steady gaze.

Pausing as he looked around for the briefest moment, without further discussion Jacob switched the conversation. "Where's Rena?"

With a blink of the eyes and a nervous cough he clears his throat. "She was in the shower when I got here a few minutes ago—she's probably still there."

Hearing the shower running, Jacob turns to go into the kitchen. Pouring himself a cup of leftover morning tea and not really looking at Rup. "Say you just got here Rup?" says his father taking a sip, looking out the kitchen window. The tone of his voice is one of suspicious speculation.

Rup is becoming more and more nervous with his father's persistence. "Aaah—I dunno—I guess it was a little while ago. Why do you ask?" stammers Rup.

"I was out behind the tool shed loading my truck when you pulled in. That was close to an hour ago."

Rup's blush is quickly turning to a pale glower. "Yeah, it could have been." For a brief moment he wants to blurt out a confession of all his deceit and relieve his aching guilty soul, but he catches himself with yet another lie. "You know Dad, I'm starting to get sick again. I think I'llgo home to bed." With that he gives his father a quick hug and walks out the door.

Jacob remains staring out the window sipping his tea and pondering his suspicions. Finally opting to leave his showering wife alone, he heads out to the corral, saddles his horse and heads out for a long ride hoping to make sense of his suspicions.

It's after dark when he returns. After rubbing his horse down, he calmly enters the house. It's quiet except for the TV in the living room.

Rena remains sitting. It's clear she's nervous. Trying to make small talk, she asks, "Did you enjoy your ride?"

Jacob can't help but pay attention to her obvious restlessness and it's obvious to her she's being studied. It's making her even more agitated. Ignoring her question, he poses one of his own. "I saw Rup here earlier. Did you and him have a good talk?"

"Yeah, sort of," says Rena with a reluctance and avoiding eye contact. She too is riddled with guilt. It's only after she has crossed over this line of moral behavior that she has realized its horrible cost. Not only is she in the throes of depression over the loss of a son, but now has piled on an added burden of adultery.

Whether true or false, Rena has always felt that she lives in the shadow of her older sister, always competing for Jacob's attention. Now in this hour of deep need, they are locked into themselves. Neither are able to release themselves to the needs of the other.

The look of guilt on Rena's face as she is confronted tells her husband the whole story. Without so much as a good-bye, Jacob opts to leave and stay with Lena.

It's a lonely time for Rena. Benji thinks it's odd that his father is staying away, but has learned to stay out of his mother's and father's marital squabbles. A few weeks have passed when Rena hears the familiar sound of Jacob's truck in the driveway.

She practically leaps to the window. "He's returned" is her immediate thought as she fusses with her hair trying to prepare herself for whatever Jacob may have in mind.

"Hello Rena," greets Jacob. A kiss and hug are conspicuously withheld. It's only been two weeks but she thinks he looks as though he's aged.

"Hello Jacob." It's a rather obsequious greeting as she awkwardly wrings her fingers, not taking her eyes off her husband. Without hearing her husband speak, her mind is already playing a tape, "The jury has found you guilty as charged," is her first thought. "Why can't he just beat me and get this over with?" She willingly welcomes such verdicts. She is guilty and deserves whatever punishment her husband prescribes, it's the waiting that kills her. She continues to stare in wretched anticipation.

"The verdict, the verdict, please, please!" Her anxiousness is overwhelming. She has rehearsed this scene over and over, and is preparing for a life of shame and pain. Her escapade has stained her marriage. Losing a son was thought to be unbearable, but now she has also lost her husband. The destruction of a family always guarantees sorrow and suffering.

Letting out a great sigh, Jacob remains silent as he sits down at the kitchen table. The sun through the window has created a shadow of himself. His shoulders appear tired and rounded.

Rena timidly follows suit seating herself across from him. Tired is too mild to describe her. Her bland appearance reflects the enfeebled outcast she believes herself to be.

"I would be a fool of I didn't know what went on between you and Rup." Casting his eyes toward Rena, he pauses long enough to choose his words and then continues, "It breaks my heart to be deceived by two people whom I love and who I trusted loved me."

Tears of sorrow are once again streaming down the face of this silent wife. There are not words to describe her desolation. It's full force is tormenting. She can claim no legitimate defense in as much as the undoing of her indiscretion is seated directly in front of her. All the petty grievances she held against her husband pale in comparison to the brokenness she has caused.

Jacob has always believed that his faith in God to be a serious concern, even though at times he has not allowed God into his decisions. This time his sense of powerlessness has driven him to his knees.

Jacob pauses, again carefully measuring his words. "You and I both know your conduct is inexcusable, but it is forgivable. Over the past few weeks, especially with Joey's disappearance, I buried myself in my own sorrow and paid little or no attention to how it has affected you."

Jacob continues with yet another thought. "It has occurred to me that if God is able to forgive me a less than perfect husband, I should also forgive my less than perfect wife and son. That's why I'm here, I want to forgive you as much for your sake as mine."

Pausing yet again to measure his thoughts into words, "I am saying this is my intention—but I'm not God. I can't do this as quickly as He does. For me it's going to be a longer process.

With his piece spoken, he prepares to leave. Rena has soaked a dish towel with her tears. Placing herself before her husband, trying to hold back still more tears, she takes both his hands in hers. Softly in a near whisper, she forms the words, "Thank you Jacob."

He gives her a kiss on her forehead, for now it's the best he can do. The tornado of adultery has ripped its way through this marriage.

# 12 — WORDS CAN'T EXPLAIN

To the extent it can be measured, Rup is relieved that he has not had to face his father. The incident with Rena has been a few weeks ago, now he's hoping he's out of the woods, not realizing it's his father's footsteps he hears coming down the hall. Rup is doing paper work when his father appears unannounced in his doorway.

"Mind if I come in?" The question is moot as Jacob steps in closing the door behind him. In that split second an involuntary chill races along Rup's spine. Reflexively, he gets to his feet and pulls out a out a chair for his father.

"No, no, no, not at all. Come in," says Rup motioning to the pulled out chair. The blood in his face has drained away leaving him pale and shaking. He can feel the arrows of recrimination coming his way.

Jacob relocates the chair to his liking, dismissing any illusion that this gesture of respect is going to amount to much.

"How's the business doing?" says Jacob with a slight smile, suggesting he is toying with Rup as a cat would a mouse.

"AAAHH, good," answers a blinking, and obviously distracted, Rup. His mind is speeding like a runaway freight train before the wreck.

Jacob crosses one leg over the other with hands folded and resting on his knee, peering directly at his eldest son.

"You may be wondering why I'm popping in like this." His gaze intensifies. Leaning forward in his chair as one would before a pounce. "I want to assure you that I didn't just fall off a turnip truck—I got a pretty good idea what was going on between you and Rena."

Rup is sucking air and letting it out slowly. "I wonder if he's going to kill me—he's way too calm."

Jacob renews his piercing gaze, letting a moment of contemplative silence pass, before continuing, "Your second thought may be 'am I going to let you live?' Yes, I'm going to let you live. I'm even trying to find ways to forgive you, but as I told Rena, I'm not excusing either of you."

Rup's face doesn't look any different at this moment than it did when he was two years old caught in an infraction. He's speechless as he always is when drenched with guilt.

"Good grief, he still does that blinking thing," thinks Jacob. Not finished yet, he prevails, "I haven't heard a confession from either of you and I don't really need one. Her tears and your blinking tell the whole story."

Rup has taken these recriminations without a word. He attempts to clear his throat and with a distinct stammer and still trembling, he speaks. "Words can't explain how terrible I feel." Not able to look meet his father accusing gaze, he keeps his eyes glued to the floor. Rup's demeanor definitely reflects sorrow and he certainly will accept any forgiveness his father offers.

Remaining on track, Jacob proceeds, "You don't have to answer this question now, but I want you to think about it. Do you feel terrible about what you did or do you just feel terrible because you were caught?"

Rup is speechless once again. He knows in no uncertain terms what his answer should be, but unfortunately the reality of it is quite different.

"Oh and one more thing Rup—stay away from Rena. I mean that very literally. Is that clear?

"Yes sir," says a retiring Rup. He's uneasy, knowing he's been dressed down. Things haven't changed much over the years. Sitting in his office at thirty-nine after an upbraiding isn't much different than at ten while sitting in the basement. The results remain the same with him resolving to make a change.

Conversations like these leak out gradually. It may take six months or six years, but sooner or later differing events bring previous discussions to light.

Sam has been keeping a close eye and ear open after seeing his father go into Rup's office and close the door. This behavior only serves to increase his concern. Ambling around until after his father leaves, he then makes a bee-line for Rup's office.

Rup is wishing he could have a few minutes to himself after his father has left. His father's scoldings leave him exhausted, but with a brother like Sam that's not likely to occur. Barging through the door, Sam is on his usual full-court press.

"Whad the Ole Man want?" demands Sam slumping in to his father's empty chair.

"Nothing much, he wanted to know some costs," lies Rup.

Sam is looking hard at Rup. He knows his brother's weakness under pressure. "He didn't mention any thing about Joey?"

"No, not a thing." He's feigns disinterest, hoping Sam will leave. His head needs clearing. Since he doesn't drink alcohol or use drugs he has found an escape in sleep. He'd like nothing better than to leave the world behind with a nap. He's been known to sleep three days at a time, getting up only to relieve himself.

"If that dreamer shows up, it's going to be a heart-stopper for us," growls Sam. Brutally blunt as always, he continues with his rant, "You know if we don't take the right precautions our heads will be on the chopping block. Does that give you any concern?"

"You know it does," says Rup with a renewed sense of worry.

Sam is merely feeling his older brother out. He wants to be certain that Rup is worried enough to remain his ally. Never completely certain, but at the very least content for the moment, Sam drifts back out into the shop.

# 13 — FROM DESPERATION TO CALM ASSURANCE

It's beginning to feel like a summer day where temperatures turn the corner. Joey is stripping off his Carhartts satisfied to be in his lighter clothing. Not sure exactly how long he's been out here, he's marveling at how comfortable the wilderness is beginning to feel.

"Maybe I've been out here longer than I know." Crouched on top of a ridge, contemplating this thought, concludes that it doesn't explain, "How I would ever have been so careless as to end up at the bottom of that mine shaft?"

Rubbing his hand across the places his head suffered injury, "Nah, I never would have put myself down that pit unless I fell." But he suspects his loss of memory and his head injuries are allied.

Musing on how much of his life may or may not have been spent in this wilderness is a futile exercise. Dwelling on these kinds of distractions are luxuries one can hardly afford in this hostile environment. Sharp eyes and sharp ears gather data to produce a sharp mind. These are the tools one needs to be successful in this neighborhood. Survival is for the crème de la crème. The weak, the stupid and the inattentive are soon rejected by their environment, finding themselves at the bottom of the food chain.

Forced once again by the static reality of his situation, he quickly releases himself from his ruminations, straightens from a crouch to stand erect and gazes out across his terrain.

Surveying the landscape provides the information needed to move forward—studying the creek in particular. What has become apparent is how much faster, wider, and deeper it's become. Another eye opener is how the trees have changed from alpines to aspens. "This can only mean one thing. I must be making my way downstream." Amazed that he knows this fact, it continues to frustrates him to be aware of so many things yet be totally unaware of others.

Looking at the abundance of these young aspens begins the formulation of a new idea. "A RAFT! That's what I need." As if on cue, he's down off the ridge on to a flat spot below.

"Perfect! Perfect! Perfect!" Everything needed is available. Fraught with the excitement of this new project, his mind quickly transfers into an engineering mode. His movements become swift and purposeful.

Not two weeks ago this same man was running on fear, hiding from every perceived danger, at the mercy of everything that had a moments seniority on him. Now he's in command, conforming his environment to fit his needs. Not able to adequately explain this sudden confidence, but willing to accept it as a normal progression from his previous beclouded and timorous decision making abilities.

His are raw talents, seemingly unrefined but completely effective; need seen, need met. *Extraordinary* can only be measured against the *ordinary*. There is no standard to measure either of these in Joey's world other than his exceptionalism is rooted in the ability to survive.

After attacking a number of uniformed sized trees and cutting them into poles, he begins the arduous task of lashing them into a stable, durable configuration. Dragging fifty feet of rope around with no immediate use has been a chore. At last it's found solid employment.

Finding a great sense of pleasure in this challenge, it can only be surpassed by this contraption actually holding together under duress.

Nonetheless, for the moment skidding it into the river is the task at hand requiring all his attention.

Success brings a broad grin of satisfaction across his weather-beaten face. The next observation brings an even greater exhilaration. "IT FLOATS! IT FLOATS!" Overcome with joy, he breaks out into an impromptu dance.

What has come into view during this hoedown of sorts, sitting on his haunches panting nonchalantly while being entertained by this human's shenanigans, is his four-legged neighborhood hobnobber. A flash of embarrassment flushes over him as though he may not be meeting the standards of adequate entertainment for this audience. To redeem himself, he reaches into his cache of bear meat, cuts a chunk and holds it out with the words, "Come here fella, come get it."

Despite their previous interaction, this dubious canine views this as a whole different experience. Going through the same slow, cautious motions, the critter trusting its nose, thrusts it as far forward as it confidently it can and continue to hold the rest of it's body in abatement. In one quick surge of unaltered faith, the animal snatches the meat and retreats to a less fearful dining area guaranteeing the meal will not be shared.

Each time this unlikely creature shows up, Joey has always hated to see it leave without a particular way of phrasing the question to himself. It could be said he yearns for the companionship. He senses that he's lost something. It's like a homesickness, but having no clue where that home may be.

Resuming the tasks at hand, launching the raft away from the waters edge, he rudders the craft using a long pole, maneuvering it to the middle where it's expected to be the deepest.

The sound of water cutting away from the raft is an exhilarating gurgle. Soon it's the only noise perceived as all else is silent as the current carries him with an easy elegance.

Soon the stream has widened and is much faster with the addition of several other streams feeding into it greatly increasing its velocity. Building the craft is one thing, but managing a course is a whole other challenge. Joey is quickly learning this is definitely a skill he has not mastered.

Special attention has been given to secure his backpack and spear, also to providing an anchor system. By tying one end of the remaining portion of rope to the raft and the other end to a large rock, he is able to throw the rock overboard allowing its drag to act as a brake.

So far the combination of river and raft are remaining within a 'learn as you go' mode, not exactly a piece of cake, but with Joey's navigational ingenuity at least manageable.

This is proving to be an amazing adjustment for a man who a few weeks ago was close to death. At this very moment he feels more alive than at any other time in his memory. It's as though there is no past or future, only a now. He can't help but think that his unknown history must have included challenges such as these. "Why else would my mind tell me to 'do it'! I can't imagine a life with no exhilaration." Little does Joey realize that this sense of oneness with the universe is truly a rare gift for any modern man to experience.

The sun is creeping ever so low in west. Darkness comes quickly in these mountain ranges. The river is taking on a new twist as it is bending more often slowing his progress.

Using the lowering sun as a time piece suggests it's time to select a campsite. Angling his raft toward shore, he scours the landscape for a suitable mooring finally settling on a space with very little rock and more sand.

The warm daytime breezes are predictably turning cooler. Happy to have a warm pair of Carhartts to slip into even as dirty and worn as they have become, he goes about his evening chores. Soon a good bright fire compromises the ensuing darkness. The reddish-yellow glow streaking through the clouds insure good weather tomorrow.

Lifting the plastic container carrying the last remains of bear meat to his nose and takes a sniff, concluding, "Not too bad yet, maybe I should cook it all up." Taking it down to the river, he washes the stickiness from it, smells it once again and decides it's probably edible. Unexpectedly an eagle swoops down grabbing a huge salmon, looking to it as the last meal of the day. Other birds are going through their age-old ritual of flocking into the safety of the aspens as they too, begin to roost yet another night.

The smoke from the fire swirls around in the breeze opening a spot clear enough to make out a familiar shape. It's his amiable consort, the half-breed dog.

"Ah, good to see you old friend, you're just in time for dinner." Holding out once again his hand of friendship containing the remains of his meal, Joey teases the reluctant creature to come closer. The mongrel, in turn moves cautiously forward, glancing an eye side to side. By now it's become a tradition as both are becoming well acquainted with each others idiosyncrasies. The yellow-gray cur snatches the morsel and for the first time is satisfied to sit and munch more or less patronizing this charitable benefactor.

A dog's DNA will augur a predictable certainty of behavior as does wolves. In this case this mongrel is half dog and half wolf, thus conflicting any predictable conduct. Either way this aberration of the animal kingdom is fully capable of pushing its way through life, taking advantage of these pleasantly-presented inns along life's highway.

"You and I have a lot in common old friend. You don't have a name and I don't know mine. I'm going to call you Schnitzel—Whada ya think of that?"

Schnitzel is neither endorsing nor opposing this ad hoc christening, satisfied to continue to munch, adding the impression of hanging on Joey's every word. Of course Joey assumes that this lack of contrariety is per-mission to bedaub this creature with this dumb name. But then humans have natural inclinations to try and tame wild things. It's always surprises the tamer when the one being tamed has been merely condescending to achieve its own agenda. Taking food from a relatively benign source is a longevity tactic for this survivalist.

Not having a watch has forced Joey to depend on indicators that aren't always static. His time piece has become the sun. His diurnal clock hasn't changed. He still sleeps at night and is active during daylight. Not being cognizant of incidentals like what year he's living in and where he is geo-graphically, his dependence on other indicators has become crucial such as the continual upward direction of temperatures and the length of days and the shortness of nights. His reactions to these changes suggest to him some sense of similarity with this animal, who also survives without knowing the 'why' of things.

These few meals provided by Joey doesn't betroth this creature to a do-mesticated future by any stretch of anyone's imagination. The boundaries continue the same for this female, fiercely independent, and only willing to pander to this human on her own terms, continuing to remain untouch-able and aloof. Satisfied with lounging in the middle of Joey's camp, she bides her time, content with fellowship at this level. It's as if this guest were saying, "You mind your business and I'll mind mine." Nonetheless they fulfill some hunger in each other by merely being in each others pres-ence—it seems to be enough for now.

Another morning arrives. Predictably, Schnitzel has abandoned camp in her own time and without fanfare. Joey staggers around rubbing the sleep out of his eyes. Scrounging through his cache of canned goods, se-lects a can of peaches and downs it with a half dozen slurps. With hunger no longer an issue it's time to begin to plan the day.

The desperation that loomed over him early on in this adventure continues to be replaced with a calm assurance that somehow he is being led by an inexplicable, overwhelming, mysterious force. There is also another strange phenomena of a seeming recurrence of the same dream over and over. It puzzles him. Watching the sun rise brings back to mind the dream. It's an odd dream in which he finds himself controlling the son, moon, and stars. He actually finds himself wondering out loud, shaking his head at this absurdity. "Why would I ever have such a dream?" Nonetheless it remains a dream that continues to prey on his mind.

The luxury of entertaining these thoughts soon give way to organizing his survival kit. The dwindling stash of canned goods pilfered from the cabin is beginning to give pause. With spear and backpack all lashed securely to the raft, he makes a conscious decision to keep his hatchet separate by placing it through his belt.

Once again it's time to go. Once again he chooses a direction without predetermining a destination. The lack of an ultimate goal continues to remain a mystery.

Forcing the beached launch back into the river, the current once again fights for control. Within a short distance, his speed is picking up. Many of the small streams that feed this main tributary come through canopy-covered routes like nerves supplying a vertebral column. In other places, high narrow, solid rock walls thread the flow into an ever increasing velocity.

With no warning this sluice conduit turns from a smooth flow to a pitching, jetted torrent of raging water. Any attempt to maneuver a less perilous path is quickly challenged. This rapidly changing river is rendering any endeavors to slow this craft compromised, that includes the time proven method of dragging the anchor.

Joey's mind is frantically trying to adjust to this unexpected threat as he careens out of control. Ramming one rock and then another, launching his helpless dingy in every direction, nearly throwing him and his cargo into these frigid, unforgiving cascades. It's all he can do just to lay on his stomach and grip on to some of the looser lashings. The angry roar of the river rivets off the canyon walls adding to his already overloaded senses.

A strong perception of powerlessness over takes him at every level; physical, mental, and spiritual. His fingers are beginning to bleed, suffering from the chaffing his soft, water soaked skin is enduring as it continues to be pinched between the lashings of the raft's shifting planks.

A stressful "AAAAGGGG" is the only human strider he can manage, adding nothing to the powerful roar of this torrent. Streaking through his mind is his dream of some strange power over the heavens and how he wishes it included raging rivers. There is definitely no questioning who is not in charge of this situation, and it's certainly not him.

Without warning the bumping and pitching has stopped, only to be replaced by the smooth, unencumbered perceptibility of falling. All he can see is a burst of spray and foam rushing toward him. With no time for the mind to even process this horrific drop over a water fall, he is with no warning encountering the full force of this cataract. Ultimately torn from the limited safety of this floating platform, he finds himself completely at the mercy of this river's unstoppable effort to drown him.

Gasping and coughing, banging from rock to rock, he can feel the weight of his drenched Carthartts pulling him under. His lungs are filling with water, forcing over and over, what small amount of air is left to try and expel it. Any attempt to stabilize himself quickly becomes an effort in futility.

What has seemed like a life time, the current at last relinquishes, winding down enough to permit him a welcome reprieve. Cold and soaked to the bone, he manages to stagger to shore, collapsing on the rugged, rocky shoreline.

His body and mind are fighting for dominance. Physically, his body is demanding sleep. Mentally, his mind is demanding he get to his feet. His body wins this debate as he gives in to an impending unconsciousness.

His next sensation is the awareness of something very rough rubbing against his face. Startled awake by what could only be imagined as an imminent danger, he comes face to face with a long, pink tongue lapping across his face. The surge of adrenaline produced by this baptism catapults him instantly to his feet. His breath is coming in short pants. His eyes search frantically for a misplaced spear only to meet a matted ball of fur sitting on her haunches staring with ears up, head cocked to one side, patiently waiting for an expected handout.

Despite the unconventional method that has brought Joey back to consciousness, he realizes double quick the extreme grievousness of his condition as his mind struggles for a survival move. With aching body and numbed fingers, amplified by uncontrolled shivering, he forces his hand into a pocket containing his butane lighter.

With a stiff, uncooperative body, underwritten by sheer determination, he soon has a roaring fire warming his numb, naked body.

His raft is long gone along with his backpack containing the few canned goods, also his sleeping bag and spear are among the missing. After taking inventory of the dried fruit and can of Spam he had stowed away in his pockets an eternal sense of thankfulness rolls over him. Also, especially grateful that the hatchet he had bolstered through his belt remained in place.

Sitting by a hot fire, still naked, and very happy to still be alive, he shares his can of Spam with his unwitting savior. The sky is overcast, leaving the sun as a bright gray spot in the sky. By all calculations it's noon.

The next ultimate concern becomes getting his wet clothing dry. Dealing with these ups and downs are taken as ordinary as breathing. With a full belly, he moves into this arduous task simply and efficiently. Having no rope left to fashion a clothesline leaves the occasion open to creative improvisation. The bounty of scrub brush provide an ample supply of materials that can be cut into poles. These in turn are placed, one end in the ground surrounding the fire pit, the other bent slightly toward the heat, each bearing dangling wet clothing and boots. By early evening, Joey is once more wearing layers of warm trappings.

While reflecting on his day in the safety of his camp, he can hear the faint, steady static of the rapids upstream. An undetermined and unrelated din slowly, but earnestly makes its way into earshot competing for the listener's attention, eventually becoming distinct enough to dominate. It's the cacophony of a struggle like something pushing hard through a barrier that's unwilling to let it pass freely. There is no question it's getting closer. Directly, not more than 50 feet above him appears a freight train slowly straining against a steep winding grade.

An undefinable sensation of excitement comes over him. Watching car after car creep by brings about an overpowering obsession to be on that train.

"I've got to go! I just know it will bring me closer to some answers—I can just feel it."

As quick as this thought has made its way into his adrenal glands, he is kicking sand over his fire, has his hatchet back through his belt, all the while keeping one eye on the crawling cavalcade.

Within minutes, Joey is up the embankment scouting his options. Suddenly a freight car approaches with an open door. With cat like reflexes, hell-bent-for-leather, and making flying a leap, he lands on his belly, flipping one leg over to secure himself more on the train than off.

His first reaction is to turn around and marvel at what he has just successfully accomplished. It elicits a chord of amazement and gratitude.

He then spends the next few moments sadly watching Schnitzel trot off in the opposite direction.

"Good-bye old friend. Good luck to both of us."

Continuing to contemplate this strange companion, he watches until the train rounds another curve leaving the two of them eternally separated.

Finally beginning to assess this new and foreign environment the very first reality that hits him is how much he misses the warmth of his fire. The freight car is cold, dark and drafty. The only light is coming from an open door with a soon to be setting sun behind it. The floor is littered with cast off pieces of card board. It doesn't take him long before he discovers that cutting strips of this material and sliding them inside his Carhartts is the perfect barrier against the cold night. Further scrutiny reveals that the door is able to be slid shut assuring a lot less draft. Gathering all the cardboard in a close proximity and tucking it up, under, and around himself is proving to be as warm as the lost sleeping bag. "Adapt and over come," comes to mind from some lost oracle from the past. Soon the hypnotic rhythm of rail wheels meeting track lull this homeless vagabond to sleep.

# 14 — WHERE DO APPLES FALL?

Parents should know their children better than anyone. As a fundamental Mormon polygamist, Jacob has tried very hard to put his family in the forefront all of his decisions. The circumstances surrounding the disappearance of Joey is bringing new challenges in this regard, especially on how he views his children. The seeming loss of this much-loved son is far from settled.

He's seen the bloodied jacket, but what troubles him is the lack of any other physical evidence—no body, not even the minutest of body parts. It's as though his son has been assumed bodily into paradise.

What further distresses him is the half-hearted attempt by some of his brothers to try and find him. Jacob is not prepared to go to war with his progeny on this issue, but is determined to know the truth.

The disappointment with Rena's indiscretion is further adding to his anguish. Although he continues to have a bond with her through shared children, for the present he has found it impossible to set aside the hurt caused by her betrayal. It's further exacerbated by his fundamental expectation that women by nature are monogamous. Not indifferent to these circumstances, for him to have a physical relationship with her at this time is emotionally impossible. Nonetheless, he continues to partner with her in her devastation over the loss of Joey. He hopes, for her sake as well as his, to have some closure on this issue.

Despite his age and failing eyesight, Jacob has made a decision to return to work. The frustration of a missing son, an adulteress wife, compounded by profit percentages headed in the wrong direction prompts his decision.

This choice is not shared by Lena. "Jacob I wish you would reconsider. You're not exactly the energetic youngster you think you are."

Jacob hears her plea, but is in no frame of mind to pay any heed. His mind is made up. Not measuring his words, he replies, "I've built this business from my own sweat and toil, to sit back and watch these efforts disappear through these boys mismanagement is more than I'm willing to hazard."

Lena is not about to let this judgment against her boys go unchallenged, like so many mothers, her sons could be sliding through the gates of hell and she'd slide in after them.

"These boys have put in a lot of hard hours for you Jacob and don't you forget it!"

From the disparity in his wife's voice, Jacob measures his words, "I know, I know." Pausing for a moment paying close attention to how he's framing his words. "They've all worked hard, but there's a reason buried somewhere in all that hard work that we're losing profit."

Lena's demeanor is taking on the same tone it did years ago when the boys were little and she'd complain to Jacob how he needed to get after them and then attempt to manage the discipline. Her next question is fraught with the same anxiety, "Well, what are you going to do?"

Growing weary of his wife's over-developed sense of responsibility for these adult sons he shoots back, "Lena you don't have to run interference for these guys, they're grown men and expected to take on the responsibilities of grown men."

Placing a couple fingers to her lips, conceding to her husband, she's compelled to add, "I know Jacob. I just know they are trying to do their best."

Not to be outspoken, Jacob gets the last word, "I'll give them that, but their best is losing us money. I didn't build this business to watch it fritter away. I'll get to the bottom of their shenanigans one way or another."

This last statement is where Lena realizes she is running an end game and resigns herself to whatever her husband plans to correct this problem. In spite of Jacob's adherence to Mormon teachings regarding trust in God for his daily needs, when push comes to shove, he soon moves God aside and takes over, especially when it involves the business he feels that he's built.

Sam is happier than ever to pick up the slack left open by Joey's absence, if for no other reason than to prove to his father how much he had overrated Joey. So far his father's estimation of his efforts is below par. On the other hand, Sam's persistence to play a larger role in the business is undaunted.

"Dad, I know I can do the job Joey does, just give me the chance."

The confidence Sam is hoping to portray to his father is unwittingly patronizing and churlish in view of his father's affection for Joey. Jacob didn't graduate from a business school and is not versed in elite business terms such as "The Peter Principle", nonetheless, he knows common sense tells him not to give Sam any more responsibility than he can successfully master.

This is not a new game for Jacob. Back in his younger years he recognized his twin brother's inefficiencies, able to convince himself of the rightness of his actions for the good of the business, he then tricked their father into giving him total control. Short of being ruthless, Jacob always puts business principles before personalities.

"I'll tell you what Sam, I'll work out in the field with you for a while, you show me what you got and if I like it and it makes us money, I'll consider your request."

Much like his father, Sam's idea was to rid himself of anyone competing with his personal ambitions—his tactics may be more horrific than Jacob, but after all, didn't the end result in the same met desire? But now he has the added concern that he failed. Men like Sam prefer to eat their prey if necessary. Somehow his brother has managed to escape and he doesn't have a clue where he is. Much of his thoughts through the day are centered on how to handle this dilemma.

As the afternoon wanes, Rup has left instructions not to be disturbed, with his door closed, and ignoring all phone calls or messages, he has retreated to his office couch.

This may be fine orders for employees. His father, on the other hand, is not putting up with this dereliction.

Bolting unannounced through Rup's closed door, he confronts him with the incriminating evidence.

"What in the Sam Hill are you doing sleeping in the middle of a business day? This crap is ending today, is that understood?"

Without a word in his own defense, Rup forces himself up from his sleep. The look on his face is blank. Little does his father realize the deep depression his son's guilt is causing.

"Listen to me Rup and listen to me good. First you invade my house and take what doesn't belong to you and now you sabotage my business with your apathetic behavior. Despite you are my son, I want you out of here now!"

Rup is about as responsive as someone that is either drunk or drugged and he's neither. Finally rising to a sitting position, still remaining silent, continuing his blank stare, he pulls his coat up over his head and flops back down. Ravaged by guilt, the guilt associated with his involvement in Joey's disappearance would be sufficient for anyone, compound this with his adulterous affair and it becomes unbearable. His thoughts continue, "I wish I were dead. Anything but this."

Not able to withstand the pressure of guilt, his conscience erupts into a bumbling confession. "I'm so sorry Dad, I don't understand what came over me. I deserve what ever punishment you choose."

Listening to his sobs, Jacob contemplates his son's seeming anxiousness. Continuing to study Rup, Jacob fights an overwhelming feeling of contempt for this son. He has always been aware of Rup's character weaknesses, but never in his wildest nightmares did he ever suspect that he was capable of this kind of deceit against his own father.

Jacob takes a deep breath. He's tired. These past few weeks are taking their toll. "Get the hell out of here," is the best he can come up with, at least for the present.

No one doubts Jacob's business savvy, he's very capable. His "my way or the highway" attitude serves him well in the business world but remains a hindrance in family situations.

Sam is unwilling to leave his father and Rup alone out of fear that Rup in one of his many weak moments will blurt out a confession regarding his implication in Joey's disappearance. He lives with this fear as much as he does the likeliness of Joey reappearing.

Hearing none of the content of his father's anger, Sam remains ignorant of the liaison between Rup and Rena, he is only aware of his father telling Rup to "Get out!"

Sam's eyes dart from brother to father searching for a quick solution. Jacob says nothing, mindful that Sam nor anyone else become informed of Rup's and Rena's secret intimacy. Sam says nothing not wishing his father acknowledge Joey's disappearance. These are the pauses that incubate lies.

"You want him out of here Dad, I'll take him home," is Sam's hasty rejoinder.

Traffic is light to non-existent in this part of the world. A few bugs are hitting the windshield as Sam drives a forlorn Rupert to his house.

Sam begins to scold his older brother. "I thought you were brighter than this. You signed on right along with the rest of us with the decision we all made about Joey, so it's your responsibility as well as ours to protect each other."

Trying to keep one eye on the road, he continues his glances toward Rup hoping for a favorable response.

Rup turns his head, looking out the passenger's side window, looking at nothing, seeing nothing, lost in his own trespasses. He's like a rudderless ship bouncing from wave to wave, having compromised most of the convictions that he may have held dear at one time, his life is slowly ebbing away like a dying ember. He remains silent.

Soon arriving at Rup's cabin, Rup remains speechless as he exits the vehicle. Sam runs his window down, making one last imperative, "Don't do anything stupid, Rup."

Rup soon disappears into his cabin. He sees his future as extremely bleak. With barely enough energy left, he flops into his unmade bed, and falls into a coma like sleep removing the past and having no future. It's the closest a person suffering with depression can come to oblivion without dying.

Rup has remained a bachelor for various reasons. Partly because of a lack of eligible women. The custom in these male-dominated polygamist communities is that the older men are usually assigned the younger women and these men will choose as many as they feel they can support. The result is that the younger men are often driven out of the community or they remain single until middle age. In Rup's case, he lacks the fundamental drive to seek a marriage partner, beside that, the only female he has ever had feelings for is Rena.

Sam, on the other hand, is married to only one wife. Her name is Doreen—he calls her Dori. This is an arranged marriage, not a lot of romance which fits both their pragmatic personalities. It's not that he's opposed to multiple wives, it's more to do with economics. Dori has produced seven children in the ten years they have been married. All of her children have been brought into this world with the aid of an Indian midwife.

She's a lean woman, always accommodating to her family's needs, having no other aspirations other than being a wife and mother. She wears her hair pulled back into a simple ponytail, not given much to good looks, but she is tough as nails.

Shortly after dropping Rup at his cabin, Sam arrives home unexpectedly, opting to let his father rant alone back at the plant.

"You're home early," says a surprised Dori, folding a basket of laundry, "you coming down with something?"

"No, I thought maybe you'd like some company," says Sam with a sardonic grin.

"Don't get any ideas big boy, I've more work than I'll ever get done in one day." Her tone is blunt and to the point. There is no doubt who the household engineer is in this family as her dexterous hands magically glide from one endeavor to another.

"You gotta slow down once in a while, Dori," says Sam with some concern.

"Why you gonna stay home and do this work?" says Dori continuing her undertakings.

It's a thought. Lately his mind has been filled with tornado-like thinking hurling panicked thoughts in every direction. He stayed home for a week when his last child was born. This kind of distraction grounds Sam once in awhile.

Sam's dichotomy is that he's not the same person at home as he is with his brothers and others. He's very devoted to his wife and children in a kindly way. Looking around at his home, his wife, his children, he imagines how safe he feels here. The elements of his life that appear to others as evil, bad, antisocial and the many other descriptive adjectives that are used to describe him are not evident in this sheltered environment.

Dori knows nothing of Sam's world outside their home. She is always surprised when others paint a darker side of her husband. They seem to partner seamlessly in raising their children, taking care of livestock, and the other endless farm chores.

What she has noticed of late is how Sam seems to be distant, preoccupied with things that don't seem to include her and outside their common mission.

"Sam is everything all right with you?" questions Dori. She's giving Sam the look that warns him to tell the truth.

"Yeah, everything's fine. It's just a thing with my Dad, he's decided to come back to work."

"I thought he was turning the plant over to you and your brothers," she further inquires.

"Well you know Dad, he can't stay away," Sam answers.

Dori suspects there is more to Sam's mood swings than merely having his father come back to work, but for her own reasons, she doesn't push any further. Her experience is that he'll work it out in his own way and in his own time.

There is an old saying that says that apples don't fall far from the tree. In deference to this thought, Sam isn't much different than his father in some respects, for many years ago, Jacob had coldly swindled his brother out of his share of the family business. In Sam's case, he intended on murdering his brother for the same basic reason.

There are periods in some lives where people lose the fear of God. Like so many other men who profess to follow Christ—they fail. Their religious standards have barely captured their heads much less their heart and soul. When this occurs they no longer suffer the terror of violating the laws of either God or man. What usually tries to replace it is some self serving and perverted sense of good.

His personal terror does not lie in that he attempted to murder his brother, but in the retribution he may suffer from failing. What had been clear and concise just few weeks ago has become muddled and confusing. Many men like Sam have cloistered themselves off to the very periphery of civility. Rare is there a companion who will give him comfort. These men are destined to share their pain alone.

"What am I ever going to do if Joey reappears?" It's a ceaseless mantra—and a tormenting one at that.

# 15 — TINY

Any time one awakes in a strange boxcar, it has the strange effect of bringing about a cautious uncertainty. In Joey's case it's the realization that his recent familiarity with the wilderness has been replaced. Things, simply put, are not clear. This contrivance needs to be analyzed. In the meantime it has all the makings of some monstrous contraption speeding him to some intractable destination.

After relieving himself through the partially open door, he rejoins his curiousness. Inquisitiveness is the uniqueness of his survival. He surveys the new dawn, not with the wonderment of a tourist, but rather with the brain of a modern man and the instincts of a savage.

New light allows him to see clearly, but to also be seen. He instinctively steps back from the open door as any wild animal would do. Not knowing the 'why ' of it—it just seems safer to remain in the shadows. Survival is also a studied strategy, it can't be done haphazardly if one wishes to remain on the top of the food chain.

Out of nowhere a hand shoots decisively from the shadows behind him pushing the door open a bit more. Feeling a burst of adrenalin shoot through his body as one would a jolt of electric current, he involuntarily, jerks back. His mouth opens to scream, but no sound is produced. The fight or flight modes are in such conflict that they are forced to give birth to a third mode—frozen.

The hand belongs to a huge black man. Instantly regaining himself, Joey is ready to jump from this moving train to the misconceived safety of a rock strewn rail bed. In the next flash, he is fixated on the big disarming grin of this intruder.

"Whoa, whoa there, ha, ha, I don't mean to scare you. I thought you knew I was here," says the big man trying to play down his unceremonious greeting.

While desperately trying to process the danger of this unexpected interloper, Joey's hand has found its way to his holstered hatchet. He can feel the shift of blood draining from his face to every muscle in his body. He stands pale and blinking, staring into the face of someone with a neck as big as his own thigh. The stranger's broad grin continues to over ride Joey's ability to discern the breadth of danger. He stands frozen.

The big grin broadens and breaks out into a robust laugh. "Oh hell man, I didn't mean to shut you down like this. I ain't here to unroof ya Dude. I'm sorry." The big man sticks out an even more formidable hand gesturing a truce.

Much like the first encounter Schnitzel had with him, he cautiously studies the uninvited offer of brotherhood. Big Afro hair, big-bearded face, big teeth with large spaces between them; his eyes are bloodshot and watery, big hands, six-foot-six tall, 350 pounds but not fat. Just big.

"Here take a drink of this." Back comes the big hand once again. This time it's holding a half-empty quart bottle of clear liquid.

The enfeebling panic that had gripped Joey for what seemed like an eternity has finally submitted to the need to breathe. A gasp follows as his brain refuses to function on dead air and forces him to suck in a deep breath.

The last human beings he has seen were a few weeks before and had created a similar reaction. Once again, he finds himself standing inches from another human. With a rigid gaze and an obsequious hand, he accepts the bottle.

Thirst is generally satisfied in humans without much thought. The generous presentation of this bottle of clear cold liquid brought it, without thought, to his lips. Just having recovered from his previous bout with oxygen deprivation, his breathing suddenly stops in mid breath.

What had been assumed to be a generous gift of water is proving to be moonshine. Never having had liquor pass his lips, it's causing him a great whooping gasp for air. When he wants to exhale, he finds himself sucking in, when he felt the need for air, his lungs force it out. His chest feels like it will split wide open. Still shakily grasping the bottle in his hand, the big man lunges forward with both hands wide open quickly retrieving it as one would a falling child.

With a mixture of saliva and moonshine stuck to his scraggly several weeks old whiskers, Joey takes a deep breath simultaneously trying to wipe the snot from his face.

"Good God Almighty bro, you gonna be all right?" Still hoping to prompt an alliance, the man pats his big hand on Joey's back.

Joey is bent over bracing both hands on his knees, in one long, loud expulsion, he belches swallowed air. "Ya, I think so." These are the first words he can recall with another human.

"I never met a man who didn't like 'Shine' before," says the big man. His face and voice are flooded with contrition. More apologies follow. "I sure didn't mean to piss you off like this."

"My name is Albert Proudfoot. Most people just call me Tiny." Tiny is proving to be a contradiction not only in name and size, but also in his gentle disposition.

Joey's thoughts are twirling like a tornado. His only response is to stare speechless. Chunks of memory fly forward with no real context. The muddied vision that he recalls is remembering some bodiless voice calling the name "Joey". It's like the memory one would have of being down some *Alice In Wonderland* like rabbit hole. Feeling like a bystander to himself, he begins to hear raspy sounding words start to form from his recent over-burdened trachea.

"Joey, I think my name is Joey."

Tiny accepts this revelation unquestioningly. In this world vagueness is a common reality. Most of its inhabitants hang to life by a thin thread hoping to bury their devils before their hope runs out.

In a span of five minutes Joey's life has enlarged from what felt like a near-death experience to a sense of safety. Tiny has a disarming charm about him, it's deeper than an ordinary magnetism suggesting he hasn't been riding the rails long enough to become disenchanted.

Despite a rib cage stressed from retching, Joey feels the warmth of the morning sun through the open door. An immediate sentiment of acceptance has developed between themselves. It's the kind of stuff that grows between two people or proves to have been a false sentiment and evaporates fast. Nonetheless, what ever forces brought these two vagrants together, they are very quickly tapping into what they need from each other.

"Where the heck did you come from? I thought I was in this car alone," asks a recovered Joey.

Still smiling his big, gapped-toothed grin, Tiny points to the other end of the boxcar amidst a pile of empty crates.

"Right back there, man. I looked you over for awhile, you didn't look too dangerous so I went back to sleep."

Joey is feeling a wince of shame for the reaction he had given Tiny. "I'm really sorry for acting so stupid." The regret can be seen in his eyes.

Taking another pull on his bottle, Tiny slides it back into the side pocket of his massive top coat. The cashmere top coat accessorized with the once white silk scarf suggests yet another contradiction surrounding this drifter.

"You don't need to apologize. I'm the one that should." Still chuckling his affecting laugh, once again extending his huge black hand. This time Joey accepts it, feeling an exaggerated smallness in his own.

For his size, Tiny is not slow at all. Quickly moving to the sliding compartment door, peering out, moving his head from one direction to another, and then with the certitude of a seasoned tour guide, turns to report, "We're about five miles out of Anchorage. We should be there in about fifteen minutes. You hungry?" Not waiting for an answer, he gathers up a large dufflebag, tossing the strap over his shoulder.

"Yeah, I'm getting that way. I've eaten what food I had," says Joey readying his backpack following Tiny's lead.

"If you can hold out for another half-hour, I know just the place," says Tiny, energized by the thought of it.

Joey is quiet, off to himself in thought.

Tiny takes one last pull from his bottle and tosses it through the opened door. It makes the unmistakable sound of breaking glass. Using the moment to study his new companion, he asks, "By the way where you comin' from?"

The question is followed by nervous blinking. It's caught him off guard. "I been in the woods. I got on back there a ways."

Transparency is at a premium in this underworld. It's not as if Joey is trying to purposefully evade the question. If there is a reason for a clearer answer, it's going to have to wait. "How about you, where did you get on?" He asks the question as much out of curiosity as he did to avoid any more questions directed at him.

"I been ridin' the tracks since Fairbanks." Unlike Joey, he's able to reveal more of his past, but remains somewhat guarded. Giving anyone to much information in this fringe of society could prove to be one's undoing. For the moment neither can give or are unwilling to give any more details and it doesn't seem to be important enough to pry any further.

As predicted it's 10:30 a.m. when they arrive in Anchorage. The train has slowed to a crawl. Both are sitting in the open door. It's been agreed that Tiny will give the signal to leap off.

"We've gotta keep a damn good eye open for the Railroad 'dicks'. They think these are there personal cars and that guys like us are intruding on there property. They take great pleasure in busting us in the head."

Tiny has taken on a much more somber tone, keeping an eye open for anything and everything. Pointing to a building a quarter mile up the tracks he says, "See that big red brick building, that's where we get off."

Tiny spends the next few moments adjusting his bag over his shoulder, frequently checking on Joey's progression. His signature grin is on hold, his eyes dart, his muscles are taunt. The train has slowed to under ten miles an hour, still at a pace where a careless jump can result in a broken ankle or leg.

"Okay Joey, here's where we get off ," says Tiny. In a split second his feet safely hit the ground.

"I'm right behind you," says Joey. With that he makes his leap only to find himself stumbling out of control toward the undercarriage of the rolling boxcar.

Before he can recover, he's feeling himself jerked backwards, rolling on the ground. Tiny's big hand has shot out and grabbed him just as he was about to be severed in half by an unforgiving rail wheel.

"Bro, you tryin' ta kill yourself?" says Tiny snatching the back of Joey's collar, pulling him to his feet.

Still reeling from the near fatality a trembling Joey manages to form a grateful appreciation. "You saved my life Tiny. I thought for sure I was a goner. I can't thank you enough."

Not willing to dwell on the past too long, Tiny speaks out, "Well bro, ain't neither one of us dead so let's go get ourselves some breakfast."

With that Tiny's off at a determined pace. It's all Joey can do to keep up with this giant of a man. His two steps equal one of Tiny's. Passing down through a brushy area along the tracks Joey struggles to see anything that appears to be familiar. The smell of a wood fire catches his attention. It's the only common place sensation he's experienced so far in the otherwise roof-lined horizon of this city.

"Hey Tiny whose your little girly boy?" cries out one of the grinning men sitting around the fire. Joey's small frame has caught the attention of this group of boozers. Many of them have spent years in the penitentiary and have used smaller, weaker inmates as sex objects.

Not waiting for an answer, the heckler continues as Joey turns his head long enough to catch a glimpse of this would be tormenter. He's got bulging, watery, bloodshot eyes, and a broken, flattened nose spread across his booze soaked, tattoo littered face.

"Yeah, you good buddy. You ever get tired of that big son-of-a-bitch just come see me. I can make that little girly ass of yours twitch like a home girl."

Ignoring the trash-talking drunk, Tiny keeps his arms and legs moving in a synchronized gait.

"Don't pay any attention to these morons. They wouldn't have a clue on how to treat a real woman. They'd screw a rock pile if they figured they'd be a snake in it."

Joey picks up the pace to keep in step with Tiny. He's feeling less jittery over all the unpredictability of this strange world and more confident in having such a formidable ally.

At this brisk pace they soon find themselves standing in front of an unpretentious white-framed, Cape Cod house. A big sign in the front yard announces to one and all DOWN TOWN SOUP KITCHEN.

"They got the best damn ham and bean soup you'll find any where in this whole damn state. That includes any up-scaled Beaneries," declares Tiny as he deftly stoops passing through a side entrance. On the other side of the door, an enthusiastic female voice boisterously blurts out an announcement, "Hey Tiny, good to see ya back." She's a fifty-something, gray-haired, matronly lady named Gertrude O'Connell.

"Hell ya lady. I can't stay away from you or your bean soup." Tiny's contagious laugh is back in full force exploding across the room. "That's good darlin' because we come as a pair. You get two for the price of one."

"Oh you a flirty little hoe, but I love ya anyway Gertie." With that, Tiny grabs her around the waist, twirling her in and out amongst the tables and chairs as she burst into a raucous, child-like laugh loving every moment of it.

Soon the place begins to fill up. It's the city's down and outers who find a meal here. Some find themselves at the bottom of the cities social scale by choice, others by circumstances. Either way, there is a sense of community among them and for many, it's the only stable thing in their lives.

They all have their stories to explain why it's not their fault they have found themselves here. It seems they have succumbed to a victim mind set. For a share of these folks, mental illness is their culprit, for others not being able to cope with changing environments becomes their nemesis, and of course the quintessential alcoholic/drug addict occupy many of the chairs. In all cases, as coping skills become less and less capable, hope fades and hopelessness fills the void. After all it is a law—nature abhors a vacuum.

"You stay the hell away from my hangins'," says a toothless middle-aged woman (referring to the plastic bags hanging from her grocery cart) to a younger, very thin woman wearing a red stocking cap pulled down covering everything from her eyes on up.

"I ain't messin' with none of your ole crap bitch," says the red-hatted lady. Anger and sarcasm trump any semblance of true fellowship. Poverty always brings its own brand of miseries and in this world that type of desperation is never quiet, it's always loud and to the forefront. But then the devil is never in a hurry for those he's sure of so they continue to muddle their way through their miserable lives.

This barrage of human misery is taking its toll on Joey, without warning a wave of emptiness, a sickening loneliness, a strong sense of loss—it's a kind of shocking grief he's never experienced before—it's like he can't breath. "I gotta go outside for a minute Tiny. I think I need some fresh air," says Joey, simultaneously nearly leaping to his feet. As he's looking into the faces of all these miserable folks, he wonders if their world is his world.

Tiny follows him out. "You gonna be okay, Bro?"

Joey is nearly hyperventilating, he's fixed on his reflection in the glass door. Ignoring Tiny's question, he asks his reflection a question, "Who the hell are you?" He's repulsed by and disconnected from the seeming stranger staring back at him. Finally coming to himself, he turns, looking hard at Tiny. "Tiny answer me true, is this all just a bad dream we're having?"

Tiny stares back at Joey for a moment with his own thoughts. "If it is Bro, it's the worst there is."

Joey remains silent. Then as if an epiphany suddenly came to him, he says, "Tiny I gotta talk to somebody before I fall completely apart."

Tiny recognizes an urgency in Joey's voice that he has experienced himself. Motioning toward a small cluster of outdoor plastic chairs he says, "Go ahead Bro, I got a good ear."

Joey takes his story back to the only past he knows, beginning his story with his struggle to get out of the mine shaft. It's a short legacy and obviously a small legacy within a much-larger legacy.

"It's like I can remember to tie my shoes, but I don't remember why I know. I feel like I'm living on the edge of fear all the time because of what I don't know. Much of the time I find myself in a crouch just watching hoping nothing gets me."

"Damn Joey sounds like you got some kind of blackouts. You drink a lot?" asks Tiny. He studies Joey for a moment then adds, "I get like that if I get into the hooch to damn deep."

"I don't think I do. That stuff you gave me this morning wasn't something I'd try again," says Joey with a firm voice. So far it's the only sure thing he'd bet on.

"No you probably don't," says Tiny. He's studying Joey as one would a project. Prior to this road trip, he had been a restaurant manager. He became very aware of the habits and actions of heavy drinkers. Joey possesses none of these.

With this thought behind them, Joey continues his chronicle. "I have a hard time with what's real and what's not. It's like the things I'm aware of came from a dream. It's like I'm dreaming a dream."

Tiny is trying to process all this. It's like looking at a file cabinet where all the drawers are locked. "You been to see a doctor?" asks Tiny. Catching himself he bursts into a chuckle as he answers his own question. "Well hell no you ain't seen no doctor — unless you saw one while you was 'frontierin'." Pausing for a moment, Tiny takes on a more serious tone. "You wanna see a doctor?" Continuing his trustworthy gaze he adds, "Cause if you do, I know where we can get a free one."

Joey rolls his foot around as if he had a corn cob under it. "I got nothin' to loose. Maybe, at the least, I can get rid of some of this anxiety."

With that settled, Tiny is to his feet. "All right Bro, follow me." Within five minutes walking distance, they find themselves standing before a large stone church. Without a word, Tiny makes a left turn heading to the church's rear entrance, down some steps and stops. There before them in big bold letters FREE CLINIC. Entering, they take a seat. It's obvious it's going to take a while. The place is full of overweight women with small children.

Within a few minutes a lady in a flowered smock appears with a clip board. "Are you both here to see the doctor?" Tiny, saying nothing points toward Joey. "Okay sir, if you will please fill this out for us and someone will see you soon."

A closer scan around the room reveals a young man about his own age. He's wearing a gaudy pair of orange and black checkered pants. His leg is seemingly bouncing involuntarily. He's thin and pale. It's apparent that he's agitated.

"Nurse, Nurse," he shouts over and over while waving his hand.

The nurse continues to wear her professional demeanor, hesitating for a moment as if to collect her composure.

"What is it, sir?" says the nurse trying hard to remain courteous.

"I can't wait any longer or I'll go nuts. All I need is a methadone script and I'm out of here." Hoping that his plea is effective enough to move him to the head of the line.

"I'm sorry sir but the doctor needs to see you first," she replies with the same confident tone.

"That's bullshit!!" shouts the belligerent man, "I need somebody to see me now."

"Mr. Lindsey, if you insist on disrupting this office, I'm going to ask you to leave and if you don't comply, I'll call the authorities and have you removed."

"No, no, please don't do that. It's just that I'm really hurtin'."

Without further comment, she turns, going behind the closed door leaving the disrupter to fend as best he can. Rifling through his pockets he manages to come up with a few Percodan, struggling with a dry mouth, he finally manages to get them down. Within a short time a much more complacent "Mr. Lindsey" has his head back, mouth wide open as the effects of the pills have pulled him tighter into his preferred state of oblivion.

The door opens once again. The same calm nurse looks about the room. "Mr. Joey. The doctor will see you now." Her eyes have enough wetness that when her mouth smiles so do her eyes.

This is the sweetest face he can ever remember. Allowing this angelic figure to lead him is a pleasure. She placed him in an examination room closing the door behind him. He sits staring at pictures pasted to the walls of human meat from the various parts of the human anatomy. It's raw and it's red. It's reminding him of the meat from the bear he killed.

Soon the door opened. A smallish man with a blue shirt, khaki pants, and cordovan loafers steps through the door with a stethoscope around his neck.

Looking somewhat puzzled at his clipboard. The paperwork is blank with the exception of the word Joey in the name section.

"What can I do for you Joey?" asks a perplexed doctor.

Struggling for the right words, Joey hesitates. "I can't remember anything from my past."

Looking rather intent the doctor asks, "What drugs are you using?"

Taken back by the insinuation, Joey reels forward with a vehement protest, "I don't use drugs!"

The doctor has heard these protestations many times. Undaunted, he turns to his nurse, "Do a urinalysis and a blood work up and we'll go from there."

A compliant Joey moves from room to room allowing whatever the nurse asks of him. After what seemed like a life time, the doctor finally re-enters the examination room with a confident smile.

"Well Joey, I can tell you, you have no drugs in your system."

Feeling the pressure mounting on his temples, Joey fears his head may implode from anger, and for the moment he can only stare back dumbfounded. "You had me sit here all afternoon only to tell me I have no drugs in my system—I told you that hours ago! My problem is that I can't remember my past." Joey's voice has become much more anxious, and has turned to a shout.

Not appearing to be angry or surprised at Joey's reaction, the doctor calmly says. "All the cases I see with memory deprivation result from either alcohol or drug abuse. If your memory loss is from neither of these, then let me ask you, have you received a blow to the head recently?" asks the doctor.

"I think I may have, but I can't tell you for sure because I can't remember." Joey still has a frustrated feeling that things aren't going to get better. It's times like this that waves of fear roll over him leaving him feeling helpless and alone.

"Well tell me why you think so," returns the doctor in the same calm voice not rushing him.

Disarmed by the doctors assuring presence, Joey apologizes, "I'm sorry for my outburst, but I'm so frustrated over this." He settles down sinking back into his chair feeling comfortable enough to venture into his saga of finding himself bruised and bleeding at the bottom of a mineshaft.

The doctor listens very carefully, interrupting only when he needs something answered. Finally as Joey finishes, the doctor sums up his thoughts.

"Joey from what you have described my opinion is that you have retrograde amnesia. You've profiled your symptoms perfectly with this condition." Hesitating for a second, he adds, "What bothers me is the amount of time since your accident. You should have begun to recover by now. My suggestion is that you see a neurologist. I don't recommend that you put this off." With that thought he writes out a name of a colleague and hands it to him.

Joey takes a deep breath and lets it out slowly. It's a bittersweet relief. At least he has a name for his condition other than 'crazy'. Holding the papers the doctor has given him, he makes his way back to the waiting room only to find that Tiny has disappeared.

"Maybe I overwhelmed him with my problem and he's taken advantage of the opportunity to leave," is his haunting thought.

By the time he's made his way back out to the street he's resolved to return to the wilderness where things are more familiar. While deciding which direction will best serve his decision, he spots a familiar swagger. With a huge coat swaying from one side of the sidewalk to the other its proprietor charges his way straight ahead. A strange relaxation ripples over him as he recognizes this huge hulk of a man twisting and swinging his way toward him. Joey takes a deep breath swallowing hard. His face and body suddenly loose their tensions. The sight of Tiny grinning his huge gap-tooth grin is one of comic relief. The world takes on a new reality, less chilling and more focused.

"Did that old witch doctor screw your head back on straight," Tiny asks.

"Amnesia, he says I have retrograde amnesia," says a much more accepting victim now that it has a name.

"Whad he say you gotta do about it Bro?" inquires Tiny a bit further.

"Nothin," says Joey.

Tiny begins to sing a little song he remembers from somewhere, "When there's clouds in the skies just keep smilin, what's the use of cryin."

Joey gave a second thought to this little refrain as he as he wads up the doctor's referral and tosses it aside.

"Well good, now that we can take a chance on your sanity we got some other stuff happenin. I been checkin the shelters out. There's one over by the river we can get into tonight. I been there before. They got good showers." With that same broad grin, he adds, "They got one callin your name."

In a matter of fifteen minutes, they arrive at the shelter. Every evening it's the same scenario, it's as though every day the city's exiles are all drawn off the streets at the same time. Coming from every direction, some pushing grocery carts or pulling wagons draped with every color of plastic bags imaginable. They give the appearance of a pilgrimage as they make their way toward the various homeless shelters. To get there late could mean no bed for that night. All are mistrustful of each other and avoid eye contact with anyone. To expose any weaknesses is to invite a predator, so most remain privately stoic hoping to hide their desperation.

The dumpster at the corner of the building provides an opportunity for those who wish to rid themselves of any contraband not allowed inside. Some are gathered there tipping up near empty bottles hoping to get one last drink.

Signs at the entrance with big bold letters read:

BROTHER FRANCIS HOMELESS SHELTER

NO ALCOHOL - NO DRUGS - NO WEAPONS

Anyone not complying will be escorted out.

All this is routine to Tiny. None of this is even remotely familiar to Joey. Someone bumped him from behind and he jumped like he'd been goosed.

"I don't know if I can do this Tiny," says Joey nervously looking around. "I don't think I've seen this many people in one place in my life." What he is puzzled over is how there isn't much variation in the behavior of these men, in how they all portray themselves as victims. It seems to be the bond that holds them altogether.

The shelter typically has cots for up to a 100 men during nice weather and up to 300 as it begins to cool down.

The staff is accommodating and informative when necessary and condescending and patronizing when dealing with the wet-brained and drug-induced paranoiacs. These are all part of the daily buffet of God's children struggling their way through life.

There is a receiving desk available to check in valuables. Both Tiny and Joey opt to hang on to their own by storing them under their cot. For this time of year there are at least 150 cots separated only by enough room to walk sideways. The din made by this swarm of humanity is highlighted by any number of toothless men shouting vulgarities.

"You muddapucker, get dapuck off my pucken bed," flaps a pair of toothless lips at a perceived trespasser.

Volunteers wearing BROTHER FRANCIS emblazoned across their shirts patrol the various common areas trying their best to maintain order.

An older vagrant trying to voice his dominance over a younger man can be heard saying, "Shit kid, I've spilt more booze than you ever drank."

Not to be out flanked by this old geezer the young gun returns a volley of his own, "That's too damn bad cause if ya hadn't spilt so damn much and with a little luck you'd be dead by now."

Civility is practically an unknown. If anyone was ever charged with being too courteous there wouldn't be enough evidence to gain a conviction.

Joey is struggling the best he can not to bolt out of the door. "Ya doin okay Bro?" breaks in the voice of this tutelary saint. Tiny's garrulity can't help but cut through all the commotion. Having a six-foot-six-inch black man running interference is more than mere luck. It's obvious this is a place where God is preferring to remain anonymous.

"I'm trying." It's a true response after spending weeks in the wilderness without human interaction. To find himself in this crowded environment is like a looming crisis waiting to happen. His thoughts hark back to some of the crises already behind him, but he's becoming more and more dubious about overcoming this one.

The normal course of action is to get a bed, get something to eat and then try and get what Tiny refers to as a "damn good hot shower". The menu tonight features something referred to as "slumgullian", consisting of vegetables held together with a thick chicken paste like gravy. The effort is to make it filling as well as nutritious.

With this particular phase of the evening agenda out of the way, Tiny takes the opportunity to lead Joey to the shower room and introduce him to the joys of a shower.

In a short time, Joey is reliving this simple pleasure. Both of his hands are stationed above his head planted firmly against the shower surround allowing the full force of the cascading water to massage each muscle in his body. A picture is taking shape in his head of having done this before, but not remembering where. Tiny has finished his shower and is heading back to his cot to do some reading, leaving Joey alone to pamper himself.

Having finished his shower, Joey moves to another section of the shower room to review a beard that hasn't succeeded in merging into any vision of who he hopes he is. It's unsettling to look at his face in the mirror. "Damn I'm ugly. This face looks like it wore out ten bodies. This crap has gotta come off," he says out loud.

Without notice two other men have made their way into his area. Politely moving his backpack out of their way and between his legs, he continues to probe his mode of attack on his beard.

One of the men, wearing a dirty blue hoodie silently appears on his right side, the other wearing an orange stocking hat pulled down to his eyes stations himself on his left. Joey's eyes meet an unfriendly stare from both of them. This unexpected change of events is suddenly leaving him feeling vulnerable. His eyes dart around for an escape. Nothing is apparent as both of these uninvited strangers continue to move toward him. Realizing that the same fear that sent him looking for a quick way out is now preparing him to fight. In a flash, Joey has grabbed his backpack with one hand while the other wraps itself around the handle of the concealed hatchet.

"What you got in the bag there, little man?" snorts the hooded character. He's moved in close enough now so that Joey can smell the alcohol on his breath. Managing to back away, he positions himself in such a way to see both of them without moving his head from side to side.

"I think he's got the feeling we're invading his space," says Mr. Hoodie with a smirk.

By this time Joey is acutely aware that this situation is not turning out well. Attempting once again to work his way to the exit only to find Mr. Orange Hat step in front to block the way.

"What'sa matter Huckleberry, don't you like our company? Now les see if you any smarter en yo dumb ass face say you are."

Joey is not moving. His hand is still firmly griping the hatchet hidden in his backpack. Mr. Orange Hat has taken the confrontation to the next level by popping open a switch blade knife. "Jus hand over you backpack asshole before I cut you a new one."

In one quick move Joey has his hatchet out and raised above his head in a striking position with the other hand positioning the canvas bag as a shield.

WHAP! An excruciating pain, seeming out of nowhere, shoots through his bare leg. Mr. Hoodie has extended a car antenna turning it into a whip, lashing Joey's leg and nearly bringing him to his knees. Mr. Orange Hat takes advantage of Joey's distraction and lunges at him with the stiletto only to have it deflected by the make shift shield. Trying to keep an eye out for both of these miscreants coming from different directions is proving to be impossible as WHAP he feels the sting of the antenna once again. Mr. Orange Hat sees an opportunity lunging again with the speed of a rattlesnake but once more having his blade deflected by the equally quick reactions of Joey.

Mr. Hoodie's antenna is raised ready to lash but has found his arm unable to move. "Wha the hell...." is as far as gets before he is spun around facing the most formidable foe he has ever encountered in his entire criminal career. Before he can process all of this, he finds his feet are dangling in mid air, his nose is spurting blood like a gusher as this fearless opponent has lifted him off the floor and given him a textbook headbutt. With the same swiftness this benefactor slams this low-life cretin to the floor. The poor thing lets loose of the antenna as he lay crumpled in a pool of his own blood screaming, "You son-of-a-bitch, you broke my nose."

Mr. Orange Hat witnessing his partnership dissolve in a matter of seconds, drops his knife and makes a bee line for the exit. What he had deemed only moments before as a good idea has turned into his worst nightmare. Before he can take another step the biggest hand he has ever had laid on him has grabbed a hold of his hood and jerked him back with a force never before experienced. His screams are soon only hollow echoes as they bounce off the walls of a porcelain toilet. Gasping for air, he finds himself sucking its unflushed water down his miserable gullet and into his lungs.

"Stop! Stop! Stop!" they shout as several volunteers are attempting to pull Tiny away from his drowning nemesis. Tiny is not about to stop until he's satisfied this miserable wretch has swallowed enough of this unseemly beverage to never forget it.

"Drop it now!" are the shouts directed toward Joey as he stands buck-naked with a hatchet poised to strike. Hardly able to hear apart from his own adrenaline soaked thoughts, he is frozen as two volunteer security guards have him disarmed, face down on the floor and handcuffed.

Tiny has at last relented and has been pushed back against an opposite wall. Mr. Orange Hat is vomiting profusely. Mr. Hoodie is still on all fours holding his nose and moaning a low, mournful groan. His blood drenched clothing stands as an unsightly testament to untimely behavior.

Two security guards are holding Joey. His twisted hair and matted, month-old beard give him a demented look. Anyone coming on this scene will have a difficult time separating the good guys from the bad.

Four good sized policemen arrive. There is such an aversion to the police in these shelters that only when weapons are found do they involve the authorities. Mr. Hoodie is shouting over the top of everyone. "These two assholes jumped us. We were minding our own business when Big Foot and Candy Ass went off on us.

The police are attempting to segregate all the participants from the gawkers while the volunteer security force encourage people back to their cots.

Joey's heart is racing, his body is convulsing as his system struggles with an adrenalin assault. Somehow he knows it's important to remain calm. He's been placed in a small room off to the side. After removing his handcuffs and allowing him enough clothing to dress himself the policeman notices the large welts on his legs.

"Are you hurt, sir?" he asks.

"Nothing serious," says Joey, running his fingers over the raised skin, "I got whacked a few times with a car antenna."

The policeman agrees that these wounds aren't life threatening and moves on with his questioning. Joey gets the sense that this is by no stretch of anyone's imagination a casual conversation.

"I'd like to see your identification," asks the policeman.

"I don't have any, sir," replies Joey.

"What is your name?" questions the policeman.

"Joey," he answers.

"Joey what?"

"I don't know. I have retrograde amnesia and don't remember."

After writing a few things in a small note pad the policeman moves on with his questions.

"Tell me in your words what happened."

Joey begins by telling how these two men came in demanding his backpack and how they pulled a knife and the car antenna and began to attack him and how he pulled out his hatchet to protect himself.

"You stay put here, I'll be back in a minute," says the policeman. Joey can see him through the open door conferring with what appears to be a sergeant. Moments later he returns. With no fanfare he motions for Joey to stand up, "Turn around sir," he commands as he replaces handcuffs on him and reads him his Miranda rights, adding, "For the present time I'm placing you under arrest for brandishing a deadly weapon. You may be innocent but it takes awhile to sort through cases like this and in the meantime you will be housed in the county jail until you have a hearing."

With this phase completed, he's quickly whisked out a back door to a waiting patrol car. From the back seat window he spots Tiny shackled in another car. As he passes by they catch each other's gaze. Tiny gives him a reassuring wink.

In spite of all this craziness, Joey has calmed down with an indescribable sense of serenity. It's as though there is an inner, unexplained sense of something much larger leading him. Staring at nothing, his thoughts are no longer assailing him. "I know there is a life in all this insanity. All I need to do is keep fishing' for it."

# 16 — A NEW ALLIANCE

Jacob has taken over the day-to-day operations at the Mueller and Sons Smelters. Being well aware of his failing eyesight brings with it a sense of urgency about what he is yet able to do. Recently, he's begun a regime of special shots in his eyes anticipating at least a delay in losing his sight allowing him a welcome reprieve.

The recent rise in precious metal prices has brought with it a whole influx of greenhorn miners into the region. There is hardly a stream that doesn't have claims running its whole length. For every egg-sized gold nugget that's been found in-turn has brought several thousand would be miners selling everything they own for a grubstake hoping they'll find several more just like it.

Rup is much relieved to be out of the office. His guilt over his affair with Rena has detached him even further from his father. He's more than willing to play a minor role, staying out of the way of any patriarchal business privileges his father may exercise.

There are no smiles among the Mueller family members. The loss of Joey and the deceptive roles each of these brothers are playing not only against their father, but among themselves is not merely shameful, it's also dishonorable and above all dishonest.

When a lie replaces love and respect in a family, becoming the unseemly common bond that unites them, that family is at its weakest point. It's a model that will soon implode destroying all within it unless drastic measures are taken.

Whenever the four sons of Lena have time together the sinking feeling that accompanies guilt always surfaces creating a fellowship of discord.

As usual Sam's personality dominates. His voice becomes loud and boisterous "Why do you guys want to keep going over this? I did what I thought was best for all of us. Things don't always go as planned, but we're brothers and brothers stick together."

"Sam that's just like you. You make a decision without us and want us to willy-nilly go along with it," says Justin.

Sam's head snaps around. This is an attitude creeping in that he's not had to deal with. He's hoping his aggressive demeanor will be enough to thwart this mutiny.

Embolden by this older brother, Levi enters the fray. Locking his dark eyes on Sam, "Justin's right. None of us like it." Being a younger brother, it's not like Levi to take such a bold stand against Sam. Now he's looking around the room for support. Rup is fidgeting with a grinder trying as best he can to appear too busy to be bothered.

Feeling he's left alone in his rebellion, Levi tries to engage Rup. "Come on Rup, you know we've talked about this."

Having more on his plate than he can deal with, Rup waves his hand in a dismissive gesture, "I've had it with these conversations. I say let's just give it a rest."

Sam's complexion is darkening along with his mood. Digging his heels in a little deeper, his eyes dart from brother to brother. "You all supported the decision to tell the Old Man that the bears got Joey. Now you think you can just back out of it. Well let me ask you, how do you propose we do that?"

Silence as usual. Sam has been successful in bullying his brothers all his life. It doesn't look like it's ending any time soon.

Levi breaks the silence. "Ya but that was before Rup laid all that stuff out in front of the mineshaft that all disappeared."

Hoping to end this revolt quickly, Sam attempts to re-assert his dominance. "That doesn't mean a dead man crawled out of that hole. Anybody could have come by and stolen that stuff."

As usual Sam is able to get the last word leaving them dangling with their feet on nothing. All three of them have wanted to walk away from Sam, but lack the strength of character to carry it through. Each of them catch a glimpse of themselves in the face of each other, forcing them to resign themselves again and again to their own improbability.

Despite the disturbing undercurrents of conversation that have forced their way to the top in the last few minutes, Benji, who is seldom if ever privy to any of these parleys, enters the room with his lunch pail under his arm. Being the youngest of Jacob's children and still a teenager, he doesn't expect to be privy to most of his brother's conversations. Because of his age they sometimes indulge him, but mostly dismiss him.

Much like his older brother, Joey, he's of a slighter physique. Earning straight A's in school, he's quietly reserved which leads his brothers to consider him, at least on the surface, as naive. On the other hand, Benji's brightest moments are when he's in the presence of all his older half-brothers. Perhaps he may be on the naive side or it may be youthful presumptions, but he still believes their father is the common bond that holds him to his brothers and them to him. Having finished their conversation, they force a little smile, patronize him a bit and get on with business.

Despite his youth, he can't help but notice how things have changed with his brothers. Tiny suspicions have begun to steal their way into his thinking. He's paid particular attention to how often they avoid him and how anxious it makes them when he wants to talk about Joey. The natural trust he feels he should have within his family is beginning to erode.

"Knock, knock, knock," says Benji slowly cracking open his father's office door.

"Come in, come in," says Jacob. Noticeably affected by his youngest son's visit, he's up out of his chair putting the boy in a bear hug. "How's school going?"

"Oh fine I guess," says Benji helping himself to a chair. It's soon apparent that this is not a social call.

"What's on your mind son?" says his father taking a seat opposite him.

"Oh a lot I guess," pausing for a moment. "I can't stop thinking about Joey, Dad."

Jacob lays some papers he had been holding aside, letting out a noiseless sigh, he drops his head, folds his arms, silently sitting back in his chair.

Benji interrupts his father's silence. "Dad, I think Joey's still alive."

Hesitant to dismiss his son's misgivings as he is also struggling with the same disturbing thoughts. "Why do you say that son?"

"Because they're not sad, Dad. Whenever I want to talk about Joey to my brothers, they get angry and leave," says this grieving brother straining to choke back the tears

Benji's words are striking hard against Jacob. He's up from his chair immediately and with great purpose makes his way to his grieving son. He holds him close, feeling his son's wet tears on his creek as they mingle with his own.

Not wanting a split between his families, Jacob takes advantage of this momentary halt to measure his thoughts into words lest they become corrosive. "I'm not entirely convinced that Joey is dead myself. I agree that your brothers are noticeably insensitive, but we need to be careful that we don't read more into this than what they are demonstrating. At the same time, I continue to ask myself, if I'm so sure he's alive, why doesn't he come home?"

Benji's at an awkward age—too young to be a full participant in the adult world, but too old to be ignored.

Jacob's response is an assuring nod. A new alliance has been formed between father and son blending the sentiments of youth with the pragmatism of age.

Each of these participants in their own way are subject to anger and frustration, but neither are willing to merely suppress their apprehensions. Both seem to be aware that a make-believe calm is tenuous at best and can only lead to despair. The hope of a miracle remains more than a golden dream with these two today as together they form a new alliance of hope.

# 17 — DREAM DILEMMA

Meanwhile, back in Anchorage the patrol cars carrying these roustabouts make their way to a precinct lockup. To be sure this is a rag-tag cavalcade. It would be easy to aim the harpoon of guilt equally among all four of these dregs of humanity.

Mr. Hoodie and Mr. Orange Hat are playing the tough gangster role. They're both barely out of their teens and already have extensive criminal records.

K.C. Randolph, the jail turnkey, knows both of these local desperados very well. No one would dispute his ability to keep an orderly jail. He's been doing this work for years and seen it all several times over again. In an interview he has been heard to say, "This job's like herding a bunch of sixth graders all trying to get away with something."

K.C. looks up from his desk as the uniformed guys are bringing in their latest quarry. "You guys back here again?"

He's gazing directly at Mr. Hoodie. Neither Mr. Hoodie nor Mr. Orange Hat have anything to say—at least for the moment.

"Okay Raymond, (Mr. Hoodie) you know the routine, I want all of your piercings out and put in this envelope."

"Bullshit, man! Why you make me take these out? You act like I'm gonna stab somebody with 'em." says Raymond.

Giving him a good hard stare, K.C. allows him only one chance to comply. "We go through this every time you come in here Raymond, so I'm gonna tell you what I always tell you: either you take them out or I take them out with wire cutters."

"Damn you K.C., why you gotta be such a hard-ass?" asks Raymond. He is already beginning to untwist a dozen or more contrivances that make him look like a walleye coming downstream with a bunch of lures hanging off him.

K.C. gives himself a satisfying little chuckle. When he can make these guys lives a little harder, he knows he's doing his job. Satisfied that Raymond is under compliance, his attention turns to Lester (Mr. Orange Hat) who is much mouthier.

"If I didn't have these shackles on, your ass 'ed be mine," mouths Lester toward K.C. He still reeks of booze, stale cigarette smoke and sweat.

"Lester, you stink. Nobody wants you in a cell with them or even near it. Get those clothes off," says K.C. still chuckling. He's aware that they won't be arraigned until the next morning and then they'll get jail clothing. For the time being, he's messing with Lester for his own entertainment.

"Eat shit and die you freakin pig. I'd like to see you make me get out of my clothes." Lester is definitely ramping up his verbosity as he continues his diatribe. "That's probably what you get off on isn't it, lookin at some guy's bare ass? Well you big ass freak, you ain't gonna see mine any time soon."

K.C. continues his bantering with these two. A jail is one of the few places in the world where a criminal's attitude can be neutralized. The continual reminder to those who find themselves behind its walls is that they are no longer in charge. K.C.'s view is that the quicker they realize other people run their lives, the better.

The booking process is routine for those who comply. For Joey and Tiny the procedure goes orderly and systematic. They soon find themselves cell mates.

"I hope you boys find our accommodations to your liking," K.C. says with a wry little smirk. The clank of the door serves as the period at the end of his sentence.

The only words Joey can come up with that seem pertinent to the moment are, "Well, I guess we're in jail."

Tiny nods a knowing nod as one would who may not be exactly at home with this situation, but expected it.

"For me it's come a little sooner than I'd hoped for," says Tiny stroking his massive beard.

"What does that mean?" asks Joey. His voice reflects a duress while finding it odd that Tiny is so nonchalant.

Tiny is pensive for the moment, not exactly sure how much he wants to reveal to this new friend. Deciding to risk it he begins his story.

"I got accused of embezzling on my last job." Sitting on the edge of his bunk, Tiny is watching Joey's face for any reason to stop his story. Joey's expression is one of puzzlement, not contempt, so Tiny chooses to continue.

"My bail was set at $5,000 dollars. It was all the money I had in the world. So, with no job came no money, which meant no apartment, no car, no nothing. I soon found myself homeless, and then missed my hearing which means I've jumped bail. I've been on the road ever since." Reliving these events has moored Tiny in a heaviness Joey has not, up until now, seen in him.

With the same puzzled expression, Joey presses the issue. "How'd you ever get charged with embezzlement?" He's only known Tiny for a day, but he feels he has seen enough of his benevolent character to view this charge as a contradiction.

Still seated on the edge of his bunk, Tiny toys with his interlocked fingers as he considers Joey's question. "Have you ever heard of Gore Amzlov?"

"Not unless I've met him in the last couple weeks," says Joey with a sardonic grin. A life time of worries and concerns have been erased and now singularly replaced by anxieties over not remembering them.

Tiny's black eyes quickly take on an apologetic look. "I'm sorry about that Bro, I forgot that you forgot," says Tiny in an attempt to be diplomatic.

"Don't worry about it, I can't miss what I don't know," says Joey waving his hand dismissively, expecting it will happen if he says it often enough.

Tiny continues his introduction, "Mr. Amzlov is a first class business-man in these parts. He owns hotels, a rail line along with several different mining operations.

"I managed all the watering holes in his chain of hotels. An unex-plained shortage of cash materialized. Somehow it was made to look as though I had been skimming cash. The guy that handled the restaurants pointed the finger at me.

"Mr. Amzlov doesn't take stealing lightly. The next thing I know, I'm arrested." Tiny's head is down with elbows resting on his knees, his fingers are interlocked. He looks defeated.

As Joey listens, he is trying to spot any insincerity or weakness of character in Tiny. What seems to be more and more apparent with this new friend is that he is much too transparent to be a deceiver.

Placing a reassuring hand on Tiny's stooped shoulders, Joey says, "Tiny I have to tell you that in my deepest soul, I believe you."

Tiny lifts his head, gazing directly at Joey. His appreciation for Joey's vote of trust is told in his voice. "Thanks Bro, you're a good friend."

Wrapping his blanket around himself, Tiny lies down on his bunk. He's soon sound asleep.

Joey lies on his bunk listening to the sonorous snores of his big friend. Soon a diaphanous-like veil envelopes him. An unprecedented reassuring calm overtakes him. Immediately he drifts into an anesthesia like trance. Suddenly his whole being is lit with a brilliance way beyond anything he has ever experienced. He finds himself in a beautiful field of golden grain basking in the warmth of a brilliant sun so bright one can hardly behold it.

He begins to harvest the grain with a scythe, tying it into bundles. Other men in the field are also doing the same. He feels quite at home with these other men as though he has a familiarity with them. Then another strange phenomena takes place. All of their bundles of grain begin to bow down to his. The realization of a strange, mysterious unearthly power taking up residence within him is unquestionably accepted. Joey has felt this phenomena many times over the past few weeks, nonetheless there remains a strange transcendence about it all.

His first conscious thought on waking is his dream. He knows intuitively that this dream is placing a responsibility of authority on him. What's not apparent is the when, where, or how of this perplexing phenomena.

It's 6 am. Jail house noise is seldom quieted. As usual the volume is picking up momentum as the breakfast cart is making its way from one group of cells to another. The restlessness of incarcerated men is expressed in the hollow din of voices as they echo off cement and steel.

Tiny is also awake. He's sitting on the edge of his bunk.

Not his usual enthusiastic self, there is an unsettled comportment about him. He's stumbling around trying to use the steel-rimmed toilet. Scratching his head he mutters to himself, "What the hell was that all about?"

"What was 'what' all about?" questions Joey. Watching Tiny becoming slightly unhinged.

"I had the weirdest dream Bro. It was as real as you and I right this moment. I've never had anything like this crazy dream happen to me—not even in my worst drug days," expresses Tiny, pausing long enough to pay the proper homage to something as unusual as this. He is up off his bunk pacing the small area striving to form the right words that will give this experience all that it's due.

Joey can't believe what he's hearing. Two different people in the same room having a similar experience at the same time. For some strange incomprehensible reason, he cannot disregard it as mere coincidence.

"Tell me about it, Tiny," says Joey.

Tiny can hear something in Joey's voice that tells him that his interest is more than idle curiosity. Now more than willing to share this weird chimera, Tiny begins, "Joey it was the damnedest thing I've ever dreamed in my life. I actually saw a vine in front of me, it had three branches that began to bud and blossom. Joey they were so damn real, I could smell 'em. All of a sudden there were three clusters of grapes in their place. I was holding Mr. Amzlov's wine glass in one hand and in my other hand I held the clusters of grapes. Then I began to squeeze the grapes allowing his glass to fill with the juice. When I had finished I placed the glass in Mr. Amzlov's hand." Tiny finds himself looking at his hands as though expecting to see grape stains.

Joey has climbed off his top bunk and is sitting on the edge of Tiny's bed watching and listening to this drama as it unfolds. It's been observed by others that when the longings of the human heart and mind are intense and persistent enough, they often make their way into dreams.

"I know what your dream means, Tiny. I don't know why I know, I just know that I know." Joey makes this statement with the same assurance he would if he were asked the color of a clear sky.

A look of puzzlement comes over Tiny. It's obvious that Joey got his attention. The only seat in the cell not occupied is the commode. Tiny plops his big behind down over it, giving it the appearance of a miniature pot. He's all ears as he waits for Joey to begin.

"The three branches mean three days. Within three days your Mr. Amzlov will find you and take you out of here. You will then be reinstated back into your former position." Joey has a look of satisfaction in being able to give Tiny this good news.

Tiny is sitting listening objectively. Still not smiling, he suddenly bursts out, "Where you comin up wid this shit man? Don't be messin wid me Bro." He's clearly agitated.

Before Joey can respond, K.C. appears at their cell door."You guys got five minutes before I take you to see the Judge so be ready."

Both their minds are twirling as they eat in silence what little is left of their breakfast. These dreams have created a great impression on them both, enough to generate hope and confusion all at once.

If this is not enough, their emotional roller coaster is promptly kicked up to the fast track as K.C. returns. "Okay Mutt and Jeff step out here one at a time. You're on your way to see the Judge." Manacling them together, he leads them across the parking lot to the court house. It's short and sweet as these procedures are inclined to be for these garden variety scofflaws.

Tiny is charged with assault and battery. His bond is set at $500. Joey is charged with brandishing a deadly weapon. His bond is set at $1,500 dollars. Their bond may as well been set at one million dollars since neither has enough to buy a decent cup of coffee.

Consequently, they are returned back to their cell to either be bailed out or wait for trial. Meanwhile their street clothing is replaced with orange coveralls. Joey is making the exchange fairly easily. Tiny, on the other hand, is trying to stuff his big body into a sausage-like casing of jail house coveralls.

"You look like a wiener, wearing scarecrow clothing, Tiny," says K.C. viewing Tiny's pant cuffs well above his ankles. Trying his best to make the adjustment Tiny bends down attempting to pull down the pant legs when-RRRIIIIPPPP the seams give out. K.C. is in hysterics.

Tiny's protracted silence and indignant look suggest to K.C. that he needs to get himself under control and fix this problem. The solution to this dilemma is soon remedied with K.C.'s return lugging a bright orange pair of sweat pants and matching orange sweat shirt bearing the stenciled letters of the Anchorage City Jail.

The next couple days are uneventful with the exception of Tiny teaching Joey how to play chess. Tiny is really amazed at Joey's cleverness.

"Hey Bro, you sure you never played this game?" as Joey is beginning to win a few matches. "Man, you playin' me like you a ringer, Joey," says a wary opponent.

Neither have brought up anything more about Tiny's dream and Joey has kept his own to himself.

The third morning begins uneventfully. Breakfast is over and another jailhouse day begins. The next thing they know K.C. is standing in front of their cell. "Mr. Proudfoot, you got a visitor."

Tiny's head snaps around and narrows his eyes at Joey who is smirking his "I-told-you-so" smirk.

Maybe out of some old leftover habit Tiny asks, "Who is it?"

"How the hell should I know. Wadda do I look like, yer personal secretary? All you dumbasses think I work for you—think again," says K.C., adding his signature little sarcastic chuckle.

K.C. proceeds to walk Tiny down the corridor to a small room. "Sit down here and wait," he says pointing to a steel table jutting out of the wall along with a steel seat all painted in a battleship gray. The room is so small that a person the size of Tiny leaves very little room for anyone else. The clank of the closing door of this exceptionally small room engenders an uninvited event. The sweat begins as the walls close in around him. It's a claustrophobic attack that's about to make a full-scale assault. The air is dank and reeks of mildew, void of any ventilation.

The door could not have opened soon enough. There in the doorway stands Mr. Amzlov's attorney, Clark Shanhizer. Totally lost for words, Tiny remains speechless.

"Hello Tiny. You're sure a hard man to track down as we've been searching for you for a month," says Shanhizer, his hand outstretched toward Tiny. He's a fifty-something man wearing a dark suit and his signature fresh-cut, red rose through his lapel.

Tiny, as yet unable to form words, gives him his hand. The sight of this man, who previously pushed to have him prosecuted, can only mean trouble. For the moment, he's left with disgust for himself for being so stupid as to have been found. Finally clearing his throat, he manages to form a sentence. "Ya, I know I planned it that way."

Shanhizer, still standing, continues, "You can relax. I've got good news and some better news. The good news is you're off the hook for any embezzlement charges. It took awhile, but we finally got to the bottom of it all. It turned out the guilty person was the very person who accused you—Mark the food manager."

Shanhizer purposely shuffles some papers around pausing long enough to allow Tiny to digest what has just been said.

Tiny has quickly processed the whole scenario and is reacting with a defensive posture. It's making Shanhizer nervous to be locked in a small room with Tiny considering he was the one who initiated the warrant for his arrest.

Not looking real happy yet Tiny asks, "So what's the 'better' news?"

Trying his best to put a good face on himself as well as his words, he forces a smile. "Mr. Amzlov is willing to give you $10,000 to cover your expenses as well as give you your job back and a substantial raise to go with it."

Tiny muses for a second, then bluntly inquires, "How's this all going to happen with my ass stuck in this hole?"

"That's all taken care of. Your bail has been paid and I'll take care of the legal matters."

Tiny's expression has relaxed. "You mean, Mr. Amzlov is willing to go through all this mumbo-jumbo for me?"

Shanhizer is still not real sure he's out of the woods with Tiny. "Yes, on one condition," he adds as he pushes a paper across the table, "that you sign this agreement not to sue."

Tiny scans over the document not really taking time to thoroughly read it. Shanhizer continues to try and read Tiny's response. "Mr. Amzlov is willing to admit a mistake has been made and is willing to compensate you."

Not willing to let Shanhizer know how thrilled he is inside, Tiny plays the cool, courteous role as he obliges him by signing the papers. It's like his world just came back to life once again. His bitterness is evaporating by the minute.

"Good," says Shanhizer. All the i's are dotted, and the t's are crossed, he's satisfied he's done his job. That's as good as it gets in his world.

Only a few minutes have passed before Tiny is returned to his cell. Joey knows what has taken place without being told. Plopping down on his bunk Tiny begins to weep. It's like all the tensions from the past few months are leaving in his tears and all the black clouds that have been pressing down have all evaporated.

"Thank you Joey, thank you," says Tiny with tears streaming down his face.

"Don't thank me, thank God," says Joey, still as puzzled as Tiny as to how he could predict this outcome. "He's gotta be the One doing all this." Pausing as his thoughts try to comprehend all that's happened, he concludes, "Evidently, I'm some kind of messenger boy."

Joey watches as Tiny gathers up a handful of his personal items. Choosing his words discreetly, not wanting to come across as needy, Joey tries to laugh as he says, "If you remember, put in a good word for me somewhere ... and maybe a prayer or two."

With all sincerity Tiny assures Joey, "I'm going to do everything I can to help get you out of here, I promise." As is true of words, they are powerful and these are the most intimate symbols of communication Tiny could have spoken. Joey smiles.

Without notice, standing in front of their cell is the unmistakable presence of K.C. "Okay big man, you've been busted out of here. Gather up what you need and get going. There's people waiting for this room." His ever-present chuckle is interrupted only by him snapping open a plastic bag for Tiny's paltry possessions. Filling what he needs, he turns toward Joey. "My friend, and you truly are my friend, I will see you soon." With that, he bends his huge frame over and embraces Joey.

Impatient and not one for jailhouse sentiments, K.C. blurts out, "All right you lovebirds. Let's get this show on the road!"

Tiny is up and ready to go, looking back just once to his friend who already appears at a distance with each footstep he takes forward.

# 18 — A CAUTIONARY TALE FOR BETTER THINGS

The winter has been typical for Alaska, little sun light and plenty of overcast snowy days. Many of the miners are, as usual, chomping at the bit to get an early start. The evidence of blue tarps are every where as camps are reappearing up and down the snow covered riverbeds. These all guarantee an ample supply of mud as the warm rains pull a layer of frost from the ground

The days have turned into yet another season and still no word from the elusive son and brother, but then with the natural progression of time less and less thought is given to his disappearance. Time has also had its way with the long-honored Mormon principles centered around family values. In the Mueller family, much to the disappointment of their father, his sons' values are more and more taking a differing direction.

"Sam, I want you back out in the field," says Jacob. He has pondered his alternatives for each son as they continue to mature in the business. He's decided that Sam's rough and tumble temperament best fits with the attitudes of working miners. Nevertheless, Jacob remains suspicious of what he has described as "Sam's cancerous weakness of ambition," especially the way in which Sam uses questionable methods to achieve his goals.

Benji is a different case. He's still trying to find his niche. He's done everything from running errands to making payrolls. He's always willing to do whatever needs to be done for the good of the business. He prides himself on his ability to learn fast and achieve his goals regardless of how big or small.

Rupert, on the other hand, has willingly let go of any desires for any type of upward mobility. He's content to be back in the lab doing testing and especially much more able to stay out of the way of his father.

Justin and Levi are especially fit for handling laborers out in the plant and its security.

All in all the family continues to manage their business affairs fairly adequately. It's their private lives they continue to sabotage. Their pride, anger, greed, gluttony, lust, sloth, jealousy and envy have proved to be the very pallbearers of an otherwise pious Christian character.

Sam has never made an effort to conceal his discontent with his father's "old-fashioned" business practices. Jacob, being far from willing to give this son a free rein, has come up with a strategy Sam won't like. "Sam, I want to spend less time in the office this season and more time out in the field."

The look on Sam's face tells the whole story. His first thought is to find a way to avoid this, but his second thought is to not rock the boat. By complying, he may be able to counter any negative notions his father may be harboring toward him.

On schedule the next morning, Jacob climbs into Sam's pickup as the shotgun passenger. Sam is far from comfortable with this new arrangement and is straining to give his father the respect he knows is expected.

Sam does not hesitate to try and call the shots for the morning agenda. "I think we can begin with that new operation up on Raccoon Ridge. I'd like to get up there and see what's going on with them. They pulled a thousand ounces with us last year."

Jacob remains silent. He particularly recalls Sam handling that account and only entering 945 ounces. Somewhat numbed by this inadvertent admission, he chooses to remain silent—at least for the time being. Aware for some time of Sam's tendency to lie, he's hopeful with all his heart that he will be able to redeem within this son a sense of integrity.

For the present time, the weather is in a seasonal flux. The days have been warming and the nights are remaining above the freezing mark. The roads remain free of packed snow only to be replaced with a slick, perennial mud.

Sam has taken an old two track logging road around the mountain, when suddenly they come upon a rough, homemade sign adorned with a skull and crossbones with the announcement DUE TO AN AMMUNITION SHORTAGE NO WARNING SHOTS WILL BE GIVEN.

"Nice welcome," chuckles Jacob.

He's done business with these miners his entire life and is accustomed to their paranoia. There have always been the old-time miners, but since the price of gold has escalated it's attracted a large population of people from the Lower 48. Many of these have mortgaged everything they own in order to buy the best equipment money can buy hoping this will increase their chances against the elusive gold.

A few of the old timers have caught on to a new way of doing business by allowing these newcomers with all their fancy new equipment to mine their claims for a percentage. The claim they're coming up on is such an arrangement.

Approaching them is a gray-haired, bearded, grizzled looking, sixty-something miner. "Jacob Mueller, you old hound dog, looks like we made it through another winter."

"Burt Webster, I thought for sure you'd be dead before spring," says Jacob. These two have grown up in these mine fields together since their fathers began doing business a lifetime ago.

"Ah you know the devil's never in a hurry for them he's sure of," returns Burt with a wry grin.

After a hearty handshake Jacob asks, "What the Sam Hill are you doin down here with this bunch?"

"As you've noticed neither of us is gittin any younger. This group of young fellas with all this big new equipment approached me about leasing. Hell, Jacob that junk of mine has been bailer wired for years. These guys want to work around the clock and I cut out my fourteen percent sittin on my ass."

"Can't hardly turn down a deal like that," says Jacob as he looks around at all the new shakers, dozers, trenchers and every other imaginable piece of modern equipment.

Letting out a little sigh along with a knowing grin, Burt adds, "All I'm doin now is tryin' to protect my claim. This is the same crew I had in here last year. I'm just gittin 'em started again hopin they ain't muckin stuff up too bad."

"I hope you do good," says Jacob pausing long enough to change the subject, "I'd like to do business again with you this season, Burt."

Burt, somewhat self-consciously looks away sort of pawing his foot into the dirt avoiding eye contact for the moment until he can regroup.

Jacob has known this old friend too long not to sense when something isn't right between them. "You're hesitating Burt. Is there something we need to work out?"

Still hesitant Burt takes a deep breath, "Ya there could be. Could I have a moment in private with you?" It's easy to tell Burt is not comfortable with this conversation and reluctant to continue.

"Yea sure," says a puzzled Jacob as he motions for Sam to take a hike.

Sam's face turns an ashen white as he walks away knowing what the rest of this conversation may entail.

Burt begins, "Jacob, you and I have known each other since our fathers did business together. I trust your honesty without question. I wish I could say the same for your son, Sam." The tone of his voice is telling. The last thing he wants is to have this kind of conversation with an old friend.

Looking embarrassed with this public revelation of Sam's actions, Jacob asks the obvious question, "Tell me, Burt what happened between you and Sam."

Feeling more comfortable knowing Jacob is not adversarial, Burt launches into exposing Sam's business practices the previous season. "These boys were green as hell last year. I assured them that your boys could be trusted. Sam tested their gold light, claiming there was too much copper in their samples. After he paid them, I looked the paper work over and ran a few tests on the same dirt we hadn't shaken out yet. Jacob, I gotta tell you there was no copper in that run."

Jacob's face has gone from an embarrassed to a painful appearance. He has always thought of himself as a humble man, not because he needed to be humiliated like this first, but because he has always been willing to go the extra mile to please a client.

"Burt, I want to assure you that if my family cheated you in any way, I'll personally make it right. You have my word," with that Jacob extends his hand.

Burt accepts it, while still holding a reservations. "There is no doubt in my mind that you're a man of your word Jacob, but I'm not the one that needs the convincing. These guys been negotiating with Amzlov Refiners. I'd rather be dealing with you, but they got a big stake in this operation and don't want to risk being taken again."

"Can you arrange a meeting for me with them so I can get this straightened out?" asks Jacob. The shame he's feeling is reflected in his voice.

"I'll do what I can," promises Burt, "get back with me in a few days." On that note they shake hands and go their own ways.

Jacob returns to find Sam sitting in the truck. Sam has a sheepish look, letting out a nervous little cough. He knows without asking what the topic of this discussion was about and that he's down for the count.

Nonetheless it doesn't prevent him from attempting to play the role of a responsible member of the Mueller and Sons Smelters team.

"Did we get them again this year, Dad?" asks Sam trying his best to sound enthusiastic. Mentally he's on his knees but outwardly he's still trying to save face.

Jacob looks long and hard at this son hardly knowing where or how to start. "Do you know what Burt wanted to talk to me about Sam?" Not willing to wait for an answer he blurts out, "He says that our company cheated him, Sam. Did you know that, Sam?"

Sam looks away without saying a word.

His father is not willing to let this slip by without getting right to the bottom of Sam's chicanery. "Don't turn your head on me, Sam, I want you to look at me." Jacob is relentless.

Sam won't look at his father. Unfortunately his relationship is based more on fear than love. His shame is not in offending his father as much as it's because he's been caught like a boy with his hand in the cookie jar.

"Well, those guys hardly know what the hell they're doing, Dad. I mean they probably didn't get all the gold they hoped for and put the blame on me."

His answer has left Jacob looking as stricken as a man taking a bolt of lightening. Sam's lack of remorse leaves him with more than a little concern. Harking back to the last conversation he held with Joey on that fateful day was over this very issue. He's fighting his mind as it tries to revisit that dreadful occasion—it's too malevolent.

Heaving a deep sigh of resignation Jacob points his finger forward, "Okay Sam, let's get on the road. We've got more work to do."

This is said not so much to banish the problem, but rather to temporarily set it aside.

It's begun to rain as Sam fires up the truck. Little waterfalls are channeling their way down the truck's windshield. He's not at all convinced this episode is over and that his father is letting him off the hook this easily.

The rain is making the road a slick, slimy mess. Even with all four wheels locked in place, they slip and slide causing the truck to strain on even the smallest inclines.

Deep into their own thoughts, neither are speaking allowing the truck to perform without much scrutiny. After lumbering up a steep grade the crest finally succumbs. At this opportunity the vehicle reduces its effort, smoothing its performance to a cruise mode. This plateau is a man-made cut dividing this part of the mountain. There is a towering snow-packed slope on one side ascending 1,000 feet and a sharp decline on the other side breaking out in shelves at various points.

Without warning both are jolted into an emergency plight. The heavy wet snow on the slope above them has sufficiently lubricated the drier snow beneath resulting in a thundering avalanche. Both understand at the same moment what comes with this crisis.

Sam reacts with cat-like reflexes with his foot pushing the accelerator to the floor, but not before the road before them is filling with what can only be described as a rushing twenty-foot wall of snow, moving anything and everything in it's path.

Jacob has already grabbed the door pull with one hand, the other is pressed against the dashboard in a futile attempt to brace himself. A crashing torrent of rock and snow slam against the passenger side, lifting and pushing the 3,000 pound truck effortlessly over the rim of this precipice along with its passengers. All in the way of this relentless, surging deluge of half-frozen fluid are held completely in its mercy as the truck is turned upside down with the roof acting as a toboggan coursing its way down, leaping the shelvings as mere inconveniences.

Sam's grip has long been torn from the steering wheel. He's been slammed headlong into the windshield, crushing his chest full force against the steering column as the truck slams through boulders, trees and gravel. The further they are carried down into the canyon, the faster they find themselves traveling. Finally coming to an abrupt halt on the riverbed at the very bottom of the canyon.

Both Jacob and Sam are a crumpled mass. It's difficult for Jacob to untangle himself from Sam.

"Sam are you okay?" shouts a frantic Jacob. There is no answer.

"Sam, Sam talk to me!" shouts his father all the louder.

Sam lies crumpled, cramped into the corner of the cab. Blood is flowing from a wound on his forehead mixing with the snow packed around his neck giving it an odd pink color.

Jacob's attention is quickly diverted to a burning electrical odor. The cab is beginning to fill with a choking black smoke. His eyes dart frantically around the upside down truck cab. The thought rips through his mind to get out of this thing now.

With burning eyes and gasping for air, Jacob manages to kick out the back window. There appears to be a ray of daylight forcing its way through a veil of white snow. With the physical strength God seems to supply to those who are intent on rescuing another, he reaches through the shattered back window and manages to get a grip on the jacket collar of his unconscious son and drag him free of the noxious fumes.

Digging his heels into the packed snow he's exhausted but continues to talk to his unresponsive son, if only to motivate himself to move forward. "Come on Sam. We've only a small ways to go." The added threat of gasoline fumes is further adding to the urgency to be out of this situation. "God give me strength!" becomes his mantra as he tugs his 250-pound son out through the broken out tailgate.

It is an answered prayer. No sooner has he cleared the truck, than a muffled WHOOSH sound is followed by a ball of fire that engulfs the whole vehicle.

Physically exhausted, Jacob's turns his attention to this unconscious son. His body is limp and lifeless. "Oh my God Sam, you're not breathing." Jacob's chest is heaving from exhaustion, nonetheless he doesn't hesitate to put his lips to his son's and force what air he has into his fallen boy. Sam is unresponsive. In a near panic, he begins to beat on Sam's chest.

Suddenly in the midst of all this mayhem Sam lets out a choking gasp. It's the first living response in minutes of not breathing and no heart beat. Immediately his eyes roll back up into his head as he falls back into unconsciousness.

Finding his phone to still be intact, while cradling Sam in his arms, he makes a 911 call. Since avalanches often exceed more than a 100 miles per hour the amount of time that's lapsed since the encounter is probably no more than six or seven minutes. It's another 40 minutes before the helicopter from Anchorage will arrive.

Any disgust Jacob may have had for this son earlier has been replaced with a true fatherly concern. For the present time a higher calling has set any animosities aside. The unconditional love this father carries for his family remains intact, in spite of Sam's obvious recalcitrance.

A clap of thunder shakes the canyon wall. Sitting quietly Jacob stares into the rain waiting for their rescue. All other vexations can wait to be settled. For the time being his concentration is on getting this son out of danger and into a medical facility.

It's noon and Sam has been flown to a hospital. They have him wired to a monitor while he undergoes treatment for bruised kidneys and a concussion. He's regained consciousness but there is something very unusual about him.

Jacob is just finishing a call to Lena when the doctor enters the room. His face reflects the magnitude of his concern.

"That was quite a fall you men survived," says an amazed doctor. Still intent on monitoring Sam's recovery, he points toward Sam saying, "I'd like to keep you overnight. I'm concerned about some other internal injuries other than those that we're already aware of. Otherwise, I believe you're on your way to a good recovery." Finished with his examination, he removes his stethoscope from his ears to resting around his neck adding, "With luck on your side, you men will be on your way home tomorrow morning." Exiting the room, he gives them a knowing little smile leaving the two of them alone.

Sam is propped up in his bed with pillows supporting his back. He's silently picking at the leftovers of a lunch on the tray in front of him. Pushing the tray away, he tosses his napkin aside. Looking pensively at his father sitting across the room, he struggles for words. Finally he breaks his silence. "Dad something happened to me today that I can't explain."

Hearing a tone in his son's voice he has never heard before, Jacob squints a bit cocking his head slightly with a gesture that indicates that he's all ears.

"I watched us go down that mountain, Dad." Sam is looking at his father with a perplexed look as sons do when they're seeking an answer.

Instead Jacob looks just as puzzled. With no answer, his eyes hold Sam's for a moment as he forms a comment. "What are you saying you 'watched us go down the mountain'?"

"I'm saying I was outside and above the truck watching it snowball down with that avalanche. I saw it when it stopped at the bottom. I saw you pulling me out of the cab through the back window. I saw you trying to resuscitate me."

With an equally unhinged comportment, he hesitates as something even more incomprehensible is troubling him. Jacob remains attentive but hardly able to offer any kind of explanation. "That's when I left, Dad." Sam is staring, eyes wide open, unblinking, expressionless as he begins to relive something he'd rather not revisit.

Jacob has gone from puzzlement to grave concern. He has never seen his son this fearful.

"I'm trying to follow what your saying son, but I'm not sure I understand," says Jacob. His voice is full of uncertainty.

Sam picks up his napkin and mops the sweat beads forming on his forehead. Clearly not comfortable, he continues, "It was like I was being sucked down. I couldn't stop. What made it horrible was that I was all alone." Pausing for a moment as the chilling aftermath of reliving this is having a similar effect on him. "I have never experienced this kind of loneliness. Suddenly there were other people. I saw them and they also noticed me, but the awful loneliness was with all of us. We were all totally and completely self-absorbed. It's like I had become death. The stench was horrible.

"Then a voice came from somewhere. It filled my whole being. All it asked was a simple question, not loud, not angry, but very meaningful, 'Is this what you want?' I became so full of fear that I became the very essence of fear itself, where it became who and what I am. What was strange was that I also knew everything about everybody. I feared them and they feared me. Along with the agonizing screams of fear, it made my loneliness unbearable.

"What kept running through my mind was, I know this is hell, but I'm a Mormon and Mormons don't go to hell! I don't belong here! Why am I here?!

"Then I was led into what appeared to be another chamber. There was a long hallway with many doors. The voice ordered me to choose a door. Afraid to disobey, I did as I was told. When I opened a door the aroma was beyond any worldly smell I have ever experienced. It was the most wonderful smell of food I could never have imagined. It was rising up from a huge cauldron in the center of the room filled with wonderful meats and nutritious vegetables. Around this huge pot were many people. They were all gray and sickly in appearance as starving people appear. Their most significant feature was not their gauntness rather it was their strange spoon like arms that were so long that when they would scoop the stew from the cauldron they couldn't get it into their mouths. They continued to starve.

"I was told to close that door, leaving them to themselves. I was then told to choose another room. When I opened that door, I was met with a similar scene. The aroma was the same breathtaking lusciousness, the cauldron was the same, people were also sitting around the same way and they also had long spoon-like arms. There was one significant difference, these people were healthy and joyous.

"The voice spoke again asking me if I would like to know the difference between these similar rooms. I said that I would. I was then told to look closely. When I did, I noticed the difference, these people had learned how to feed each other."

Jacob is sitting dumbfounded. There is nothing in his life that can compare to this. On the other hand, Sam is gathering more and more resolve as he continues. He is reliving a mysterious rescue from what can only be described as something very dark.

"When I was allowed to leave that room full of death and drawn to that room surrounded in love and wholeness, I was only allowed to look, but not participate. It was then that I was invited to follow. I knew immediately this person is Jesus. As He showed me His cross, He looked me straight in the eyes. His were full of a love I never knew existed. All he said was, 'I sought you, don't walk away'. Then He did something I didn't see coming at all. He pointed to His cross and said, 'I did this for you'. It was then that He told me that He has given me the key that will open the gate that allowed me to leave."

The two of them remain silent. Neither can make words that are relevant. This revelation is too profound being completely out of the dimensions of any ordinary experience.

Jacob wants to say something and realizing much of what Sam claimed to have experienced is at variance with his Mormon beliefs, he nonetheless still wants to validate his son's obvious profound, heartfelt experience, he can only say, "Boy that was some dream."

Sam can hear a reluctance in his father's voice. The excitement of this journey and the novelty of it comes back to him in words that never crossed his mind. "Dad, I believe I had to undergo this for a reason. I think it's going to begin a new journey for me." There is a boldness in his voice that is different than his usual bluster. It's the voice of fear turned to courage.

"You are also right when you accused me of stealing. It's true. I was stealing for my own selfish reasons. I'm asking you to forgive me. But either way I'll replace all that I've stolen with interest."

Jacob is taken back by this sudden transparency. He doesn't doubt Sam's sincerity, but it's so far out of character for Sam that he hopes he won't be disappointed. Nonetheless this is the answer to a prayer, although he just wasn't prepared to have it answered this way.

"Sam you know I can forgive you. I certainly believe we can work through this together."

When Sam steps out of the hospital the following day he's convinced he's a changed man. Although he's not prepared to reconcile the disappearance of his brother with his father just yet, he wants to begin to deal with it.

# 19 — COMING HOME

The morning is giving way and early afternoon is making its unheralded entrance. Mr. Amzlov's, Clark Shanhizer is giving Tiny his itinerary. They have left the jail and are sitting in Shanhizer's Lincoln Town Car. It has the distinct smell of cigar smoke.

Shanhizer prefers to keep a comfortable distance between himself and clients. Being confined with Tiny in this small place takes him out of his comfort zone. Even though he's driving back to Fairbanks and could easily transport Tiny, he has made arrangements for Tiny to take the train.

Still maintaining his professional demeanor, Shanhizer hands him one envelope with a ticket and another envelope with cash. "Here's your ticket for the 2:30 pm passenger train to Fairbanks and $500 for expenses when you get to town."

Tiny's face is distorted in a twisted facade of intentness.

"Thank you sir," says an appreciative Tiny.

Shanhizer isn't finished, handing Tiny one more paper to sign. "This states that you received the tickets and the cash."

Without reading it, Tiny signs it and hands it back.

"When you arrive in Fairbanks go immediately to the hotel, a room will be waiting for you. If you have any questions, call me," says Shanhizer handing him a card.

Without offering Tiny a ride to the train station, he dismisses him, driving off leaving him barely an hour to make his connection. Professionally, Shanhizer's credentials are impeccable, on a social level, he is left wanting.

Tiny hardly sees this as a slight. He has known Shanhizer for years. Spending three hours in the same car with this cigar smoking, socially-handicapped attorney is not in his opinion three hours well spent. Besides it was Shanhizer who signed the warrant to have him arrested.

Calling a cab to get him to the station is the first luxury he's enjoyed in months. On reaching the station, he finds himself filled with angst. Ever since he began to ride the rails, he's had to keep an eye out for the railroad detectives or "dicks" as they're commonly known. This is the first time he's going to ride as a ticket holder and he's not sure how he'll be perceived.

Without warning a voice he recognizes immediately comes from behind him. "Hey Tiny, how you doin' today?"

It brings to fruition this very concern. He reactively swings his huge body around to be met by the official presence of Detective Bernie Wenzel. He's a middle-aged man with years of weather having carved his features. His all business 5'8" frame has the uncanny ability to intimidate even this 6'6" giant at will.

"Hello sir. I'm doing fine," says Tiny forcing a smile.

"I'm gonna cut right to the chase son, either you got a ticket or you breedin a scab on the end of your nose. So which is it?"

His no nonsense mien has Tiny fumbling around for the correct envelope. Finally producing it, he triumphantly waves it as though it were a winning lottery ticket, "Right here, sir. I got it right here."

Bernie stares first at the ticket then at Tiny. "Well, I'll be damned—a miracle happens somewhere everyday." Handing it back minus any fanfare, he turns to continue his rounds.

Tiny lets out a sigh of relief. His shoulders are back along with his signature stride as he makes his way to the boarding platform. "This ol renegade is makin his way," he announces through his big, genuine gap-toothed grin.

The train ride is anticlimatic. He does as he always does whether in a club car or a box car — he sleeps.

Arriving in Fairbanks several hours later, he takes a cab to the hotel. The familiar face of Sylvia Bouman greets him at the desk. "Nice beard, Tiny." Despite the seeming approval, her tone of voice suggest the opposite.

With a big grin Tiny plays along. "I'm pretending I'm a serial killer and I'm lookin for a smart-ass victim. You wanna play?"

"Absolutely not," says Sylvia with a wry little smile, adding, "Welcome back. I heard they found you."

"I was in plain sight all along, just not in their sight," says Tiny. He takes pleasure in her flirtations. Smiling to himself he heads for his room. The familiar sounds of the hotel add to his sense of arriving home. He's more than ready to take on whatever task his job puts on him. As the days turn into weeks, his short connection with Joey begins to fade. Soon he never comes to mind.

# 20 — BEWARE OF THE DEVIL'S LIE

Unable to bail himself out and the legal system's problem with his lack of identification, Joey continues to languish in jail. His strong sense of being led by some Providential force convinces him that at some point things will become clearer. This impression is much more than a feeling — it's an awareness buried deep in his being.

With nothing much to do, Joey spends much of his time focused on himself, trying to make sense of the bits and pieces of disconnected information floating around, bouncing off the walls of his mind. Growing weary of this exercise, he really hopes the gaps will begin to fill in. Other times are spent looking at the countless messages left on the walls by some hopeless soul wanting to leave a trace of his miserable existence.

A welcome interruption sounds out, "Hey Joey, you wanna get out of here for a while?" It's the unmistakable voice of K.C..

Joey is on his feet. "Heck yeah. That would be great! What you got in mind?"

"The kitchen needs some help. You interested?" says K.C. already unlocking his cell.

"Just call me Chef Boyardee," says Joey. He can't hide his excitement. His eyes move from side to side as if to clear any obstacles that may prevent his escape.

K.C.'s clean, crisp khaki uniform contrasts against the dullness of Joey's faded orange jail jump suit. Joey can't help but be impressed with K.C.'s organizational skills. Somehow there's a familiarity he shares, but has no idea how.

"Whadda yah got for me K.C.?" says Dakota. She's the wife of sheriff Ben Watson, also the jail's matron and the head of the kitchen. Dakota is a striking, athletically-built woman with well-formed angular features, some where in her mid-thirties.

Standing in the door of the kitchen, Joey finds himself overwhelmed with emotion. The brightness and cleanliness of this facility contrasted all the more the gray, dullness of his cell.

"I got a new recruit for ya," says K.C.

Dakota stops what she's doing, wipes her hands on a towel and for a moment gives Joey a once over.

"Can you cook?" she asks with a direct attitude.

Joey is still gazing about at the size of this room. The sensation of not being confined causes him to hesitate.

Catching himself, he stammers, "I don't know until I try."

Maybe charmed by something in the way he answered, Dakota can't quite put her finger on a strange attraction she finds for this young man. Maybe it's his strange quiet assurance that's not readily seen in the average inmate.

"Good, because we've a lot of work to finish. You can begin by emptying this dishwasher. Just look around and you'll figure out where everything belongs," says Dakota with her arms folded under what can only described as ample breasts. Her stance is awkward off to one side amplifying a narrow waist and a bubble butt. Her eyes have fixed on Joey as he begins his task.

The intensity of her stare is beyond one of concern over the correctness of his task. He's not particularly handsome. Nonetheless, it's as though she recognizes something in this young man that is not apparent in other inmates.

Joey is trying to hide his uneasiness as Dakota continues to scrutinize him.

"What's your name?" she asks as she continues to move closer.

"Joey," he replies still trying to keep his focus on the task given him.

"Joey what?" She continues to search.

"That seems to be the question that everyone would like to know, including myself, but unfortunately I've been diagnosed with retrograde amnesia and can't answer that question." A hint of embarrassment is in his answer.

"Okay then, Joey will do," says Dakota.

Uneasiness with the uncertainty that goes with this task is enough to deal with, but as the day wears on Joey has become aware of Dakota's presence in areas that don't require her assistance.

"How you coming, Joey?" she inquires back near the laundry. Her voice is taking on a much more mellifluous tone.

Not sure why he's getting all this attention, he tries to remain matter of fact. "Good. I think I'm catching on."

"In my opinion you've caught on faster than anyone else I've had doing this job," says Dakota adding an unneeded touch to his shoulder.

Realizing she is his superior, he wants to interpret this gesture simply as a reward for a job well done.

Joey has spent much of the day pushing carts with food trays to the inmates.

"You expect me to eat this shit? Dogs eat better than this! Take it back and bring me something fit for humans," or "Come on Dude, give it up, I can't live on this. You're starvin me." The former is often the new inmate decrying his new found lifestyle or the latter an old inmate trying to get more than his share. What Joey is discovering is how offensive many of his fellow humans can behave toward one another.

Late afternoon is soon followed by evening and Joey is back in his cell lying on his bunk reviewing his day. Some new thoughts are bombarding him. "I do find her attractive and she's obviously flirting with me. It's a fact she has a husband, but damn, I'm so lonely. No, no I can't keep thinking like this, I've been given a trusty job and I can't violate this trust. But who would know? Her husband is so busy he hasn't time for her. After all I could make her happy and if she's happy her husband will be happy.

"Joey, listen to yourself! You're just asking for trouble." His arguing with himself continues until he drifts into sleep.

The next morning arrives with the contentious din of hundreds of inmates. It seems everyone has the sense that someone else is violating their rights. This remains the same jail house theme from time immemorial.

Joey has already been summoned to the kitchen to begin preparing the first of three meals for the day. He spots Dakota immediately. She's at least thirteen years his senior, but when lust enters into the mix, hell's out for breakfast.

She is looking exceptionally good. Her shoulder length hair is pulled back in a ponytail, accentuating an already long linear neck. Her skin is an olive color contrasting a set of greenish blue eyes. Adding a pair of tight fitting jeans only serves to tantalize an already overactive fascination.

Considering the impact Dakota's flirtations made on him from the day before, Joey has vowed to stay his distance hoping not to have to deal with some maleficent thoughts for another night.

By taking his morning assignment from her in a group gives him the space he's hoping to maintain for the rest of the day, but her ardor continues to keep tensions high. She has deliberately assigned him to assist her.

"Do you have a wife or girlfriend waiting for you when you get out of here?" she asks. Even though the question seemingly is cosmic in nature it's making him very uncomfortable.

"No, I don't think so," answers Joey. The question catches him off guard as it occurs to him that he has never considered that possibility.

"I can't believe that." Her statement is posed in such a way that it becomes a question that requires an explanation.

Dakota sees the confusion she's able to create in Joey. She relishes this as much as any predator enjoys toying with their prey. Her cross hairs are on this trophy and to her that's paramount.

Not wanting to be drawn into this conversation any deeper, Joey doesn't answer letting the statement remain her thought.

Realizing their conversation has staled out, Dakota immediately takes command putting her official boss hat on once again. "Joey, I want you to take this grouping of food items and work it into a menu. Do you see it as something you can do?" Like many "cougars" she can as quickly become assertive as fawning.

Joey finds himself much more comfortable with this relationship and wishes it to remain that way.

"Let me look it over, but I'm sure I can take care of it," answers Joey in the most professional tone he can.

"Good. Take this folder and go back to my office and use my desk, I'll check with you later."

Dakota's demeanor has once again become staid, but not being one to be dismissed this easily she is already scheming her triumph. Women like Dakota are opportunistic. They aren't born that way, but because of the way she feels men have misused her in her younger more impressionable years, she has learned how to turn the tables. In these older years, she boldly takes what she wants and because of her uncompromising good looks, she usually succeeds.

She has been married to sheriff Ben Watson for five years. He is twenty years older than her and nearly at the end of his term. Having no plans to run again, he is ready to enjoy a lucrative pension.

Her plan is to outlive him and receive widow's benefits as well as her own indemnification.

Taking the folder, Joey makes his way back through a storage area to a corner door. The only outstanding feature this area offers is the high-gloss finish on the tan tiled floors. Canned and dry goods are neatly stacked on shelves against the walls creating an aisle through the center.

Once the door is opened it exposes a neat little office, decorated with a feminine touch of bric-a-brac and wall hangings. Everything is neat and in its place revealing its owner's penchant for organization.

Soon buried in his task, he hasn't noticed Dakota has slipped in and is sitting on the couch.

"Good grief you startled me," exclaims Joey.

"Don't let me bother you," says Dakota pulling off her apron. "I need to take a break."

"How you coming?" she asks getting up and placing herself behind Joey. While looking over his work, she places her hands on his shoulders. It sends an electric shock of adrenalin surging through his body. It carries with it an unrelenting wave of desire. His pen drops involuntarily from his hand as she begins to massage his tense shoulders.

"Oh you're so tight," she exclaims while reaching around unzipping his coveralls. As she folds the top down around his waist exposing his physique, her hands continue to massage his bare flesh. For a moment, he actually finds himself placing his hands over hers as she continues to move down the loosened uniform toward his crotch. Her hands continue to lightly squeeze and massage. It's driving him crazy as Dakota lets out a soft little moan and sigh.

Suddenly an authoritative voice echoes from some unidentifiable recess of his mind and rages through his head, "Thou shalt not commit adultery!" This dispatch dulls the moment long enough for him to force his way out of the chair and to his feet. He's holding up his oversized coveralls with one hand and holding the other in a defensive position in front of himself.

"I can't do this Dakota." He pauses, hoping she gets the message. "It's not because I don't find you beautiful. You're the most beautiful women I can remember seeing. It has to do with me. Your husband has allowed me this trust. You're his wife and I can't violate that trust."

Standing in front of him staring wide-eyed and speechless, she suddenly screams savage epithets. "You bastard! You son-of-a-bitch! Do you actually think you can reject me that easily?" Lunging at him, her fingers forming claws, she lashes at him she with the energy of a cat. "YOU RAT BASTARD!!!"

Desperately attempting to protect his face, Joey throws both hands out in front of him, resulting in his coveralls falling down around his ankles. Her rampage is relentless. She continues to claw and curse him until he completely stumbles out of his outer garment, left standing with nothing more on than a pair of jail issue boxer shorts.

"Nobody does this to me! You're going to pay for this big boy. You're going to pay big time!" With that she rips her blouse open with buttons flying in every direction. She then tears open the door, recoiling out of the room as though she's been launched, she runs out screaming, "Help! Help! Somebody please help me. He's trying to rape me!"

To her first responder, she screams, "Get K.C. in here now!" Feigning desperation she staggers down to one knee then appears to struggle back to her feet.

Dakota's office quickly fills with kitchen help including K.C. Joey is confused and left standing stunned, nearly naked in the middle of this fiasco. Before he can respond, he's thrown to the floor and cuffed. Next he finds himself being dragged to another office plopped into a chair and left to wait.

News of this kind of mayhem travels fast in a prison community. The buzz is everywhere.

Meanwhile Dakota has hidden herself in her private bathroom waiting for the most propitious time to emerge. Her husband, being the sheriff, is brought in immediately away from an appointment in the courtroom. He's a large man, more in girth than in height. He bursts through the door in a flurry, and in spite of the weather being cool, he has large beads of sweat forming on his forehead.

Told that his wife has hidden herself away in the bathroom, he calls through the closed door, "Are you all right, Babe?"

Reacting as an actor would, having fabricated her mascara to imitate tears streaking down her face, she thrusts the door open throwing herself into the waiting arms of her doting husband.

With heaving sobs, she wails, "Dan, that bastard tried to rape me after all I tried to do for him. Take him out and shoot him!"

"Don't worry about it Babe, he'll rue the day he was born." At this point his desire to seek retribution against this interloper overrides any deep concern to comfort his wife. There's fire in his eyes as he turns on his heels and heads for the door.

Risking impertinence, K.C. is right behind him making a plea, "Sheriff maybe I should handle this until you cool down. If you rough him up, all it will do is piss the Judge off and give some attorney a lawsuit."

Still charging forward Sheriff Watson speaks in no uncertain terms, "You may damn well be right, but I want this peckerwood to get one hard look at me and know his ass belongs to me."

The accumulated confusion over the past twenty minutes has overwhelmed Joey. Looking up from where he's seated, he's confronted with the unmistakable demeanor of his pitiless jailer staring back at him through a glassed partition. The very sight of this dead-eyed husband glaring at him motionless is enough to give him a horrendous discomfort.

The potency of what has come to pass in the past few minutes is making its full impact on him known. His state of undress only lends itself to exaggerating his emotional nakedness.

"I thought I was doing the right thing," Joey thinks to himself. Catching this thought, he reconsiders it in the next second. "God help me, I know I did the right thing." Courage is slowly making its way back into his life in direct proportion to how he deals with his fears. After all, courage is nothing more than fear that's said its prayers.

K.C., having successfully distanced the angry sheriff from Joey, returns. Placing himself behind a desk, he fusses with some papers, finally tossing them aside, reeling back in his chair, placing a inquisitive finger on his lower lip, he stares at Joey. It's clear he's struggling with this situation.

"Just what in the hell were you thinking?" demands K.C. Not waiting for an answer, he ushers Joey back to his cell.

Once again finding himself alone, the battle begins anew. It's like he's fighting the devil himself. "You're a dumbass Joey. All you had to do was go along with her program and everything would have been fine. You'd be happy, she'd be happy—but no, you had to get all sanctimonious. This bullshit of pleasing God first, everyone else second and yourself last doesn't work in the real world.

"If you were smart you'd have taken her up on her offer. Rotting for years in some jail cell for some damnable ideal only brings grief.

"Look at yourself! You have no family, and no idea where you came from. You don't even know your name. How far do you think your high-hatted ideals are going to carry you in this world? You don't even have to answer yourself because you're right where you belong. Dumbass! Reality can be hell even if a person is only visiting."

Self-deprivation, clearly the devil's lie, is forcing its way into his thoughts. Frustration and self-disgust end in Joey throwing a cup of coffee across his cell splattering against the cement wall. It's as though this act is his resolve to extinguish the lurid, dark, looming shadows obscuring his thoughts.

"Go back to hell where you belong," he shouts out loud hoping to regain some peace. Despite his harrowing circumstances, he soon falls into a deep, restful sleep.

The following morning breakfast has been served when K.C. arrives. "Joey, you got a date with the Judge this morning."

Joey remains motionless. His heart, soul, and mind have melded. It's as though by having named his enemy and dismissing him all his emotions have remained in check.

He's obsequious in presenting himself to be manacled. K.C.'s resentment toward Joey is apparent as he silently arranges his shackles. After all, isn't he the person who recommended Joey to Dakota's tutelage? Now he feels his reputation is in jeopardy. A bad call like this, especially involving the sheriff's wife, is the kind of stigma he doesn't need besmirching his record.

As he's being led out of his cell, he happens to glance up near the ceiling. There some previous scribe has left a timeless vestige scratched into the wall, "Cease panic and start praying." A chronicled footprint left by some anonymous notary indicating the devil isn't always at home here.

The physical trip across the parking lot is a bit more challenging this morning as K.C. has purposely shortened his ankle shackles forcing him to make little hopping steps. It's leaving him with the overwhelming sense of falling making him wonder what he would look like with broken front teeth.

Soon after he is placed in the court room, he's called to the bench. The plaque on top states 'Judge Terry Brinknan'.

"Mr. Joey—is that your name sir?" asks the judge.

"I'm not sure what my name is Your Honor. I've been told I have amnesia."

Looking puzzled, he gazes out over the top of a pair of glasses perched on the end of his nose, he then poses another question, as much out of curiosity as a legal issue. "Who told you that?"

"A doctor at the free clinic here in Anchorage," states Joey, as a matter of fact.

"Okay Mr. Joey, we'll get on with this. I've got good news and bad news for you. Let's start with the bad news first. You're being charged with attempted rape. How do you plead?"

These words have a knee-weakening affect on Joey as he tries to form his words. Finally regaining enough composure to form the words, "Not guilty."

"Your plea is entered into the court record. You have the right to an attorney. If you don't have the financial ability to hire your own, the State will provide you with one. The State also regards you as a flight risk and is setting bail at $5,000.

"Now for the good news." He continues to peer over his glasses. "The previous charges brought against you have all been dropped. It appears your accusers have modified their accusations to the point that the court can no longer believes they're trustworthy."

"You mean I could have been out of here today?" says Joey with a slight hint of irony in his voice.

"Unfortunately that's not going to happen unless you meet the court's bond requirements," says the Judge not bothering to look up as he strikes his gavel.

"All rise!" says the bailiff.

Disappointment is quickly falling toward despondency. Still standing before an empty bench when K.C. comes to retrieve his prisoner, the words of the Judge stating that he could have been released today are re-emphasized over and over in his thoughts. A resentment is brewing. He's on the verge of a pity party. "God give me strength to bear this injustice" becomes his quiet reflection.

On his way back to the jail it would be hard not to notice how the weather has turned rainy and cold. Surprisingly, he finds himself actually looking forward to lunch and a warm cell.

# 21 — KEEP YOUR EYE ON THE HORIZON

It's a brilliant day sunny day a mere 100 miles from the Fairbanks City Jail. Sam is making his way to the smelting plant when a large elk vaults out of a swale bounding alongside his truck, then deviates into the protection of a wooded area. It reminds him that in spite of Alaska's frontier hardships this is why he lives here.

While watching this, something else catches Sam's attention. It's a flash of color in some rock formations. These formations often suggest that gold formations are in the neighborhood. He wonders why he has never noticed this before. Since his accident he has become more and more aware of things he has never taken note of.

Parking in his usual space, Sam is met by his father. Jacob is not exactly smiling from ear to ear, but appears to be more lighthearted than Sam recalls recently.

"What say Sam we get an early start? There's a new bunch of 'Johnny Newcomes' over by Clawson's Creek. They called this morning asking if we'd be interested in meeting with them," says Jacob as he climbs in the passenger seat.

His eyesight is getting progressively worse and he's beginning to drive less and less. Up close objects disappear until they get a ways out in front. Studying the dashboard as it warps into different shapes makes him hope he'll be a candidate for a new treatment that will slow its progression. It's disconcerting but he's learning to adjust.

A week has passed since Sam's 'Come to Jesus' meeting. His left arm is still in a sling forcing his right arm to meet all the driving maneuvers.

Jacob is paying close attention, remaining suspicious of Sam's new found scruples. He's well aware how oftentimes a person will have a life-changing experience and make reference to having been 'born again' in a religious sense only to discover that it may have been merely a 'conception' and simply put, they abort. Jacob is watching with a suspicious eye how Sam reacts when the realities of life come in on his blind side. Whether he is going to grow with the ebbs and flows of life or if he aborts.

Sam is fussing with something under his seat. "Before we get started, I'd like to get something cleaned up," he says tossing a zippered bank bag on the seat.

Jacob's face is taking on a foreboding look as his eyes glance unblinking at the bag. It's a look that suggests something significant is about to happen. Unzipping the bag, he can't help but be attentive to the heft of it. Again glancing at Sam before he peers inside, maybe watching for any unrevealed clues, Sam's face only reveals peace. Definitely not a look his father is accustomed to.

Peeking inside, Jacob catches a glimpse of a familiar looking cylinder. Along with the weight of the bag and years of handling metals, Jacob quickly discerns that this container is filled with gold. 331.1 grams is written on the container.

"What have we got here, Sam?" questions Jacob still not sure what this means. Although he's still clinging to the old-fashioned idea that fathers and sons are to be forthright.

"That's the gold I've been holding back," admits Sam. Pausing for the moment he then adds, "I should have put it in the inventory, but I didn't. Can you forgive me?"

Both sit looking at the other saying nothing. There is an unmistakable display of humility in his disclosure. On the other hand, as soon as Sam made his confession and restitution, a sensation of regret overcomes him. He realizes that without a doubt he has opened a Pandora's Box. He does not hold a regret for confessing, but regrets not having the courage to confess what he did to Joey. Unfortunately, the confession of one sin always leaves the question of how does one deal with those left unconfessed.

Jacob breaks the silence, "I can forgive you Sam. Now let me ask you— is there anything else you want to tell me?" He suspects there is much more, and is attempting to seize this moment of truthtelling to lead it in another direction. It's an encounter he's been praying for.

Sam feels a wave of fear overtake him. He shudders from the chill it leaves. He rightly suspects that his father is probably alluding to Joey's disappearance.

"No Dad, not at all," says Sam looking at his father with as much sincerity as he can muster. This lie has so convoluted his whole psyche that he feels he has no other choice than to continue to conceal his deception.

At least getting this milestone in their relationship to a head holds a large degree of satisfaction. It certainly has been an exhausting journey. Eventually it's settled enough that both conclude it's water under the bridge and time to get back to work.

It's not long before they drop in on their day's first 'Johnny Newcomer'.

"Mr. John Simpson?" says Jacob extending his hand.

"Yeah, I'm Simpson," he says grasping hold of this outstretched hand. A friendly hand shake culminates in a new business relationship.

"My name is Jacob Mueller. My son and I are gold buyers and we're here to see if you have any gold to sell."

"I wish to God I did. I've sold everything I owned to open this mine. So far it's been a bust." His frustration is unmistakable.

Jacob gives the operation a once over. Like so many people pouring into Alaska's mine fields, they usually have no clear idea on how to mine for gold, or for that matter even what capabilities their equipment can produce. After inspecting Simpson's wash plant, Jacob concludes the chances of them recovering gold is zero.

"I'd like nothing better for both our sakes' than you brighten your season with some good color, but let me tell you, the way you have your shaker set up, you're throwing your gold back into the creek," explains Jacob.

Sam has also taken this opportunity to walk across the claim. He's come back with a proposal. "Mr. Simpson, I'd like to hang out here for a while this morning. I believe I can help you get on track — that is if you'll let me."

Simpson's immediate reaction is a mixture of suspicion and relief. He's boondoggled so much of his time already that he's tenderized enough to set aside his suspicions in hopes he can save his claim.

Without much hesitation, Simpson quickly agrees. There is such a sincerity in this offer that to misapprehend it would be difficult.

Turning to his father for approval, he adds, "What do you think, Dad?"

Jacob is at a loss for words. This concern Sam is demonstrating for a stranger is unprecedented. "Yeah, Sam we can manage this. I can see all right on these back roads to drive. I'll pick you up this afternoon on my way back through."

On his way back to his truck, Jacob swallows hard shaking his head in disbelief. This is a face of Sam he has never seen. "Thank you Lord. I hope it continues."

Jacob is happy to have a day by himself. Despite the risk he's taking in driving, his stronger compulsion is to attempt to repair the damage Sam has created with long-time trusted clients in the region.

As the day wears on, Jacob is experiencing the full extent of Sam's riding roughshod over every inexperienced miner in the region. "Yes, I know we could have been fairer at times, but things are changing for the better." "In order to get back on track with you, I'm willing to round up to the next whole gram on gold we buy from you if you'll continue doing business with me." These are just a few of the concessions Jacob is making in order to cover over Sam's shenanigans.

There has never been any doubt that Sam is bright and capable of performing many tasks well, but now Jacob is again and again in camp after camp forced to listen to how Sam took advantage of their lack of expertise.

Trying as best he can to remember Sam's heartfelt confession, by the end of the day, he has an overwhelming desire to kick Sam's ass up around his neck and then kick his head off.

Arriving late in the afternoon at the Simpson claim, it doesn't take Jacob long to spot Sam. They have just finished cleaning out the sluice box. It yielded a little over two ounces.

Simpson couldn't be more elated. His small operation can make money on two ounces a day.

Sam can't help but notice his father's downcast demeanor. He knows without asking what his father has dealt with all day on his account. Hoping to make up for the disappointment he's certain he's caused, he chances to interrupt his father's dolefulness. "We got over two ounces today." Letting this good news sink into Jacob's mind for a moment, he adds, "And he said we can have his account."

Jacob is silent for the moment, seemingly nursing a small scab on the back of his hand. A slight smile is creeping into the corners of his mouth. He's shaking his head in disbelief. It's the kind people do when something going bad suddenly turns good. "Good work, Sam. I gotta say you done good on this one."

On the way home, the beautiful snow-capped mountains loom like perpetual custodians. For most people, it's a tireless sight. Adversely, Jacob is in no mood for sightseeing. In spite of the day ending on a positive note, his irritation over spending his entire day dealing with Sam's shady business dealings needs to be aired. His struggle now is how to make this a positive experience and not merely a blame fest.

"Sam, I gotta tell you, it was probably for the best you didn't go with me today. We would have been thrown off most claims."

Sam listens quietly. It's an emotional moment. After all, he's the one caught with his hand in the cookie jar. His resolve remains ready to work diligently to change things. He's trying to conceive a meaningful response. Even though sensing the urgency and his father's seeming patience, it's coming slow. Nonetheless, he's resolved to work through it.

Looking straight ahead, taking a deep breath, letting it go in a sigh, he acknowledges, "I'm certainly guilty as charged." Taking a moment to gather his thoughts, a flash back of his near death escape comes to mind.

The terror it brings with it fosters an even stronger resolve to work diligently toward righting his wrongs. Continuing, he fastens an even more steadfast commitment to his response, "I'm going to give you my solemn word that I will do all I can to make my wrongs right." There is no doubting the sincerity in his voice.

"I sure hope so Sam." The frustration is heard in Jacob's voice as his hand unconsciously runs through his hair.

Retirement is not in Jacob's field of view. After spending most of his life making his family and business blend together, it has become unthinkable to try and separate any of it. He's grown accustomed to the everyday hustle and bustle. Still keeping his eye on the horizon, his priorities remain toward growing the business. Not that wealth is the end in itself, rather each dollar is a vote of certainty for a job well done.

The sun is as low as it gets this time of year. It has a golden glow to it, turning the work truck into a golden chariot for just a moment before it hides behind a misty cloud. The air is heavy with the smell of a blossoming tundra. With Sam driving again, Jacob tilts his head back and drips his eye drops into his eyes. He's only doing what has to be done. To be a true Alaskan one adapts and overcomes. Jacob has met this criteria his entire life.

# 22 — GORE AMZLOV

Gore Amzlov is a sixty-year-old Russian immigrant as well as a self-made billionaire. He made a harrowing escape from the old Soviet Union across the Iberian sea. He qualified for political asylum and soon began his career as laborer building track beds for railroads.

He has always been enamored with any company that has the name "American" in it. As a young man steeped in the American dream, he would invest his money in companies with names like American Motors or American Telephone and Telegraph, among many others. This strategy proved to make him a very wealthy man over the years.

In the Soviet Union, he had learned the machinist trade, but because of language difficulties he never pursued it in the United States. That held true until the Banko machine shop in Fairbanks became available. Old Lester Banko had died and his widow wanted out from under the struggle of running the shop without Lester. Amzlov made an offer and the widow accepted. He soon landed a contract with the U.S. Army making firing pins for army rifles. Not satisfied with this alone, he began to add machinery to build commercial machines for large gold mining companies. His penchant for a high-quality product soon made him a trusted name within the industry. Now he has expanded his financial empire to include hotels and short line railroads, as well as diamond mines up north.

Amzlov married a young Alaskan woman. Her mother is a member of the Athabaskan tribe, and her father is an Italian immigrant. Her maiden name had been Maria Melba Scaleone. Melba, as she prefers to be known, is an old-fashioned girl with an old-fashioned name. She was first drawn to him by his accent and handsome features and then by the depth of his dreams for their lives together.

They have a twenty-six-year-old son named Andrew, who has settled on being referred to as "Drew". He graduated from the University of Alaska as a certified public accountant or more commonly referred to as a CPA.

They also have a twenty-two-year-old daughter named Carrie who is currently enrolled in a nursing program at a nearby college.

Drew is chomping at the bit to get out into the work-a-day world, separate from his father.

"Drew, you come vwork vwiz me. I vwant make you prezident zomeday," says Amzlov. He says this with a pitiful expression, hoping he can make his son feel guilty.

Drew continues to hold out. "Dad, I need to get out on my own for awhile. It's not that I don't want to join you. I know I will sooner or later, but I have some things I need to prove to myself."

Knowing that his father has done well in the business world and that he is not very receptive to business changes, Drew knows that working with his father would be more challenging than he wants to deal with for the present time.

Not one to be dissuaded easily, Amzlov continues his pleadings. "I got pretty goot ztuff teach you zon. You go long vays in company."

Drew chooses his words carefully. "I'm sure there're many things to learn. My hope is that when the time comes, I'll have something of value to share with you."

"Vell at least you be honest viz me," concedes his father.

Drew has seen many young college friends immediately enter into the family business. The results are usually disastrous. The father expects to remain in control and the son to remain subservient and for daughters it's even worse. Generally speaking if there is a confrontation the son or daughter is reminded as to who signs their paycheck. Those that fall into this trap usually remain an employee as long as their father lives.

For the next few weeks he spends his time sending resumes all over the region. Drew has found that opening his eyes to the world outside the hallowed walls of the university is the strangest and most difficult thing he's had to do. Nonetheless he is prepared to meet the challenge.

Confiding in his sister he laments, "I know Dad will try and pull some strings if he knows where I'm interviewing."

"I know exactly what you're saying and I won't say a word," promises Carrie. She is four years younger than Drew and has spent her life living in his shadow. It's a shadow she has never minded, as she idolizes her older brother.

Melba spends much of her time doing volunteer work at St. Catherine Catholic Church. The empty-nest syndrome has begun to sneak up on her. She has never doubted her role as the guardian of Christian values in the home, and accepts her responsibility to insure that her family remains firmly consecrated in the Catholic faith.

"It like I be married to nun," says a half-laughing husband. In the old Soviet Union the Amzlov family had remained Orthodox as much as the State would permit resulting in Gore having little or no contact with the church.

Amzlov's penchant for good Russian vodka and a bias for black market suppliers is never far from his mind's eye. An evening with him is an adventure in itself. Sharing the fruits of his labors has never been an issue, and in so many ways he can be as generous as he is demanding. It's never unusual for him after work to invite all the help in the house to get drunk with him.

Well endowed with the mind set of so many immigrants, he believes this to be the country for achievers. He has never believed that he couldn't accomplish all his dreams.

"Vwhen zingz goez vwrong, I getz buzy—getz it done. Melba zhe vwaitz for Jezuz do it. Zhe still vwait." He howls with the laughter that comes to those possessed with a self-assurance. After all didn't he cross the frozen Iberian Sea in the middle of a blizzard on a dog sled with only a compass?

It's always easy to tell when he's getting excited because he uses his thumb to roll a gold ring studded with bright white diamonds around and around his right ring finger. He shamelessly adorns himself with gold bracelets and neck chains as well as a 24-ct. gold crucifix centered in the open neck of a shiny, black silk shirt. When things do go wrong, Amzlov is fully capable of unleashing a barrage of Russian curse words that if it were not for his accompanying scowl could be mistaken for poetry. Nor is it totally out of the question to have him try and barter under the table using gold and diamonds to buy some goods and services not readily available. It's a habit he brought with him from the old country. It's one he finds useful and difficult to break.

"Everybody Russia vwant come Amereeca. Get beautiful womenz, vwork hard make big money. In old country black market only vway make money. Government full stupid politicians who vwant be big shots. Zay never figure business, only vwant power. Russian black market have both," says Amzlov with a knowing grin.

Often times he finds himself laying in bed thinking of times past, of life in the old USSR. Not a particularly religious man in any church way, he nevertheless always finds time to tell anyone who is willing to listen, "Tank Gott for Amereeca."

# 23 — GET DREAM GUY

Several times a month it's Amzlov's habit to personally make an un-announced visit to one of his dozens of enterprises. On this particular morning he's chosen his flagship hotel, the North American.

When Amzlov bought this hotel, the previous owners had been forced into bankruptcy and the bank was happy to get twenty cents on the dollar. Having fallen into ruin, it had lost much of its original charm. Now with a face lift and Amzlov's management design, it is back on the road to its original splendor.

The hotel's decor is accented with the rich colors of red, white, and blue along with the muted hues of these same colors in various tones of mauve contrasted against lighter or darker shades of blue giving a taste-fully elegant appearance.

These colors add to his sense of pleasure and comfort as well as to his gratitude for having been allowed to participate in this great democratic experience, always remembering the repressive political system he fled.

"You vwant know vwhat freedom eez? You go Russia you zee quick vwhat freedom ain't." He always gives a knowing little chuckle with a nod of his head when this subject comes up. Still chuckling he likes to add the American maxim, "Been zer, done zat."

He slips in unrecognized and secures a room. This now puts him in a position to observe his enterprise undetected. For this particular occasion Amzlov has become concerned with how he can keep a superior edge on a new competitor who is beginning to worm into a domain he is building for himself.

Taking a seat in the lobby during a busy period allows him to take note of how the hotel staff is dealing with the public. For the most part, he's dressed and acts in such a way that the employees find it easy to marginalize him.

He has sent his secretary, Doris Lang, under the guise of arranging a sales meeting for a fictitious company. It's his way to bring his own team in to overview the hotel's day-to-day operation.

"Hello," says an unsmiling Doris. She's giving every indication that she is just another exhausted traveler.

"Hello, how may I help you?" inquires a male clerk barely looking up from his computer and remains expressionless as he continues to be absorbed with his keyboard.

"I'm here to make arrangements for the Lang sales group," continues Doris with the same look of fatigue.

Playing off her fatigue, the clerk gives every indication that he too is tired.

Meanwhile, Amzlov remains in the background paying attention to how the baggage staff treats Doris's luggage. She's left with no assistance to load a luggage cart. Making her own way alone through the long corridor to her room, she is met by another cart being maneuvered by hotel staff taking up much of the aisle. The belligerent employee barges his way through first, forcing Doris to stop and allow him to pass. The man is consumed with his conversation with another staff member. Both ignore Doris's struggle.

Amzlov also steps aside mumbling under his breath, "You Vwant whole Damn Road?" Without a split second wait a booming voice seems to fill his head, "Yes Gore I want the whole road!" Amzlov stands alone in the aisle stunned and shaken. It's obvious the two men didn't hear the voice as they continue their conversation down the corridor.

Amzlov on the other hand tries to recount the circumstances surrounding this odd phenomena. Not having much luck, he dismisses it as nothing more than a curious aberration. Without an encore it quickly fades into a non-event.

It doesn't take him long to refocus on these two obvious miscarriages of duties in less than fifteen minutes declaring, "Zis place go to hell in handbasket."

As soon as all room arrangements are in order, Amzlov regroups with his committee. His face is set in stone, laying out his instructions to his would-be reconnoiters, "You all be vwatch dog. Keep eye open, zee how everybody pay attention to job."

There is no question that he is in charge and expects nothing less than an acme of first-rate from housekeeping to top management. There is also no question as to his generosity with those who put a finishing touch on a job already well done. On the other hand, he can just as easily be a thorn in the side of those who fall short in both.

"You alvways gutz zink bout vwhat you do. Very zimple. Treat people vway you vwant be treated, only do first and better. Vwhen you understand zis, you getz gut job vwis me, but you not understand zis, I geeve you vone more chance, zhan you gone," he says with a quick reflexive hand gesture.

With this finished, the day begins to unfold like a well-scripted play. Still undetected, Amzlov's crew begins their sleuthing. Each person has their assignment, including Amzlov. He particularly loves this part, having set aside his signature dark suits with the red accessories in favor of shlumping around in an out-dated warmup suit, a nondescript fishing hat, a pair of aviator sunglasses, and some off-brand bargain-Benny athletic shoes.

Amzlov has insured that he has transformed himself into the type of person who can easily be seen and just as easily be dismissed. His advantage is that he can now avail himself of access to such places as the housekeeping section or the grounds maintenance garage and merely appear as a straggling old man seemingly lost. This allows him to take note of all aspects of every job, as he has done each of these at one time or another himself.

Behind the hotel, Amzlov finds himself engaging a middle-aged man stumbling along with a full garbage can. It's obvious from his struggle that the man is either physically handicapped or under the influence of drugs or alcohol.

Weaving and stumbling the man attempts to pour the smaller can into the larger with much of it missing the mark and landing in a heap in the front of the dumpster.

"How you do?" asks a smiling Amzlov touching his hat.

The man looks somewhat puzzled not expecting to be noticed. His blank-looking, bloodshot eyes glisten against the morning sun striking the moisture besetting each of them.

"I've done better," says the man unveiling a slur. This slight interruption results in his loosening his grip on the small can. Unable to retrieve it, it crashes to the ground with a loud bang spilling the remainder of its

contents. Stooping down, he cups the loose garbage in his hands attempting to place it into the dumpster. Instead he falls squarely on his buttocks.

Amzlov's quick reaction finds him catching the man under his armpit
avoiding any further injury. While getting the man to his feet, he can't
miss the undeniable smell of alcohol coming from his breath.

Without a word, the man grabs his now empty trash can and stumbles
his way back into the hotel. Amzlov's eyes follow him. For a moment,
it takes him back to his native Russia, remembering similar incidences.
Working while drunk is the norm in much of that culture. A quiet gratitude overtakes his thoughts. "Had I not come Amereeka, zat man be me."

With the day drawing to an end, each member of the team readies
themselves to give a full report. Still clad in his old sweat suit, Amzlov gives
a hint of a former, less-formal life. Nevertheless, even in this humble ap-
parel, the strength of his personality has no problem dominating the room.
His energy level remains high, waiting to process each of their findings.

Soon this leg of his multi-pronged salvo is complete and he's making
arrangements to meet the following morning with the hotel's managers.
He's asking his team to continue to fraternize with the hotel's personnel
through the evening, but not to disclose their primary purpose for being here.

It's getting late and Amzlov is ready to bring the evening to a close.
The many infractions his hotel staff are assiduously addicted to will be
dealt with in the morning.

The thoughts running around in his mind are preventing him from
readily falling asleep. He has a hard time understanding why natural-born
Americans have a problem understanding integrity. "Vwhy I gutz keep eye
on all zeez guyz all day? Zay should come up, do gut job. I vwant only do
best. Zat vwhat get me out bet in morning."

When he finds it difficult to fall asleep, he relies on the sure Russian
sleeping aid, vodka. Pouring himself a half glass, he climbs into bed to

wait for the inevitable drowsiness to occur. Soon the vodka has its way and he drifts off into a slumber.

No sooner entering into what is described as REM sleep, he becomes aware of strange, and at the same time a very real phenomena. It's the same clear voice he had earlier in the corridor. This time it's way too clear to be dismissed as easily as the last time.

"Gore Amzlov, I want you to come with me. I have something very useful and important for you to do."

In an unexplained reaction, Amzlov without question is somehow intuitively aware that this foreshadowing is safe.

"Gut. Vwat you show me?"

Willingly and even enthusiastically, he agrees to accompany this voice. They are soon effortlessly flying over mountains and valleys until they reach the ocean. It all seems very natural. Ironically, Amzlov recognizes the spot immediately. It's the very spot his dog team carried him to land many years before after crossing the ice-covered sea. It is bringing back a torrent of memories. How safe he felt not having to contend with jagged ice formations along with huge cracks in the ice. How joyous he was at the prospects of a new life. Even the cold breeze blowing off the sea is the same. It's the kind of dream that he doesn't mind visiting. As a child Amzlov didn't like his dreams. They were more of the nightmare type. He was always trying to avoid punishment for crimes he didn't know he was committing.

Abruptly his dream takes a different turn, not frightening, just odd. Unexpectedly the ocean begins to shudder. Seven heads begin to break the surface. At first he can't distinguish what kind of creature these heads belong to. As they come into view and as their bodies begin emerge, he's surprised to discover that they belong to cows. Gradually these seven beautiful, healthy cows come ashore. They are the embodiment of strength and vigor.

A sense of contentment comes over him in watching this fine example of living vibrancy as they begin to feed off the lush pasture at the water's edge. It's one, he feels he could never tire of.

Something with the ocean shuddering once again catches his attention. Seven cow heads appear the same as before, but as these cows make their way to shore, he notices they are not robust like the first seven. These are skinny and sickly looking. Instead of feeding on the lush grasses, they begin to viciously attack the seven healthy cows until they consume them hoof to horn.

Whatever sense of contentment Amzlov may have enjoyed earlier in the dream is changing to fear. Shocked now to the point of terror, Amzlov awakens soaked with sweat and gasping for air. Sitting straight up in bed shaking and confused all he can think of to say is, "Vwat da hell is goin on here?"

Unable to cast this supernatural vision aside, he pours himself another slug of vodka, sitting up in bed until some forty minutes later he grows weary once again and falls into another trance-like sleep.

As if on cue the same intense, demonstrative voice seeks his attention yet again. Once more Amzlov finds himself enjoying the same exhilaration as he effortlessly glides over tree tops looking down on the roof tops. Every color is more brilliant. The reds are redder, the blues are bluer. Again his sense of well being is freshened as he finds a sense of oneness and a longing to stay here.

Unanticipated the landscape abruptly changes to an endless sea of golden ripened wheat. The voice beckons him to take special notice of the bounty. Amzlov can't fathom the greatness and beauty of this sight. While they continue to glide over this opulent harvest it is further imposed on him to pay special attention to the fourteen stalks isolated in a group in the center of the field. In this grouping are seven full ears and seven gaunt ears.

As before the events begin to take a turn. The peace and serenity imposed by this vision rashly turns to violence as the seven gaunt ears violently attack and eat the seven full ears.

Shaken once again at the unsettling nature of these dreams, he awakens.

"Vwat za hell goin on here viz all zeez crazy dreamz. I moost be luzink my mind."

Not wanting to risk going back to sleep again, he stays awake for the rest of the night. Not disconcerted often, the reality of these visions are way beyond anything Amzlov has ever encountered. He would prefer to dismiss the whole occurrence as some kind of surreal nonsense, instead the reality of these visions leaves him with a nagging feeling of helpless.

It's 7 am and time to think about how to confront the managers. Shanhizer has driven in for the occasion in the event his legal advice is required.

Hoping to put the night behind him, he carefully puts his mind to choosing his wardrobe. It's time to get down to business. A blue pinstriped suit catches his eye along with a solid-colored, dark maroon silk tie over a French-cuffed white dress shirt. A maroon breast pocket-kerchief and a pair of black Bostonian shoes sets his tone for the day.

The morning is progressing on schedule. Each department head is given a list of grievances and ordered to fix the problems. The discourteous clerks behind the front desk are discussed as well as housekeeping and groundskeeping problems. Tiny is the bar and restaurant manager and is the last to be brought in.

"I want to thank you from the bottom of my heart for getting me out of jail a few months ago and putting me back to work."

"Ya vwe vfind out zat vweazel of a chef eez da tief. Vwe gut heez ass in whoosh-cow now. I only vwant be fair, put you back vwork. Hell Tiny you damn gut manager," says Amzlov. His laugh is infectious when he's done a good deed.

Shanhizer is his usual all business, expressionless self.

"I also have some good news for you Tiny," says Shanhizer shuffling a few papers around.

Tiny cocks his head to one side posing a quizzical look, "What's that Mr. Shanhizer?"

"All charges against you regarding that assault have been dropped," adds Shanhizer peering over the top of his glasses.

What Shanhizer doesn't make known is that he has had this information for months but has opted to keep it from Tiny. His thinking is it would insure a stronger allegiance to the company as long as Tiny was under the impression that the company was keeping him out of jail.

"Well halleluiah, praise the Lord," says a visually grateful Tiny continuing, "I knew all this was going to happen, it was all in my dream." By this time he's become even more jubilant.

Amzlov's interest is suddenly piqued. "Vwat dream you have?"

"I had a dream while I was in jail. I didn't understand any of it because it was so weird. My cellmate was the guy that was with me on those trumped-up assault charges, he knew spot on what my dream meant."

"Three days later you showed up just the way he said it was gonna happen," continues Tiny, nodding toward Shanhizer.

"Zeez guy tell you vwat dream mean?" quizzes an even more interested Amzlov.

"Yes Mr. Amzlov he did. He told me I'd be freed, and hired back to work. What's more he told me who the person was who stole your money."

Amzlov is mentally jousting with every word that is being said. His eyes dart in rhythm with these words bouncing off the walls of his mind.

"Vwhere in hell vwe vfind zeez guy?" interrogates a demonstratively excited Amzlov. The tenor of his question suggests that he is doing more than gathering interesting information.

It's quickly becoming apparent that his boss wants something more than a passing conversation, his interest is something other than a mere curiosity. Continuing, Tiny weighs his words very carefully. A well-fabricated flow of words begins to flow from Tiny as Amzlov hangs on his every word.

In a very thoughtful question Amzlov asks, "How long go zeez happen?"

This slight pause shifts the conversation into a new emphasis. Amzlov's impetuousness is beginning to center on Tiny's ability to recall what he considers mundane details. On the other hand, Amzlov's intensity about these details indicates they are anything but mundane.

Without any further explanation, Tiny is doing all he can to recall details he has had no reason to remember.

"It was the day before I got out of jail," answers Tiny. The perpetuity of this line of questioning is making Tiny's mind grow weary.

"How longk go you geets out jail?" fires Amzlov.

"I can't remember exactly," says an overwrought Tiny searching his frenzied thoughts.

Shanhizer is sitting by waiting for an opportunity where he can interject. "It was two months ago Mr Amzlov," says Shanhizer with precision.

"You zinks ziz guy still jail," asks Amzlov turning away from Tiny in favor of the more precise information.

"A phone call will tell us," says Shanhizer in his usual determined tone and already scrolling his phone.

Tiny quickly tries to tell the story of Joey's amnesia telling Shanhizer, "Just ask for a guy named 'Joey'."

Tiny is more than curious by this time over Amzlov's interest in Joey and is hoping he's not being squeezed out of the loop of this growing enigma.

While Shanhizer is making his call, Amzlov turns back to Tiny. "Vwat hell zeez guy do go za jail?"

With questions coming at a staccato pace, Tiny tries not to stammer. "He was charged with brandishing a deadly weapon."

This pronouncement leaves Amzlov more than a little unsettled. "Vwat kind maniac zeez guy?" His indignation is as thick as his accent.

Before Tiny can be speak, Shanhizer's is speaking with someone. He is definitely employing his lawyer voice. Concluding his conversation, he turns back to Amzlov. "They are still holding him in jail. The what-the-hell-are-they-trying-to-pull now charge has been dropped and they are now holding him on an attempted rape charge."

Tiny's eyes pinch in a curious fashion. "What the hell are they trying to pull now?" is his immediate thought.

This incessant attention Amzlov is giving this jailed itinerant has raised the eyebrows of Shanhizer, but he is also well aware that with patience his boss will sooner or later reveal the reason behind all this interest.

Tiny, on the other hand is not nearly as patient. Risking an impertinent question he nonetheless proceeds, "Mr. Amzlov, how can this guy possibly be of any service to you?"

Wide-eyed and fearlessly forthright, Amzlov shoots back his answer, "You say zeez guy know bout dreamz. I need dream guy."

In a quick move, he turns toward Shanhizer, slapping the table with both hands and at the same time giving him an imperative, "Get zeez dream guy!" With that he turns and leaves.

In this rare instance Tiny and Shanhizer are on the same page. They share the moment staring in wonderment at one another. Tiny finalizes his perplexity with a shrug leaving to go back to work and left Shanhizer with the unconditional ordinance to "Get zeez dream guy!"

# 24 — EXODUS 23:3

Waiting for his trial in his accuser's jail has been far from a cake walk for Joey. Not waiting for the court to pass sentence and already confining Joey to his cell, Sheriff Watson has another opinion, "That son-of-a-bitch is going to start his sentence right here and now."

Remarkably, Joey has adapted to his imposed confinement, even with a degree of solace. He's been severely isolated thus limiting his contacts to his food server and K.C. In spite of this, he has remained friendly and engaging when he can. To his advantage K.C. has continued to treat him humanely.

Clad only in his jail jumpsuit, he is met with a request. It's K.C. standing in front of his cell. "Hey Joey, there's an attorney out front by the name of Shanhizer. You wanna see him?"

Joey's mind races for an explanation. "An attorney? I didn't ask for an attorney."

Staring directly at Joey, K.C. rather candidly replies, "I don't know anything about him or who sent him. I'm only the messenger boy, wanna see him or not?"

Recognizing K.C.'s less than patronizing disposition, he quickly assesses that at the least it will get him out of his cell for awhile. He's soon led down a corridor to a small room with a steel table, the same room Tiny had been led to a few months before.

Gazing over the top of his glasses with sheets of paper before him sits Shanhizer. First, he looks at Joey then at a transcript in his pile. He's attempting to make sense out of a piece of identification available for this new client is simply the name "Joey".

Shanhizer, not satisfied that someone hasn't missed something, begins to question Joey a bit further.

"It says here your name is 'Joey', is that all? Just the single name?"

"Yes, Sir," answers Joey. Because of the frequency of this question, it brings no more than a bland matter of fact answer.

"Well Mr. Joey, I guess we'll just have to deal with what we have available, won't we? Do you have any idea who Mr. Gore Amzlov is?" asks Shanhizer still peering over his glasses.

Pursing his lips while speculating on the question, he surmises, "Is he the man that got my friend Tiny out of here?"

"You're close. I'm the man that got your friend Tiny out of here. Mr. Amzlov hired me to do that. He has also hired me to do the same for you."

Joey hesitates for a moment. He has been cut off from the simple joys of life for such an extended length of time that he is not sure how to handle the thrill overtaking him, he breaks into a quivering grin. "You mean you've come to get me out of here?"

Not looking up from his work, Shanhizer opts not to acknowledge Joey's elation, instead he continues to flip one document after another adding, "All of us do only what the law says we can do. For the present I can get you out on bail."

"I want you to know that I didn't do what I've been accused of doing," says Joey with a sigh, as he forces the words through a dry throat.

Joey's words fall on indifferent ears as Shanhizer continues to shuffle his papers around.

"Mr. Joey we're taking this one step at a time. For now I can get you out on bail, but that will be only under one condition. Mr. Amzlov has an issue he wishes to take up with you," replies Shanhizer.

With this final statement, Shanhizer puts down all his paper work, clasps his hands together and looks Joey straight in the eye. This stare is the kind that pauses long enough to solicit a response.

Without hesitation, Joey blurts out, "Yes, sir, I can do that. I'm very grateful." In his excitement, he is to his feet reiterating what he has just agreed to one more time, "Yes sir! That I can do. Just tell me what you want of me."

In his most bland lawyer voice Shanhizer pushes papers toward Joey, "We'll get to that soon enough. For now sign these papers and go back to your cell and wait until I can get things taken care of."

A mixture of hope and anxiety battle for dominance with Joey as he is met by K.C. to return him to his cell.

"Things looking good for you?" questions K.C. as he goes about his routine handcuffing.

"I think so," says Joey still wearing his nervous smile.

After gathering a small bag of his belongings, he hastily changes into his old Carhartts brought to his cell. K.C. escorts him toward the front door passing by the Sheriff's office. Watson is standing in his doorway, arms crossed begrudgingly, staring at Joey as he unashamedly marches to freedom.

"It's not over yet big boy." With that said, he turns back inside closing his door behind him.

With a mixture of anxiety and happiness, Joey tries to put Watson's words behind him. The front door opens and he breathes deep the cool refreshing, uncloistered air for the first time in eight long weeks. Something familiar catches his eye. It's the unmistakable swagger of a huge black man sporting an even larger gap-toothed grin making his way through the parking lot. The sun is casting a shadow in such a way that it leaves the impression of a dancing marionette escorting this mountain of a man. It's by far the most welcoming sight Joey has had in two months.

Tiny's big hand stretches its way toward Joey. Grabbing his hand he pulls him into an embrace along with his irascible laughter. The big smile on Joey's face supplies an occasion for Tiny to relive his own first day out of jail all over again.

"Hey Bro you're bringin' back some good memories. I'll bet you thought we forgot all about you," says Tiny blissfully slapping Joey on the back.

"I thought everybody in the whole world forgot about me," says this grateful evacuee picking up his fallen little bag of belongings, readying himself for whatever Providence has in store for him.

Within moments of this reunion, Joey's past troubles are giving way to a new sense of joy. No amount of earthly treasure could supplant the simple pleasure of this experience. Even the sound of traffic is like soft music compared to the din of yelling voices twenty-four hours a day. Free of bondage, Joey struts along with Tiny across the parking lot to the waiting car.

Catching a glimpse of his skin color against Tiny, howling with laughter, he blurts out, "Look at me Tiny, I'm so white the crows would spit me out."

Joining along in the lighthearted moment Tiny comes back, "Yeah Bro you sure as hell got that jailhouse pallor—even I got light skinned in there." This brings on a good belly laugh with them both.

By this time the sound of a remote controller unlocking the doors of a very intimidating black Chrysler 300, tricked out in chrome trim around dark tinted windows becomes primafacie.

"Hop in and I'll take you for a ride," says Tiny with a bit of mock puff coloring his voice.

While adjusting his seat belt, Joey can't take his eyes off the interior of this luxury vehicle. It's a mixture again of frustration and pleasure. He expresses a familiarity with these encounters but has no recall of knowing how or why, "This kind of stuff sure looks familiar, I just can't put my finger on why or where."

Tiny is still. He's never tried to overthink his friend's condition. "Oh hell Joey, you'll get past this. If you live long enough you'll probably just outgrow it."

Tiny's laugh overpowers Joey's frame of mind once again as he loosens the ostensible garment his life is forcing on him. "Yeah, you're probably right," shrugs Joey, "let's get something to eat."

"Now you're talkin'. I know just the place," says Tiny. Soon they are riding along a familiar street. Tiny pulls up and stops at an even more familiar looking place. DOWN TOWN SOUP KITCHEN are the bold letters greeting them.

"Oh my gosh Tiny, I can't believe you picked this!" says Joey. His enthusiasm can not be sold short. "Do you think they'll remember us?" he continues. The expression on his face translates his feelings far more than his words.

"Yeah, Gertie's always had a good memory. She remembers every lie I've ever told her." Tiny's face says he's confident.

Joey revels in anything of a past he can recollect. He's clearly happy to see something familiar.

"Hey Gertie, you good lookin' hoe, how Yah doin'?" says Tiny barely through the door.

Swinging around from some chore, she fixes her eyes on Tiny's face. It's obvious she's suspicious of what she's looking at. Continuing to check him out from head to toe, with her hands on her hips and wagging her head from side to side she finally lets out a shriek, "Good God Almighty is that you Tiny?"

"You know it's me," laughs Tiny.

Gertie has a quick engaging smile that gives a lonely man pleasure. "What happened to that wild lookin' man I know? You all shaved and prettied up like you some kind of executive."

In this neighborhood a person is measured by how they treat others since clothing is usually nondescript. Tiny's expression is, as always, one of self-contentment, certainly not smug. "You're getting pretty damn close girl, but sure as hell not executive enough to keep from stopping by to see my favorite girl friend."

Shaking her head at his persistent flirtations while unconsciously adjusting her hair, she says, "You're full of it right up to your eyebrows Tiny, you know that?"

Changing the subject, Gertie spots Joey. She's giving him the ole once over, "I see you still got your partner in crime with yah. Good Lord boy, you jus get out of jail? You got the color of hawk bait."

Joey manages a grin, happy for any female attention. "You're right Gertie. You gave me my last meal as a free man and I want you to give me my first one as a free man," says Joey pulling up a chair.

"Well then I hope you boys like goulash cause that's what you're gettin'."

"Perfect!" says Tiny, "Gertie you make the best damn goulash in town."

She's always had Tiny in her cross-hairs and makes no bones about it. "Tiny you're such a BSer. You'd tell the truth even if you had to lie to do it, but you know I love every minute of it." Gertie's heart is as big as her ample hips. If anyone can make matronly alluring, Gertie's able. Her frame is well dispersed across the room as she makes her way, still giggling, back to her kitchen.

The afternoon wanes on. They have finished their meal, still nursing a cup of coffee, Tiny at last points to the door and his watch. "We gotta get on the road, we got another four hours of drivin' to do." He then reaches in his pocket, pulling out a couple hundred dollar bills and presses them into Gertie's hand. "You always got somthin' needs doin' around here."

Gertie gives each a big hug, holding on to Tiny a bit longer. "Thanks Tiny, you a damn good man."

Soon they're on the road. Joey is uncommonly quiet as a dose of reality is making its way into his thoughts.

Tiny has taken notice. He's taken up smoking cheroots. The smoke is filling the car in spite of a window cracked open.

"Smoke bothering you, Joey?" asks Tiny as he pulls the cigar from pursed lips. The acrimonious vapors stream out like steam from a locomotive.

"Not nearly as much as what your Mr. Amzlov could possibly want with me."

"I'm not real sure myself, but I suspect it could have something to do with dreams," says Tiny tossing the last of his cheroot out the window.

Now that the wheels are in action, Joey's mind changes course. "What exactly did he say about his dream?" The expression on Joey's face tells that he isn't asking for a sketchy answer.

Tiny turns directly toward Joey, pausing for a moment to reassess Joey's changed sentiment. "He didn't say much. I could tell from the conversation that whatever dreams he had were bugging him no end. I told him about my dream and how you were dead on in unraveling it. He got all excited and ordered Shanhizer to do whatever it took to spring you."

Joey doesn't turn toward Tiny, rather he continues to stare directly ahead. He is nervously digging the cuticles surrounding his thumb nails. His lightheartedness and spirited wit have turned to a tense introspection.

"Here is the problem with that Tiny, I can't turn this on and off like I'm some kind of conjurer. When I explained your dream, I knew that knowledge was coming from some outside and unexplained source."

"That's kind of spooky don't you think?" Not waiting for an answer Tiny poses another thought, "Do you think this may have somthin' to do with your amnesia?"

"I really don't know, but I do know that when I explained your dream, I knew without a doubt that it was true. I had no hesitation or doubts of any sort. I've never experienced that kind of assurance in getting my pants on right.

Armed with a better understanding of Joey's concerns, Tiny opts to measure his views more carefully. "You think it's God doin' all this?" further questions Tiny. He tone has taken on a somberness.

Joey is quiet again. His thoughts seem to have entered his soul. "Yah, I do Tiny. I'm sure it's not of me and I'm sure it's not something evil." Weighing his thoughts for a moment, he continues, "Yah, I do believe it's through God in some way."

This is a reaffirmation of Joey's strong sense of being led toward something of which he has no understanding nor its purpose. He also recognizes that in some unexplained way, this unearthly power has allowed him to overcome daily obstacles that seemingly baffle others.

In turn, Joey poses a question of his own. "Who exactly is your Mr. Amzlov, anyway?"

Tiny's thoughts meander around endeavoring to measure the scope of Joey's question. "He gave me a job when I was just a kid. This was at a time when big black kids like me were either in prison or getting ready to go. He claims that he saw something different in me and was willing to take the gamble. I can truthfully say that once he sees a strength in a person, he'll find a place to make use of it."

Letting the moment slide by without further comment, Joey mulls over Tiny's assessment wondering how he's going to fit into the scheme of things.

The road is steep at times and winding, having been carved out of either thick foliage or walls of jutting rock. The beauty of a full moon presents itself as the undisputed sovereign of the night sky, shimmering its way through the trees. With only an hour left before they arrive at the hotel, Tiny navigates the road as skillfully as a Tennessee rum runner.

The closer to their destination, the higher Joey's anxiety level rises. Now with only a half hour left, Joey sorts through his sensibilities, "This is crazy. I feel like I'm climbing out of that mine shaft again." He says it loud enough to be heard, but more intended to shout down some gnawing apprehensions.

Everything about himself begins to bug him. "Look at me Tiny. I'm in no shape to be interviewed by anyone, I look like crap."

In a motion designed to emphasize this apprehension, he unzips his Carhartts. In doing so, he feels something strange in his pocket. It turns out to be a folded sheet of paper the doctor had given him listing his diagnosis.

"According to this paper, I'm some kind of loon stumbling his way through life without a clue as to who he is or where he came from. Where in God's creation does someone like this fit?" laments Joey oscillating between being led by a Higher Power and the languidness of his human poverty.

Upon entering the city, Tiny has taken to softly humming, wheeling his way through traffic as one does with the familiar. Joey on the other hand, sees only looming fortresses that are singularly designed to seal his doom.

Without warning Tiny whips a hard left, crossing a traffic lane and stops under a canopied parking area in front of a huge digital sign announcing THE GRAND AMERICAN HOTEL.

"Here we are Joey, home sweet home," says Tiny handing his keys to the parking attendant. It's near 10 pm. on Friday. The evening is young with flashing neon luring the young revelers and the young at heart to partake of its revelry. The hotel also attempts to bewitch those whose lives have become ordinary, presenting a seductive, captivating soft yellow glow to their lighting.

With the best minds that money can buy to produce these masterful diversions, Joey only becomes more bewildered. He's like a puppy in the center of traffic with its tail between its legs hoping something will save him.

"Tiny there is no way that I belong here. Everything here is totally foreign to me. At least in the woods I knew how to survive. Even in jail, I knew where I stood."

"Don't get your shorts in a bind Joey, you'll do just fine," assures a smiling Tiny.

"Yah easy for you to say. What happens if I can't provide enough to satisfy his whims? I'll probably go back to jail, right?

Joey is dreadfully agitated, more than at any time since he emerged from the mineshaft. He's struggling with what he believes to be the enormity of what he assumes is going to be required of him.

"Don't wet your pants till the water comes Bro, you're projecting an outcome to something you don't know the questions to." His voice echos an almost parental appeal — be patient but forthright.

Meanwhile, on the top floor of THE GRAND AMERICAN a party is on going. It's happening in the presidential suite. Amzlov has brought his wife and two children to the hotel along with senior management and their families. It's Carrie's 22nd birthday, and Amzlov is sparing no expense. Russian caviar, black market vodka and roasted lamb.

Amzlov delights in these kind of parties. He sits back in his chair watching all the people enjoying themselves. This gives him great satisfaction.

Melba is at least a dozen or so years younger than her husband. She has a ready smile and can be as gracious as circumstances require. Even though she is married to the single most wealthy and powerful man in Alaska, she possesses an independent spirit that remains undaunted despite her husband's position — as he will readily attest — "I first one findz zeez out."

Drew and Carrie have never experienced a lifestyle less than opulent. This, of course, has troubled both Amzlov and Melba as neither of them possessed much of earthly value when they were the age of their children.

They both have found this to be a bone of contention, an enigma for which neither have a workable answer. Short of abandoning them on the streets, they are left to deal with their own creations.

"Za tootpaste out za tube. How you ever getz back in tube?"

On the other hand both children have chosen working careers rather than live on their inheritance. This is much to the delight of their parents. Amzlov and Melba have always hoped that by their example their children would choose to become productive members of their communities.

Nonetheless, tonight is a celebration. Carrie and Drew have included a number of their respective friends to enjoy their father's cornucopia. By this time the party is in full swing with a karaoke machine inviting each guest to strut their stuff.

Unnoticed by all except Amzlov, Shanhizer has slipped in. Drawing Amzlov aside he confides, "Everything has been taken care of. I've been able to get him bonded out. I believe he and Tiny have just arrived. I instructed the desk to place him in a suite down the hall from you. It should be easy and private when you wish to see him."

It's a habit of Amzlov to purse his lips in and out like halibut when he's contemplating things. "Invite him breakfast tomorrow morning."

"That sounds good sir. Where would you prefer that to be and what time?" questions Shanhizer in his usual matter-of-fact legal voice.

"Vwe meet here in room 7 am," says Amzlov.

Down the hall Shanhizer is met by both Tiny and Joey preparing to settle Joey into his room.

"Mr. Joey, Mr. Amzlov requests that you have breakfast with him tomorrow morning at 7. I have also arranged for a change of clothing, a razor, and a set of clippers with several attachments for you to run across your hair."

Nodding appreciatively, Joey says, "I want to thank you for everything you've done Mr. Shanhizer. I was beginning to believe I was just another forgotten man, lost in the legal system."

Shanhizer says nothing, but manages a slight knowing smile. His ego definitely reacts to a stroke now and then. With that, he turns, leaving Joey to manage alone.

The reality of this situation continues to weigh heavy on Joey. "Tiny, this is like a bad dream that I can't wake up from."

"Hell, Joey, you didn't have a heads-up for my dreams, you just shot from the hip," says Tiny trying his best to be reassuring.

"I guess you're right. So far things have worked out despite my fretting," says Joey. Something is once again fighting back against the demons of doubt. It's coming on amazingly strong. Joey is always dumbfounded how gentle, but powerful this awareness becomes.

Without a Providential symposium, Joey has calmed down enough to peacefully shower, shave, eat a light supper that's been sent to his room and soon falls asleep.

Time quickly eats the night away. As peaceful as it was for Joey, Amzlov, on the other hand spends a restless sleep. If these dreams hadn't been so graphic, they would have been long forgotten, blamed for the moment on vodka or indigestion. But because of the clarity of these dreams, he finds it impossible to dismiss them. Like all things in his life, he dislikes leaving things undone.

Amzlov has not built his life around running from the unknown. To him it's logical to confront, and unmask the illogical so it can be reasonably analyzed. There remains the hope that this strange young man with an unknown past will bring light to this haunting chapter and bring it to a close.

Amzlov's habit is to rise early and take control of his day before it gets away from him. This morning is no exception. He's awake by 6 am, having showered and shaved. It's now time to check the overnight markets and make notes on what he would like his financial people to do.

A similar scenario is developing down the hall. Joey is also up. Looking at himself in the mirror after attempting to replace a professional barber the night before, he is pleasantly surprised. Not willing to kiss the devil good morning, the strong assurance that everything is going to be okay remains in place. It occurs to him that his faith must be something that's been left over after he's forgotten where it originated.

Answering a soft knock on the door, Joey is met by a large black man in blue pants, a white shirt, blue tie, and a red blazer with the insignia GRAND AMERICAN HOTEL. "How ya doin' this morning Joey?" says Tiny. Not waiting for an answer, he continues, "Hey Bro, you look like the lead man in a B-film."

Joey is not smiling or frowning. The clothing that had been laid out the night before are now bedecking him, blue blazer, white shirt, red tie, white trouser, blue socks and white loafers. He has the look of a man who is at one with his mission. "Yah Tiny, I think everything going to be fine. I feel as though I could bring the world to its knees."

"Good. Let's get started," says Tiny, short of grabbing Joey by the hand, heading down the long hall.

Tiny's soft knock quickly produces a man of short-to-medium height, sixty-ish looking with an equal portion of black and white hair pushed back in a deliberate tasseled style. He definitely has the appearance of a man who listens to his own drummer.

"Come een. Come een," is the smiling invitation.

Tiny takes the lead in making the introductions, "Mr. Amzlov, I'd like you to meet my friend, Joey. Joey I'd like you to meet my long-time employer, Mr. Amzlov."

The two shake hands exchanging the traditional, "Nice to meet you."

Hardly finished with the exchanged courtesies, Amzlov is already moving into the next facet of this orchestrated get together.

"Tiny, you ztay breakfast?" says Amzlov. This is said with the unmistakable intonation of an imperative.

Tiny has worked long enough for this man to realize this request is not something that's up for debate.

"Yes sir, I can do that," says Tiny without the slightest hesitation. He has arranged for the kitchen to set up a small breakfast buffet in Amzlov's suite.

Small talk ensues through the scrambled eggs, bacon, sausage, toast and coffee. But soon Amzlov gets to the core of this meeting.

"Tiny tell me you pretty darn good trippiting dreams, Zat zo?" questions Amzlov.

Finishing his breakfast, using his napkin to wipe the corners of his mouth, Joey calculates the question carefully.

"I don't believe that I do the interpreting. I think it has something to do with God, but I can't prove that either. It remains as much a mystery to me as to you."

Having scrutinized Joey through breakfast, this answer is good enough for Amzlov to begin. "I have dream — I make correction — I have two dream. I call lady who say she medium, zshe don't know zsheet bout dreams. Maybe you tell me vwat dreamz mean, eh Joey?" says Amzlov, arms crossed, cocking his head to one side while doubtfully giving Joey the evil eye.

"I'm sure Providence will have it's own reason for withholding their meaning, but right now I don't sense that's going to be the case."

With enough conversation behind them, Amzlov begins telling his dreams. "I vwas standingk on zea zshore venn suddenly seven big fat healthy lookingk cows come up out za zee. Zey begin eatingk za grassez. Zenn seven more cows comez up out za vwater. Ziz bunch eez skinny, zay vwas ugly cows. Zenn zeez skinny ugly cows zstart eatingk za good cows.

Eet don't help zem a bit, zay zstay skinny and ugly. Here vwen I vwake up. I go get glass vwarm milk and go back sleep."

From the look on Amzlov's face it's apparent that he's reliving the dream. His eyes are wide open, his arms are waving around, his voice is more animated than Tiny has ever seen it.

Now Amzlov begins the saga of his second dream. "Zeez time I fly-ingk around in za air like zsome kind zsuperman. Now I lookingk at big vwheat vield. I zinkingk eet een Russia zome vwhere. Zeez time I zee zseven head gut grainz on vone zstalk. Now crazy zingk ztart happeningk. On zame zstalk come zseven shitty lookingk head. Zen zay do zsame damn crazy zing skinny cows do, zay zstart eatingk up za gut vwheatz. Vwat za heck goingk on?" It's the same question he had days ago when these dreams first occurred.

Joey is attentive to every word. He seems impervious to Amzlov's heavy Russian accent. Without any forethought or evasion of mind Joey begins with a very emphatic explanation.

"Both dreams mean the same thing. Both the seven good cows and good heads of grain mean the same thing. They are seven good, produc-tive years. But here is where they differ. The seven lean cows and the seven empty heads scorched by the sun are seven years of bad times."

Amzlov sits quietly contemplating every word Joey is saying. "Vwat all zeez zstuff bout cows—I got no cows."

Joey continues, "The next seven years are going to very prosperous years. You will become even more wealthy than you are now. But seven years from now there will be seven years of economic decline and many people's wealth will be wiped out. There will be tremendous unemploy-ment and bankruptcy as people lose their homes and businesses through bank foreclosure. Things will get so bad that no one will remember the good times.

"Now I want to add to this that because you had a similar dream both times that this experience is beyond some earthly coincidence. I believe this to be something sent by Divine Providence.

"You can expect these events to begin immediately. My suggestion is that you find the wisest people in your organization and place them in charge of moving your wealth into positions of strength. This will insure that when the seven years of depression come, you'll have wealth to spare."

Amzlov sits with one elbow resting on an arm crossing his chest, stroking his chin contemplating these strange premonitions, this unexpected prediction.

Melba has not been in the room, but it's not her nature to be left out of the loop of any affair taking place within her family's lives. She has surreptitiously placed herself where she can hear, but not be seen. Not able to contain her silence, she surrenders her furtive cover. As graciously as she can, she approaches Amzlov.

"Gore dear, I couldn't help but overhear. Would you introduce me to your friend."

Amzlov has learned over the years that his wife of more than a quarter century will enter into his life when she senses a need to. Amzlov quickly complies. It doesn't take her long to zero in on what she heard, especially about his talk implicating a "Divine Providence." Directing her concerns to Joey, she asks in a rather patronizing voice, "Are you in the church?"

Joey is taken by surprise at her question. To him it's a strange question since his amnesia has cut him off from any recollection of worship forms or for that matter anything called "church."

In an attempt to run interference for Joey, Tiny speaks up in his defense, "He has amnesia Mrs. Amzlov. He doesn't remember anything."

Soon enough Joey recovers from his momentary disconnect with Melba's question and addresses her concern.

"I'm not sure I know what you mean by church, I have no specific memories of it."

Melba remains equally disconcerted as Joey, only because she has no reference for "Divine Revelations" coming to anyone outside the church. It's as though she's expected to believe that sacred truths float through the air by caprice, ignoring the church and choosing this near pagan to reveal essential information impacting their lives.

Not knowing what a proper reaction should be, Joey remains quiet leaving a moment of uncomfortable silence.

This time it's Amzlov who comes to Joey's defense. "Well we know he not from devil, Melba."

"Just what makes you so sure?" shoots back Melba.

"Cause he look out for me. Devil never look out for nobody." Amzlov is predictably steady in purpose as he makes his counterpoint a point of finality.

Amzlov has always known how important church is to his wife. Even though at times it provides her with a gentleness, at other times it provides an occasion to appear smug. (One can only wonder how many people are kept out of the church by those professing to be in it.) Amzlov is trying to head her off from this annoyance.

It's Melba's intention to remain a faithful Catholic as well as a faithful wife. She has given ascent to both believing that one won't contradict the other.

"I believes Got tell him vwat He vwant me know," says Amzlov. Melba knows her husband well enough to know that she won't be able to win if he believes he's right. For the time being she is willing to give him a pass.

Turning to Joey, Amzlov continues, "You knowz, zat makez you real smart guy. I makez you in charge everyzing. You gonna be manager guy now. Only one bigger zen you eez me."

Joey is motionless. This is all coming at him faster than he can process it. He's experiencing all kinds of nameless emotions. Mostly he feels like he's been dropped to hang in mid-air with his feet on nothing. Finally after a series of confused blinks, he manages to spit out a few words.

"Mr. Amzlov, I don't want to sound disrespectful, but you have the wrong man. Having a revelation concerning dreams is a lot different than what you're asking me to do. I'm not prepared in any way to take on that kind of responsibility."

Amzlov is standing beside Joey shaking his hand and with the other wrapped around and resting on Joey's opposite shoulder. He's smiling from ear to ear, like he always does when he's completed a successful project. "Nah, I zink you vwrong. You gotz zome goot brains. Nobody vwork here vizout goot brains. You say you getz brains from Got—goot zat kind brains vwe needz vwork here."

Tiny is looking on along with Melba, both are as surprised at this shift in events as Joey. Tiny manages to catch Joey's attention long enough to give him a nod of confidence.

Over the past few months Joey has managed to develop an elaborate defense mechanism that blocks out much of the frustration over his memory loss. Nevertheless there is also the re-emerging realization that a lot is missing.

In one form or another, his life has been one of struggling for survival. Now he's being challenged to exchange his hand to mouth existence for the permanence of hearth and home. Over the months he's found a strange kind of comfort in the miserableness, maybe because of its predictability. This offer by Amzlov is not predictable in any way.

Tiny is about to explode. He fears Joey has been down so long that he'll prefer to stay there. Interrupting this moment of silence, Tiny blurts out, "Mr. Amzlov, let me have a minute with him."

"Yah zure take all za time you needz," says Amzlov.

Motioning to Joey, they step out into the corridor. "Joey he throwin' you a life line bro, don't screw it up."

"Yah I know, Tiny, but I'm scared," says Joey. His face says he's telling the truth.

"You been showin' us you got somethin' goin' on with these dreams, why ain't you showin' us you still got it?" It's clear that Tiny is beyond frustration with Joey.

"I don't know, I think this is different," says Joey turning away.

"That's what you doin' man, you turnin' on God like you turnin' on Mr. Amzlov. Why don't you do this like you been doin' it? That time you told me you was bein' led, I could see you was really believin' it even if everyone else thought you was crazy. God ain't leavin' you in this deal Bro, you leavin' God."

Tiny's words are hitting Joey hard. Words are powerful and these are coming like a right hook squarely on Joey's heart.

"If you need a human hand to hold for a while, you can hold mine," adds Tiny.

"Okay Tiny, let me think about this for a minute. Right now it's overwhelming me," says Joey. His shoulders are slumped as he follows Tiny back into the presence of this generous benefactor. At the moment, he has a conflicting desire either to escape back to the woods where he imagines things to be easier or to fight back his cowardly desires.

Still standing behind Tiny, Joey becomes aware of his servile posture. Straightening his shoulders, he attempts to confront his ever growing dread.

Amzlov is not waiting for Joey to speak. "Look here Joey, I vwant people vwork me have goot time, zo vwe takez zings zslow. You zsmart guy, you catch up fast."

Something in Amzlov's smile takes the edge off Joey's anxiety. Slowly his anxiety is being disarmed and replaced by an overwhelming assurance that he is ultimately being led toward a great good—how, when, or where remain cloaked in mystery. For the moment it's enough to give him pause. Without a full awareness of all that is happening to him the essence of his character is changing. Taking a deep breath he lets it out slowly, "Okay Mr. Amzlov, I'll give it a try."

In his excitement Amzlov impulsively reverts back to his old country ways, grabbing Joey and kissing him on both cheeks. "You make damn gut decision Joey. You vwait, you see."

Surrendering his misgivings is enough to leave Joey empty. He can only hope, as a riderless horse that courage jumps on his back and digs its heels in.

Highly suspicious of this innovative prophet, Melba retreats to the side lines until such time she can find a point of re-entry. She is already plotting the missionary work that needs to be started on this ostensible interloper.

"What fun we are all going to have, I can't wait," says Melba. Her voice is carefully crafted to sound submissive to this latest pronouncement made by her husband. All the while her mind is calculating how this heathen can become a Catholic.

Where Tiny had been earlier hanging on to his hat and fastening his seat belt preparing himself for a bumpy ride with Joey has smoothed out for the present.

With this occurrence behind him, Amzlov is turning his attention back to confronting his department managers concerning the neglect some of the hotel's personnel have fallen into.

In particular he is concerned with the over-all condition of the fellow emptying the trash can. He has learned from the grounds manager that the man is dealing with an increasing struggle with alcohol addiction.

"I vwant you deal vis zeez guy. Vwe gotz goot insurance. Zend him dry out. He refuze go — fire him."

Amzlov does not expect long discussions with any of his managers. He lays out a strategy and expects it to be carried out. Those that don't comply, Amzlov dismisses them with the indictment, "Zey lookingk for horzes teethz in vwrong endz."

At last Amzlov has finished his directives with the hotel staff and is returning to his room. As he passes through the lobby, he is confronted by a familiar figure. It's the same stumbling drunk employee he had helped to his feet the day before. He's caught off guard by the man. Evidently he turned down the offer for rehab and chose to lose his job.

"You big shots are all alike. You don't give a damn about us poor bastards. You think since you got all the money you can shit on the rest of us cause we're poor. Well I hope you and all your money rot in hell." The man is still shouting curses as security carries him off the premises.

The man's words bring back old feelings. Amzlov knows what it's like to be poor. He remembers very well the feeling of being powerless and disenfranchised in a world controlled by others. He can't get the man's words out of his mind, especially the part of being rich and not caring about the poor.

Still stinging from the man's exploding epithets, he carries this thought back to his room. Pouring himself a small glass of vodka, he sits down in his chair. Suddenly he feels a drowsiness, and falls into a slumber. The guilt feelings the drunk man aroused in him follow into his sleep. Unexpectedly a loud, clear male voice breaks into his catnap, "EXODUS 23:3." Not to be ignored it recites itself once again, "EXODUS 23:3." It startles him, but only in his dream. Soon awakening from his nap, he notices that only a few minutes have passed. Pouring himself a cup of coffee, the memory of those resounding words EXODUS 23:3 boom once more across his mind.

Amzlov is soon interrupted by the door flying open. It's Melba and Carrie returning from a shopping trip. It's a welcome intrusion. Their girl chatter has always enlivened him as he tries to engage them.

"Here my two best lookingk vwimins."

"Oh Daddy that's just your vodka talking," says Carrie kissing him on the cheek.

"We don't pay any attention to you, you say that to all the girls," further teases Melba.

"Zat zo zsweet you zay zat, zsweet like you Momma's keezzez." (This is Amzlov's rendition of the sarcastic remark that something distasteful can be about as sweet as a mother-in-laws kiss.) Looking at each other, Melba and Carrie both shake their heads in some strange appreciation for this ridiculous moment with this charming husband and father. Amzlov's attempt at American humor always leave his family amused. They find his blundering a punch line funnier than the joke he attempts to tell.

"We brought you a sandwich Daddy," announces Carrie. Fumbling with the deli wrapper she spreads it out on the folded paper.

Amzlov picks at it for a few minutes still befuddled over the strange voice. "Melba, vat you know about Exodus?" he asks chewing on a piece of the sandwich.

"Exodus what?" inquires his wife rather puzzled about such an odd question coming from her husband.

"You know — zat Bible Exodus?"

This is without a doubt the most surprising question her husband has ever asked her. Following through she asks, "What is it that you need to know about it?"

"Vat it zay at Exodus 23:3?"

Melba is examining her husband from head to toe. "Gore you have asked me a lot of odd questions in the past twenty-five years, but this one takes the cake. What in the world would ever possess you to ask such a question?" She asks this at the same time she fumbles getting her ever present St. Joseph edition of the Bible open. She has carried the same worn book since her grandmother gave it to her at her confirmation.

"It says that you shouldn't favor a person who has done wrong just because they're poor."

Amzlov sits stunned. He seems to be paralyzed.

"Gore, what in heaven's name is wrong with you?" shouts Melba as she watches the color drain from her husband's face.

"You ain't gonna beleef vat happen here again Melba," says Amzlov becoming more animated.

"Believe what, Gore?" she shoots back even more urgently begging for some explanation.

"Got's talkingk me again!"

Seeing no other way out, Amzlov quickly gives his now very agitated wife and daughter what had transpired with the inebriated man and the ensuing dream.

Not used to seeing him perplexed like this, Melba's only comment is that she is going to talk to her priest about all of this. Her first inclination is that her husband is undergoing some type of demonic attack. She's seen movies about this and knows the church has priests who can exorcise people, or as she has been heard describing them as "snake wigglin', foot washin', tongue talkin' Baptists".

"I know Father can get to the bottom of all this." The tone of her voice unmistakably declares that she, in no uncertain terms, is going to get the answers she wants to these enigmas.

Something has piqued the attention of another member of the family with all this talk back and forth about some guy named Joey.

"Who's this new guy I keep hearing you guys talking about?" questions Carrie. She is quite sure the demur little sophomoric smile she is evolving will not go unnoticed.

Her mother is the first to react, "It doesn't matter who he is, in fact no one knows who he is. He supposedly doesn't know who he is." The sarcasm is dripping from Melba's words.

"I zink he geeft from Got." Amzlov says these words with the same assured expression he would declare that the sun is shining.

Carrie is used to her mother's devotion to the church. What she finds strange and at the same time surprisingly attractive is her father's sudden embrace with those things usually only discussed by members of the clergy.

"Now you've really gotten my curiosity up. I want to meet this guy," says Carrie. Her enthusiasm is paralleled only by her broad smile displaying a row of perfectly straight, white teeth contrasted by her olive-colored skin.

Melba's eyes and mind compete with the other. This is truly a complication that is hitting her blind side. She searches for that elusive reason to dissuade her daughter from searching out any such liaison. She has prayed and lit candles for her family to be united under the Church and they seem to be doing all they can to have this remain in the prayer stage.

Amzlov on the other hand sees no threat in this young Sibyl. "I know zeez guy ain't buulsheeter. He tell truth. You vwait, you zee."

Melba's thinking is beginning to get murky. She always works best when "Father" gives her a good Catholic answer. "I wish he were here right now." Her second thought is, "I'm going to have to take care of this myself."

# 25 — HEALING THE WOUNDS

The mining season of Jacob Mueller and Sons is in full swing. The snow has all melted. The mud has dried making access to some of the more uncompromising areas easier to service.

It's Jacob's week with Rena. The wounds of Rena's indiscretion have barely begun to heal. There has not been an open confession on the part of

Rena nor Rup. But then Rena's apology and implied complicity is enough for him to begin to give thought to mending their relations. Jacob is not sure that hearing all the details is that important anyway. He's decided it would serve no good purpose, realistically he can live without it.

Rena is nervous, having a stricken look much of the time. Her whole life is upsidedown. She has lost her normal channels in which to trust her confidences, namely her sister and husband. Having no one to confide in, she is struggling to ease her way through this distress alone. "It's my punishment." She's sure of that. Jacob has chosen not to resume intimacy with her, isolating her even more.

Benji is always happy to see his father when he comes. It gives him an opportunity to have a one on one without his older brothers' interference. Like most teens when parents aren't getting along, he senses a rift between them, not exactly knowing the details. He stands by hoping the air will clear.

He and his father are outside repairing a window. Handing his father a tool, he reflects, "Everything has changed since Joey disappeared Dad. It had to of been the worst day of my life. I just can't imagine him dead. I sure hope he's alive somehow."

Benji finds times like this are therapeutic. He's talking as much to himself as he is to his father.

Jacob can feel a surge of compassion as Benji lays his heart out. "I realize your brother means a lot to you. I want you to know your mother and I love him dearly and miss him along with you." It's impossible for Jacob to disguise the tear following a crease in his cheek. He continues, "It's times like this that we are going to have to learn how to depend on one another to get beyond.

When Jacob's inabilities to take care of the concerns of his family surface, his frustration turns to anger. He tries to hide it, but after this many years of truthful transparency, it becomes nearly impossible to disguise his emotions.

Just in time for a change of thought, Rena brings out a tray of hot chocolate and fresh baked chocolate chip cookies.

"Mom, you're the best," blurts out an appreciative son.

Since her and Jacob's estrangement and her oldest son's disappearance, she has found herself focusing much of her motherly attention on her youngest son.

What she is particularly noticing is that her husband is smiling. Their eyes meet only fleetingly. His eyes have always given his feelings away. Rena can tell immediately that things between them are beginning to change for the better.

Stepping down off his ladder, Jacob bends down to receive her handheld cookie, placing his face directly in front of hers. His smile continues. "Thank you," is his simple reply.

Rena's eyes are now locked to Jacob's, taking a step back. "You're welcome," is her simple reply. It's like a bolt of electricity shot through the air to clear all the unwanted sulking and guilt, allowing a renewed relationship to emerge.

The last thing either of them wish for is that one of them appear pitifully wounded beyond healing, even though neither couldn't help but feel reproached in the presence of the other — Jacob for failing to meet the needs of his young wife; and Rena for entertaining pent up lust as a part of her life for so many years.

Like so many of the devil's ploys, it leaves them full of a hopelessness. The thought of their shortcomings makes them both realize the tremendous cost both have paid. So much of their joy has turned to disappointment through either a self-loathing or blaming the other.

Trying to move forward in a casual way, Rena carefully chooses her words. The next few moments could be the most she's exposed any affection toward her husband in weeks.

Jacob in turn, is ready to stop sulking and withholding forgiveness.

The beginnings of smiles on their faces have quickly nudged to life a youthful appearance both had lost. Their eyes begin to moisten slowly, both trying to constrain any unfettered display of emotion. The attempt fails as they fall into each other's arms. It's a timely relief for both.

"Okay you guys what's going on?" asks a bewildered Benji. One thing is for certain, he is not going to figure his parents out any time soon.

"I love you." Speaking quietly, she's not willing to have Jacob release her just yet.

"I love you, too," says Jacob through rheumy eyes, surveying her affectionately.

Benji can't imagine what might be going on with his parents. They aren't throwing even a few scraps of information he can put together. However he's relieved things aren't so tense and that his Dad is showing up.

Rena self-consciously smooths out imaginary wrinkles in her dress as she then gathers up the empty tray. Carrying it back to her kitchen she hopes her home is returning to normal.

There is a sliver of sunlight making it's way through a slit in her curtains. It's been there all along but unnoticed. She sees it as a small sign of brightness making it's way into her life.

Setting her tray on the counter, she sits down for a moment contemplating that ray of sunlight straining it's way through her kitchen window. The pent up emotions of the last few weeks begins to pour out of her in gasping breaths followed by a torrent of tears. Her hands reflexively grasp a dish towel hanging on a lone hook, forcing it against her mouth, she hopes to muffle her sobs. It's not a sad sob rather one of gratitude and hope.

After Rena has left, Jacob turns to Benji, "Son, I hope that when your day comes where you have to face the 'man role' in your own family that you will focus on those things that sustain a healthy family."

Benji isn't sure what has transpired between his parents, but he's certain that this event must have some strong significance to them both.

Jacob continues on with his project noticing a burst of energy he hasn't felt in a long time. What could have easily ended in disaster has ended in reconciliation. Even though each of them will have to deal with their own shortcomings they won't have to do it forsaken. They have left each other alone long enough.

# 26 — RUP'S GORDIAN KNOT

It's a late summer Sunday morning, and as is the habit of this fundamental Mormon family, Jacob leads the family worship. Both families gather at the home of the wife he's spent the week with. This has been his week with Rena.

His heart has not been in this activity since the disappearance of Joey, compounded by the problems arising between Rena and Rup and Sam's horrendous business practices. To say the least it's been an effort. Nonetheless, he knows he has to perform this duty despite his own feelings

Over the years Jacob has become a man who to a large degree has learned how to overcome adversities that would have left other men wanting. He has come to realize that focusing on his own problems, his own needs and wants cannot supersede his commitment to the needs of his families. The quality of his life, along with that of his family, has certainly benefited from such an uncommon dedication.

This particular Sunday finds him just short of an irrational exuberance. It's a nice warm day. The trees have leafed out allowing adequate shade for outdoor worship. Chairs are lined in rows under the huge maple tree adorning the front yard.

The focus of Jacob's message to his family today is an attempt to bring to mind the great blessings they share as a plural family. Not all his children share the same thoughts he and their mothers have about the benefits of such marital arrangements.

Rena's mind is especially light. The hurtfulness of the past few months has turned a corner allowing her a lightheartedness. Watching her husband as he stands before his family giving a well-defined, veritable message on family and family values, she finds her thoughts wandering back to the night a little over a month ago when she and Jacob re-consummated their marriage bed.

She remembers how she waited for him to come into the bedroom as she fussed with her hair and how anxious she became when she heard his steps. When he began to kiss her shoulders and neck how within seconds she could not imagine life without him. How lost she had become in that moment. She could feel him deep inside her. It was as though that moment had no beginning nor end, that it would last forever. How she lay in that darkened room feeling the strength of his body on hers. How even their breathing was in concert. How truly free she felt succumbing to the stipulations outlined in the pledge they made to one another on their wedding day.

As Jacob concludes his message, his eyes meet Rena's for just a moment. It's that moment two people share without words.

The human mind is capable of all sorts of wonderful hi-jinks. Things it finds too difficult to deal with can be shoved into the cricks and crannies of the mind until they become almost dead from lack of use.

Rena is purposefully burying her and Rup's behavior into those dark folds of her own mind. It's too dark to share with anyone. She doesn't know anyone she believes is strong enough without being hurt to hear her confession. It's left between her and God.

Without conversation, Rup and Rena have prudently set boundaries for any further interaction. Rup has had to seriously re-evaluate his boyhood history with Rena. It's true they had been adolescent admiration for one another other, but that all changed when his father took her as his second wife. In this culture whatever hopes he had had with her should have come to an end, but as with all humans, ideals often remain just ideal.

Rup remains unenthusiastic about following rules set down by his sect's leaders, but as is his nature, he remains secluded most of the time thus avoiding a closer scrutiny. He certainly does not share the freeing feelings Rena has come to appreciate inside these parameters.

He is also truly reproached by his father's seeming goodness. In contrast to this strength, it is difficult for him to see anything but weakness in his own character. It depresses him, resulting in yet more resentments. Sometimes he finds, he lacks even enough character to lose his character.

After the worship service the women are busying themselves with a Sunday dinner. Meanwhile, Rup has separated himself by going out alone for a stroll. Jacob, seeing him leave, takes advantage of the privacy he wishes between himself and Rup.

"Hold on a minute, Rup. I'll walk with you," calls out Jacob.

The sound of his father's voice directed at him finds him ill-prepared. Since his affair with Rena and his part in the disappearance of Joey, he has found a demoralized comfort in avoiding his father. It's been tolerable in group meetings with his father but this one-on-one liaison has caught him off guard.

"Sure Dad," says Rup, clearing his throat, giving himself enough time to coordinate his mind with his body. His mind is telling him to run, but his body refuses to obey. It's as though it knows better than to try.

"I've got good news," says Jacob.

"What's that?" asks Rup.

"We're up 25 percent over last year," reports Jacob.

"I've noticed, I've been a lot busier in the lab," says Rup, also remembering that he was in charge last year at this same time. He is also aware that he had known of Sam's pilfering but lacked the courage to confront him. Rup isn't any more comfortable with this reassuring news than he would be without it.

From the look on Jacob's face and his eyes surveying the area, seemingly to insure their privacy, it's become apparent he has something important to say.

"Rup have you given any thought to getting married?"

Rup's throat has all but closed off. It's so dry his words stay stuck in his mind. Once again his mind is screaming "Run, run, run," and once again his body remains paralyzed. His eyes are blinking rapidly as they dart around looking for refuge behind, under, or on top of anything. His body still refusing to move, he clears his throat.

"No, Dad. I haven't. I used to think about it some, now I'm content with my life the way it is."

Rup uses the word "content," not because he is, but the word "fear" is unbearable.

Parents always believe they know their children better than anyone. It's true they may have a general idea of their child's character but it always disappoints when they discover just how bad it can be. Rup is no exception. He may be a physical adult, but his mental and spiritual development remain immature.

"Well at least give it some thought. The last time I spoke with the Bishop, he indicated that the Schultz family over near Fairbanks have six daughters of marrying age."

Rup feels undue pressure from his father to make changes in his life when he would much prefer hiding out for its remainder.

Sam has taken special notice of their father holding a private conversation. This makes him nervous. Despite his seeming "come to Jesus" experience, he as yet is not ready to relate the full details of Joey's disappearance. He's fully aware of his brother's weaknesses. It terrifies him that Rup will blurt out some untimely information that he'll be forced to deal with.

Feigning a retiring disposition he makes his intrusion.

"Hi guys. I'm not interrupting anything am I?"

Rup could not be more relieved. "No come join us," he says motioning him in with his hand.

"Hey there, Sam," says Jacob trying to appear lighthearted. "We were just talking about your brother giving some thought to taking a wife."

Sam's face lights up with a mischievous grin, "Why did you find an ugly one that needs marrying off?"

"Come on you guys give me a break," says Rup. He's certainly welcoming his brother's interference as it eases his father's intensity. At least for now, the course of this conversation is taking a much less serious direction.

Meanwhile back in the kitchen, Lena and Rena are putting together a pot roast dinner. This has been a family tradition for as long as anyone can remember.

Waiting for things to finish cooking, the sisters find a spot at a smaller kitchen table to catch up on their lives.

"Rena, I must say, you look a lot more at peace than you have in some time. I know you have been through hell and back with your loss of Joey. My prayers have certainly been with you," says Lena as she places a loving hand over her sister's, hoping to share some of her sister's hurt.

Rena has chosen to wear a modest but cheerful yellow dress. Her blondish hair is pulled back into a twist giving her neck an elongated look.

"I know it's those prayers that are helping me get through this. It's hard to lose a child and especially difficult when I don't know what happened," says Rena squeezing her sister's hand.

"I think we should thank God every day for our strong, loving husband. I don't believe our children could have had a better father. He gives us so much."

Listening to Lena, Rena's thoughts swirl. "More than I can ever tell you, my dear sister." Rena's eyes are beginning to moisten with these thoughts.

BREEEEEEEEE! Just in time. The pressure cooker announces a finished pot roast. The two sisters quickly unwrap themselves from their concerns with each other for the moment and with deft hands center on the task of feeding a hungry family.

Jacob takes his place at the head of the table. After the blessing, he gazes at each bowed head as it is raised up. A smile makes its way across his face. He couldn't be more content.

# 27 — SVOBODA

A day has gone by since Amzlov's meeting with Joey. He's also finished his business with the hotel staff and is preparing to leave for home. He is his own impetuous self, making everyone and anyone within hearing distance look for a way to avoid him.

"Okay, okay vwe getz on za road now," barks Amzlov.

Spotting Joey in the breakfast lounge, he approaches him with waving arms. "Vwhy in hell you zit here? Vwe gutz zings do!" he rants.

Amzlov has always plowed his way through life, not always aware that he's many times several steps ahead of everyone else.

Joey's mouth is full of pancake. Making a hard swallow, simultaneously wiping his lips with his napkin, he spontaneously stands. With his mouth still half full, he manages to stammer a few words, "What things, where are we going?" Without an answer, he watches his new mentor speed off toward some other undone business.

Joey is trying his best to keep abreast of what may be going on without appearing to be overly anxious.

"Don't be so jumpy, you'll be okay." The voice is definitely female and attempts to be reassuring.

Before Joey can turn toward the voice, it speaks again, "Daddy's just having his normal ADD morning. Don't get too worked up over it."

Finally able to make a full turn, swallowing the last of his pancake, Joey comes face-to-face with a very beautiful young woman. He stands doubly dumbfounded, still speechless and reeling from Amzlov's imperatives, he finds it impossible to respond with anything other than a stupid looking, wordless stare.

With a wry little grin she returns his stare with a much more confident one of her own. "You must be the new guy my Dad's been talking about." Making full use of her seeming advantage over this handsome young man, she thrusts out her hand in his direction along with the announcement, "My name is Carrie Amzlov."

Still desperately trying to make his mouth form some words, Joey finally regains enough composure to shake her hand. "Hi. I'm Joey," is about all he can muster for the moment. He definitely realizes he is out of his element.

"I understand Daddy is putting you up in the guest house."

"Guest house, what guest house?" There is an unsettling sound to his voice as he attempts to assemble a group of words that don't make him sound stupid but satisfy his curiosity.

Without the satisfaction of a reply to his question another female voice interjects, "That's just like your father. He tells us nothing. He just expects everyone is a mind reader."

Still on a full court press, Amzlov re-enters the room.

"Gore stop it! No one has any idea what you're doing or where you're going," says Melba trying her best to be discreet and not bring undue attention.

"Vwe headingk home. Vwhere elze you vwant go?" Amzlov talks as much with his hands as with his mouth.

He's finished with what he came to do and is ready to move on. "All you guyz eez rose zmellers. I gutz no time rose zmellingk," says Amzlov still moving ahead.

Each member is aware of Amzlov's impatience with the rest of them, consequently they all drive their own vehicle finding it not imperative they all leave on his schedule. It's just his way to herd everyone together then force a stampede.

With his back to Joey, ignoring everyone, motioning with his curled finger, Amzlov declares, "Come Joey, you ride vwiz me."

He orders his secretary, Doris, to bring his SUV around to the front of the hotel. Shouting orders in every direction, his arms are as busy as if he were directing an orchestra. Most of the front desk clerks to the groundskeepers are still smarting from the dressing down their managers gave them. Since none of them care to go through that again, they are doing all they can to keep their boss happy.

"If that man doesn't slow down, he's going to give all of us a heart attack," says Melba trying her best to exit the hotel and allow things to take an orderly course once again.

The bag boys are scrambling around behind Amzlov waiting for his next directive leaving Melba to take her bags in hand. Opening her car trunk, she quickly loads them in. Able to avoid much of her husband's insanity and without as much as a good-bye, she sets off down the road in the direction of home. Following her lead are Drew and Carrie, both undertaking a quick exit, sidestepping their father's asininity.

Despite Amzlov's rantings, Joey is adamant to locate Tiny. There has grown a comfortable familiarity between them. He believes when friends part, they need to say their good-byes and reassure each other of meeting again. Finally locating him in his office, "Tiny I want to thank you from the bottom of my heart for everything you've done for me. I wish I could better show my appreciation." With that said he grabs his friend in an embrace.

Tiny looks him over, scrutinizing him as best he can. "You gonna be happy, Bro?" asks Tiny displaying his huge, reassuring gap-toothed grin.

"I'm sure gonna give it a try," assures Joey.

"You startin' a whole new life. It beginnin' right now so go for it. Don't worry about thankin' me. We'll catch up later brother."

"I think you're right Tiny. I need to start living life instead of hiding from it."

Suddenly and impetuously there is a familiar voice behind them. It's Doris. "There you are. Mr. Amzlov is throwing a fit to get out of here. Please, for everyone's sake let's not keep him waiting a minute longer." The look of near panic is loud and clear. It's become evident that Doris has also lost her sense of humor.

Saying one last good-bye to Tiny, he grabs his small duffel bag and heads down following Doris' frenzied lead.

"Unless we can get on the road, he's going to be a beast for the rest of the day," continues Doris speaking as much to herself as to Joey. The hall ends in the lobby where they charge through without a shred of politeness, out the door and into the waiting van. Men are mowing. The smell of fresh mowed grass fills their nostrils. Joey's heart leaps with excitement at the prospects of this new venture.

A great burst of raw horsepower sends the big SUV through a pile of loose grass clippings on down the road. Amzlov is behind the wheel with

Joey in the passenger seat, Doris is in the back seat with pen and note pad in one hand and her phone in the other. The muffled almost hushed tones of her voice are an indication that she has found ways to finish her work without having to compete with Amzlov for air time.

Instinctively, Joey finds himself trying to brake with his feet as Amzlov cuts in and out of traffic and at the same time pay attention to his incessant nattering.

"Gut Got, zeez guyz need get off road. Zay poke lonk like gotz nozingk elze do." With that said another burst of unbridled horsepower launches his machine past more vehicles poking along at the speed limit.

No sooner has he pulled back into his lane when a dated cement block building catches his eye.

"Zee zat buildingk?"

Joey's head snaps in the direction Amzlov is pointing before it can only be seen in the rear view mirror.

Amzlov's eyes linger as long as they can watching something go by at 80 miles per hour. "Zat my old machine shop. Got lotz goot buzinezz done zere." Despite his speed, the softer tone of his voice languors a little longer as his mind loiters around the memory of these long past years. But then he catches himself, "Now vwe move better zingz." He releases a little chuckle indicating he's satisfied with his life decisions.

Amzlov has never thought his broken English to be the slightest hindrance to his business pursuits. Doris has been his secretary for more years than she cares to admit. She serves not only as his secretary, but also as a translator and adviser and at times a referee.

"Oh he's a persistent one. He can convince the devil he needs a furnace and he's got just the one to do the job," Doris has been heard to say.

She has kept her private life private. She has never married and appears to be content with that. Amzlov is not privy to her life outside the office nor does he give it much thought. His major concern is what would he do without her. He would be humbled very quickly if she ever threw in the towel and quit. He is aware of his erratic behavior at times and is very grateful that Doris has the strength of character to put up with him. So far she hasn't given any indication that things need to change. As with most things in his life, he is far from stingy, paying her well thus eliminating any financial worries she may have.

With his foot hard on the accelerator, it's just a matter of time before they'll be arriving at their final destination. "Ain't goink be lonk vwe be home vor lunch," says Amzlov.

Joey hasn't given his stomach much thought with Amzlov chief priority being that he can never bear to have another car, bus, or truck in front of him. For the past several hours it's been Joey's concern for his life that's nudged its way to the forefront with Amzlov passing as many as four vehicles at a time, but now with that behind him, he can safely add a hungry stomach to his list of concerns.

Five minutes later Amzlov is fussing with a remote control. As they round a curve, it becomes clear why. Joey has noticed for the past quarter mile a stone masonry wall, maybe ten feet high with ornate, iron pike pole artifices detailing the top. It soon ends at a juncture of two towering pillars of the same materials joined together by a formidable but ornate double iron gate displaying a huge bold plaque above scrolled with the Russian word "SVOBODA" (FREEDOM).

With Amzlov's eyes darting from remote to gate, it becomes clear the relationship between the two. Predictably, the gates slide open presenting a red brick, paved driveway. This meanders a quarter mile under a canopy of imposing Norway spruce. As genteel sentinels, each offering its branches as a gallant courtesy only to end at the most elegant Romanesque mansion imaginable.

It's constructed of colored corner-cut field stone with hues of pinks, reds, blues, grays, blacks, and white. In spite of its stone structure the sun's rays cast a warmth as it brings out the brilliant earth-tone of each stone.

The windows are all accented with rounded arches. The whole structure finalizes itself with a conical tower on each corner jutting some three stories, ending slightly above the roof line all with vaulted windows.

The front door is beautifully hand-carved from solid oak and arched with leaded cut glass above transoms embellishing the entire portico.

Joey is noticing windows on at least three levels indicating that the house must be a minimum of three stories. To make a statement that this house has "country charm" would be an understatement; it would be adequately described as "country elegance."

There is no question that this house is built and maintained with Amzlov's wealth, but to say this is Amzlov's house would also be an understatement. Melba's hand is seen everywhere, even in the choice of Romanesque architecture celebrating her father's Italian heritage. If Amzlov lived here alone, it could be referred to as a large house, but with Melba's touch it's been transformed into an elegant home.

All the furnishings are mostly from high-end local craftsmen made from the best that gold, silver, and diamond money can buy. Melba's choice in furnishings and art works center around the strengths this house portrays. As a result she has chosen large furnishings with bold colors, all large enough to compliment the oversized rooms with a smattering of feminine frills. It's a home in which both she and Amzlov feel comfortable.

Joey can't help but gawk. The wilderness and jail cells have been his only memorable homes. He remains speechless. Amzlov pulls the SUV into a circlular drive and stops in front of the main portico. Grabbing his bag, he shouts at Doris, "Take heem to guest house and boz you come back to lunch."

Without a word Doris is in the driver's seat, following more of the brick road down a lane to the guest house. It's also constructed of the same cut stone as the main house. Directly behind is a river separating in the middle around a small island.

After Doris fumbles with a number of keys, she finally manages to get the door unlocked. To say that Joey is overwhelmed would be an understatement. The first thing he's greeted with is a massive fire place. The room is large and open with groupings of chairs and sofas. Under windows are desks or small tables supporting lamps or pieces of art. Along the walls are book cases and an assortment of large plants. At one end of the room is a kitchen with a table and chairs. There is also one convenience he will readily reacquaint with—a big screen TV.

"Drop your bag, Joey, we're going back for lunch," says Doris. This is all in a day's work for her. Being Amzlov's secretary often involves chauffeuring clients to and from the airport and acting as hostess, especially if he's late for an appointment.

They make their way back to the main house, coming in through the kitchen. They are met by Tillie Tilson, who's been the family's housekeeper for a number of years. Her duties consist of general housecleaning as well as making lunch. Today she has prepared cold salmon and hot tomato soup. It's one of Amzlov's favorites. (Melba still prefers to make the evening meal herself.)

Tillie is a matronly woman with ample breasts resting on an even larger stomach. She has lost her top teeth and refusing to wear a plate, she has a tendency to suck in her upper lip causing her chin to appear exaggerated.

Her husband is Burt Tilson. He works as full-time maintenance man with duties ranging from gardening to all around handyman.

Making their way into the dining room, they convene with Amzlov, Melba, Drew, Carrie, and Shanhizer all coming from an elevator. Soon they are all seated. Without a word being said, they simultaneously make the sign of the cross as Melba recites a table prayer.

Joey sits dumbfounded, barely uttering a word since arriving. He feels like an alien in a foreign land. He's the only one not at ease. This makes him even more uneasy. He feels like he's sitting in a classroom being given a test he's never studied for. It would be a great relief if someone would just kick him out. He just wants to run.

Food is soon being passed and conversations begin. Since Joey is the new guy much of everyone's attention is in his direction. All at the table are aware that Amzlov got him out of jail. Over the years his family has grown used to his sometimes compulsive actions. This latest has everyone's curiosity piqued.

Drew begins, "So where do you com from?"

It's obvious to everyone that Joey is nervous as he clears his throat hoping to give, at the very least, a trustworthy answer.

"I'm not sure. I've been diagnosed with amnesia," says Joey. It's a simple answer, but also the most forthright he can give. Looking around the table, he judges this response to be at least satisfactory for the present.

Carrie is the next to ask a question. "I've heard you called 'Joey'. Do you have a last name?"

"I'm sure I do, but I have no idea what it may be."

Melba is sitting quietly sipping a cup of tea with one hand while toying with the crucifix adorning the chain surrounding her neck with the other. She lets a few more questions be asked before she cuts loose with the question most concerning her since she laid eyes on him, "Do you believe you may be Catholic?" She's taken aback that no one else in her family thought it important enough to ask.

Joey is taken back by the pertinacity carried along in her voice. He's sure that this is a question that needs to be answered satisfactorily.

"I...I really can't answer that question because I really don't know for sure," he stammers. When he doesn't see a look of approval in her demeanor, he quickly rethinks his answer, "But maybe I am though."

Melba is willing to accept this answer as the beginning of his conversion she is plotting.

"Oh Momma don't badger him about that..." says Carrie as her mother cuts her off in mid-sentence.

"I'm not badgering him, Carrie. I'm merely asking a simple question. I'll bet Joey doesn't think I'm badgering him." Then turning toward Joey she reiterates, "Do you, Joey?"

Not wanting in any way, shape, or form, to be the center of attention, he tries as best he knows how to rectify himself, "I BELIEVE IN GOD!"

The whole table went quiet, turning to look at him. He had actually shouted over the top of their bickering about this. Realizing what he has done, he tries to recover once again by restating in a quieter voice, "I believe in God."

Amzlov has sat quietly through this whole inquisition, not impressed with any of it.

"Vwe needz getz you last name. You gotz be legal." Turning to Shanhizer he continues, "Getz Joey here lazt name?" Shanhizer nods agreeing. Amzlov has learned very early in his career to, "Getz allz 'iz' viz dots and 'tz' viz crozzez."

Joey has been so busy turning his head to address each person's question that his food remains on his plate uneaten. At last things quiet down enough for Joey to get a few long overdue bites down. By now the parents have turned their attention to their two children.

"Drew, you know you make beeg meestake not come in beezniz," says Amzlov for the hundredth time. He has said it so many times expecting the same results that he barely pauses between bites of salmon. He already knows that Drew's responses will be about wanting to get some outside experience, but nonetheless he enjoys the challenge. Turning to everyone now except Drew, hoping to gain some allegiance from the rest of his family, "I pay beeg collage moneey get beeg zhot CPA guy here. Vwhat he doez? He goez vwork ozzer guyz. Vwat kind zanks I getz? Beeg kick in azz!" Amzlov has used guilt on Drew before to no avail, but then he doesn't give up easily.

"I know Dad, but when I do come work for you, I'll have something from my experience to bring to the table," says Drew in his own defense. Drew realizes his father is far from finished with him. He's hoping he can get hired somewhere before his father figures out what he's done.

"Gore let him be. He's old enough to make his own decisions about what he wants to do with his life," says Melba. Drew has always had his mother as a buffer between himself and his father. Amzlov is well aware that when his wife gets involved, things are not going to go in his direction.

Carrie, on the other hand has always been the apple of her father's eye. The DNA contribution of Russian, Italian, and Indian has given her the best of all combinations. Her complexion is beautiful with the brown and yellow blended into a smooth creamy color. Her hair is a dark luster, with blond streaks announcing themselves as only an accent to the much stronger darker pigment. Her eyes, slightly slanted reveal themselves to be a deep Russian blue. She has a smile that captures the attention of anyone engaging her and her figure is such that it completes any outfit she chooses to wear.

Amzlov has forever considered Carrie as his baby princess, giving no indication that anything has changed.

"Carrie you gotz goot zmartz. Talk zeez crazy brother zome zense."

"Okay Daddy, I'll try," says Carrie looking at her brother with that silent look that says, "I got your back."

Parents never understand the relationships their children build amongst themselves. They can only be included at their children's whims. In turn, their children can sense very quickly what kind of relationships their siblings have with their parents, especially how favors are distributed.

Carrie and Drew both are well aware from which parent they can gain the most support. It's a rare thing to find both parents on the same page when it comes to dealing with their children.

"Gore, don't drag Carrie into this. This decision is up to Drew. You have to let him live his own life," says Melba.

Amzlov reluctantly accepts, at least for the present that this conversation is not going in his direction. Finishing his lunch, he wipes his lips with his napkin, takes a deep drink of what appears to be ice water, clunks the finished container to the table, slaps his knees with both hands, and kicks his chair behind him. Standing up, he takes a deep breath. Letting it out, he turns to Joey, "You viz me go today," motioning him to follow.

Joey bolts out of his chair following along behind like a lemming, having no idea where he's being led. Amzlov says no more as he practically sprints as one does when one knows exactly where one is going. Joey does not have this luxury and is content to trot along behind.

The destination is an elevator at the far end of the house. Amzlov pushes the access button allowing the doors to open, at the same time motioning Joey aboard. A whooshing sound emitted by the lift accompanies them all the way to the third floor. As the doors slide open, Joey is met by what appears to be a series of offices on each side of a long corridor extending the whole length of the building.

He immediately spots Shanhizer talking on the phone. He had slipped out from lunch to return to work. He doesn't look up. Shanhizer prefers to keep what he refers to as a "professional distance" between himself and others. The only person who can penetrate his self-made fortress is Amzlov.

"Shanhizer," shouts Amzlov still moving forward into Shanhizer's office.

"Yes Mr. Amzlov," says Shanhizer ending his phone conversation abruptly.

"How you comingk on makingk zeez last name?

Shanhizer is required to wear several lawyer hats for Amzlov. Some days he's a corporate attorney, other days he's may be called on to handle defense, patent, or civil cases and occasionally an immigration problem. Amzlov makes no distinction between legal disciplines. To him a good lawyer does it all. Fortunately, for Shanhizer, he is respected well enough in the legal community that when he needs council on something, he generally can get it. Without hesitation, he switches legal hats.

"You have any paper work diagnosing your condition?" questions Shanhizer now choosing to look at Joey.

"Yes, a doctor at a free clinic in Anchorage diagnosed me with retrograde amnesia," volunteers Joey.

"We're going to need more than that," says Shanhizer using a very knowing and official sounding tone.

Amzlov permits Shanhizer's arrogance only because he has earned it by his stellar accomplishments. Posturing himself this way without results would have him quickly looking for another job years ago.

Shanhizer continues shooting from the hip long enough to gain Amzlov's confidence. "We're going to have you see a specialist to start with, then we'll take the next steps."

Amzlov has always been besotted by Shanhizer's legal babble. "If he not dazzle vwiz brillianz, he bafflez vwiz buulsheet," he's been heard to say with a knowing, wry little smirk.

"You getz buzy vweez it—vwe gutz have eet done." In the same breath he has turned to Joey with the same curled finger motioning him forward, "Comez vweez me Mr. Joey, I show you beeznez."

They spend the rest of the afternoon pouring over different aspects of Amzlov's empire. Joey is discovering a strange, unexplained sense of community where he truly had expected contention.

It's already 5 pm as they are concluding. Amzlov hasn't changed his mind about Joey's abilities. As a matter of fact, Amzlov's fervor for taking Joey on has been reinforced by the type of questions he's been asking. Many of them could not have been asked unless one had upper management skills.

"Zo vwat you zink here Mr. Joey, you gutz kahuna getz job done?"

Joey's confidence level is back to a comfortable stability, much like he enjoyed toward the end of his wilderness survival.

"You know, Mr. Amzlov," says Joey adding a confident pause, "I believe I can." He finds it encouraging that he is impacted with the sense that much of the knowledge from his past is pushing itself into his present faculties. All in all it serves to buttress his confidence.

The next few months prove to be challenging, but very rewarding for Joey. Much like a person going through a physical rehabilitation to regain the use of their limbs: he is stretching, bending, and crunching his mind trying to recall certain procedures that he is more and more beginning to believe have played a role some how in his past. He's finding that he has the abilities to make the level of business decisions expected of him with precision and confidence and he demonstrates a rare quality. Amzlov couldn't be happier.

# 28 — RUNNING STOP SIGNS

The hope of every Mormon is to serve God significantly and to have God notice and grant eternal life on some level, based on how well they've done. Jacob's family is no exception. But as is true of all God's children, selfish, self-centerdness has more or less dominated the human condition since its inception in the Garden Of Eden.

Jacob has not been granted an exclusionary writ by anyone to be omitted from this stain on humanity. He once had a twin brother, who is now deceased. His brother's name was Ezard. Jacob had always considered him as a weak business partner, Ezard didn't share the same zest for business that he did. Instead his brother found his life spent hunting and fishing.

In spite of being born twins, Ezard had always enjoyed the family status of being the oldest since he had slipped through the birth canal first and pulling his brother through after he had allegedly grabbed his ankle. (The family insisted it happened that way despite the doubters.) Ezard remained an impulsive man, buying when he should have been saving, never considering the consequences until it was too late.

Jacob was always looking for an opportunity to persuade Ezard to relinquish his share of the business.

He soon found what he perceived to be a perfect opportunity. From youth on, Ezard had never been a good manager of his personal finances resulting in a mounting debt that was threatening his family's well-being. Jacob took full advantage of his brother's misfortune by offering him a job for life and his debt paid off in return for his portion of the business.

It was not out of character for Jacob to grab more than just his brother's heel. He has always shown traits of a business opportunist. His business skills have always been text book perfect. In the moment of his brother's anxieties he offered a fast fix, aware of his brother's weaknesses. As well, Ezard had long ago abandoned their fundamental Mormon faith by marrying a Lutheran. When the Prophet, along with the rest of their small congregation began to marginalize his family, he permanently converted.

One common human trait to justify another person's questionable practice is to diminish that adversary's value as a human. In time, Jacob rested much of his denial of complicity on the sentiment that his brother had become apostate by leaving the faith. Deceit driven by selfishness can be disguised in many different ways making a person blind to a personal unrighteousness.

Shortly after this, Ezard was killed in a mining accident. His widow left the area, moving to Anchorage. Not much has been heard of the whereabouts of their children and no one seems to care.

Over the years, Jacob has reflected back on those younger years realizing that the devil didn't care how close he felt to God, just as long as he wasn't. He has come to realize he needs God's goodness much more than God needs his. He continues his struggle never sure he's done enough to purify himself in God's eyes or his own.

The people, good or bad that have leadership abilities, eventually stand out from those of lesser capabilities. Often what brings this person's special skill to the forefront is an occurrence to shine successfully with a problem where others fail. Generally, what is common with those possessing this gift is an outspoken decisiveness and then followed up by a controlled action.

Jacob had first recognized this leadership ability in Joey at a very early age. Now that Joey is gone he's turning his attention toward Sam.

The truth of it is that Sam is still smarting from his near-death experience. He has known the difference between right and wrong since he was a child. As a former avowed opportunist, his driving force had often been to gain from the miseries of others. Nowadays he is doing many right actions and his father commends him for it.

"Sam, I want to tell you how pleased I am with your turn around. We're having a great season and much of it has to do with your new attitude in the field."

"Thanks, Dad. You know I'm trying to do the right thing. That dream or whatever it was certainly put me on the right track," says Sam.

Jacob is standing in the doorway of his office, surveying Sam. This son has come a long way, but Jacob hears something in Sam's voice that gives him pause. It's the lack of an important ingredient for character building that he believes Sam needs, something Jacob has learned over a span of sixty years.

Still staring at Sam, he purses his lips in and out (when he does this Sam always knows there is more coming).

"Sam, I want you to think about my next question. When you run a stop sign do you ever feel a sense of gratitude?"

Sam scrutinizes his father for a moment, feeling he's studied the question long enough. "Your damn-tootin I do!" says Sam considering the question too straight forward to give it any length of thought.

Jacob presses forward. "What do you consider to be the origin of your gratitude?" searches his father.

"That's easy enough. That I didn't get a ticket. The way these cops are around here, they'll ticket a person for anything they can."

"That's a good, honest answer son," says Jacob still pursing his lips.

Sam knows his father well enough to recognize his father's body language is saying something different. This answer will do for now, and he's happy he's off the hook.

The next morning comes as expected. The seasons are moving on. It's September and it's Alaska where it can snow from now until next May.

Neither Jacob nor Sam are coffee drinkers, first by religious law and second because they have never acquired a taste nor a need. Consequently, their mornings are slow getting started.

Gathering all his boys as well as various other employees into the foyer, it's Jacob's habit to have a brief prayer asking God's blessing on everything he can think of for the day.

When Sam and Jacob are loading the work truck for the day, Jacob is moving a bit slower than usual. His poor eyesight is beginning to have a greater effect on what he's able to do.

"Dad, if you're not up to it, you really don't have to go out with me today," says Sam after noticing his father's battle.

"I know that, Sam. I don't have to do a lot of things, but I can't imagine not going," says Jacob still loading their gear.

However, Sam continues to carry the burden of guilt that accompanies his dishonesty and lack of forthrightness about Joey. He's well aware that there is a good chance his father won't be able to forgive him and it would ultimately wipe out this new found relationship they've began.

It's not relieving his nervousness that this particular morning his father has chosen a work sight along the same road that Sam had his altercation with Joey. His tortuous re-enactment of that day is reeling non-stop through his mind.

Many of the back roads in this part of Alaska are treacherous, requiring a great deal of skill to maneuver. It's not at all unusual to come across vehicles off the road in a ditch or even worse down a steep embankment. It's always been the unwritten rule for Alaskans to stop and assist any stranded motorist. One never knows when it becomes their turn for that same needed assistance.

Sam is hoping that he can quickly get past the never-to-be-forgotten spot, but this morning that is not to be. Instead, as he crests the hill just below the mine shaft intended to entomb his brother is a pick-up truck with its hood up and a motorist standing by with a helpless look.

Sam's gaze darts between the mine opening and the open road. He tries to ignore the stranded motorist who has unwittingly parked in the same spot he believes he may have killed his brother.

Jacob shouts, "Don't leave this guy. We gotta stop."

The tone of his voice is a telling disappointment in his son's seeming decision to ignore this person in need. It would have been an easy decision for Sam to have left this piece of geography in the dust were it not for his father's insistence they stop.

Reluctantly, Sam complies and pulls his truck to the side of the road. A flash of the events are mercilessly plowing their way through his psyche as his father has run his window down asking the motorist what the problem is. He barely hears the conversation over the cracking echo in his mind of his fallen brother's head smashing against the rock.

"I'm not sure," says the stranger, having pulled a scarf up a bit further against the wind.

No sooner have they exited the truck, than they find themselves surrounded by two more men wearing ski masks holding them at gunpoint. One of the strangers pulls Sam's keys from his hand. Sam can smell liquor on the man's breath.

Jacob involuntarily lunges at the man. He is straight way struck down by another of the men. Sam jumps to the aid of his fallen father in the same spot he had left his fallen brother for dead. The crack that echoed this time was a rifle butt against his own head knocking him and his hat to the ground.

Dazed, they are both pulled to their feet by ropes lassoed around their underarms. The stranger wearing the scarf grabs their cellphones blurting out, "One more dumb-ass move like that and you'll both find yourselves dead sooner than later. If you're smart you can both avoid being dead. Listen hard. We know you have a half million in gold at your plant. That is going to be the price for your release. Your hope is your family considers you worth it."

Meantime, the other two thugs help themselves to the cash Jacob uses to buy gold along with the guns they carry for security.

Finished with this they are promptly dragged along the trail leading to the mine shaft. Once again, the presumed spokesman for this clandestine gang makes yet another warning. "You are both going down this mine shaft. There are only two options for this to happen. Either we lower you," pointing to the ropes wrapped around them, "or we throw you down."

Jacob and Sam manage to get a single glance at one another. Not given the chance to make any decision, they are pushed to the edge. They both have a look between frustration and desperation as they reluctantly begin their descent down the shaft. Both are able to feel the tension of the ropes tightening against their weight as they're being lowered at the mercy of their captors. Not at all sure how long these predators will agree and not drop them, they make their way down the steep walls of the shaft.

Lost in thought, Sam is beginning to imagine what will be found at the bottom of this pit. The lower they go, the darker it becomes. Soon darkness overtakes them as Sam begins to panic imagining he will be lowered onto his brother's dead, decomposing body. Unutterable terror is grasping him.

Soon, but hardly soon enough, they find themselves at the bottom. Just as quickly all the tension is off their ropes. The next sound is as though someone else is making their way down after them. It proves to be nothing more than the other end of the ropes.

The smell is the dank odor of damp earth. On closer inspection it has the feeling of wet soil and gravel. Their eyes eventually adjust to the very dim light supplied by the opening some fifty feet above them and just enough for Sam to see no sign of a body. Instead a cheerless alternate of gloom and despair has replaced it. "This is my punishment and well deserved," is his hopeless thought.

Jacob, on the other hand is of a much more sober mind. His hands are methodically assessing the walls of this six by six foot hole. The hardened dirt and stones that form their prison are too steep to scale. There is no sound except their mutual hard breathing and the dripping water from some unknown source. A chill begins to make its way into their sweat-soaked bodies.

Realizing, as most Alaskans are forced to if they expect to survive, that frustration with a present reality is paralyzing and must be replaced vigorously with a calmer, more calculating mind. They also notice that the dripping water is confined to one lower corner. The floor is riddled with debris from years of hunters and hikers casting their non-usables off.

Jacob is the first to set aside his frustration and begin to study the situation. He can sense Sam's panic as Sam mindlessly scrambles from one side of the shaft to the next.

"Sam take it easy. We can't just start pawin' at the dirt here. I want to get out as bad as you do, but your jumpin' around isn't going to get us anywhere."

Sam wavers long enough to let a second thought find a resting place. "I know you're right Dad, but right now that's not an easy choice." This reaction is not a new one for Sam, he has always left those around him with the notion he prefers a world of chaotic impulses rather than one of careful evaluation.

"First, off let's get these wet t-shirts off before we take a chill," says Jacob already out of his.

Having put their dry jackets and heavy work shirts back on they are reasonably comfortable.

Kicking around some more of the debris brings to light exactly what this hole's use had been. There're a couple of old rusty pails with rotted pieces of rope still attached, a broken pick ax and an equally decayed handle along with a 100 years worth of tin cans.

"This was dug as a test hole back in the gold rush days," says Jacob. "They must not have found gold they'd hoped for and abandoned the site."

Sam listens to his father in disbelief. He's finding Jacob's sudden concern over the historical significance of their soon-to-be-tomb annoying.

Turning one of the rusted pails upside down, Jacob sits down leaning back against a sidewall, arms folded, he peers toward the distant light at the top. "For the time being, I believe we're stuck down here unless God chooses to send a rescuer," says Jacob.

His matter-of-fact attitude is further annoying Sam. He hasn't opted to sit down yet. He too is peering toward the light at the top. "I can't believe we're stuck down here with no way out. There has to be some way out of here," says Sam still continuing to stare helplessly at the top.

Finally giving in, he turns the other pail upside down and joins his father. His gaze suddenly catches sight of a faint luminescence at his feet. Picking it up for a closer inspection sends a chill over his entire body. He immediately recognizes it as the luminous face stares at him. It's JOEY'S WATCH! Gasping, then recoiling as though he had just touched the head of a Burmese python, he's torn between throwing it or stuffing it away from his father's over-curious reaction.

"What are you finding, Sam?"

Depending on his father's poor eyesight, Sam says, "Oh nothing, just a sharp piece of junk." Opting to stuff it in his pocket rather than risk his father finding it. It's one his father would recognize since it was a gift he had given Joey years back while he was in collage.

Sam's mind is incapable of rest. The multitude of destructive circumstances surrounding his life continue to come back to stalk him. He's well aware of the prison that he's built around his conscience hoping to prevent his guilt from exploding into a full-blown confession. At the same time knowing he will never be free from the regrets of his past until he somehow settles this account with his father. For now he fears the consequences of such a confession greater than continuing to live with all of its agonies.

The day wears on. Soon it's ending. The two that have not reconvened with their families are getting some attention. Sam's wife Mattie is the first to ring the bell of concern. Not willing to wait any longer, she telephones her mother-in-law Lena.

"Has Dad come home yet?" she asks.

Lena considers the question for a moment, hearing an insecurity in Mattie's voice. "I'm not sure," says Lena then adding, "is something wrong?"

"It's way past 9 pm and it's not like Sam to not call if he expects to be late. I've called both their cellphones and all I get is voice mail."

Lena promises to call around to the other boys and get back with her. No one has seen nor heard from them since devotions earlier that morning.

Taking the next step, Rup agrees to drive back to the plant hoping he will come across any activity on their part that will suggest they got busy and over looked the time.

When he reaches the plant, he gave a sigh of relief noticing Sam's pick-up parked under the bright mercury light.

He's met by Jim Hartman, the night security guard.

"Jim have you seen my Dad or Sam this evening?"

"No, but about an hour ago Sam's truck shows up parked under the light. I thought it was odd because he never parks there. I checked the plant all out and didn't find hide nor hair of either one."

While listening to Jim, Rup takes a closer look at Sam's truck. "Ah they left a note," says Rup relieved. Reaching in on the dash, he retrieves the folded paper. When he finishes reading the note the color has left his face and a knot has formed in his stomach. The unbelievable is forcing its way into Rup's world.

"Jim, this damnable thing is a ransom note," blurts out Rup. Looking on as best he can, Jim reads along with Rup its demands along with its warnings.

"...Jacob and Sam Mueller are being held underground with no food and water... If you choose to alert the authorities or if you choose not to arrange payment of a half-million dollars worth of gold they will be abandoned..."

Rup steps back in retreat as he folds the paper in an attempt to keep it away from Jim's investigative eyes. Jim is a retired policeman and Rup has the warning about "the authorities" strong in his mind and not sure who Jim may want to involve.

"Jim, please keep this information to yourself. We have to handle this and I'm not sure how yet."

Stunned as well, and being a retired policeman, Jim knows how delicate these situations can be.

"Okay Rup, but don't leave me out of the loop. I've handled cases similar to this in the past. The only concern we can focus on is for the safety of your Dad and Sam."

Rup's thoughts are shredding his brain. He jumps from one scenario to another hoping for a quick solution.

"Jim do you think this is true or could it be just a gag?"

"Gag or not, we have to figure it as true until something tells us different."

Rup is mulling all this over. "I'm going to have to inform the rest of the family," says Rup talking as much to himself as to Jim. He then adds, "Will you stay and help me with this?

"You know I will, Rup. Your family has always been good to me. I'll stay as long as it takes to get this resolved." Jim says this with the determination and resolve of not only a family friend and employee, but as a professional.

"Do you think I should call the family tonight or wait until tomorrow?" asks Rup. His fretting is obvious and he's quickly becoming dependent on Jim.

"You may as well get it over with tonight as no one will be sleeping much anyway," responds Jim. "As a matter of fact have them gather here in an hour for a meeting. We'll put our heads together and hopefully agree on a direction."

Rup is as aware of his limitations, but this awareness doesn't always prevent him from a foolish knee-jerk attempt to get involved. After working with the family for a number of years, Jim is mindful of this trait and knows he's going to have to work around Rup's pattern of overreacting especially when the situation calls for underreacting.

Within the hour the families have gathered. There is an overwhelming feeling of disbelief turned to fear and ending with anger. Their longing over the loss of their loved ones is already making their faces look worn. Carrying the burden of having to live with an unknown is frustrating. Frustration can only be viewed as a luxury in this case, as valuable time is flying by. By the time Jim has outlined where he believes their efforts should be focused the family has become mildly composed.

Jim is well aware of the fundamentalist Mormon views toward law enforcement. It comes with the law taking a dim view toward their practice of polygamy. He knows better than to push the idea of involving the law at a deeper level than the unofficial capacity of just himself.

Rup has established as fact that the amount of gold demanded by the malefactors is in the vault. There isn't a second thought by anyone that if it should come down to the wire it will be sacrificed for the safe return of their two loved ones.

Levi and Justin have never been accused of being overly patient. The more the reality of their father's and brother's fate sink in, the angrier they become. "I don't think we should just roll over for these dirtballs and let them run the whole show. I think we need to keep our eyes and ears open for any mistakes they make," says Levi.

"Yah, Levi, I agree with you. We can't just sit around and let these guys make us dance to their tune," says Justin.

Jim is listening politely to all that the family is speculating. Realizing on the one hand where his paycheck comes from and on the other hand what should and shouldn't be done to eliminate jeopardizing the safety of these two men. He's trying to work a balance between the family's sentiments and the more professional direction he'd prefer this case to go. In other words, he's hoping to keep heads cool and not allow unnecessary emotions to screw things up.

Levi and Justin have already left the room and are muttering between themselves of organizing a Mormon militia, to "hunt these bastards down."

What Jim is asking for is that they simply wait patiently for further update from the kidnappers that would allow for any new assessment. "Let's all go home tonight and try and get some sleep. I know this will probably be difficult, but believe me when I tell you we all need rested minds to make clear decisions."

Jim decides to finish out his regular night shift, but will also try and get some sleep in hopes of intelligibly sorting through what needs to be addressed tomorrow.

For everyone rest is a struggle. Jim is no exception. He has never thought of the cluttered couch in Jacob's office as an inviting place to lie down, but tonight it's going to be a pallet for sleep.

Like it is for all those involved it's difficult to shut the mind down. His head is holding a virtual conference reviewing how he had dealt with other cases that started as this one has. Insights blend as they drift in and out of half dreams.

As dawn is barely lightening the sky, Jim is startled awake by what sounds like vehicle tires rolling over gravel. A quick trip to the window reveals an older model four-wheeled drive Jeep creeping past with its lights out. It's just slightly out of the shadows of the plant's outdoor mercury light. A shadowy figure makes a veiled appearance at the plant's mailbox mounted at the road's edge, depositing what appears to be an envelope, and darts back into the shadows, slowly driving away with lights still out.

Jim continues to watch from the darkness. Grabbing his notebook, he makes note of time, date, make of vehicle and what he could make out of its occupant. Satisfied the perpetrator has left, he grabs his flashlight, touches his holstered .45 out of habit, and cautiously makes his way out to the mailbox.

Shifting the beam of his light around the dirt road, he notices where he had seen the Jeep stop. He also takes note of an odd heel print impression left in the soft dirt around the mailbox. It indicates it's the heel from the left boot with an odd wedge shaped cut in the back suggesting it's probably a home-made heel.

Following the heel print back to where the Jeep had stopped, it comes to an end on the passenger side indicating there had to be another person driving.

He also takes note of the road where the vehicle had stopped paying particular attention to the tire prints. Much like the odd heel, all four tires are different tread patterns.

In full daylight, Jim is diligently taking pictures of these unusual combinations of boots and tires. He's beginning to form some preliminary judgments about these characters, "I don't believe we're dealing with the sharpest tools in the shed. I think they're probably as disorganized as their boots and tires."

Benji is the first of the family to arrive this morning. Jim is still in the road. He's attempting to get as much of his investigation concluded before traffic obliterates all trace evidence or before he has to include Justin and Levi in on his investigation.

Seeing Benji's vehicle approaching, Jim waves him to a stop. He's making it quite clear that for this task he needs no assistance, all he needs is to be left alone to finish.

Benji has arrived in hopes of being able to help in some way. Some where between prayer and worry he managed to get a few hours of sleep. His heart is broken yet again. Just months ago he suffered the loss of Joey, now life is threatening him another blow with the loss of his father and another brother.

"Anything I can do to help?" His voice carries fatigue.

Jim is finally finishing what he hopes to be a thorough investigation. With a pause he mulls over the question.

"Maybe there is. Let's get out of the road and take a drive out back before anyone else gets here," says Jim entering the passenger side of Benji's truck. He says this with an air of authority that gains Benji's trust.

Benji gives an agreeable nod as they make their way to a point where they can have some privacy and still keep an eye on who's coming or going.

"I know you must be feeling pretty bad about all this, Benji. I want to let you know that I think the world of your family and I'll work my ass off to bring your Dad and brother home."

There is an intensiveness in Jim's voice that Benji finds to be reassuring. "Thanks, Jim. I think I can speak for all of us when I say we appreciate any help you can give us." A little smile marked with assurance, makes its way across his wearied face.

Jim immediately gets to the point of this meeting. "You work out in the yard around the plant quite a bit, have you noticed anything out of the ordinary lately, or anyone strange, you know, like somebody catching your attention in some odd sort of way?"

Benji muses over the question for the moment. He finds it to be encouraging that Jim is asking such pertinent questions, but also a tenseness in answering in a right-minded way. "I'm not sure I know what you mean?" Benji is still a very young man and not always comfortable in judging adult's behavior.

"I mean did you at any time recently notice or hear your father or brother involved in any out of the ordinary confrontations with anyone? And don't worry about how insignificant you may think it to be."

Benji is trying very hard to retrieve any memories of incidents he found unusual. The last thing he wishes is that his bumbling will bring about a road block in Jim's investigation. Suddenly a moment flashes.

"I remember an incident last week when I was doing some work here in the parking lot. Three guys come pulling in. They wanted to know who they needed to talk to about buying some gold. I referred them to my father."

Jim is listening without interruption. Benji hesitates for a moment. Jim is getting the impression that he's wrestling with something about this event that he had found disturbing. The silence continues until Benji has satisfied himself that he can adequately relate the incident.

"These guys didn't look like miners. They looked more like bar guys. They didn't have the clothing miners wear. They looked like they had not done anything like work in a long time. What added to my dislike about them was after they talked to my Dad they were bitching among themselves about about how tired they were with all these rich bastards lording it over them."

Jim is listening intently. "Did you ask your father what kind of business he discussed with them?"

"Yes I did. He said they were asking questions about our gold operation. When he asked them a question pertaining to their claim they sidestepped the question. That's when he told them he wasn't interested in their business and asked them to leave.

"I also noticed that one of these guys, the shorter one, had some kind of dumbass home-made heel on his boot. What brought it to my attention was that it sounded like wood when he walked across the parking lot," he clarified.

Hearing this last sentence has Jim doing all he can do to remain calm. He's almost holding his breath for his next question as a higher pitch takes hold of his voice, "Did you happen to notice what kind of vehicle they were driving?"

Benji doesn't have to pause for a second on this question. "Yah, it was some kind of an old beater four-wheeled Jeep."

Jim almost comes off his seat with excitement. He is visibly stunned. "I think we're on to something Benji!"

Not comprehending Jim's new excitement in the least Benji is surprised as well as confused.

Meanwhile Jim's thoughts are toppling one over the other as he grapples with what to do next.

Jim's exhilaration is spilling over to Benji, "You got it figured out Jim?" asks Benji giving voice to his excitement. What he is hoping is that all this excitement means the problem is solved and everything is going to be back to normal very soon.

Jim sees what his excitement is creating in Benji. He doesn't immediately answer Benji's question. In thoughtful silence Jim weighs his choices. He finally opts to include Benji in on his discoveries with the hopes he'll have an ally.

They spend the next hour attempting to put together a comprehensive plan. The envelope also contained instructions about a drop point.

On the other hand, Justin and Levi have abandoned Jim deciding to seek support for a posse made up of church members.

# 29 — MORE ABOUT STOP SIGNS

Morning has arrived for Jacob and Sam. The night went as well as one could imagine. To stay warm they found they needed to huddle together. This was a whole new experience that had not been visited since Sam was a young boy.

Restlessness in such close quarters eventually overtake even the most patient. Being forced to grow accustomed to each other's idiosyncrasies begins almost immediately with even the most routine of life's requirements. Even small things like where they can agree to place their toilet facility is requiring an inordinate amount of discussion. Weaving themselves into each others lives in such close proximity is proving to have its challenges.

Another hour passes, then two. Each is busy with their own thoughts. Every breath, every move they make are the only sounds heard. Jacob is busying himself attempting to style a tin can into a receptacle to catch drinking water. A discarded beer can is fitting the bill.

Sam sits slouched leaning back against a wall opposite his father. He can't help but be aware of Joey's recovered watch as it's the only thing left in his pocket. As he rolls his fingers around it, he feels his jaw twitching, not with anger but with anxiety. The bitter pill he has chosen to swallow is doing all it can to wreak havoc with his emotions leaving him very uncomfortable. The only thing that is immediately in his favor is the dimness of the shaft and his father's poor eyesight to conceal his struggle. "I know without a doubt, You, God, are punishing me for what I did to Joey, but why my father? Dear God, if I've somehow dragged my father into my punishment just take me now. I can't live with that!"

Without notice Sam's mind flashes back to an earlier discussion he had with his father. "How did that go about stop signs?" is the thought he's battling to recall.

Jacob is so far continuing his quest to solve their drinking water problem. It's a business he feels that has a productive purpose and therefore worthy of his time.

Speaking out from his dark corner, Sam questions his father, "Dad I'm trying to remember what you and I were discussing the other day about running stop signs. What was it you said?"

Jacob stops his work long enough to hand Sam a drink of fresh ground water. "Why something about that bothering you, son?"asks Jacob taking a drink from his own can.

"Well, I'm not sure yet, but I think something may have become clearer about it. I remember you putting the question in some odd way of looking at it that I didn't quite understand what you were trying to get at," says Sam barely able to make his father out through the dimness.

Jacob has decided to let Sam try and reconfigure what he believed was said without his interrupting.

"If I remember correctly, you ask me if I found anything to be grateful for after I had successfully run a stop sign or something like that," posed Sam

"That's good enough to get the idea," replies his father.

Sam again attempts to assay his previous reply. "I believe I told you I was grateful that no cop caught me."

"That's what I remember, too," says Jacob now fully engaged.

"I want to add some new light to my answer. I really could get hurt doing stupid things like that. I'm grateful I'm still in one piece."

The walls of their chamber seem to have absorbed Sam's new revelation. The echoless silence left by Sam's "new light" hang in Jacob's thoughts for the moment. Sam, on the other hand, tries to look into his father's face as a child seeking approval. This wait holds him more captive than the steep walls entrenching them.

Hesitantly honoring his son's new revelation, he meets Sam's gaze, darkened as it is. "Good Sam. You're heading in the right direction," says Jacob choosing to give Sam the "atta boy" Sam desperately craves from his father.

"Heading in the right direction? Is that what you just said?" asks Sam sounding even more intent. "You mean there's more?"

"There's always more, Sam," says Jacob with a slight sigh, resuming his water collecting.

As long as Sam can remember, he's tried to make himself look larger in his father's eyes. Even as a young boy he would boast of his abilities hoping his father would be impressed. This conversation is just a continuation of this ongoing confabulation.

Sam has built his character around his attempts to become more blusterous. Jacob, on the other hand, is much less impressed with bluster and more with a quieter integrity. Consequently in contrast, Sam has always remained small.

Self-centered egotists don't usually give up easily and Sam is not the exception. He knows that he's self-centered, but doesn't always view it as a negative. His father has always caused him discomfort. The result has been, more often than not, a displaced anger against this challenger. He's too often of the mind set that his successes gained by his bullying others should account for more than his father allows.

Since his "come to Jesus" meeting during his accident, he's at the very least beginning to permit a second thought to have a place in his thinking. This is proving to be one of those times.

"All right, Dad, I'll stay with it," says Sam dropping his eyes allowing new thoughts to challenge him as his emotions continue their battle. He's discovering the hard way that old resentments don't die easily, that only strength from a Higher Power kills them and even that requires his permission.

Sam slides off his pail to the damp floor, leaning against the rough wall, he toys with a handful of dirt. "Dad do you think we'll get out of this mess?"

Even through the dimness, Sam can feel the intensity of his father's gaze. "I not sure son. It's not in our hands."

These words aren't particularly comforting, but Sam is finding that he's taking comfort in the quiet sturdiness in his father's voice.

As much as Sam wants out of this place he knows it's useless to continue with these thoughts. Instead he begins to study the walls. He notices how they have a slight banana like bend to them. Concluding that the probability of successfully scaling these walls is probably zero, his imagination is devising another scenario.

"Dad, take a look at these walls," says Sam still studying the structure.

Jacob looks up from his water collecting. "I know what you're thinking son, that you can scale these like a climbing wall. It's way too loose and all you'll accomplish is a cave in."

Sam continues to study the walls, especially the part that corresponds with the banana like bend. "That may be the answer, Dad. If we start carefully picking rock and dirt out of this wall," says Sam pointing to its loose corporeity, "We can start a carefully controlled cave-in that we can continue to stand on until it lifts us up out of here."

This proposal has caught Jacob's attention long enough to give it some thought. "It sounds like an idea that may work, but it also sounds like it could be pretty risky." Still wrestling with the whole notion he takes a couple of minutes pulling out small bits of material and watching where they come to rest. "We'll bury our water supply in a hurry..., but then it may be worth a try while we still have the energy."

Sam is surprised to get such a swift consent. He immediately feels around for the broken pick-ax. Using one end as a handle he begins his arduous task.

The sound of falling dirt and stone is both unsettling and hopeful. Within an hour, he has about twelve inches of dirt and rock to stand on. He's slowly but surely beginning to make his way up the wall. With minimal light he's depending as much on his sense of feel as he is his eyesight. The tips of his fingers are numb from digging into the semi-packed walls of this unforgiving grotto. His arms and shoulders are beginning to show fatigue from the overhead work. As always, necessity becomes the mother of invention. Soon they are wetting their undershirts, ripping them into masks, wrapping their nose and mouth to prevent much of the unwanted debris from filling their lungs. Jacob in the meantime, has managed to collect a couple quarts of water, filling every empty can he can scrounge.

Between the two of them, they have managed to keep the dirt in a five-foot pile rather than filling the whole floor. For the time being this tactic is prolonging the water supply located on the opposite side of the trench.

The daylight has once again shifted in favor of darkness. Huddling together for a second night, they lay exhausted both from their digging efforts as well as going a day without food.

The penetrating silence of their prison is suddenly shaken as both are battered awake. Sam is the first to sound the alarm. "CAVE IN! CAVE IN!" he shouts into the darkness, grasping out directionless for his father. All he can feel is a tremendous weight as his brain struggles to catch up with what's happening.

Above the sound of rushing stone and dirt is the clear sound of pain. "AARRGGG." It's the only human vocal sound in this whole dramatic turn of events. A falling forty pound rock has struck Jacob in the shoulder, breaking his collar bone. Both are struggling to their feet and are battling against all this vengeful chamber can propel against them.

Panic enhanced by darkness and confinement is pressing in on them. With the slide subsiding as suddenly as it started, Jacob's pain is on the forefront of his concerns. He can feel the bone trying to press its way through his skin. The only thing filling the air for now is dust.

"Dad, are you okay?" Sam's voice is raspy and rough between sporadic fits of coughing.

"I think something is broke, I can't move my left arm," grunts Jacob, lying back he tries as best he can to find a comfortable spot to rest his arm.

Just as if nothing has happened the whole chamber has returned to its previous silence. As if by some outside force the darkness is abruptly turned to light. The moon is full and orange and its incandescence has found its way into this obscure hole in the ground pouring in its welcomed festival of color and light. Nonetheless, for its inhabitants sleep is fitful for the remainder of the night as hope and doubt continue to trade places.

The morning arrives on schedule. The full outcome of the night's calamitous feature event is bearing witness to itself all around them. What's left is a precarious ledge hanging over them. Their safety is tenuous at best as pieces of debris no longer supported by ground beneath it continues its inability to defy gravity.

Their water supply lies under at least four feet of rubble. Jacob's arm is in constant pain. At the moment he has removed his belt and is fashioning a sling in hopes of relieving some of the pain. In real time the likelihood of facing a day with no food or water only adds to the mental fatigue already facing them.

Beginning to have serious regrets as to the rightness of his now seeming-impetuous effort to free them, Sam sits back against the wall next to his father. Both are silent, lost in their thoughts staring at the blue sky which has opened as a result of the cave in. Neither has made a sound except for the continuous clearing of their throats.

Sam is becoming weary. His outlook is jaded and confused. This is the closest he is coming to crying, but fearful of giving his dreads a platform, he cries out silently, "God have mercy!" It's devoid of any Sunday worship method and without a doubt it's the most heartfelt prayer of surrender he's ever prayed.

Sam finally breaks the silence. With his head braced against the wall, rolling it negatively from side to side he speaks clearly and emphatically, "I can't believe how simple it is."

"How simple what is?" questions his father.

"The stop sign question," returns Sam looking neither right nor left, but lost in the moment, staring straight ahead.

"Oh so you're back on that?" poses Jacob turning so as to give his son a greater degree of his attention.

"I'm not sure I ever left it," says Sam with something between a grunt and a chuckle.

"So what have you come up with?" further questions Jacob.

Sam braces himself with a movement that suggests he's having some sort of epiphany.

"You remember back when you first asked what I was grateful for if I would successfully run a stop sign and I told you it was because I didn't get a ticket and then it later occurred to me that it was because I didn't get hurt," says Sam filtering a handful of dirt through his fingers. "What I've come to realize is that much of my life has been built around fear."

In spite of Jacob's discomfort, Sam's conversation is grabbing his full attention, allowing him to continue uninterrupted.

"This idiotic escapade has brought something to my attention that probably never would have occurred without it. I'm sure the avalanche experience began the process, but this situation has brought it full blown to my attention." Pausing again, Sam searches for the right words.

"When that damnable slide started last night and I couldn't find you, I panicked. Not because I was afraid, rather I feared for you. Up until that moment my fears were centered around losing some possession I had worked for. For the first time I found myself more concerned with you than myself."

Jacob, setting his injury aside, gently slaps Sam with his good arm. "That's amazing Sam!" announces his father.

The satisfaction Sam is undergoing from the gentle "atta boy" smack by his father is dwarfed by the simplicity of this life-changing revelation.

"I'm not sure why all this new light is coming my way now," says Sam in a speculative tone.

A smiling Jacob says, "Oh, I think it's always been there. It's just now that your dirty window's been broken enough to let a little more light through. Darkness, you'll notice, has a way of increasing the size of fears. You see how much they've shrunk? Radiation shrinks the size of all kinds of tumors, including tumors of fearfulness."

Sam is basking in the consolation of these new breakthroughs. "Thank you for being my father and thank you for your patience," he says expressing an unprecedented gratitude.

Jacob slips his arm around his son. "Don't worry. There's more to come"

Sam's hand is fingering his brother's watch. "Yah Dad, I believe it."

# 30 — A JUBILANT DISCOVERY

Dressing quickly, Benji doesn't take the time to shower. He is to meet Jim and the other brothers at the plant. At the recommendation of their Prophet the rest have rejoined themselves to Jim's leadership. The five of them arrive within minutes of each other.

Justin, Levi, and Rup were at first reluctant to have a security guard in charge of their father's recovery, but at the advice of church leaders, Jim Hartman is the best alternative next to getting the authorities involved.

The days and nights are more or less equal this time of the year. Dawn has broken and for this region it's one of those rare September mornings where a south breeze is bringing clear blue skies and warm temperatures.

Jim has been retired from the Fairbanks police department for several years and spent his last few years behind a desk. Nonetheless his knowledge on how to conduct an investigation far exceeds anything the family is capable of.

Quickly bringing everyone up to speed he explains, "We're supposed to make a drop today over on Mastodon Pass. Before we do that I'd like to go over a few other details.

"Benji and I spent yesterday attempting to retrace your Dad and Sam's route. We stopped at several sites, none of them had seen them yet, but were expecting them.

"There's a mine over on Porcupine Ridge that they may have started with. I think we should make a trip over there this morning and check it out before we make any decisions about a drop.

"Benji, you and Rup ride with me. Justin, if you and Levi would watch the main highway for that Jeep. More than likely it will be carrying three men all in their mid-twenties. The most I could get for a license plate was X8; not enough to get an owner and an address. The consensus is that it is more than likely a plate from this area. I suspect that these guys are not going to be the sharpest tool in the shed so if you run across them just keep an eye on them. Get a license number if you can, but do it without making them suspect anything.

"Okay it's 7 am and let's get as much as we can done before we have to seriously consider paying a ransom. If anything breaks, we all have to be available so keep your phones open."

The eager wordless expressions on the faces of this posse exhibits their commitment to this effort. Sitting around waiting is not an option for men like these. The term of their earnestness is driven by a single-minded agreement that they will all work tirelessly to bring home a father and a brother. Within minutes they are in their vehicles making their way to their stations.

The roads can be treacherous year around in these parts. In the winter months they are covered with layers of packed snow making them nearly impassable for anything less than a snowmobile. In the spring everyone battles mud. This time of the year the fall rains can bring about a washout in a matter of hours.

Jim is doing the driving for himself, Benji, and Rup. Without warning he suddenly swings his truck to the left side of the road. It quickly becomes apparent that a large hawk had mindlessly dove at prey on the opposite side of the road. This is evidenced by a thudding sound resonating from the explosion of feathers drifting behind as they continue on down the road.

"Holy shit, whad I just hit?" says Jim trying to shake the image of that poor bird fulminating from the front of his vehicle. "We're damn lucky that little bastard wasn't any bigger or he'd ah had us for lunch."

This brings a laugh at Jim's irony giving each a welcomed moment of comic relief. The intensity of this campaign to find Jacob and Sam has eroded anything resembling recreation so any light moment like this has a direct effect on moods. The somberness is lifting long enough for each to become objective enough to be driven on more by a hope of finding them in time rather than a fear of losing them.

This moment of lightheartedness is true for all except Rup. Being the type of person who's more inclined to try and hide from trouble, he spent the previous night helplessly wringing his hands, worrying about the outcome of this atrocious state of affairs. He is extremely tired and in need of a strength not available through his fellow passengers.

The imagery of his adulterous affair with his stepmother is a vision that continues to convict him over and over along with his concealing his part in Joey's disappearance from his father. It's as though this unrest for his indiscretions is the punishment he'll have to endure for eternity.

"The devil is sure having his way with me," thinks Rup alone in his thoughts.

Many of the roads in these remote areas are kept in repair by the miners themselves. More often than not, they are the principle agents making use of these out lying pathways. Jim's big Ford barely changes it's sonorous hum as it effortlessly conquers even the steepest grades and curves.

It's Rup who all of a sudden recognizes the terrain. "This is where we lost him!" The distress in his voice brings everyone to attention

Benji's head nods in agreement even though he didn't share with Rup and Sam the deceit that went on that day concerning Joey's disappearing, he nonetheless recognizes it as the region where they hunted for his brother.

"Lost who?" questions Jim, slowing his vehicle.

"This is where we lost Joey," adds Rup as his thoughts shoot through his mind of that early spring day. Without thought his eyes dart to that mine opening barely visible above the road. Almost simultaneously these same darting eyes catch sight of something very familiar along the road.

"STOP, STOP!" he shouts at the same time beginning to exit the still moving truck. On a full run he's to the side of the road. There close to the ground and caught in some brush overgrown with weeds is a visable distinct gold patch on the front of a black hat reading "Mueller and Sons Smelting."

Rup's heart is racing at the prospect this discovery will bring. "This is Sam's hat," he shouts. His eyes and body are moving in concert as he turns, leaving the road to a trail concealed by outcroppings of rock and scrub brush.

By this time, Jim has parked along side of the road. He and Benji are giving him their full attention despite not knowing where he is leading them. Rup in the meantime is scrambling up the trail like a man immersed in an undertaking knowing exactly what he's about.

Jim and Benji have caught up to Rup. They pause long enough to pay attention to Rup's frantic hand gestures pointing at the trail. There before them, distinct in the soft dirt on the trail lie a flurry of confused boot prints. The ones that immediately catch Jim's eye are the notched-heel impressions.

They all display a helter-skelter, chaotic, out-of-step struggle. Some look to be made by someone pushed or dragged.

Rup is still leading the way, charging up the slight incline to an all-too-familiar dense outcropping of brush on the side of the unwelcoming hole. As devastating as this experience is, his eyes sweep every memorable incident this location holds for him. The same small budding tree that he tied Joey's escape rope to is now beginning to turn its leaves to a fall yellow.

Jim and Benji, for the time being, are content to be followers. It's becoming obvious to them that for some unknown reason Rup is very familiar with this old mine shaft.

The footprints all stop precisely at the opening. It's very, very apparent with all the disturbed ground giving evidence of a struggle, that something ended here. Stopping for only the briefest second, all three of them are now on the same page.

Rup is the first to break the pause. "Dad, Sam are you down there?" Not waiting for an answer, he impetuously continues his shout. "Hello, hello are you down there?"

Immediately, over the top of Rup's shouting, excited voices in unison lift up from the pit. "Yes, yes we're down here!"

Simultaneously, both groups celebrate the moment with a jubilant embrace.

It's taken only a few minutes to assess the situation. "We need rope and a fifty-foot ladder," come the instructions from below.

Quickly taking the lead on this, Benji drives the mile down the gorge to a working claim, borrowing a rope and a ladder. In less than half an hour he's back. They lower the rope securing it to the same tree Rup had used for Joey.

Benji being the youngest and the most agile makes his way down the shaft only carrying a flashlight. He soon finds himself at the point where the cave in undercut the wall.

"Don't come any further, son. If you drop a ladder we can climb to where you are," says Jacob staring up at the most wonderful face of his savior.

"No Dad. I need to come the whole way," comes back the voice of his youngest son.

Within the hour they have made all the necessary preparations and have, despite Jacob's injury, managed to get both out safely.

The jubilation is quick and intense as a wave of emotion overtakes them. All realize there is much more to do and getting these two home is a first priority. The recall of Justin and Levi has quickly gone out along with notification to meet at Lena's.

Within the hour they are gathered reviewing the next phase of this travesty.

# 31 — THE ABDUCTORS

The toughest part for the family is behind them now that Jacob and Sam are safe at home. A lot has been explained about their abduction but a future with these thugs continues to loom over them. Rup had spent the day before preparing the ransom, but the setup has drastically changed.

Jim Hartman is still the de facto leader, but willing to abdicate now that the family is reunited. "We have a few important things we need to discuss. Jacob, I work for you. My only objective was to get you and Sam back home safely. The authorities were never brought into this because I know how your family feels about any type of government intrusion.

"Of course, the ransom will never be paid, but the question as to what to do with these three men that kidnapped you still remains."

Standing at the back of the room are Levi and Justin. They share a silent glance, knowing their father well enough to already be aware of the answer to that question.

Sitting comfortably with his arm in a sling, Jacob pauses long enough to give the question more than a trite reply. "I believe we should be done with this. Any reprisals on our part will only be viewed as vigilantism and bring the law in."

Sam, on the other hand is wrestling with his father's decision. After having a summer of sharing these differing encounters with him, he's still finding it very difficult to abide with anyone who is so evil as to inflict the kind of pain these men demonstrated toward his family. In Sam's eyes this wrong must be punished.

Jim carefully weaves Jacob through the labyrinth these men had devised for the payoff. How the drop off was to be in an area not familiar to them in an old hunting blind.

"What do you suppose will happen when they discover there is going to be no pay off?" asks Levi.

"My experience with these ruthless types is that when they discover they've been stiffed it won't rest as easy with them as with us. As much as I'd prefer to be finished with this business, I don't believe they will. They probably aren't aware of this latest development and are greedily looking forward to their payoff later today," says Jim.

"Well for me, I sure as hell don't think we should just let these slime-balls walk away," declares Justin. He and Levi, even as children, have shared a more ruthless reaction to wrongs perpetrated by outside forces. To the two of them, all this talk is just wasting time. They have bonded together over the years in such a way that in almost everything they do, they have almost a telepathy between themselves.

Glancing at one another once more the pair know that between them they have no intentions of letting these guys off the hook.

Before anyone realizes, they have slipped unnoticed out the door. Making their way back home, they make preparations, arming themselves with rope, duct tape, food, water, a couple of bed rolls and two pair of binoculars.

"I know damn well where we'll find these scumbags," says Justin.

"If you're thinkin' what I'm thinkin', when they figure out they ain't get-ting' paid, they'll come back to the mine to check on their quarry," says Levi.

"You've read my mind little brother. We can get over there while these idiots are waiting for their drop," says Justin.

They are about ten miles from the mine shaft. With the self-assurance that they will see justice dispensed, they set out to bring this to fruition.

These two seasoned hunters know about every road, lumber road, or miner's road in the region. Even if these malefactors are from around the area, they will be hard put to equal the hunting skills of these two brothers.

They've decided to drive their big GMC. It's painted with a camou-flage design and stenciled across the windshield are the words "AMBUSH WAGON." This hardy vehicle has poked its way through every hill and ravine in the county. It's not their everyday vehicle which adds to their chances of remaining anonymous if they should encounter the trio.

It's only noon when Justin and Levi arrive at the old mine. The drop point is nearly twenty miles from them. Allowing for the trio's agitation level to rise after realizing their efforts have been thwarted, eventually obliging them to check on their captives, the brothers feel they have an advantage of at least several hours.

Across the road from the location of the mine is a two-track trail. Years ago it was cut in the hill by a lumber company, but now it's used by hunters and snow mobilers. It has no name and doesn't appear on any map.

Looking the location over Justin makes an observation. "I think it's dense enough that we can back up in there unseen and still see everything that comes up or down this road."

Agreeing with his brother, Levi says, "I doubt they'll be too careful. From Jim's and Benji's description, they don't sound like the brightest bulbs in the closet. I doubt they have any idea that we're on to them."

The two brothers assign themselves to the task of waiting. In many of life's day-to-day situations they often appear to be impetuous. But in hunting, they display the patience of a sniper. They are fully capable of turning tables on these would-be hunters so that they discover they are now the hunted.

A few vehicles drive by as the afternoon wanes, none of them fit the description of their target and more than likely have something to do with the mine operation down the road. Their focus remains such that hours go by without a word spoken between themselves. Occasionally a head gesture or a slight hand signal suffices.

With darkness only an hour away, suddenly, and in unison, Levy's head and hand pose a straight ahead gesture along with the word, "There!"

Creeping along the road is the long awaited Jeep. Justin has snapped up a pair of field glasses and is focusing in on their mark.

"There's three of 'em all right and I'll bet it's the three we're waiting for. I knew these bastards would be back."

With the predatory instincts of men whose lives depend on such inherent aptitudes, they analyze everything they can about these strangers.

The Jeep's occupants are definitely trying to be cautious. They drive past the mine by a quarter mile, turn around and drive slowly by in the opposite direction. They appear to be carefully surveying the area. One more pass satisfies their cautiousness as they park directly across from Justin and Levi, in front of the mine.

Justin's binoculars are bringing life to their every move. Their heads bob around anxiously as they look for phantom observers. He can see the whiskey bottle passed from man to man and their compulsive smoking as they nervously try to determine their next move.

After sitting there long enough to convince themselves that they are alone, they exit the Jeep and make their way to the path above leading to the mine's opening. Having barely reached sight of the opening, they catch sight of the ladder and ropes still strewn around haphazardly. This is enough to cause them to bolt like scalded dogs, stumbling over one another down to their waiting Jeep.

In their preoccupation with getting to the mine they hadn't noticed until now that Justin has pulled his huge "AMBUSH WAGON" directly in back of them. All three of them stop in their tracks, obviously stunned at their unfolding predicament. There is not the slightest hint that these three are going to do anything other than attempt an escape.

Stumbling, lurching, and tripping, they manage to fall into the Jeep, spewing gravel behind it as it haphazardly propels its anxious cargo forward. Dusk is intensifying the bright Halogen high-beams directly behind them further intimidating their flight.

It would be an easy task to overtake them if it were not for the driver's weaving from one side of the road to the other. These roads were cut out of the wilderness more for convenience rather than safety with no guardrails. The paths wind through rolling foothills of a mountain range, putting at risk even the most capable driver. The ravines are straight down several hundred feet of jagged rock. Justin and Levi know these roads like the back of their hand.

Justin is steadily increasing their speed forcing their opponents to do the same or risk being overtaken. It's becoming apparent that the opposing driver is far from being a brilliant motorized technician. His increased speed and continuous swaying has increased the frequency of his vehicle nearly sliding out of control. The bright headlights from the GMC reveal the frenzy in which these three have now found themselves. Every pothole sends them flying off their seat as their tires go airborne.

The roar of the engines echoing off the canyon walls warn anything that wishes to live to get out of their path. The danger is far from exaggerated. There would be absolute carnage should another vehicle come around one of the many blind turns. On some of the straightaways speeds are reaching nearly 80 miles per hour with neither party willing to relinquish. These back roads are not paved and none of the hairpin curves are marked. The dust is billowing out behind this procession creating a jet-like plume. Justin is focused ahead solely on a pair of red tail lights, positioning himself only inches behind forcing the other driver to ever continue to increase his speed.

At this point they are traveling a road that parallels a river. They rip past a thick stand of willows, not permitting the river to be seen from the road, onto a gradual grade that soon rises above the tree line giving way to a rocky outcropping, leaving the river far below.

Justin knows this spot very well. The Jeep is beginning to struggle against the incline causing it to slow considerably. As if on cue, Justin drops the truck into a lower gear and presses the accelerator to the floor. The big Suburban lunges forward, slamming its sturdy push bar into the rear of the Jeep and pushing it easily the rest of the way up the incline. The Jeep's driver is visibly shaken along with his passengers as they try to recover from the whiplash created from this unsuspected rear-end collision.

Justin is propelling them faster and faster up the hill. The Jeep's brakes are burning out as the driver attempts to slow the vehicle. This conveyance is totally out of control with burned out brakes and now a blown front tire.

Unbeknownst to this carload of apostates the top of the road has a quick left turn away from the steep gorge leading down to the river. Justin maneuvers the hard left and stops, leaving the Jeep to hurl off the edge of the rocky precipice. It's silently airborne for what must have felt like an eternity before gravity brings it crashing into the side of the rocks. The rest of the way to the river results in a series of end over end flips, finally plunging into the cold, swift current only to sink out of sight.

The two brothers stand on the rim staring down at a very peaceful scene. The visual image of this event is already lost in the past never to be viewed again. The sun is leaving a very beautiful red glow in the western horizon.

"Red sky in the morning, sailors take warning. Red sky at night, sailors delight," they recite in unison. Giving each other a high five, Justin adds, "It's going to be a great day tomorrow." They return home satisfied that nothing has been left undone.

The next morning the whole crew is back at the plant. Jacob is anxious to have his life return to a manageable hum rather than the roar with which it's been coming at him most of this year.

Jim has hesitantly acquiesced to Jacob's insistence that they neither involve the authorities nor seek revenge. All in all the whole family is adjusting. Wisely deciding to keep their actions between the two if them, Justin and Levi also make adjustments along with everyone else.

# 32 — ELK RAPIDS

Not to disappoint, Joey is becoming the asset Amzlov had known him to be all along.

"Zeez Mr. Joey, he a natural. He gotz more brain een little finger zan zome gotz in whole head," brags Amzlov.

It seems as though the winter had come on a bit faster last year, but then there are always those who aren't prepared the morning it shows up. All of the Amzlov mining enterprises slow to a mere skeleton crew during this time of year. Joey took this opportunity to pour over every aspect of Amzlov's records from quality control to financials. By this spring he has acquainted himself with every aspect of the business.

He's proving to be an inspiration to those who are having to relinquish their former familiar systems and adapt to his suggestions. He's gained the same respect and dignity back that he's conferred to those who have no other choices other than to follow his leadership.

"I've never experienced working with anyone as perceptive as this man. He's going to save us a lot of money," is the perception of a diamond mine manager. Of course Amzlov can't be happier.

"Zeez guy geev me time go fishing," laughs a satisfied Amzlov.

It's a fine spring day for Alaska. The lower 48 are sharing warm southerly breezes bringing the spring temperatures to a comfortable seventy degrees. Joey has finished his breakfast and has made a decision to take full advantage of such a rare day. He's going to do a bit of outdoor exploration.

Not only does Amzlov have a love affair with automobiles, he also has a full stable of horses. Thoroughbreds, Quarter horses, and Arabians to name a few.

Charlie Greer has managed this equestrian herd for years. He's the breeder, vet, bronc-buster and all around trainer.

Carrie is off from college enjoying her spring break. She too is more than ready to get away from the mundane rigors of a winter indoors.

Spontaneously, they have together shown up at the stables, both primed for some outdoor action. So far there have been some time constraints on them becoming better acquainted. This is proving to be an exceptional moment for them both.

"Well, good morning, Carrie. You look fantastic this morning. It's good to see you," says Joey grinning like a Cheshire cat.

Equally surprised, Carrie unconsciously toys with her hair. "I might say the same for you. I understand from my father that you are doing a great job," responds Carrie still fussing with her hair.

Attempting to downplay his importance, he replies, "I hope so. Your father wouldn't put up with anything less. You planning a ride?"

Charlie is standing patiently by staring at both, waiting for some indication of what they have in mind for him to do.

"Yes, I think I'm going to take a ride up river to Elk Rapids," determines Carrie with a tone of finality, and still self-conscious over her appearance.

"I'm not real familiar with the area yet. Mind if I tag along?" inquires Joey. Their eyes fumble around until they meet just long enough to have that uncomfortable feeling of trespassing. Embarrassed, both quickly look away.

Trying her best to remain demur, Carrie extends a slight nod in his direction. "I welcome the company," she says with a forced forbearance.

Charlie takes this as his cue. "How about I saddle a couple of Quarter horses? I think they'll be more sure-footed along that trail."

The day is young. Carrie and Joey try their best to conceal any overt excitement for what being together for a day could bring.

Charlie saddles Big Red for Joey. "This one look all right to you?" questions Charlie as he brings the horse around for Joey's inspection.

Joey surveys Charlie's choice for a moment. He has no specific memory of a riding event, but has some recall as to its nature. "Yah, I believe you made a good choice, Charlie," says Joey massaging the side of the horse's bridled face. The horse in turn gives Joey a knowing eye, sizing him up as well.

"He's a good strong fella, but you gotta let him know right off who's in charge," adds Charlie. Turning to Carrie, Charlie's sporting a big wide knowing grin, "I got 'Lil Darlin' out for you, Carrie. I remember how well you and that horse get along." Charlie had also taught her how to ride when she was just a small child.

"Thanks, Charlie. You're right. That horse and I've been buddies since I was a little girl," she says continuing to stroke his long, shaggy mane.

Charlie follows Carrie into the tack-room, watching as she fills a saddle bag with energy bars and a full canteen.

"If you folks ride up river pay close attention to the water. The current's faster 'an hell this time of year with all that ice and snow melting above the falls." It's Charlie's fatherly way he still deals with Carrie.

"You're as bad as my Dad, Charlie. Neither of you want to admit I've passed my twelveth birthday," says Carrie.

Charlie merely gives her an affable smile. "Carrie darlin', even if you double that, I've got boots that old," he adds.

"OAGgggggaaa, you're impossible," replies Carrie as she turns and walks back to her horse.

Joey has taken a silent back seat to all this good-natured bantering, but not to attending to a full canteen, a handful of energy bars, a holstered .45 Colt revolver along with a buck knife and a hand full of extra cartridges.

In deference to Carrie's self-proclaimed emancipation, Charlie doesn't want to push too hard against her plans for the day, but he has some serious misgivings about her planned field day, especially for this time of year. With Carrie out of hearing range, Charlie takes this opportunity to spend a moment in private with Joey.

Quickly turning his attention to this outing. "Keep an eye on her. She can be foolhardy." The apprehension in his voice is apparent.

Having finished with her saddlebags, Carrie returns. She has a somewhat smoldering look about her. Suspicious that there's some 'man talk' going on behind her back, she links her arm through Joey's giving him a light tug. "Yes, Joey, in spite of what Charlie may be telling you, I am a big girl now. Let's get on the trail."

In an impromptu move, she pulls her hair back into a ponytail, further accentuating her angular neck and back. The breeze is causing her hair to blow across his face. It has the sweet smell of lilac as it caresses his skin.

Nervousness causes him to clear his throat. "Okay. We can leave anytime you wish."

In another swift move, she mounts her horse, turns toward the trail, leaving Joey the option of catching up or being left to himself for the day.

Charlie still has the same nervous look. He remains skeptical about this trip. He feels predisposed to give Joey one last piece of advise. "She can be a handful. Don't let her talk you into anything foolish." Joey touches the brim of his hat with a slight nod of the head as he acknowledges Charlie's concern.

His heart and mind are already at logger-heads. His horse is far from being warmed up and against his better judgement, he kicks him to a full gallop hoping to overtake this elusive date. Her compelling beauty and her open desire to be with him has completely befuddled him. A sensible head quickly seizes him compelling him to pull back on the reins, slowing his steed to a healthy trot. He can readily observe her horse's hoof prints in the thawing ground allowing him to easily track her.

The aspens are shaking their winter bareness and giving birth to spring buds as they paint a beautiful pastel composition of pale yellows, greens, and whites.

A simple pleasure surges through him triggered by the splendor of his surroundings. As he continues to barely trot his horse, he can feel the sun's warmth not only on his skin, but also on his spirit. All this is causing his thoughts to drift around some. "I know everything happening to me is taking me in a direction that feels right, but I also get the sense that there's more to this than I know. Something is missing. I just can't put my finger on it."

The sky remains cloudless and his horse is enjoying the pace. He's also hoping that Carrie will suddenly appear on the trail.

Without warning, he feels the harshness of some foreign physical object suddenly enveloping him along with a shriek of female laughter. Out of nowhere, she has thrown a lasso around him forcing him to bring his horse to an immediate halt or risk being pulled off its back.

"What the...!" is all that spontaneously enters his mind. She had laid in wait behind a large boulder and roped him as he rode by. Joey remains terrified for the moment and not at all sure what is happening.

Carrie, in turn, continues to laugh as she applies even more tension on the rope. "Goin' somewhere cowboy?" says Carrie in her best attempt at a John Wayne imitation.

As quickly as the terror had overtaken him, the irony of it follows and he too begins to laugh. "Charlie warned me to keep an eye on you," says Joey, still chuckling as he clumsily pulls the loop back over his head.

"That old geezer! Wha'd he tell you?" interrogates Carrie trying to give him a hand.

"He said you were full of piss and vinegar," returns Joey handing her his end of the rope.

Musing over this for a moment, she gives her butt a defiant little twitch as she returns her rope to her saddle horn.

"If it were up to my Dad or Charlie, I'd still be in a little sundress playing with Barbies," she adds.

"I think you'd look just as perky," says Joey mockingly agreeing in a back-handed attempt at humor.

Her eyes dart, hurling a mutinous, non-compliant glance without the slightest hint she is about to discontinue her diatribe. "Hell will freeze over first," she says defiantly throwing her leg over her saddle. Mounted and far from defeated, she has no problem leading out once again.

With Carrie well out of earshot, Joey feels safe enough to voice his own afterthought, "That apple didn't fall far from the tree."

For the moment Joey's impulse is to follow her lead. As much as he may not want to admit it, he finds her tenacity titillating. She is definitely her father's daughter. Amzlov teasingly made the observation, "She too young go avway leeve, to old leeve vwis mommy and me."

Joey is willing to set aside his inclination to be in charge, as long as she has something she is skilled in leading. For the time being, he's satisfied just viewing all the crooks and crannies of her personality, besides he finds her enthusiasm alluring.

"Hey don't be in such a hurry," he shouts at Carrie as she forges ahead. He's getting the feeling she's purposely trying to keep him on edge.

"Keep up or go home," she challenges. In her own way, she is also studying her date. Her taunts are her way of throwing her entire personality at him. She finds him handsome, but there's plenty of pretty faces available.

She imagines that he must have some kind of strength of character in order to catch her father's attention. Her hope is that he will prove himself to be what she is imagining him to be. "Please don't cave in on me. I hope you're all I think you are," she confides to herself.

"She glances back noticing he's not putting his all into keeping up. He also has that annoying, but cute smirk that suggests he may not be willing to play along with her game plan. She's not real sure how she should react. The last thing she wants from him is to only be seen as the cute little girl in the sundress, but by the same token she doesn't want to come across as a pushy, bossy type.

Seeing this as a time to switch strategies she condescends, "Okay, Okay I'll slow down for you."

She has had several boyfriends since high school, never anyone she would consider as "serious." At this stage of her life she is looking for something more than just someone to date on a weekend. For the most part she has outgrown her suitors. They find her beautiful. She finds them shallow and incapable of being more than a simple Friday night wonder.

Not exactly sure what it is that she's looking for in a man, she doesn't hesitate to cast those aside she finds objectionable. Her thoughts continue as they resolve to ride side by side.

Of course, to say that Joey is merely struck with Carrie's physical beauty would be to understate how her energy and spontaneity are impressing him. Nonetheless, he finds himself ever so cautiously fixing his eyes on her physical attributes as the last thing he wants is to be discovered leering.

"Okay, Carrie no more games. Let's just enjoy the day and get to know one another," says Joey as forthright as he can be.

His quiet approach is disarming. Carrie is giving second thoughts to her original "competitive" plan of attack. What is becoming apparent is that this man is unabashedly transparent and candid. The only thing about him that remains hidden is his past and that remains hidden even to himself.

Within a few hours they reach the falls the natives refer to as Elk Rapids. It's a place where the river is separated by a steep cascade of water tumbling down from from melting deposits of winter ice and snow. The river has become a boiling, churning current that is carrying huge ice floes that begin breaking up along with the rising temperatures of spring. The river has already risen some ten feet above normal levels with the continuing threat of rising even higher.

Pointing to the only flat spot this piece of ground has provided, Joey suggests they stop and let the horses graze on the new spring grass. It appears that the water has done little to tame this rugged terrain. There is a trail that leads up the side of this staircase of water falls. Each level rises approximately twenty feet until it reaches a 100 feet to the upper portion of the river. It's a rugged yet beautiful in a way that humans, with all our cleverness, have never been able to duplicate.

The horses whiny, bobbing their heads and stamping a front foot. "They're acting like we got a mountain lion somewhere close by," says Carrie first turning in one direction then another as she continues to remove their saddles and blankets.

"Yah, something's sure spookin' 'em," agrees Joey all the while fingering his Colt.

Still keeping a wary eye, Carrie wraps the center portion of her rope around an aspen so each end can serve as a lead for each horse.

"If it were a cat, these horses would be long gone," surmises Carrie.

"You're probably right. Somethin' else is spookin' 'em," admits Joey cautiously looking around with pistol in hand.

The horses continue their vigil, ears back and eyes heedfully reconnoitering the area. Their grazing is nervous at best.

Satisfied for the time being that they don't have an impending emergency, Carrie and Joey turn their attention back on one another. Each are on their best behavior trying to do something courteous for the other.

Determined to put his best foot forward, Joey has taken it upon himself to arrange the saddles in such a way that they can double as a chair.

"Would you like some of my peanut butter power bar, Joey?" she asks while charmingly tossing her pony tail with her every move.

Joey is nervously toying with the brim of his western- styled hat, tilting first forward against the sun then uneasily tilts it on the back of his head.

"I appreciate the offer Carrie and I'm more than willing to share with you a few chocolate chips from Charlie's private stash."

Their hands brush each other as they playfully exchange cereal bars. Hardly noticing they've eaten, they continue their lighthearted frivolity.

In an attempt to continue her ever-growing fascination with this mystifying strange man, she initiates some chit-chat. "How do you like working for my father?"

Joey's face shifts from carefree to dead serious and without a moment's hesitation he says, "Your father has given me an opportunity where others would have run the other way. For that I will be forever grateful."

Carrie listens to this unrehearsed testimony with interest. "Of course, I've known my father my entire life. He's yet to come up with something that doesn't surprise me. My father's life has always been driven by his passions and many times it gets driven into the lives of other—like it has your life," she says.

"I have to believe that somewhere in my past I must have done similar work. Your father has provided me the opportunity to regain a vitality and enthusiasm I must have enjoyed somewhere back there."

Carrie is listening not only with her ears, but also with her heart. "I have to admit that since I've gotten older that I'm beginning to appreciate my parents more. I mean my mother acts like a whacked out nun most of the time, but I can't help but admire her values and Dad would do any-thing for our family."

Listening to Carrie, Joey can't help but sense a longing within himself for a similar family experience. This yearning serves as a landmark to him for something he believes he once had but has now lost. This awareness prompts him to say, "I'm ashamed of my envy for the family you have. My mind aches when I try to bring any such memories to the forefront." His eyes have taken on a new sadness, dropping them as if in search of something that has fallen out of sight.

Carrie gives his insight a few seconds consideration before revealing her own. "It's just been recently that I've begun to appreciate my parents. I see where I've been pretty self-absorbed most of my life. It frightened me a lot when that drunk guy at the hotel threatened my Dad. It made me think that someday they aren't going to be here." She pauses getting one of life's "hmm" moments and then hesitatingly adds, "I too will have to learn to live without my family."

"I remember last year at this time when I was living in the woods. Every day I spent concerned with how I was going to survive. Then an old feral dog came into my life. I soon found myself beginning to show more concern for that mangy ole critter than I did for myself. I think I could have given my life for that dirty cur — I mean that was the closest thing I had to a family."

The two of them have become so lost in one another that they've forgotten time. It's at least a two-hour ride back to SVOBODA. Along with the horses continuing strange behavior and the advanced hour Joey concludes, "These horses haven't really settled down much this afternoon. I think we should start to pack up and head home."

Carrie replies by making excuses for her horses, "Oh they're probably reacting to having been cooped up all winter. After all this is the first time they've been ridden since last fall." With that settled she unties them as Joey brings both their saddles.

Suddenly with no warning from seven stories up comes a thundering CRAAACK. Both their heads almost separate from their necks as they snap upward long enough to see a cascade of water carrying huge, thick pieces of tumbling ice beginning to charge its way down the staircase of waterfalls.

Joey leaps toward Carrie grabbing her around the waist, jerking her out of the way of a two-ton chunk of ice bouncing less than ten feet from them on its way to a lower energy level followed by a surge of backed up water.

His adrenalin is supplying him with strength of several men. Carrie, on the other hand finds herself paralyzed, not by fear but rather the sudden confusion that's burst upon them. Not having her immediate wits about her, she willingly surrenders to Joey's rescuing effort.

Joey has whipped her up into his arms, carrying her up twenty feet to the next plateau just as the another ice dam holding back a palisade of ice and water breaks. It's a form of raw power that is not deferential as to who or what may be in its path.

The untroubled landscape has been instantaneously transformed from a friendly pastoral setting to a sea of foam, mist, fog, and plowing shards of broken ice. It's as though the force of the whole planet has turned against them.

The horses are nowhere to be seen. The very spot they had been grazing only minutes ago is swollen with broken pieces of trees bobbing aimlessly in the twisting current.

The temperatures have dropped in favor of the dominating ambiance of the icy waters. Carrie is still clutching the horse blanket she was holding when Joey grabbed her. It's rough texture is gladly overlooked for the immediate warmth it's providing.

Joey's eyes dart from one concern to another. He sees danger below and above. Staying put is not an option.

"Carrie, are you all right?" shouts Joey above the raging torrent.

"I think I'm okay," returns Carrie.

"We're going to have to climb out of here. It's way too dangerous with the ice breaking down on us to stay at this level. Here take my hand, I'll get us out of here."

At this point she willingly submits to his lead. As her body and mind are finding a path to bring them together again, she suddenly remembers a major concern. Her look of despair cannot be mistaken. Breaking loose from Joey's grasp, eyes desperately searching the turmoil below.

"The horses! What happened to the horses?"

Joey is taken back by her sudden concern for the horses at the expense of her own safety. Realizing they are going nowhere until that question is satisfied, he surmises, "I honestly can't say for certain. I suspect they got swept away, but I'm sure they're hardy enough to swim ashore at some point."

Meanwhile, Joey continues to see the falls widening its borders making allowances for the extra overflow. In this case the danger is more than imminent as another large chunk of ice bounces past them. This disaster is proving to be truly of epic proportions. It's showing no mercy to anyone or anything in it's path.

Fully aware that the spot they are standing on is about to change, a move has to be made. Shouting above the ever-increasing rage, Joey dictates a command, "Grab my hand, Carrie. We have to get out of here now!" He pulls her up the precarious rocky precipice with only the protection angels can supply.

At last they manage to reach the crest. Exhausted, they seat themselves on a fallen tree trunk well above the rampage. What becomes evident makes them ever more grateful. Pack ice had begun to clog the narrow mouth leading to the falls creating a huge dam. What they managed to survive was the force of the water behind the dam finally breaching and creating all the havoc as it slid toward them at the bottom of the falls. This phenomenon is certainly an example of nature's treachery.

Silence, or at least the lack of the fall's overpowering roar, is the first sensation of which both become aware. Lost for words, they give themselves the next few minutes to reflect on the past life changing fifteen minutes.

Still grasping the horse blanket close to her breast, the reality of what they have survived suddenly makes an impact on her whole body as she begins to tremble, followed by a bursts of tears.

Discovering that he's been hurled into this sort of difficulty is not a new experience for Joey. He readily transitions back into an old, familiar survival mode.

Carrie on the other hand is tossed outside her comfort level. "What the hell do we do now?" There is a marked signal of bewilderment in this question. She is demonstrating a characteristic of which he has yet to take note. It's a beleaguered appearance.

Not at all out of his element, Joey responds with a focus she has yet to observe in him. "We are going to do the next right thing," he says with a little wry, but assuring grin. It's the only reassuring moment she's had in this whole trial by ordeal.

The beach is littered with the tangled debris of old dead trees, and tree branches, not to mention the ubiquitous supply of cast off plastic bottles. What catches Joey's eye is a rusted antiquated flashlight. He can't believe his eyes. "Whoopty-do," is his singular exclamation.

Carrie is looking on with a curious facial expression. "Whoopty-do, what?" is her only reaction.

"Look at this old thing," he says, tapping the rusted screw on portion holding the lens against a rock.

Carrie is looking, but only sees an old rusted piece of junk. Meanwhile, in spite of the sun's warmth, she gives a little shiver through her damp clothing. It's a small remaining reminder of her recent jeopardy. Happy that she had the presence of mind to hang on to her horse blanket, she throws it over her shoulders.

Joey continues with his soliloquizing making more of his "whoopty-do" noises. Along with his continued fanfare, Carrie is given pause as she notes smoke wafting over his hunched body.

"How'd you do that?" she exclaims with the excitement of one watching a magician's demonstration.

"This old lens is convex," says Joey as though this statement is more than enough explanation.

"So?" is Carrie's frustrated rejoinder.

"So...if I angle it toward the sun like this, I can start a fire," he says as he demonstrates on some dry grasses.

"How'd you ever know how to do that?" asks Carrie with a truly puzzled demeanor.

Joey pauses for a moment. A visible look of frustration abruptly replaces his enthusiasm. "I don't know!" is all he expresses, silently turning back to his fire tending.

Carrie realizes she has hit a touchy spot. Hoping to redeem herself she asks, "I'm sorry Joey, I keep forgetting. What can I do to help?"

Joey has a moment to reflect on his response. "I'm sorry. I didn't mean to snap at you. I hope I didn't hurt your feelings. I just get frustrated over this damn amnesia." There is a tinge of remorse in his eyes.

Taken back for the present moment, not used to the males in her life so quick to apologize, she is pleasantly surprised. "Apology accepted," says a smiling Carrie, jutting her hand in the air to promote a high-five gesture.

With the air cleared, Carrie starts a new page. "So...Mr. Joey, what's our 'next right' move?"asks a much more relaxed Carrie.

Looking at his watch with one eye and the other at the sun, Joey surmises, "We only have an hour before sunset. Let's take stock of what we have to get us through the night." Emptying his pockets on the ground reveals a half dozen energy bars. Through all the ruckus he managed to maintain his half-full canteen still strapped across his shoulders, a buck-knife and .45 Colt belted around his waist, a handful of cartridges and a packet of wet matches.

Carrie looks on sheepishly as she reveals she has absolutely nothing to contribute. Her pockets are totally empty. She keeps them that way so as not to add any unnecessary bulges to her figure. Her energy bars, her canteen, and her cellphone were all swept away.

"Looks as though I'm destined to die of hunger and thirst," says Carrie feigning desperation.

"There are probably a few surprises waiting for you in this predicament, but starvation and dehydration are not any of them," says Joey holding the unscathed victuals of energy bars and a canteen of fresh water. "Besides, we're only ten miles from home. With a little luck we can walk that tomorrow," adds Joey.

Carrie is somewhat taken back by Joey's seeming quick adaptation to their plight. Up until this point in her life, this kind of situation was only a chapter in an adventure novel or a segment in reality TV. Today it's become the real thing.

"You seem to know what to do out here. I'm surprised. It's like you've done this before. Anyway, I find it comforting," says a more subdued Carrie.

Joey listens to her with a steady, intent gaze as much of his life a year ago becomes a life-size memory. Not wanting to get into a deep revelation concerning his past, he is content to let it wait until another time.

"Yah, I've spent a little time outdoors," says Joey satisfied he's said enough for the time being and at the same time surveying the skies "but right now we have to find a shelter. I'm sure after a warm day like this, especially this early in the spring, we'll get some rain through the night."

Carrie listens to Joey's calm assurances that everything is manageable, letting it chip a way at her fears and doubts. Considering that she has spent far less time with him than many of her other suitors, she finds his openness a refreshing mystery. She is discovering that she can't expect Joey's emotional reactions to conform to the less acceptable standard she has experienced with other males. Thus far he's demonstrating that he is in a class by himself. She's finding that with Joey as a safety net, she has the luxury of relaxing and permitting this to become an adventure.

"Tell me what I need to be doing. I want to be a help not a liability," says a much more animated Carrie.

He's taken by her prompt willingness to adapt and overcome her fears. "Good, good," says Joey excited to share a common goal with her. "Let's get this fire out then we can search for something with a roof over it."

Shortly they are off exploring their options. "Keep your eyes open for an overhanging ledge or a cave," directs Joey, pausing for a moment before he adds with a grin, "I prefer a ledge. This time of year bears are emerging from their winter naps. Caves are often their economic choice. When they emerge they're hungry and not too fussy what they eat."

"Oh thanks, Joey that's real comforting," says Carrie. The sarcasm can't be missed.

Studying her concern for a second, he replies, "We have to remember that the wildlife is full-time out here and that we're only part-time. They're very wary of part-time intruders, so the more we're aware of their rules the fewer unnecessary confrontations we'll have."

Joey is enjoying her seeming dependence as well as her independence. Carrie can easily switch from a dependent girly girl to an independent, active outdoor type, but in neither case she is able to set aside her natural attractiveness. Her honest unaffected movements have been known to dull the senses of many otherwise reasonable men.

Joey is certainly not clear of her bewitching qualities anymore than other men, but at least for the moment these feelings must be set aside for the greater good of finding shelter.

The river has subsided some ten feet from the high-water mark along its banks already. The shoreline is littered with almost as much man-made material as nature has provided. The river has a series of flood seasons seemingly to discharge its gorging of plastic bottles; fish line; lures; life jackets; various qualities of ropes; a single shoe; and various articles of twisted clothing half buried in the sand.

But on a sweeter side, it's quiet enough to hear the melodious song of the river as well as the mating call of nesting birds. It's now late afternoon with the sky displaying a deep purple to gray. Perhaps the storms are not too far off.

They have traveled about a half mile upriver all the while keeping a keen eye open for anything remotely inviting enough for even one night.

Before abandoning their fire, Joey had lit a small bundle of dried and green sticks which he's carrying in hopes of using it as a starter for a more permanent fire.

The banks are thick with foliage. Carrie's eyes are more alert for anything that may move rather than in finding shelter. Occasionally she will spot something moving only to have it turn out to be a plastic shopping bag caught in a shrub flopping at the mercy of the wind.

The river is beginning to make a slight ascent up steep defiles. The scrub brush along the river's edge is giving way to a more permanent stand of 100-year old cedars. Behind them are the craggy promontories suggesting the promise of a suitable overhang. One in particular catches his attention. Not too far from it is a small stream of water having over time forced it's way through the rocky walls creating a small pool of fresh, pure mountain water.

"This is exactly what we're looking for," announces Joey with his attention on a singular projection. The day is much more noticeably coming to a close as the clouds grow darker. Reading into what they may be threatening, Joey plans a wood gathering mission along with cutting enough cedar boughs to comfortably insulate them against the hard rocks that make up their shelter.

Meanwhile, Carrie is busying herself filling the canteen along with various plastic containers. She is actually beginning to enjoy this contest. Another thing she is finding worth noticing is how this simple event is having an effect on her thinking. She is paying special attention to how an uninvited deeper development of feelings is impacting her actions toward this new champion.

Unguarded, she lets her thoughts wander as she follows how Joey methodically performs task after task. "I know that much of the vision of men I have has been formed between me and my Dad. I love my father, but this man doesn't fit anyone I've ever experienced. I'm not sure I know what this is, but I'm finding it refreshing and I welcome it."

Joey is finishing his wood gathering and is tackling the bough-cutting project. Carrie is proving not to be the only one of them with wandering thoughts as Joey too is experiencing a similar phenomenon. "I can't believe how quickly Carrie has come around. She had her cry and immediately began to adapt to our situation. She's one tough babe. She's sure proving to be a lot more than just a pretty face"

The night and the rain have arrived as predicted. With a thick layer of cedar boughs as a floor and bed as well as draped as a barrier to the wind and rain in front of the overhang, the fire is proving more than adequate to keeping them warm and dry.

Secure in their make-shift abode, content to share a portion of their cornucopia, but not ready to share thoughts, they silently stare into the fire anchoring their own feelings in their inner most sanctum sanctorum. Sharing feelings for each other at this time is considered by both to be too dangerous an undertaking. Their imaginations may be presumptuous and risk an embarrassing rejection.

Sleep soon overtakes them. Joey takes Carrie's hand in his; her hand a willing hand only waiting to be taken. Together they find this level of intimacy comforting and, for the time being, sufficient.

# 33 — DELIVERANCE

Things are not so calm back at SVOBODA. Darkness and rain are dampening any hopes of Joey and Carrie returning that night. It's well past 6 pm when Amzlov makes his way to the stables. Charlie is finishing up for the day and is hanging around waiting for Carrie and Joey to return.

"No vword yet?" asks Amzlov running his window down far enough to be heard, but up enough to keep the pounding rain from pouring in.

"No, nothing. I don't get it. Mr. Joey left his phone here but I saw Carrie put hers in her saddle bag. I know she would call if she needed something," says Charlie with more than a little concern.

"Zay not back tonight vwe getz zingz goingk een morningk first zing."

Of course, Amzlov is making this effort because of his concern for the safety of his daughter, but also lurking over him is the full understanding that he will be returning to her mother with no good news. This can become as bad as his concern for Carrie. On the other hand, knowing Joey as he has come to, he knows she's in capable hands, especially, God forbid, if there's been an accident.

Melba wastes no time getting the door open. She studies him for a brief moment. The look on her face tells everything. Amzlov knows he is going to dread the rest of the night. She is overcome with motherly impatience.

"You're going to tell me she's not back yet and no one has heard a word or knows why." Her arms flit back and forth from folded across her breast to clamped to her hips. Not waiting for an answer she continues, "What in heaven's name is the matter with that girl? She can be as irresponsible as she was at twelve."

Melba fears letting her mind travel any further than the thought that Carrie is being merely irresponsible. She and Amzlov attempt to have a quiet supper, each buried in their unspoken worry.

Out of the corner of his eye, Amzlov can sense his wife's fidgeting. Unable to contain her restlessness, she elects to share it with her husband.

"Tell me truthfully Gore: do you think she's okay?"

"I don't know vwhy not. She viz Joey, he know how zings go."

Amzlov and Melba abruptly stop all conversation as Charlie interrupts having made his way through the kitchen entrance. He's visibly uncomfortable, lending credence to Amzlov's and Melba's uneasiness. He quickly becomes aware that the two seconds that have lapsed have taken too long to hold their attention without a rebuff.

"For Got's zake Charlie, speak up, vwat you gotz zay?" barks Amzlov.

Charlie stands hat in hand blinking nervously. "I just got off the phone with my cousin up near the falls. He says that earlier today they had an ice dam give way on top of the falls causing a flash flood below. He maintains that the water came up twenty feet in just minutes. They were doing repairs on some fences and barely got out with their lives."

He stops talking but his body language is still speaking. Amzlov knows Charlie well enough to know that he's not telling all.

"Don't be azzhole Charlie. Vwat elze you know?" Amzlov is understandably ready to throttle him.

"They found two dead horses with our brand," says Charlie, his voice breaking up with emotion.

All are silent.

"I'm sorry Mr. Amzlov, I'm really sorry," says this clearly despondent friend and employee.

"Okay two dead horzez not two dead peoplez," says Amzlov minus his previous bluster. "Tomorrow at daylight vwe headingk out, vwe findz zem. Okay Charlie?"

"Yes sir Mr. Amzlov. I'll have the quads ready and waiting at the crack of dawn," says Charlie. Never sure how his boss is going to react to negative news.

Melba is far from relieved. Clearly agitated, her hands run through her hair as she nervously tosses her head. Her whole being is reflecting an unfettered desperation.

On the other hand when Amzlov faces these hard situations, it's much easier for him to isolate, starting with a couple shots of vodka. Caught in their individual frustration, unable to comfort each other, they choose to retreat to a lonely desolation.

Melba soon finds comfort in her rosary and Amzlov in his vodka. Each method eventually produces sleep.

Morning breaks with the rain trying to give way to a rising sun. Amzlov has also drawn Drew into helping search for his sister.

Assuring everyone the night before that he would hold himself responsible for having everything ready by dawn, Charlie has kept his word.

"Good morning Mr. Amzlov," says Charlie in an attempt to be as upbeat and optimistic as the circumstances allow.

He has rigged two quads with canvas enclosures. One for himself and Amzlov, the other for Drew. He and Amzlov are in a four-seater pulling a trailer with several days worth of provisions. It can also be utilized as an ambulance if need be, although it is not presented as its principle use. All three are fully aware of the chances of running into a tragedy as it can't help but weigh heavy on their minds. Each chooses to keep the thought to themselves.

"Okay Charlie vwe go zee vwat kindz mezz zeez guyz getz into." When Amzlov starts a project all hell is out for breakfast until it's finished.

This group is definitely focused. There is a father whose daughter is in harm's way; a brother whose sister is also his best friend, and a surrogate father who probably spent more learning times with this woman than her own family and she is missing.

In an attempt to remain pragmatic, Drew is the first to openly grapple with his misgivings. "I want to believe that since she's out there with Joey everything is going to be okay."

Thinking back on some of her antics as she was growing up Amzlov recalls, "You know how head strongk you zsister be zsometimesz I hope zshe not do zsomezing zstupeed." He is thinking back to one of her college antics where she went missing after a night of bar hopping with friends only to be found the next morning passed out on a toilet by the bar cleaning crew.

"I fully agree with you, Mr. Amzlov. I warned that young Joey not to let her lead him into some foolhardy chase," says Charlie shaking his head.

"Vell vwe zoon findz out don't vwe?" says Amzlov as a final word indicating it's time to be getting on.

Spring in Alaska is another word for mud. The sun's rays penetrate the permafrost only enough to turn the top layer into a river of slippery slime — and especially after last night's rain.

This morning is no exception. These powerful ATVs bully their way through the wet environment like war horses. Each knobby tire spews out a path formed of grass, dirt, and water arching behind in a plume like so much cast off debris.

Considering that it's a ten mile jaunt as the crow flies they expect to arrive in several hours. The rough terrain offers each of the drivers a better than average chance they may tip over. Pushing their speed absolutely guarantees a mishap. Even Amzlov, as impatient as he is, is aware of the pitfalls should they choose to ignore the demands of this twisting, unpredictable trail.

The rain has moved out and the sky is clearing. Amzlov checks his GPS for their location. He's not familiar with this area and is totally at the mercy of Charlie and Drew. These kind of circumstances always leave him uneasy. Periodically he will order Charlie to stop. He'll scan the vista for any sign of the elusive twosome, but it's also a reminder to Drew and Charlie that he is still in charge.

"How longk for vwe getz fallz?" asks Amzlov in his usual commanding intonation.

"Maybe an hour, hour and a half," estimates Charlie as he maneuvers just one more of the many mud slicked mounds.

Amzlov is hanging on to both sides of his seat creating the impression of a mud surfer. He's trying his best to remain calm as he finds he's completely out of his daily environment and totally at the mercy of Charlie. He finds this disconcerting and from time to time takes the role of the back seat driver.

As much as possible, Charlie tries to ignore his boss. He knows much better than Amzlov how to negotiate this type of trip. Amzlov knows this as well, but it's nearly impossible for him to settle down.

With the diligence of not only being a long-time employee, but also of one who is genuinely a friend, Charlie realizes that Amzlov is worried sick and his way of dealing with it is to fuss about everything

After a surprisingly decent night's sleep, both Joey and Carrie find themselves well rested. The firewood gathered the night before is much appreciated as the sun is taking its time heating the air. Continuing to warm themselves, they munch on an energy bar. Carrie is somewhat quiet and pensive. Joey takes note and is compelled to ask, "Are you all right this morning?"

Breaking her silence, Carrie responds. "I'm damn mad at myself for the way I acted yesterday," she laments.

"Mad at yourself for what?" asks Joey.

"For being so damned needy," she replies with a shout, turning her head away in disgust.

Joey can see the animosity she is building toward herself. "Well, if it will help you any, I been there, done that and got the t-shirt. I spent a good part of last year alone in the wilderness and believe me, until I had a few hard weeks with the odds against me, I barely managed to survive. During that time I never had the luxury of being relaxed and if I did it was very short-lived. So go ahead and kick yourself in the ass for awhile if it makes you feel better. But I also want to tell you how much you impressed me with how fast you recovered and caught on. Believe me when I tell you Carrie, you are one strong woman," says Joey.

She listens intently for a few minutes as she sits with her knees drawn up to rest her chin, her eyes remain lost in the distance. "Thanks, Joey."

Joey gives her a reassuring hug along with a little cajoling, "Don't worry about anything Carrie, as nothin' goes right anyway."

Relieved, she responds willingly to his embrace with one of her own.

Joey is able to strike her feminine sensibilities in a positive manner. She sees a strong inner man that is rare among other young men his age. "I'm beginning to see what my father saw in him months ago," is a prevailing thought.

With the diligence of a professional woodsman, Joey begins to break camp. His focus is on salvaging anything that will aid in their survival. With the sun warming the air, he douses the fire, refills the canteen along with a few of the rescued plastic bottles. He then checks his pistol and replaces his buck knife back into its sheath.

"We have about a ten mile hike back to SVOBODA. Are you up for it?" asks Joey.

Carrie is pulling on her boots, chewing on the last bite of her energy bar. "Yah, I'm sure I can make that. These boots were made more for riding than for walking, but I'll make do," she says standing and stomping her foot further into her boot.

Making a last look around Joey exclaims "Okay, let's get going and remember what we discussed about bears. Keep an eye out especially if there are cubs. That could definitely make it worse."

"Damn it Joey, if you want me to revert back to a whiny little girl keep talking about the bears." She has lived in Alaska all her life and has heard plenty of stories involving bears and people where people always seem to come out on the short end.

"If we should be so unlucky, I want you not to panic. Our first line of defense will be to walk away putting as much distance between them and us as possible. If that doesn't pan out so well and one decides to get aggressive, I'll fire a shot in its direction or at it. If none of this seems to be doing the job — then you panic."

Staring directly at him, she clutches her sides protectively through folded arms. Declining his offer to be humorous, she blurts back, "That's not funny, Joey!"

"I'm sorry Carrie, I'm only trying to give this whole ordeal a lighter face. Don't worry, if push comes to shove, I don't know too many bears that do well after being hit by a .45 slug.

Carrie's thoughts are drifting back to some of yesterday's disasters. The unpleasant consequences of her horse being swept away is rippling its way back into her thinking. Her concern for the possible outcomes is getting a lot of free rent in her head. That horse in particular has always been there to meet her as she passed through stage after stage of her growing up years.

Not wanting to tear up again, she attempts a whisper, "I wonder if our horses made it out?"

Realizing Carries legitimate concern for her oldest friend, Joey wraps an understanding arm around her shoulder. "We can only hope." His use of the word "we" is to assure her that even in the worst scenario, he's there to give her understanding.

Wiping a bit of moisture from her eyes, she slaps her hips as a gesture of finality saying, "Okay, I'm done with my fretting. Let's get this show on the road."

Joey stands in awe of how fast this woman can get out of a negative mind set and start anew.

The reality of their environment meets them head on as they both turn at the screech of an eagle as it swoops down, not fifty feet from them on an unsuspecting rabbit. In less than a second the huge bird is off toward the safety of a rocky ledge where it'll enjoy this most recent breakfast companion.

This latest vision lends to both the thought of how important it is to remain diligent enough to always remain on the top of the food chain. Within minutes their backs are turned on all their past as they boldly forge into the future that the rest of the day has not yet unfolded.

"We can make it back to the falls within the hour. Depending on how much the river has receded will determine our next move."

Carrie finds it peculiar how familiar the area is beginning to look. She had never ventured above the falls, now after twenty-four hours, the terrain features seem like old friends skillfully leading them out. It gives her a lighthearted sense of community with the whole area.

Joey is rather quiet on this hike. His thoughts are on Carrie. He is once again finding her a very pleasant distraction.

"Joey wait. I can't keep up as these boots are killing me," says Carrie as she grabs his hand.

Overwhelmed with the growing awareness of how much he is falling in love with Carrie, he is suddenly conscious of how sweaty his hands have become. Nervously wiping them on his pants, he further becomes conscious of how smelly he must be. This fragile beginning of intimacy mixed with his lack of hygiene is causing him a nervous uncertainty. Nonetheless, he grasps her hand back into his.

"Joey, do you think that you've ever been married?" she asks.

The question catches him unguarded. "I think about that sometimes." He pauses for just a moment letting a thought become words. "I don't think I am. Seems like everything else I find familiar that that would be too — but it doesn't fit anywhere." Letting out a pent-up breath, he takes a sip of water from one of the bottles. It's getting warm but he hardly notices. All he is aware of is this beautiful woman whose hand is in his.

Satisfied with the answer, the question soon becomes irrelevant as they continue to grow their own memories together.

The first sign of the falls isn't as visual as it is audible. It's roar is unmistakable. The volume of water spilling over the stair case is tremendous, not to mention the huge chunks of ice blocking all exits.

Realizing the paths that brought them to the top yesterday no longer exist today, Joey reassesses their options. He's a deliberate man. Squatting down, he gazes out over a raging, swollen river below.

"To even imagine we can climb down here is insane as it's way too dangerous. We are going to have to create a plan 'B'."

Carrie's lightheartedness is going the way of yesterday's path as the blunt reality that this is no mere walk in the park hits her. Then she is struck with another blunt reality. Her eyes brighten and widen with the exhilaration of one whose just had an eyeopening epiphany. "My Dad, Joey. My Dad is looking for us. I know him. He's out there some where right now!"

This speculation leaves a gap in the conversation as Joey thinks about it. "You are probably right Carrie, knowing your father the way I've come to. This is the kind of stuff he would be into with both feet."

"Charlie knew we were coming up here. Knowing my Dad, he won't let Charlie rest until we're home," adds Carrie as her lightheartedness makes a comeback.

With this new speculation as a probable reality, Joey continues his gaze out over the river below. It seems to disappear into a tangle of ice, broken, uprooted trees and snarled brush. The mist forming from the cold ice mixing with the warmer air creates a surreal atmosphere. The sight bears the vision of something terrifyingly beautiful. Neither of them can dismiss it as ordinary.

Continuing his thought, Joey says, "If we follow this ridge, we could get lost. I think we should wait here for now. My suspicions lead me to believe that this is where your father will begin his search."

"Good! Let's have lunch," responds Carrie. She is back to her cheerful self.

Lunch continues to consist of the proverbial energy bar and water. It's amazing to them how hunger can convince them that this mundane food is worthy of the attention of a lavish banquet.

Speaking loud enough to be heard requires great effort this close to the falls. A more inviting area down the ridge away from the falls catches his attention. "Let's move down away from the noise," suggests Joey.

"I think that's a great idea," responds Carrie. The sun is higher and warmer. They are finding a common concordance as they take each other's hand and make their way down the ridge to an old growth stand of cedars. Their canopy creates a clearing with some of the trees having been forced through the stresses in their lives to become bent, running parallel to the ground which provides their admirers a bench to sit on and just enough clear sky to allow the sun's warmth.

Sitting on these seats nature has provided, they share their lunch along with a similar spirit. This ageless phenomena is undeniably doing its work drawing them together. They are sitting in such a way that some portion of their body touches the other's, making them become more and more conscious of the other. There is a freshness surrounding them. It's the naivete of young love.

Joey desperately wants to kiss her. Not knowing quite how to ask, he keeps his longings locked up. His breathing is becoming more rapid as his racing heart demands more oxygen. He's becoming so light-headed, he feels he's on the verge of passing out.

He senses the need to be doing something more than holding her hand. Moving around behind her, he begins to massage her shoulders. "Oh my gosh, that feels wonderful," she says leaning into his strong hands, making no effort to stop him. A quietness comes over them both and just as natural as breathing they turn toward each other, staring for only a moment then ever so tenderly, ever so softly their foreheads touch, then their lips brush which causes a deep sigh from each of them. Both are aware that this line they just crossed is the beginning of something that they both hope will never have to be undone. They will go no further. It's enough for now.

Something in the distance catches their attention. It's a faint sound carried by the wind that dopplers off the rocky terrain. It's not a sound produced by anything in nature. It has all the undertones of being something man made. They both welcome the timing of this interruption. It's perfect in that it leaves them time to digest the past day before they commit themselves to a relationship that could easily speed ahead faster than either wants.

"Do you hear what I think I'm hearing?" says Joey slowly releasing his embrace on Carrie, with his ear cocked in the direction of the faint timbre.

"Yes and there they are," points Carrie as she deliriously waves her arms. The sound is coming from two ATVs barely audible and looking like some kind of wild dancing shapes bouncing across the steppes. They are 100 feet below them and s50-foot width with water spreading out over any bank ten feet or less at least another 100 feet. It's velocity at this time is capable of moving good-sized boulders.

At the rate the ATVs are traveling, they will be at the falls in less than ten minutes. They are being forced to break new trails since the previous ones are under water.

Carrie's waving is abruptly interrupted by a three-shot volley from Joey's .45 Colt. Not even close to expecting this, it jolts her.

"Don't scare me like that Joey, you brat!" says Carrie half laughing as she clutches her chest feigning a cardiac arrest.

"I took a chance they'd hear the shots above the river noise and their ATVs. I'm really sorry I startled you," apologizes Joey.

They continue to track the riders as they stay the course toward the falls. They seem to be impervious to anything outside the sounds of their own machines and their purpose.

Joey and Carrie are about a ten minute hike back along the ridge to the falls. A warm breeze meets them as they begin the arduous task of retracing their footsteps. Being found is bittersweet. Finding themselves stranded together is how they begin to discover so much about the other. They are silent on the walk back, lost in their own thoughts. Hope of all sorts begins to envelop them.

The familiar sound of the falls is ever present. Joey is more attentive to what he can hear over the roar of the cascade. He is particularly listening for the clattering sounds of an ATV and he's not hearing it.

This time warning Carrie, he says, "I think I better signal them once more," as he points his pistol in the air touching off three more shots.

Meanwhile at the bottom of the falls all three of the men have traveled as far as their machines will carry them. The current is racing by threatening everything in its ever-growing path. The water now nearly meets the bottom of the cliff leaving them only ten feet of muddy ground.

While contemplating their next move, Charlie is the first to interrupt. "Listen, I hear a gunshot," as two more ring out. Taking time for only a brief glance at one another, Charlie grabs a rifle from rack on his ATV. Without a word of conversation, he answers back with three shots of his own.

The screen of mist, broken ice, rocky outcroppings, and scrub brush make it impossible for those above as well as those below to see the other.

Being so close yet distanced by an impossible-looking situation is frustrating to Amzlov. "Vwat you zsink here Charlie, vwe can getz up zer?"

This is one of those rare moments in their long history together that Charlie has heard a note of vulnerability in his boss's voice.

"I'm not sure but we'll soon enough find out." Cupping his hands around his mouth he lets out a yell, "You up there? Can you hear me?" His words melt into the thunderous groan of the cataract, dissolving them inaudibly.

Unnoticed, Drew has withdrawn, reappearing abruptly from behind a rock formation. "I think I may have a possible route. There's a good chance this old trail could take us to the top. It looks a bit tenuous but I believe I can make it."

It doesn't take long before they've agreed on a plan. Drew is going to attempt to carry enough rope to allow them to rappel somewhat — at least part of the way down. Charlie quickly plunders the trailer for any supplies that will bring this undertaking to a successful ending. Another reason for urgency is that they have no way of knowing what the condition of either Carrie or Joey may be.

Returning with a coil of rope he hands it over to Drew with the instructions, "This should do it, Drew. This is made of nylon so expect it to stretch a bit. But it's what we got so make the best of it."

"Wish me luck," says Drew tying one end around his waist allowing it to uncoil as he makes his way up the uncharted climb.

Back on top, Joey and Carrie realize that even with the three-shot reply, they need a better communication system if they are going to hope to resolve their state of affairs.

"How could I have been so stupid as to leave my phone in my saddle bag," laments Carrie proceeding to kick herself.

Joey has long ago stopped kicking himself for mistakes. While he continues to keep an ear to what Carrie may be rehashing, he is also preoccupied with searching for the proverbial game trail that he knows will lead to the least resistant way down the cliff.

Before he can implement his search, a human form out of nowhere appears as a silhouette against the morning sun some 100 yards down the ridge.

Not sure this stranger has seen them Carrie begins a frantic waving and hollering campaign with the full expectation of getting this stranger's attention. The stranger seems to be involved in wrapping something around a tree.

Joey grabs her arm with one hand and puts the other to her mouth. "Wait Carrie!" That's his first reaction. "Wait until we know more about this guy." Joey's primordial instincts served him well in the past and he has no intentions of abandoning them now.

The stranger also is beginning to wave running in their direction. Within seconds Carrie is the first to recognize this silhouette as her brother. "Drew! Drew! Are we ever glad to see you," says Carrie.

He's also on a full run grabbing his sister around the waist with one arm and Joey's hand with the other. "Are you guys okay?" shouts Drew in his excitement, looking them over from head to toe. Satisfied that neither of them are injured, he carries on with his usual loquaciousness without waiting for an answer. Turning to Carrie he says, "You know Dad has done everything but bring in the National Guard."

"Yah Drew, we're fine," says Joey. Noticing the beads of sweat on Drew's forehead he hands him the canteen. "You look like you had a tough climb, have a drink." Welcoming the water he takes several large slugs before handing it back.

Joey is quick to do his homework. He's already put two and two together. "You tied the end of this rope to that tree and we're going to rappel down," says Joey in a slow calculating tone.

"Rappel may be a little severe. The first fifty feet may be a bit rough, but below that is a game trail running on the bias down to the river," says Drew trying his best to be as precise as possible.

With the expectation that this ordeal is nearly over, Joey and Carrie peer over the cliff looking at the little descending white line snaking its way through the rocky brush.

With a bit of a fake laugh, Carrie adjusts her slender body for the precarious decent. "See you at the bottom, boys." Soon there is no more tension on the line and the other two follow in sequence.

The reunion is joyous. Amzlov, not given much to hugging, embraces his daughter. She can't help but notice his eyes watering. Even Charlie gets a rare hug from Carrie and he couldn't be happier.

Within moments Amzlov is on the phone making the promised call to Melba. "Yah, yah Melba, zshee fine," he says. More than happy to rid himself of his wife's incessant questions he hands the phone to Carrie.

Knowing her mother's penchant for the dramatic, she's cautious. "Yes Mamma, I'm fine." After a few more "yes Mammas," she hands the phone back to her father. Knowing her mother as well as she does, she knows however subtle her mother will try to appear, that her goal will be to weasel out how every moment was spent between herself and Joey.

# 34 — A YEAR GOES BY

A year has passed since Joey vanished. What various members of his family think about it is generally kept to themselves. For the most part it's all been talked out.

Rena has not dealt well with the events of the past year. She has lost a son and nearly lost her husband through her indiscreet behavior.

Sam also has found it most difficult to continue to live with his lie concerning his brother's disappearance. There have been so many times that he's wanted to just blurt out a confession and get it off his mind. Instead, he continues to suppress it again and again, continuing to live with the agony of deceit, only to have it disrupt his rest relentlessly compressing itself around him. He's become well acquainted with the old adage that one is only as sick as their deepest held secrets.

Jacob has been gladdened with Sam's seeming turn around, never realizing that much of Sam's humble demeanor is as a result of the depression he suffers trying to guard his secret.

Nonetheless, Sam's penchant for leadership can not be deterred. One of his remarkable changes is his willingness to listen with patience to his brothers' and father's ideas on how to conduct business. He has discovered that that it's much more satisfying to take their ideas and to improve on them. He's also managed to dovetail his sales skills with his father's insistence on fair and honest business practices. His presentations lack the arrogant, self-serving components of days gone past. Now he's much more inclined to share monetary incentives with clients rather than trying to delude them.

"Sam, I can't tell you how pleased I am with your performance. We've increased sales by fifteen percent, that's huge," says his father.

The more accolades Jacob pours on his son the deeper Sam reproaches himself. He knows he doesn't deserve them. These are bittersweet moments. Unconfessed sin has its own destructive ends. It's hardly in the stars for Sam to be an exception. His is to suffer much more noticeably by his sin rather than for it—at least in this world.

He can't help but be reminded of what he did to his brother in some way everyday. As much as he wishes it to be resolved, his failure haunts him. He's come to even avoid using the word joy because it sounds too much like Joey.

Sam has come to realize that the more of himself he pours into the business the less obsessive he is with how he is ever going to deal with the "Joey problem." There's nothing like a challenging project to snap Sam out of his past. Unfortunately, for him it's only a temporary fix.

The miners are starting a new season And it's not unusual for Sam to be on the road by 5:30 am. Since Sam's "Come to Jesus" meeting with the avalanche, he has successfully made amends to most of the miners that he had screwed over and has not pilfered for himself as much as a penny's worth of gold.

There are almost twenty hours of daylight this time of the year. Sam has been known to stay out in the field as long as the miners are still working. Some days he's taken as much as a thousand ounces of gold before calling it a day. Since the incident with the kidnapping, he is much more cautious preferring to drive an older model vehicle and making certain he is armed.

Jacob will ride along with him from time to time, but not nearly as often. He's more and more inclined to let the boys assume the day to day responsibilities of the business.

On this particular day Jacob is having a conversation with Sam's mother, Lena. "That boy has certainly come a long ways from the Sam I used to have to deal with."

"I know what you mean, Jacob," Lena says pausing for a moment, "It's a mother's sixth sense to know when something is not quite right with a child. I can't help but believe that there is something else eating at him."

Jacob has avoided this conversation with Lena because of her over-developed sense of protection for her children. He's surprised that she's being this transparent.

"I don't pretend to be the smartest at times, but I do know what you're saying. For some time I've suspected that something else is troubling him — I can see it in his whole demeanor." He says this short of expressing his suspicion that it may have something to do with Joey's disappearance. Jacob is aware of the unspoken tension between his two wives over this very issue. Rena's quiet suspicions that her sister's boys know more about her Joey's disappearance than they are admitting has contributed to her latent hostility.

As long as Sam remains obsessed with business, he's able to bury much of his despondency under his busyness. He's become much like a method actor who assumes a role in the theater until it almost becomes him. It's as though if he becomes the good business man his father wishes, he'll be able to redeem himself and his father will love him.

On this particular occasion Sam is approaching his father with a new business proposition in the hopes his father will approve. "Dad, you got a couple minutes? I'd like to talk to you," asks Sam, knocking on the door jamb of his father's opened office door.

Looking up from his work, Jacob notices Sam's voice has taken on a somberness that's much more subdued than his more recent exuberance.

"Yah sure come on in," answers Jacob, already clearing papers from a seat opposite him.

With this thoughtful expression, he begins, "I'm visiting at least one new claim a day so far this season and there are probably several more I could do but we're at full capacity right now. Since the explosion in gold prices, guys from the lower 48 are pouring in here opening new claims every day. I think this trend is going to continue. It's my thought that we should be looking at a new sight with a larger capacity to handle more product."

Jacob listens intently. This is what he has hoped all along that his sons would grow the business assuring another generation of Mueller and Sons.

"Have you talked to your brothers about this?" inquires Jacob.

"No, not yet. I didn't want to do anything until I talked with you first," answers Sam.

"Well, I think we could work it out, providing we can get all our ducks in a row." Jacob is smiling, he's taking great satisfaction in his son's interest in the health of the family business.

People who are leaders eventually will find themselves at the forefront regardless of motives. They're driven and have a penchant for getting their ideas acted on through out outspokenness, good discernment skills and the ability to demonstrate solid control.

In the past it was often noted sarcastically of Sam that he was a natural-born leader, unfortunately he just couldn't gather a following. But these days he's demonstrating a patience and humility that is maturing his skills. In the past they were shaped by the pressures of the moment. Now they seem to be guided by a quieter, more discerning spirit.

Jacob lingers, staring out his office window after Sam has left, "There is so much about these boys that I don't know." It's a transient thought. He'll often find himself looking skyward as though Divine Providence will provide his answer with sky writing. His thoughts wander until they eventually stick on something, that something is usually something to do with Joey. He searches through his thoughts with the hope that a miraculous mentation will work it's magic and give him the closure he yearns for.

This is Lena's week. He finds her in the kitchen using the last of last fall's tomatoes in a soup.

"Hello Jacob, I didn't expect to see you so early," she says wiping her hands on a clean dish towel. She welcomes him with a kiss and a hug.

"You look nice, Lena," says Jacob cupping his hand lightly around her freshly coiffed hair careful not to mess it.

She lets out a little self-conscious giggle. In an almost inaudible whisper she demurely looks up at him saying, "Thank you, Jacob, it's good to have you home." Followed by, "What have you had to eat today?"

Jacob moves to the stove lifting the lid off the simmering mixture, moving his nose across it's wafting vapors. "Nothing as good as this," he proclaims.

For more years than he cares to remember, he has enjoyed the diversity of this lifestyle. The polygamous accommodation of these Fundamental Mormons is what marries their religion to the culture. It's certainly not without it's own problems, but since it's thought to be God's plan for their lives, the problems stemming from its practice must be met and overcome.

For a moment, youth is remembered. They smile at each other as they look forward to the week together. There's a brightness in their eyes. Both are quick to accommodate the other as they sit at the kitchen table enjoying the simple pleasure of eating soup. Licking the back of her spoon, Lena uses it as a pointer toward a garden spot outside the window, "I'd like to plant more tomatoes this year." Believing that contentment insures its future by planing, she adds, "I hate running out."

After dinner, Jacob helps Lena clean up. He notices a squeaking cupboard door needs a spot of oil. Stopping long enough to find a small can of oil, he fixes it. As soon as all the kitchen chores are finished, they walk outside to review this year's garden plot.

For now the clouds in their lives have found some other home, causing anxious thoughts for someone else. The winters in Alaska can be as confining as any prison with the endless darkness, ice- and snow-packed roadways, and wind so cold that it can cut through a layer of skin as slick as a straight razor. But once again it's spring and actions run mindlessly. Smiles come with the warmth of the sun's longer stay. After all, they have cheated the death knell of another winter.

With his father's blessing, Sam calls a meeting with all the brothers. His intention is to introduce his idea to move the business forward. Jacob recalls doing something similar when he envisioned progressing from the simple blacksmith forges they used to use to the smelting furnaces they use today

Sam feels that he has found his niche. Intent upon moving this project forward and not wanting to risk any misunderstandings, he has wisely included his brothers on every phase of the project.

It's not until Rup insists on rehashing the "Joey question" in a private meeting that Sam's confidence is all of a sudden attacked by a bubble of regret and remorse arising from the depths of his being.

"Look Rup, it's over. He's gone and we don't know where. We have to move on. For that matter were he still living, he would have shown up somewhere by now." There is anger driven by compunction in Sam's reaction.

"It may be easy for you Sam, but I still have a hard time looking Dad in the eye," deplores Rup of his compliance in Sam's scheme. He's not about to inform Sam of his dalliance with Rena and that being much of the reason he feels estranged from their father. It's much easier to vent his sideways anger for getting himself involved in any of his problem toward Sam.

The unresolved anger at themselves for holding these secrets from their father continues to blemish any attempt to move past them. Protecting these fiendish demons of their past behavior precludes any successful transformation of character. It leaves each of them with the hazard of having the strength of these weaknesses continue to affront their ambitions, always to arise in unpredictable ways and places.

Both these brothers are familiar with the misery their actions have placed on themselves and are complacent enough to drag this guilt and remorse around as "my cross to bear, rather than hurt Dad any further." This has a pious enough tone to it, allowing each of them to kick the can of guilt down the road another day. On the other hand, there is no doubt in either of their minds that their father is certainly fortified enough to hear their confessions and has enough character to forgive them. At this time neither are ready to throw the shovel of pride out of the hole of guilt — so they continue to dig.

That which is silently understood between them doesn't need any more words. They both get up and go to the door.

# 35 — MELBA

The world of Melba Maria Scaleone Amzlov does not revolve around her husband's business success nor his wealth. Rather her world is the Catholic Church. She measures not only her life, but also those around her with the measuring stick provided by the Church and like so many well-meaning church people she also use it to beat those who fall short.

Amzlov is fingering his way through the newspaper, flipping pages with little or no regard as to what they have to report. Melba studies him for a moment, convinced that what she has to talk to him about will be much more enterprising.

"Gore, have you spoken with Joey about his and Carrie's goings on the past two days?" she asks in her feigned tone of concern.

Knowing where this conversation is going, a new interest in his newspaper is quickly taking precedence over his wife's penchant for news of a possible scandal involving their daughter and Joey.

"Gore, are you listening?" she asks in a demanding tone of voice that Amzlov finds too familiar. It's the tone that insures that with or without his cooperation this question will be thoroughly examined.

"Yah Melba, I hear you," says a reluctant but surrendered husband. It's been his experience that he is going to have to give in to Melba's persistence sooner or later — and to get it over with the sooner the better. "And zah anzwer eez no. I haf not spoken viz anybody 'bout nozing."

By this time it can go without saying that Melba's distrust and dislike for Joey go hand in hand. She's quite sure that he's not Catholic and the risk of a non-Catholic cavorting around the wilderness for two unsupervised days with her daughter is pressing very hard on her.

"Well, I think you should take the time. We know very little about him except he was being charged with a felony when you got him released from prison and we know absolutely nothing of his background. For all anyone knows he may have a record a mile long and to think our Carrie spent a night with him." Her hands are firmly on her hips and her voice has reached a pitch that Amzlov knows is the point of no return.

"Okaay, okay, I talk viz heem, make you happy," says a clearly agitated husband slamming his paper down. Throwing his hands in the air, muttering something in Russian, he leaves the room.

Meanwhile Carrie hears all the commotion and comes downstairs. "What are you two shouting about?" she asks stopping about midway down the stairs.

Her father is clearly agitated, passing her on the stairs on his way to his office. Turning toward him as he storms past she asks again, "Daddy what's wrong?"

"Ask you muther," he shouts, continuing to wave his hands and shake his head.

"Mamma, what's going on?" asks Carrie, with a bit more concern.

"You have to know that I worried myself near to death with you out there in the wild all day and night. I can't tell you how many rosaries I prayed, asking Our Lady to protect you."

Carrie can see the desperation in her mother's face as she makes her way down the rest of the stairs. "Well, it must have worked because Joey knew exactly what to do. I never felt unprotected the whole time," says Carrie with an air of satisfaction.

She can clearly see that her mother is upset with her less than satisfactory answer as she tosses her head removing some nonexistent hair from her face.

"Well, that may be the problem Carrie — just how protected did this 'Joey' make you feel?" blurts out her mother, her voice dripping with sarcasm.

Carrie stands stunned for a moment. She can't believe the very hero-of-the-day is the target of her mother's malevolence.

"Just what is it that you're concerned about Mother?" shoots back Carrie clearly distraught with her mother's attitude.

"I'm just saying my daughter spent a night in the wilderness with a man I don't trust," laments Melba.

With every look and gesture her mother lets her know that the last person in the world she's at ease with is this "Joey-no-name-vagrant your father has taken in" and that she is not going to rest until she is absolutely sure her daughter has not been violated.

"Mamma you're so unfair. If it weren't for this 'vagrant,' I would more than likely be dead! And NO he did not violate me. He was kind and courteous the whole time," reiterates Carrie. She has learned over the past few years of her adult life that she can stand against her mother for short periods and then she has to excuse herself or become buried in resentments against her. "Momma, I'm going to go back to my room before I say something to you I'll regret later," says Carrie with an air of finality.

"Carrie I don't mean to upset you like this. I love you and only want the very best for you. You must understand this." Her voice carries a strain that only one who has a child can understand. But then Carrie does not understand. How could she? She has no children. All she believes is that her mother is an overreacting loon who needs to be tranquilized.

"Come back, Carrie honey, don't leave me like this," says her mother, her face wet with tears.

Carrie lets out a sigh. Reluctantly walking back to her mother with only as much compassion as her anger toward her will allow. "I love you mother, but you have to understand. I'm not the little girl you still have in your mind. I don't need your constant supervision." Pausing for the moment to let what she has just said settle in with her mother she adds, "Please don't smother me. I need to have the freedom to breathe."

"Things are changing so fast since I was your age, I hardly know this world anymore," admits Melba wiping her nose with a tissue.

"Don't worry so much Momma, I still have my values," says a much more relaxed daughter. She has regained enough of her composure to at least share a hug with her mother.

"When you have children, how do you not worry?" says Melba as a matter of fact, still trying to get her nose dry.

Melba knows in her head that her daughter is an adult. In her heart it's another story. There she will remain forever the helpless little girl who can never outgrow the need for her mother.

Carrie had been sharing an apartment with another girl, but the other girl moved out leaving her alone. She enjoyed the freedom this arrangement offered her, but now with the roommate no longer there it gets very lonely. Her father talked her into coming home and moving into a vacant servant's apartment. The apartment has proven to be the right size and offers her a tolerable amount of privacy.

Joey is back to work full force. Amzlov is very pleased with him. Surprisingly enough, so is Shanhizer.

"Mr. Amzlov I can't believe how sharp this kid is. It's like he has some outside invisible force mentoring him. I've worked with a lot of smart men in my career, but never anyone like this kid. His mind works like a computer. Oh, and, by the way, I've finished all the paper work to okay a name. The judge promised he'd set aside some time to approve it," concludes Shanhizer. As they are speaking, Joey is passing by with an arm load of paper work.

"Hey Joey," shouts Amzlov through the opened door, "come here minute."

Making a hard turn back around, Joey finds himself face to face with Amzlov. "Yes, Mr. Amzlov.

"Zeet down here, make zelf at home. Vwant talkz viz you," declares Amzlov pointing to a chair. Still clutching his armload of dossiers, he obsequiously obeys.

Joey has been in Amzlov's office many times and is never under impressed with the massiveness of his furniture. It's as though he's expecting the next person waltzing through his door to be someone in the neighborhood of four or five hundred pounds.

"Shanhizer tell me he gotz name vwork all done. Vwat name you like."

With a wide grin Joey proclaims, "Joseph Finkbonner."

Amzlov remains seated for a moment musing over his choice . "Finkz-bonner, zat zound like good name," says Amzlov coming out of his chair and shaking his hand as though they had just met.

"Thank you sir," replies Joey with the same wide grin.

Motioning Shanhizer that he can leave, Amzlov returns to his chair. He can't help but see Amzlov as some kind of diminutive royalty diminished by the size of his own furniture.

Joey notices an abrupt change in Amzlov's demeanor, wondering what this could be about. As soon as Shanhizer closes the door behind him, Amzlov begins in a slow methodical tone that makes him sound uncomfortable with what he is about to say.

"Joey you know my vwife, you know how zhe be?" he says shifting from folding his hands to rubbing them together. He is clearly nervous. "Zshe vant know you do any hanky-panky viz Carrie out in woodz."

Joey is startled by Amzlov's forthrightness. Quickly regaining himself and in his most sincere and reassuring delivery, he answers directly, "No sir, not anything inappropriate. I couldn't do anything that would dishonor either Carrie, you or her mother."

Without any further thought and unexpectedly, the added words come tumbling out surprising not only himself, but also Amzlov, "That would be too great an offense against God." Joey is as stunned at his words as is Amzlov. It's as though he had learned those words in some distant part of his memory and they have become part of his person.

"You zsure you not Catholic?" questions Amzlov. The grin he's wearing spells relief.

This conversation has left Joey very self-consciously rubbing his hand back and forth across his forehead. "No sir, I'm not sure what I am."

For the most part everyone's schedule has returned to normal. Carrie is back in school and Joey has resumed his responsibilities. A few days have passed since their harrowing experience. Until now they have not had the occasion to pursue time together. But after sharing their life-changing adventure together, they have become much more aware of the other's absence.

Just finished with classes, Carrie's cell phone indicates a call from Joey. Eagerly she places it to her ear.

"Hi Carrie, Joey here."

"Hey Joey."

"Your Dad has had me so busy the past few days that I've barely had time to eat. What say we meet for dinner tonight?"

"I think that would be great," says an excited Carrie.

"I'll pick you up at 7 pm."

Closing their phones, the conversation brings a pleasant smile across both their faces. Dinner can not come soon enough for either of them.

With the clock at last near 7 pm, Joey drives the several hundred feet from his cottage to the mansion front doors. He's dressed himself in dark slacks, along with a pair of Italian cut loafers and a white sweater that is accentuating his wilderness tan.

Melba answers the door and she's shocked to have her nemesis standing directly in front of her. The pause is embarrassing especially for Joey as her eyes sweep his entire person from top to bottom with an unmistakable look of disdain.

As courteous as he can be he addresses Melba, "Is Carrie here?"

"Yes, I am," says Carrie emerging from behind her mother.

Melba remains speechless, still standing, holding the book she's reading with her glasses perched on the end of her nose as Carrie passes by closing the door behind herself.

Once outside Joey hastily recovers. "Carrie, you look absolutely beautiful," he says. His eyes always smile along with his mouth.

Her caramel-colored hair frames her face perfectly along with teardrop earrings accentuating her angular neck in such a way that her dark eyes dart out like shining twin, black onyx. Her long, dark legs emerge just above the knee from a jet black cocktail dress and end eloquently in a pair of black stiletto pumps.

"Thank you," says Carrie accompanied by a demur glance, followed by, "You look pretty good yourself." She can't help but add with a wry little grin, "Where's your pistol-buck knife combo?"

Taking a moment to catch her irony, he laughingly shoots back, "I traded it in on a knife and fork for a date with you."

Impressed with his quick wit she says, "Oh, you're such a clever man."

Glancing back at the mansion, they both catch the silhouette of a disapproving mother gracing the window.

"Gore, did you talk to that Joey about their wilderness camp out?" asks Melba, turning away from the window long enough to confront her husband.

There are only two known circumstances that make Amzlov nervous, one is losing money and the other is a subject of dispute with his wife. It's a given that she'll wear him down.

It's obvious with the look he's giving her that he wants this conversation to be over before it starts. "He say no hanky-panky. Okay, know vwe drop all zeez buul sheet now," says Amzlov.

"Well, that's just like you Gore, you always want to run from things that are important in this family. I think if he's going to be cavorting around with our daughter we should certainly know what his intentions are. That's not asking too much is it, Gore?" says Melba continuing her diatribe against Joey.

Amzlov takes a deep breath letting it out in a condescending sigh, "No Melba, zat not to much ask."

"Then I think you should ask this 'Joey' no-name to stop bothering our daughter," says Melba continuing with her ranting, "He's nothing more than a street straggler you dragged home."

Amzlov's demeanor switches suddenly from one of condescension to a defensive mode. "I tell you zsomzing 'bout zeez guy Melba, he gotz more brain zen you, me togezer. I tell you zsomzing elz, he gotz name now."

For the moment curiosity replaces her exasperation. She makes the next logical inquiry, "So what name did your genius come up with?"

"His name Joseph Finkbonner," says Amzlov with the confidence of one who hopes to put to rest a solved dilemma.

Melba can't quite believe what her husband has just told her. Her lip begins to develop a smirk. "FINKBONNER? What the hell kind of name is FINKBONNER?" Her voice drips with sarcasm. She has just confirmed a new reason to detest this gypsy intruder. "That's the stupidest name I have ever heard," she adds.

Finding himself going down for the third time in the tenth round of a ten round bout, he throws in the towel. "Melba I tell you, I don't getz how you brain vwork — you crazy zsomtimez." With that Amzlov walks out of the room heads back to the third floor where his world makes sense.


The weeks and months fly by. Melba has slowly resolved within herself that she can do very little, if anything, to dissuade her daughter's growing relationship with Joey. Instead she is implementing plan "B" which involves doing her best to influence the direction this relationship should take.

Now she picks her words more carefully with her daughter. She has become aware of how easy her feelings expressed the wrong way will alienate their relationship for weeks leaving her out of the loop.

"How are you and Joey doing these days?" asks her mother, one late summer morning, trying desperately to disguise her interest as innocent curiosity.

Knowing her mother as she does, Carrie also affects a contrived response. Wondering what her mother could possibly be digging for, she chooses to keep her answer as generic as possible. "Oh fine," she willingly reports.

The answer is noticeably honeyed. To satisfy Melba, her question demands a more profound answer, something she can sink her teeth into. By the same token, she struggles to keep her true thoughts from informing her words.

"When I ask your father about Joey he tells me the same thing. He thinks he's the greatest."

"Yes, I know," says Carrie with a smile. "He's very capable. Daddy says he doesn't know how he could get along without him."

These words grate against this mother's true core. She is least impressed with how this young man's earthly accolades have penetrated her daughter's and husband's fantasies.

With Melba there are only two classes of people—those who are under the wing of the Catholic Church and those who are not. Unwittingly, through her, the Catholic Church has become the enemy of those who are not.

She has, in no uncertain terms, let Joey know that he is teetering on the brink of eternal damnation at all times. Not at all willing to let God deal with him His own way, she is fully prepared to cast him into eternal darkness herself.

Amzlov will also admit that he found her strong moral values compelling when he first met her. He's been heard to admit that, "I know I trust her; zshe make good wife, good mamma."

She married Amzlov because she found him handsome, a good, hard working truthful man and had fallen in love with him. She also found him to be malleable in a strange sort of way.

He was not and still is not a particularly religious man, nonetheless he always held Melba's religious views in high regard. "My vwife, zshe gotz 'nough Got for bot uz," says Amzlov when the question of religion comes up.

She has never forced her way into his world of business and he has reciprocated by staying out of her Church work. She also has not missed a Sunday Mass in years, nor the observance of a multitude of Holy Days.

When they were first married, Amzlov would attend Mass with her. He had been baptized in the Russian Orthodox Church. Father Mike had always recognized his baptism and the Orthodox liturgical orders as legitimate, as a result he would allow Amzlov to receive the Sacrament. Amzlov never had the near obsessive connection Melba has with the church. As a result, he began to attend less and less until now he only attends on Christmas and Easter. It's not so much that Amzlov is without religion, rather he finds he doesn't connect well with church religion, which of course in Melba's eyes is no religion at all. The final result is that now that her children are older, they are busy with different aspects of their lives and don't attend like they did when they were younger. Melba finds herself going alone much more often.

To say that she is anything less than a pillar within her parish would be a gross understatement. To say that she is patient with other's spiritual growth would be a gross overstatement.

Like so many church goers she has become over-acquainted with all the "Thou Shalt Nots" and under-acquainted with patience and Christian forbearance toward weaker brethren. Melba falls quite piously into her calling to protect God and His church from all these heretics.

On this particular meeting with Carrie and Joey she has accepted the possibility that this near pagan could become part of her family. Joey has never been on the attack or on the defense and finds it best to patronize Melba as best he can.

"No, Mrs. Amzlov I don't have anything against the church. I don't mind going with Carrie any time she wishes to go. And I might add, I have no problem with you wishing me to be a Catholic," says Joey amicably. "I'm sure it would certainly help to keep unity in the family. With a bit of irony he adds, "and I'm sure you'll feel better about my chances of salvation."

Joey's answer puzzles Melba. She's never sure if she is influencing his life or if he acquiesces because he has already considered the content of her topic and formulated his own thoughts.

What she is discovering is the same attribute that everyone else has discovered. He possesses a mysterious strength of character. It goes well beyond the basic raw material of Carrie's previous boyfriends.

Melba's disappointment continues to be in finding nothing to form Joey into that would improve what he already is proving himself to be. Truthfully, she is realizing that any changes she would make would be like taking a major and reducing it down to a minor.

As it turns out her disappointment is for herself. Her discoveries include that his ordinariness doesn't require a whole lot of overseeing, and his common sense standards of fairness and patience continue to thwart her high-hatted and often intrusive tendencies.

As the year continues to ripen so does the day-to-day love between Joey and Carrie. Amzlov never ceases to be amazed at Joey's powers of discernment. This precludes any reasons for not seeing him as son-in-law material nor for that matter no reason to discontinue squeezing every bit of talent he possesses in furthering the Amzlov dynasty.

While not having a remembered reference point of what he may have done in the past, Joey is as surprised as anyone at his abilities. He has never doubted that with all of this unexplained competence, he is receiving Providential gifts. But as he explains to Carrie, "I have no understanding as to why."

Nonetheless, he continues to apply the principles he receives in his private as well as his business life. Beneath all the political rigors of business, the crude talk, the will for power, the struggle for monetary advantages, there remains a fairness in him that can't be ignored. This comeliness is more often than not hatched in the midst of the chaotic behavior of others.

# 36 — UNFRIENDLY NIGHTS

*"A lack of power that we think is our dilemma." Alcoholics Anonymous, Chapter 5*

*"Much of the Gospel asks us to repent and do good — not be right." author unknown.*

Nights can be unfriendly. Sam's dreams parallel the hardness of these nights. In these imageries, the sky is always a clear blue. The wind is warm, blowing across a placid lake stirring it into small waves so dazzling that each one glitters as scattering diamonds. He's rowing a boat. He's always alone on the lake with no other boaters. His rowing is effortless as he is propelled forward, enjoying every exhilarating moment.

Something catches his eye as it bobs above the water line. At first it can't be distinguished as it's being silhouetted against the brightness of the sun. No matter in which direction he looks, the image refuses to be ignored. It remains in front of him bobbing down into the water only each time to reappear closer. Closer and closer, it comes until it becomes the unmistakable person of his brother Joey. His tears are making trails down his bloodstained face. His eyes are pale gray staring straight at him. They are as lifeless and cold as stones. The sky is no longer blue, the water no longer glistens. It's dead calm except for the sound it makes as someone emerges. He's not afraid as much as he is sad. It's the kind of sadness that comes with regret.

Awakening soaking wet, he soon realizes he's not on the water. It's perspiration and that he is still firmly entrenched in the safety of his bed. An overwhelming sadness flows over him as the lingering memory of his younger brother relentlessly pursues him.

The face of a glowing clock across the room says that it's only 2 am.

The feelings of desolation and loneliness cause him to wrap his arms around his sleeping wife, yearning for her warm body to give him some comfort.

Daylight soon resurrects from its overnight death. In spite of the brightness of the sun, the feelings of dread continue to darken his joy. It's a hard way to be humbled, but it seems that the only way some of God's children can become teachable is through a bankruptcy of the soul. Sam's thoughts revolve around how he is going to respond to these dreadful visions of his brother coming to haunt his dreams. "I can easily put a bullet in my head and risk the hell I have already seen or seek God to give me the strength to resolve this dilemma I've gotten myself into."

Sam continues to nurture his perplexity hoping that some kind of answer will fly through the air that won't require any more pain than what he's already putting himself through.

Still managing to side step a fatal blow to his ego, Sam survives another dire round of these disturbing circumstances. He finds that if he can stay obsessed with work, he can let more and more time go by in hopes of minimizing his need to make any kind of amends.

Another year passes by and Sam has successfully opened a satellite over by Grover Creek, putting Rup in charge. Meeting with his father this morning, they carefully go over plans to open another plant up north at Dolger Cliffs.

"How's Rup doing over at Grover?" questions Jacob. At times the committee in Jacob's mind isn't the healthiest. How Rup violated his trust is still able to come up on his blind side and wake up the old resentments.

Sam can sense his father's lack of confidence in his choice to place Rup as the plant manager.

"I don't worry about Rup. He knows how to run the plant, besides I promised him that the rest of us would be there for him if he ran into something he can't handle. He's already managed to rustle up a hand full of new accounts."

"Well I hope you're right," says Jacob.

Sam has sensed a rift between his father and Rup, he just doesn't know what that something is. Not wanting to push the issue, Sam leaves it lay, continuing to pose the plans for the Dolger project. They spend the rest of the day wrestling over business.

Jacob's eyesight is becoming more of an issue. It's placing many new restraints on this otherwise energetic man.

As this lack of activity seizes his thoughts, his imagination's gate crash places that are better left closed. Nevertheless and without warning, he often finds himself trespassing back into old wounds, picking at the scab and taking some perverse joy in re-feeling the hurt.

Jacob finds these demons overwhelming at times. He finds himself entertaining thoughts of taking joy in seeing all those who have unnecessarily hurt him by their selfish actions suffer the way they have made him suffer, forcing them to ponder exactly what they have done to him.

When the rawness of these emotions grate against his heart and soul, he finds it overwhelming and cries out, "Please God, just take me out of this vale of tears!"

It's an unseasonably warm day. Jacob is sitting outside warming himself on this rare occasion. It's the best of days as all the summer insects are gone, killed in an early frost. His eyes close, followed by meandering thoughts, when from some recess the vision of his grandfather comes into view. "Grandpa Abe?" His lips move in a whisper, "Is that you?"

Abraham Mueller had been his father's father and had died some forty years ago. Jacob can't believe how timeless he appears from the last time he visited him. He's still wearing the same wool pants covered in horse and dog hair with small pieces of lint and firewood fragments imbedded in the fabric. Even a hint of his summer weight long underwear are peeking through his opened-necked, blue work shirt.

Jacob is overcome with joy, being in the company of this old man once more. A conversation he held with him many years ago begins to replay in his mind. Abe was a reasonable man, often drawn to the common sense of his Athabaskan neighbors.

"Jacob you seem to be troubled," says Grandpa Abe. Even in his dream, he can see the concern in the old man's eyes.

"Ezard is filling Dad's head with lies. He pretends that he's pulling his weight at the plant, but he's not. All he's doing is pissing me off. I just don't know how to deal with him," laments Jacob.

The old man listens, allowing Jacob to vent his frustrations uninterrupted. When at last Jacob has upchucked the last of his anger toward his brother, the old grandfather looks his grandson over. A small hint of an ironic bit of a grin begins to make its way across his weather-worn countenance.

"Hummm...well I believe you're a smart boy. Let me tell you a little story that may help you out. Chief Owosso told me this same story when I was about your age."

Jacob sees himself cocking his head the way he does when he's puzzled. It's also surprising how young he appears.

The old man continues, "The way the chief sees his world is as though it is controlled by the spirit of either good dogs or bad dogs. These critters live within each one of us, continuing to battle for dominance. The good dog is kind, courteous, long suffering, gentle and honest, quick to forgive. The bad dog on the other hand is dishonest, impatient with others' weaknesses, angry, rude and unforgiving. They fight and fight day after day until one of them finally wins."

Jacob remembers how perplexed he was at his grandfather's story on that day forty some years ago. He also remembers his response as he mouths the words once again, "How do you know which one will win?"

The old man's wry little smile returns as he unhesitatingly recites the same age old solution, "It's the one that you feed the most, Jacob."

Feeling a hard jerk on his shoulder, he startles awake followed by a female voice, "Wake up Jacob, wake up!" It's Rena. "You were talking in your sleep."

She's come with a tray filled with sandwiches and cold lemonade. Her smile suggests that she is amused by her husband's peculiar nap activity.

For the moment he looks alarmed as he's caught between these two seeming realities. The dream is too real to be dismissed as merely a dream.

"Were you having a good dream or a bad one?" Her question is as light and whimsical as the day is warm and sunny.

Not immediately able to discern the impact of this unexpected imagery, he fumbles for words, trying to downplay it's importance until he can sort through it.

"Oh, it's just some crazy dream," he says, waving his hand dismissively. His effort to make a smile discloses a discrepancy between thought and words. He can't shake how alive he felt watching himself interacting with his grandfather. Particularly the question he's left with, "What dog have you been feeding, Jacob?"

The more Rena tries to discuss trivial things, the less communicative he's becoming. His silent introspection can easily be perceived by her as rude, especially when she is trying her best to be engaging.

Feeling the awkward distance between the two of them, she reacts. Her arms are folded under her breasts as though they required her support. Her voice is firm and deliberate and definitely defensive as she probes for an answer.

"So what's going on with us, Jacob? And don't say 'nothing' because I know better."

Pausing for the moment he releases a sigh of resignation that should have been released long ago. He did well for a while with forgiving Rena, that was until the "devil as a roaring lion" sought out a way to destroy him by finding his Achilles' heel in refueling his resentments.

"It's not you, Rena. It has to do with me." His voice has taken on a softness as he continues, "I'm the problem."

Rising up, he kisses her. He can see the weariness in her face. It's like a mirror that reflects the hurt.

"I just want a husband I can share burdens with and one who feels he can do the same." The trauma in her voice is unmistakable.

With a new resolve to rid himself of his old familiar attraction to avenging wrongs, he commits himself to let it go.

"You're right and from now on I'm going to try and be that husband for you."

Like the soft breeze that is blowing the stray curl from her cheek, a whisper from his soul has just crossed unnoticed into a loud pronouncement directing itself straight into his will, "Stop feeding your mean dog with the time God has allotted for your good dog!"

"Oh Jacob, I hope so. I miss you so much when you shut me out."

Continuing to face her, wide-eyed and with new conviction, he says, "I want to apologize to you for my often uncivil behavior toward you. I want you to know that I love you and I don't want to hurt you anymore."

The stress she has lived with over the past year, never knowing for sure whether or not he has forgiven her, has taken its toll. Sometimes he seemed to be loving and kind and other times he could be mean-spirited and withhold his love.

"Those are the words I have longed to hear from you Jacob." Her eyes are wet with her tears as her face takes on a softening.

He feels traitorous for his actions during the past year. Saying a silent prayer, he asks God to give him the extra strengthening he's going to need to begin to feed his "kinder dog."

His words are powerful to her. She can feel herself coming back to life as she takes on the peaceful look of one who has gone through an unpleasant ordeal and is now given the hope it's behind her.

"I hope we can start a good thing from here on," she says. Her words reflect the hopefulness she has prayed for this past year.

In another part of the family, Sam continues to expand the family business. He's successfully worked out the difficulties in most cases and is finding Benji a surprising asset. Jacob has taken on the task of grooming Benji along with Justin and Levi to take over management of the coming years' expansions. All in all they are experiencing financial success with each new project.

# 37 — REUNION

Several hundred miles to the east and nine years later, Joseph Finkbonner, as he has become known, has taken the Amzlov empire from a multi-million dollar empire to a multi-billion dollar empire. Not only has he expanded into banking and property management, he has also become part of the family. Nine years ago he entered into Holy Matrimony with Carrie as a full-communing member of the Roman Catholic faith. They now have two children, a boy, nine, and a girl, eight, both baptized and catechized. All these events have been carefully scrutinized and endorsed under the approving eye of Grandma Melba.

Things have changed with Amzlov also, as he has backed out of a daily hands-on presence to allocating more to Joey and Drew.

After a number of years working for competitors, and at the persistence of Joey, Drew has agreed to come into the family business. He has proven invaluable in bringing his accounting skills along with him. Joey and Drew have dovetailed skills flawlessly. Joey remains the idea man, while Drew is content to crunch numbers and remain in the background.

In true accord with Joey's interpretation of Amzlov's dreams, the past seven years of prosperity have given this company an edge over all other competitors, who were never privileged with information of an end to come.

They are now two years into a financial depression. The Amzlov machine, headed by this hand-picked team of experts has risen like cream to the top. They are prepared to lend money through this depression and to profit from the rising interest rates.

The sun is shining and the birds are singing this beautiful April morning, but not for the mining industry. Even though the season has begun, many of the miners have found themselves not qualified for loans. Without the loans, it's impossible to get their projects developed. These dynamics have also found their way into Mueller Smelting. They have found themselves over-extended financially as a result of their rapid growth and declining markets. They are near financial bankruptcy, if they can't get the loans to see them through.

Jacob's concern is with Sam's lack of expertise especially when it comes to business reversals. The last thing he wants to see is Sam trying to muddle by without any outside financial support in an effort to pull them out of their shortfall by jerking on the seat of his pants.

Jacob arranges to meet with Sam at the plant on this particular spring morning. "Sam, from the looks of our books, our cash flow is going to be depleted pretty fast. We're going have to be proactive, if we hope to get through this mess."

"I know Dad, but right now all my time is consumed in trying to stay afloat with what we have," laments Sam.

"That may be but I want you and your brothers to head over to Fairbanks. I got some information on a bank that is willing to make loans to qualified borrowers. Before we fall off the cliff and while we're still solvent,

I want to be in a position to negotiate. I want you boys to all go and show them what we got and what we need."

Realizing his father is not to be dissuaded, Sam calls a meeting with the brothers. After a few hours of hashing things out they come to an agreement. "Rup, Justin, Levi, gather your financials and go with me. Benji you stay here and keep things going, if I need you, I'll call you."

Within the week Jacob has arranged for his sons to meet with a certain Joseph Finkbonner, the president of American Bank and Trust. The day before they are to leave, their father called them all together to invoke God through prayer for a productive outcome. The next day arrives with a caravan of four-wheeled pick-up trucks rolling into the parking lot of their hopeful lender. It's now a Monday morning.

Feeling that they are armed with the gear they'll need for this battle, they boldly and with a united front make an entrance. It's 10 am.

Within minutes they are sitting in the most luxurious waiting room any of them have ever sat in. The seating is silver gray leather with a bold red carpeting. The walls are covered in murals depicting the Alaskan gold rush era. The lighting comes mainly from recessed lights assisted by an enormous cut glass chandelier in the center of the room. On the far end is a traditional stone fireplace.

A lady in a tailored, blue suit meets them offering coffee, indicating there would be a slight delay. Holding true to their tradition, they decline the coffee settling on bottled water.

Meantime Joey is making his way into the building using a private entrance enabling him to avoid contact with clients until he's ready to engage them. This morning he is particularly cheerful as he steps into his secretary's office to check on his schedule.

"Good morning, Gracie. How are things in your world?" inquires Joey.

"Fine Mr. Finkbonner. You have an appointment this morning with the Mueller family." Her voice is as staid as the blue-tailored suit she is wearing.

"Do we have a file on them?" he further inquires.

"No sir. They're a new account from over by Anchorage. As a matter of fact they are sitting out in the lobby as we speak."

Glancing toward a glass partition, he observes a group of middle-aged men in a varying array of non-conforming attire. They look out of place. The opulence of the waiting room contrasts against their ordinariness in such a way that one couldn't help wondering how uncomfortable they may be. The men are huddled together, deep in conversation when one of them turns his head.

IT'S LIKE A BOLT OF ELECTRICITY SHOOTS THROUGH JOEY! He can feel the blood draining from his face, his breathing becomes rapid as he staggers.

Not able to take his eyes off what he is looking at, his mind is suddenly over-loaded with twenty-five years of forgotten history that's not flowing back in merely small increments, but flooding in all at once. At the sight of these brothers, his mind is unlocking at a pace that processing all this information is becoming a near impossible task.

Staggering and shaking, he manages to get to a chair. "Wa-what did you tell me these men are named?" he stammers as he turns back to his secretary. She is already on her feet, concerned that her boss may be undergoing a heart attack.

Without answering his question her attention turns to his well-being. "Mr. Finkbonner are you okay?" The obvious stress in her voice is directly proportional to the physical stress her boss is undergoing.

Joey does not respond to Gracie. Mentally, as well as physically, shaken at what he's seeing, Joey continues to stare at these men. With all that's burst into his memory, he is also unconsciously watching their body language and facial expressions to tell him if they are of the same mindset as they were some ten years ago.

"Drew, Drew come in here quickly," shouts Gracie over the intercom.

Recognizing the panic in her voice, Drew bolts down the hall from his office and through the door. Within moments he also is encountering the same scenario that provoked Gracie's panic.

He is still shaking, white as a ghost and sweating profusely. His eyes have not moved from the group of men in the waiting lobby. His voice has become louder as he continues his demand, "Tell me again who these men are."

Drew and Gracie glance at one another as if to ask, "what should we do?" Gracie finally makes a move to scurry to her desk and grab her appointment schedule to verify exactly what name she had given. "The Jacob Mueller and Sons Smelting," she reiterates.

Looking first at Drew and then at Gracie, with a dazed look that neither of them had ever seen in him before, he manages a whisper, "These men are my brothers."

Drew glances out at the motley gathering. What he sees is a group of men of varying size, with an array of flannel shirts, dark work trousers, shoes with a light hint of dried mud, and all in need of a barber.

Drew is trying his best to sort through what it is that his brother-in-law is seeking to tell him. His response is posed as a question. "You're trying to tell me that these men out there are your brothers?"

With a continuing stare and the shocked look of a man whose life has just been dealt a blow, Joey manages to form the words, "Yes they're all there except my younger brother, my father and mother and my step-mother." His last memory of his brother Sam was staring back at him in horror as he began to beat him. All he could remember was that Sam's face was the face of pure evil before he fell unconscious.

"Drew, I can't handle this right now. Can you meet with them until I can gather myself?" asks Joey as he is showing the first sigh of settling down.

"Sure, Joey I can do that. I'll get them initially started and you can pick up on them tomorrow," assures Drew.

Taking a deep breath, Joey releases a sigh and says, "I sure appreciate this Drew." Then looking purposely up from his seat at Drew, he adds, "Oh, and tell them they'll need their youngest brother present."

"I'll do all that I can," affirms Drew, nodding at Gracie to get the process going.

Joey watches with great interest as Gracie approaches the men, guiding them down the hallway toward Drew's office. He finds himself watching for clues as to what kind of men they've become over the years. He can't help but wonder if they are the same treacherous, mean-spirited men he had lived with or have they changed. He notices how they march along with hats in hands like a motley band of beggars hoping for a hand out. In that same moment, he can't help but recall the dream where his brothers were bowing down before him.

"Is it possible those dreams are coming true?" is his thought as they race unfettered around his mind, each one banging into another. He has changed from that young man who found pleasure in holding his superior intelligence over the heads of his brothers to a man secure in himself. At the present, there is an undercurrent threatening that maturity. There is no question that this situation has certainly come up on his blind side. With every moment, he is re-feeling all the anger and resentments that he held against Sam so many years ago.

Enough chairs have been brought into Drew's office to accommodate the brothers. With everyone comfortable, Drew begins his interview process. Joey has recovered enough enabling him to sneak down the hall and listen outside the room. He is surprised that even with their backs to him, he is able to pick out who belongs to which voice.

Drew is careful to keep a professional distance between himself and this new-found family of Joey's. He asks questions that pertain to items like "cash flow," or the last three years of corporate tax returns and their standards for choosing managers.

Looking at all the paperwork they submitted, Drew (in keeping with Joey's request) notices they have five plants but only four managers are present. "Where is your fifth manager?"

Sam has had the sense that he's definitely out of his element ever since he walked through the front doors. Now he's being challenged with a question he doesn't quite know how to answer. Attempting to come back with an acceptable answer, he says, "Our father wanted him to stay at home and oversee things while we're here."

Without any hesitation, Drew makes it clear that all participants have to be interviewed to proceed with this size of a loan. The brothers look at one another somewhat puzzled. They had hoped this would be a quick straight forward procedure, now they have to take several days to go home to make the different arrangements.

Arriving home the next day, Sam makes known their quandary to their father. "Dad, we ran into a slight snag. They won't consider any kind of loan until they interview our entire management team. That means they want to see Benji. We sure aren't in any position to question their tactics so we agreed," reports Sam.

Jacob muses over this for a moment. Benji is the son of his old age and he makes no bones over his fawning over him. Never in all his years in business has he ever experienced this kind of scrutiny for a loan.

"Things sure as hell have changed with all these young college-boy loan officers. I remember when a man's word and a handshake went a long ways.

I still think there's something odd about this. We're just going to have to make the best of it."

There is a conversation between the brothers as to what else will be asked of them. They want to be certain they have all their ducks in a row.

Back in Fairbanks, Joey's state of mind is no less chaotic. He's beside himself. He can't talk fast enough as he is explaining to Carrie the phenomenon of how quickly his mind recovered. "I looked out into that lobby and there my brothers were sitting. It was like the amnesia never happened. My mind snapped all at once with every memory in place. I remembered everything."

Joey pauses long enough to allow some of the initial excitement to wear off as his memory begins to include the event that caused the amnesia to begin with. For the next two hours, Carrie listens to this tale with the same interest she would were it an exciting book.

With a mischievous eye and a twisted, little grin Carrie declaims, "And my mother thought you were Catholic!"

Joey perpetually relies on Carrie to bring some comic relief to otherwise overwhelming events. "Thanks for listening, sweetheart. You're a gem. You always know when my thinking needs a tune up, but there is one thing in this mess I'm going to have to handle alone." As he pauses for a moment giving it the right amount of thought, she in turn gives back a questioning expression as to what he may have in mind.

Joey continues, "I want to test my brothers to see if they are as treacherous to Benji as they were to me." He says this with a finality that indicates he's already well into this plan.

Through the week he fine tunes his intentions. Drew has also become a confidant and has agreed to play a role.

"I'm sure they would recognize me, so if I can depend on you, I believe I can create a drama that will expose them one by one." Joey has taken the time to explain to Drew why he feels it necessary to get to the core of his brothers' true character. Drew listens and agrees becoming a willing participant.

"Drew, I want you to understand that you have been a true brother to me and your family has become my family. You believed in me during my darkest hours. I can't tell you how much I have appreciated your acceptance of me." Joey expresses this impulsively with a true sense of gratitude. It catches Drew off balance and he is at a loss for a well-drawn return. He, along with the rest of his family, has come to recognize a higher and even a truer reality in his brother-in-law than when first encountered some ten years ago. Drew has found it easy to love Joey as a brother, but is unable to express it as easily as Joey does. It's another awkward moment for Drew, but he's determined to give it his best shot. For a moment he says nothing, then with a nefarious little grin he blurts out, "But Mom always loved you best!"

Joey catches the irony of his brother-in-law's humor in time to put aside this seriousness that's crept into his life in the past few days. With a knowing grin of his own and much more light-hearted response he says, "Thanks, Drew. I needed that."

Returning to a more businesslike mode, Drew arises from his desk. Walking over to where Joey is seated, he places a reassuring hand on his shoulder saying, "Don't worry too much, Joey. We'll get through this just fine."

Not fully confident how all this is going to work out, Joey thanks Drew for his support.

The week has passed and another has begun. Meanwhile, Joey has paid particular attention to the parking lot, watching with great anticipation as his youngest blood brother pulls in. He remembers him as a gawky teen. He's somewhat taken back by the adult status this handsome young man has taken on. He's much taller and muscular than he remembers him being.

Determined to follow through with his plan to judge how well the older half brothers are treating this youngest brother, Joey moves on to the next phase of his program. Flipping open his phone, he calls Kevin Guken, the head of bank security. "Kevin, I have a little item I'd like you to take care of this morning."

Kevin agrees to meet with Joey to go over the details. A short meeting is all it takes to bring Kevin up to speed.

The Mueller brothers are once again adorning the American Bank and Trust lobby. This time, as asked, they have included their youngest brother. Their hope is that they can get all this over with in a short time and return to business.

Following the script Joey has laid out, Drew begins his part in this drama. He's continuing his very stoic non-personal business approach. Feigning going through paper work, he suddenly with no warning bangs his hand down on his desk and in a very accusative voice hurls the accusation, "You guys are not here for a loan at all. You're corporate spies aren't you? Who in the hell are you working for?"

Startled, the brothers look at one another for someone to come up with an answer for this turn of events. Sam is the first to speak, "No sir, that's certainly not true. We're all the sons of one father and nothing more than honest business men. Why would you make such a ridiculous statement?"

Joey has crept into the adjacent office and is listening over the intercom as these events are unfolding according to script. Drew is on the phone practically shouting, "Get Kevin up here immediately!"

To say that the brothers are stunned would be an understatement. Looking aghast and helpless as this whole surreal scenario unfolds, they stand dumbfounded. They have been hit on their blind side and discover quickly they have little to no defense against this sudden bombardment.

Within seconds, right on cue, Kevin and three other security men are in the office surrounding the brothers.

Once again Sam speaks up trying to defend them against these horrendous accusations only to be told to be quiet.

"I want these men searched for any bank properties," declares Drew to the security team. Immediately the brothers are lined up facing the wall and patted down for contraband.

"Here's something Mr. Amzlov," announces Kevin as he seemingly produces a computer disk from Benji's pocket.

"Let me see that, Kevin." Drew's voice is carrying an inauspicious tone. Placing the disk in his computer he goes through the motions of an intense inspection.

"Just as I suspected. These are our last year's monthly financial reports. I want you to hold him until we can have him arrested. I want him charged with corporate espionage."

Sam struggles against the men holding him. "Please take me instead. Please don't take this brother. He's our father's youngest and he has already lost one son. Please don't do this. Our father is nearly blind and not in the best of health. These circumstances will kill him. Just take me please."

Joey has tears streaking down his face in the adjacent office as this exercise continues to move forward. He's crying for his brothers as well as for himself. He feels all the hurt, both theirs and his, for the suffering everyone's going through and has gone through over the years.

While the security team is handcuffing them all to chairs as they wait for the police to arrive, Drew withdraws long enough to confer with Joey as to where he wants this to end. Joey takes a minute to compose himself. He already knows what he wants Drew to do next. "Tell Kevin to bring them to my office. Remove their handcuffs and leave me alone with them."

Within minutes Kevin has shuffled the unwitting crew of beseechers into Joey's office. Joey is sitting behind his desk, his elbows resting on its top with both his hands folded beneath his nose concealing the bottom half of his face. He says nothing, spending the next few minutes studying their uneasiness. Still concealing himself, he speaks through his hands calling out each of their names in order of age, "Hello Rup, Sam, Justin, Levi, Benji."

They all make a respectful nod, and in unison, adjudging their servile position with a, "Good morning, Sir."

Joey drops his hands below his chin, staring at each of them. They in turn remain very fearful with their eyes avoiding contact.

"How is our father?" asks Joey in a rather casual tone of voice.

Sam is the first to look up. He is silent for a moment as he mulls such an odd question. With a very puzzled look he stares at Joey hardly believing what he is seeing. "JOEY" is the only word he can retrieve to manifest the explosion that has abruptly ruptured out of his consciousness and onto his tongue as though some puppeteer has jerked a connected cord. The other men follow suit. Uninvited feelings and emotions rush over them like a tsunami carrying a mixture of guilt and shame for at least two of them and relief and joy for the rest.

Now looking directly at Sam to answer his question, Joey gives an imperative, "Come here Sam and look at me. See if I am not your brother that you tried to murder and leave for dead."

Shaking from the top of his head to the very bottom of his soul, Sam makes his way across the room stopping only inches from his brother and falling to his knees. A flood of stuffed emotions make their way to his tear ducts as sob after sob begins to pour out. "Please forgive me, Joey. I'll do whatever you ask to make it up to you."

Joey harks back to just minutes before when this very brother who ten years earlier had shown no regard for his life and wanted him dead, was now willingly offering to take the rap for his youngest brother regardless of the severity of the punishment.

Reaching down and grasping the very hands that tried to murder him, Joey lifts Sam to his feet. "Sam, from what I see of you today, you are not the same brother I knew ten years ago. I do forgive you and I am convinced a greater good will come of all this."

Both, now with tears streaking their faces, embrace the other brothers making one huge group hug.

All things work for the good of those who love God. Ro.8:28


Often times the outside world romanticizes the fervor of rigid religious sects, acting as though these folks are free of the common troubles and stresses of everyday people.

The fundamental Mormon polygamist experience of Jacob Muller is an example of such a family. They would be perfect if it were not for...

*—An envious half brother attempting to murder another half brother,*

*—A wife cheating with the son of another sister wife,*

*—A thieving son satisfying his greed,*

*—Dark secrets held between family members,*

*—Renegade sons taking the law into their own hands to seek revenge.*


The truth is all God's children create new, troubling circumstances of their own.

CPSIA information can be obtained at www.ICGtesting.com
Printed in the USA
BVOW04s1806021213

337926BV00002B/6/P